BLACK RIVER

M. TURVILLE HEITZ

"It will be safer for you if no one associates you with what is about to happen."

Ruperion couldn't even protest before he felt Denalku's hand on him—and the splash of river water closing over his head. Denalku had pushed him, with more than just his hand, a hand holding the tiny Traveling stone Ruperion had hidden in the look of white quartz, when its true face was a dark thing of unknown origin. Dark, like the deeds done with it.

Ruperion breathed deep in protest to find his lungs filled with the musty flavor of tamarack-stained Potter's Flowage and the sweet pesticides from nearby cranberry bogs. He almost screamed his rage as he surfaced among the snags and reeds, too exhausted to more than flail to the safety of the shore.

For days he glared at each surfacing fish, watched each ripple from beaver or muskrat or water spider, each passing boat wake in the hope Denalku returned to lead him home. In Metatha time fled. Had he destroyed all of Metatha? Would Denalku arrive demanding an antidote the wyseer never dared seek? Would he expect greater and greater arsenals? Where would he draw the line? It should have been before Shesta. Perhaps this would be Ruperion's punishment for mentoring such a demon: He would forever sit here in this world of dullards blind to the magic surrounding them, waiting for a dead man to retrieve him home.

Dedicated to the memory of David, soul mate and muse, who helped me discover the terrible beauty of Potter's Flowage.

A special thank you to Kandis Elliot, Jo Fletcher, Steve Rogers, Fred Schepartz and F. Paul Wilson for their invaluable feedback on various drafts of this work.

PROLOGUE

A hot wind swirled across the road, throwing the oily stench of baking asphalt into Ruperion's face as he worked the chunk of driftwood he'd carried across this world and across the greater void of water that led home. Beside him crouched Denalku. The chieftain watched with the eagerness of a boy as Ruperion's knife flicked chunks of wood away to form a small hollow like a pipe bowl.

Ruperion tried to ignore the gleam in Denalku's dark eyes and the way the chieftain grinned at some private bemusement. If only Ruperion had stabbed Denalku to death at birth—

Ruperion tugged at loose blue jeans, freeing from a pocket a tiny packet of mashed manfish leaves. He pressed the paste into the pipe bowl.

"A carriage comes," Denalku whispered.

"Car, my lord. Actually, bus. Please, take care not to call attention to your greatness in a place where your words might carry."

"The word book you provided said 'carriage' is a word for such ... transport."

"As I advised, my lord, the words of this world are often informal and change quickly."

"No one is near to hear," Denalku muttered, irritably flicking at a bit of driftwood on his sleeve. "How long before you are finished, Wyseer? The bus comes."

Ruperion looked up at the squeak of brakes as the dark blue bus made its first stop on the other end of the row of base housing. Squat beige structures that had appeared abandoned suddenly disgorged uniformed military staff whose chatter didn't carry over the din of the wind rattling the sign beside which Ruperion crouched.

"Remember this?" Ruperion asked as he handed Denalku the driftwood with the manfish paste tamped into one end. He had hollowed out the end opposite of the little bowl and tucked a thin wick running from the paste to the end of the stem.

"Ilyath," Denalku replied.

"Yes. You will be disoriented this first time. Just do not speak until I tell you it is safe."

Ruperion touched a match to the wick. A curl of smoke rose toward Denalku's nose. Soon the chieftain's jaw sagged, his gaze fixed on some distant point, as Denalku disappeared from the view of anyone who didn't bear a wyseer's seeing stone in his pocket.

The bus engine roared as the vehicle sped up the street toward them. For just an instant, Ruperion thought about just walking away and leaving the Reign Chieftain to find his own way to escape the Utah desert when the ilyath burned out. Let Denalku tromp back through forty miles of barren hills marked only by graffiti and broken glass along the road in search of the nearest civilian town. Denalku would never survive the journey. Let him shout his demands at an empty desert until his parched throat fell silent and the buzzards picked the schemes from his bones.

Denalku turned a trusting gaze on Ruperion even as the ilyath burned into his flesh. The wyseer almost heard a youth's mistaken call for "papa" that long-ago night when magic gone wild cast the future chieftain into his mentor's comforting arms.

With an angry gesture at his own weakness for Denalku—like a father's love for a murderous child, a loyalty he wished he could escape—Ruperion broke a sliver from the ilyath that, with the extra effort of a wyseer's swiftly cast spell, made him as invisible in this world as Denalku. Denalku slowly looked about himself as if he might see the mentor who took his arm.

Never again, Ruperion decided. Never again would he let fondness for anyone drive him to such foolish extremes. Never again would he so let a right and good be twisted so wrong.

That moment the bus with its austere military styling pulled up beside the sign with a puff of dust and blue exhaust. Base workers paced across dusty yards that appeared starkly green in the midst of desert, the wind ripping at their uniforms and flapping the identification badges clipped to their pockets. The two stowaways slipped aboard, Ruperion hustling his charge to the back of the bus where they crouched, almost pitching over backward when the bus lurched forward. The workers chatted amiably as the bus carried them more than a dozen miles closer to the heart of Ruperion's fear.

Denalku remained oblivious as the bus passed through guarded gates warning that deadly force would hold back intruders. Once within the installation, the bus jerked to a halt several times for herds of antelope and to drop passengers at a concertina-wire– encrusted building in the midst of open desert. The bus rumbled through dry hills, by distant bunkers and clusters of yellow barrels collected on the sides of the road, past overgrown cement platforms and blasted zones where a sinister sense of what could be lingered.

At last, Ruperion led Denalku off the bus in the tiny heart of Dugway Proving Ground, to the nondescript collection of beige buildings where the military claimed only defensive research occurred on chemical and biological weapons.

Ruperion hesitated a moment before following the last worker inside, the door slamming hard on their heels. He retraced a path he'd reconnoitered more than a Metathan year ago, although only weeks had passed here. The wyseer led Denalku over black-tiled floors framed by sea-foam green walls. He led him past defunct UV light washes and level-three biohazard labs where negative pressure hoods that sucked contaminants out of the building hummed at the arrival of the morning shift. Plastic-draped rooms held quarantined rabbits, mice and monkeys growing antidotes in their tortured bodies. Black widow spiders silently crafted webs used to capture toxin-rich dew after each weapon test. By clean rooms and emergency showers Ruperion led Denalku, at last to a room with giant, red, biohazard warning signs on what appeared to be an ordinary closet door. Black marble counters atop pine cabinets were littered with lab notes, syringes, beakers and someone's breakfast spread out in a work space that just yesterday may have held vials of rabbit fever.

Ruperion maneuvered into a corner by a rust-stained sink. Shrinking back from each passing tech, he ticked off moments of routine that would soon bring an officer to fill the morning lab order for any of the toxins stored in that closet-like chamber of horrors. Anthrax, bubonic plague, q-fever, botulism—ills innumerable for this world—a plethora of bacteria and viruses, so harmless seeming, all awaited a moment of truth when released from their tiny sealed vials. In the lab, or maybe in the vast miles of open desert, researchers would aerosolize the agent to expose it to simulated soldiers in the field. The tale would be read from the dew-coated black widow web. How far would the cloud spread? How many spores or bacteria per dewdrop might a simulated soldier inhale or find clinging to his skin?

What means would Denalku order Ruperion to use against the saber-wielding horsemen of the Pale?

In the end, his horrific act took Ruperion but a moment. His return ticket to Metatha remained too addled by the smoldering ilyath to do more than stare slack-jawed and uncomprehending. The ruler had become so much baggage Ruperion must carry with him if he hoped to see Leta and Arlin again, hear his boy speak in a man's voice now, his young wife gaze on him with a grandmother's clouded eye.

The door opened. Ruperion slipped inside behind the captain. While she checked the label of a container of botulism against her list, Ruperion snatched two vials of anthrax from the shelf, tucked them into his jeans pocket and scurried back to the bewildered Denalku. So simple. Too simple. A sign from the gods that this was part of the Plan, Denalku had claimed.

Now, water. Any pond or spring would do. The entry to this world might be tiny Potter's Flowage in west-central Wisconsin, but any body of water would take him home. He had recorded dozens of them.

His logs described in meticulous detail how he slipped on and off the emptier flights from Minneapolis to Salt Lake City, how he rented cars or jumped on buses, usually snitching at will what he needed to exist in this world. He was an anthropologist of sorts in his recordings, but in truth he was little more than a scavenger since he'd found Travel.

He tugged Denalku's elbow. The Chieftain came obediently as the wyseer paced to the exit. He grabbed an untended can of soda as he passed, tucking it under his shirt as they slipped out in the wake of a tech taking a cigarette break.

They trudged east along the melting asphalt toward a mirage Ruperion's sweat-damped square of map told him would resolve into salt flats and an alkali lake. With each step, he felt the bulge of anthrax vials in his pocket, a reminder that he was Denalku's most dangerous tool: a wyseer who Travels, yet little more than a dog on a leash held by Denalku.

He stopped walking. The "silence" of the desert fell loud on his ears—a place of clicking insects, whistling wind and heat-snapped rock. He eased Denalku down to sit in the sort-of shade thrown by twisted sagebrush. Denalku smiled up, bleary eyed, at what he couldn't see.

Ruperion hesitated, then, afraid of his own wavering will. He strode downhill toward the flats. Always Denalku fetched him home from far worlds, welcoming his pet wyseer with a friendly grin and a boyish insistence that Ruperion first hear the latest gossip. Denalku honored his mentor with lavish gifts: the finest home in the city and precious stones for wyseery, or merely for the pleasure of Leta and Arlin. They explored wyseery together, or debated as scholars and peers the role they played in the gods' plan, not ruler and ruled. Denalku turned to him when decisions weighed too heavy to make alone. Or at least he used to.

Ruperion stopped and glanced back. Denalku's forehead had scrunched up a little, still silent as his mentor had begged him to remain, patient, trusting. To go home, Ruperion needed Denalku. If neither returned, what would happen to Leta and Arlin, watched so closely in the care of Denalku's personal guard? Could he turn his back on loyalty, on a person he'd known better, longer, in many ways than his own son? Ruperion spat into the desert dust, then trudged back up the heat-soft road and tugged the Reign to his feet. If only he were stronger, more cunning. He tossed away his own sliver of carved wood, Denalku blinking dumbly at his wyseer's sudden reappearance. Then

Ruperion gently removed the ilyath from Denalku's palm so that the man stumbled into awareness with a start.

Ruperion merely muttered through Denalku's multitude of questions as they split the soda. He was concentrating on the surprising amount of life in this barren place, life that might not be if any of the vials in Dugway's lab were to walk away. Here and there he noted items of power he easily slipped into his pockets as if they were merely pretty pebbles for Leta's pleasure, a bauble for his baby, grown to manhood in the eternity of his father's Travels.

When at last they reached the crusty shores of an evaporating lake, with the calm of many ages of Traveling, Ruperion and Denalku took deep breaths, then dived together into the brine. The wyseer's hand needed only that moment of contact with the Reign to propel him on his journey. The lake they dived into might be shallow, but the void reached far deeper, the soup of the universe, the womb of the gods, they swam there, transforming through a magic greater than any simple wyseer could perform.

They surfaced just outside of Denalku's palace. Almost instantly, the clean air of Metatha burned sharp in Ruperion's lungs. His limbs, deadened a moment, responded in a flail that took him shoreward.

Many days would pass before he felt sound again. Traveling took from him more than strength, but his sense of time and place as well. It was the price to pay for metamorphosis and a taste of the gods' grand design. His only thought was to find Leta's comforting arms and pretend he didn't know Denalku's intent.

Chamberlain Shedal greeted them with soft blankets and a sly smile that had always made Ruperion uneasy. Though deep night had settled over the valley—so deep that only a few torches lit the dark river flowing beside the palace—Shedal had remained waiting, as he had for the long Metathan weeks they'd been away.

"Shedal," Denalku said, grinning through chattering teeth. He held out a turquoise scarf pin angled like the lizard of southwestern Native American design. "Do you like it? A fitting gift to Kyla in honor of her service to her lord."

In the dim torchlight, Ruperion caught the flash of Shedal's sharp glance and the hesitation an instant before a forced smile pulled the chamberlain's lips. "My daughter could receive no greater honor."

Denalku gestured at Ruperion. "Give them to me."

Ruperion almost dropped the vials of anthrax removing them from his sodden pocket. Had the spores become a part of him during the metamorphosis of Travel? Did he now bear a bit of *bacillus anthracis*? How long before blisters formed on his skin or within his lungs? Would it incubate for hours, days, years? Would the disease drag on or kill swiftly? Would it be contagious? Then again, perhaps the gods had a way of protecting Travelers. Or perhaps on Metatha, this horror of Earth might be benign, just as many of the magic devices of other worlds were merely so much junk cluttering Metathan refuse heaps.

"Ruperion! You aren't listening to me!"

The wyseer shook himself. He needed the security of a clear mind not one addled by Travel sickness, compounded by the expense of wyseery he'd used to hide them.

"Great One," Shedal said quietly as he rubbed warmth into Denalku's arms. "You must know: the unrest has grown since you left. A number of wyseers have joined the Pale and I have noted many grumblers among our own Reign supporters and staff—people who wonder if, begging your pardon, siding with the Pale might not be a better option—"

"Who says these things?"

"People, Great One. I've taken note of a few, but they grow more numerous. Not among your most trusted, I assure you."

Ruperion doubted that; Shedal's glance couldn't settle on his chieftain as he spoke.

"Shall I announce the Portioning?" Shedal asked. "More than a dozen wyseers have asked when they might collect—"

"I won't have time for that."

"But their efforts are our defense, Great One. They will wonder why you would Travel but not hold the Portioning soon after. They need the wyseery artifacts to stop the Pale—"

"We have returned with better tools for that, Shedal. We need a swift end to this, and a demonstration of the power of Valeutans. Tomorrow, Ruperion, we'll take a vial to Shesta—"

"Tomorrow? Great One, I can't Travel so soon! I've spent more than my measure of wyseery for a week. And why Shesta? That world is but a simple place—"

"Do you dispute my orders? Perhaps you forget your place." Ruperion drew in a long breath at the unmistakable undertone of menace in the Reign's words. "I will do whatever I must to protect my people from the ravages of the Pale's horsemen."

Ruperion swallowed hard and bowed his head. He glimpsed the smirk on Shedal's face, wishing he dared turn Shedal into the tree rat he so resembled, if only for a night. Certainly the Pale would find no fertile ground for rebellion among the chieftain's own subjects were he less a tyrant—one who owed his success to a Traveling wyseer, worst violator of his own bans.

Denalku, guided by Shedal, slipped into the palace as the torches sputtered out, the men's voices like furtive rustling in the eaves.

Ruperion sat long in the dark beside the river, dripping a pool of black water as dark as his thoughts. Even thoughts of holding Leta and sitting by the fire with Arlin gave no comfort. Tomorrow. Poor Shesta.

CHAPTER ONE

One leg dangling over the arm of the rocker, Kyle closed his eyes as the voices of his young nieces, nephews and cousins shushed one another. The cozy basement den had grown warm and steamy with their anxious breaths despite the patio door thrown open to a cool August night. Almost a dozen children formed a knot of sunburned and mosquito-bitten arms and legs as they sprawled around the center of attention.

Uncle Rupert sat stiffly in a straight-backed dining room chair, his wine glass set just so beside him on an end table.

Kyle's bare foot brushed his niece Denise. She swatted it as he burrowed a toe into her ear. He yanked free just as she got a good grip to tickle him, sending the rocker flying back to clip a cousin. Kyle stifled a snort and slowly repositioned to wriggle his toe beneath her ponytail.

Uncle Rupert cleared his throat and instant silence pressed against Kyle's ears. Too old and disillusioned for Rupert's stories, Kyle knew he should just stumble free of the mire of youngsters and join the other adults upstairs, but he'd found that happy medium where, without moving his foot, he could send just the hint of a presence through Denise's hair. Besides, Rupert's tales had become so much a part of being home, he grudgingly admitted to missing them. Rupert could crawl under Kyle's skin with a look, yet he partook of the man's mystique like opening his throat to chug the last of his fast-warming beer. It just was. Besides, he couldn't stomach the idea of joining the adults in their small talk, pretending he could trust them, pretending what they had to say mattered to the larger world outside of Potter's Flowage.

Rupert's glance touched Kyle, who made a show of pressing ear buds into his ears and pretending to adjust the volume. He nodded his head to an imaginary beat. Only the briefest of scowls crossed Uncle Rupert's face.

But Rupert swiftly drew him into a story Kyle's sense of the rational told him not to believe. The old man's gravelly voice implored him hear each word, to listen to something that niggled into his gut like a chigger. Rupert's mesmerizing storytelling swiftly threw him into a familiar tale.

"Metatha is the kind of world only good children can dream," Rupert began like he always had, in a light tone, if not a little weary sounding. Perhaps even Rupert tired of the same tired stories. Kyle almost instantly translated *Metatha* to "many paths" with a facility Rupert would have praised with that sly lift of one corner of his mouth. Tonight, it made Kyle frown to himself as the story seemed to take off on a false note.

"Here we have but one moon. To Metathans that would seem a dark and boring sort of night. Danat, Kylik and Siph—the grandfather, son and grandson—are generations of guardians in the Metathan night sky, and day sky as well. The gods created the moons so they could protect this very special place of Metatha, they resided there on the moons, watching the center of the universe. That's right, the center of the universe. The universe is made up of bubbles of air—those are bubbles where a moon or a planet rests in the great universal sea, all connected by spring and lake and the soup of life. The entire universe is bound together by that womb water of the gods and at its center is Metatha."

Womb water, like the little ones had a clue what that meant. He should have gone upstairs—

"But it was the gods who controlled the gates between the worlds and swam in the universal sea with the pre-born and dead. And the final rest of all those who have lived all their lives before is the moon Danat, the grandfather moon where the greatest gods ride."

Kyle shifted hard in the rocker, almost pinching a nephew's toe. He had never liked this story among Rupert's vast repertoire. It always gave him that sense of foreboding and ulterior motive, even in its innocent description of cities, palaces, fishing fleets and stark valley walls. Rupert would peer over his wine glass at his pupil—that's how he spoke of Kyle—to gauge his understanding. As Rupert rattled off strange names to the delight of children who tried to repeat them, Kyle heard only Rupert's stern tone as he taught a younger Kyle some strange word: a language, Rupert claimed, like no other.

Kyle tried to concentrate on the smell of popcorn smothered in butter, the smoldering hickory wafting in from the fire pit outside, on the distant whir of the air popper upstairs in the kitchen and voices raised to talk above it. Someone shouted "trump" and a fist, likely bearing the jack of the called suit, slammed down on the kitchen table.

Denise moved and Kyle's toe caught her in the nose. She lightly pushed him aside, too mesmerized by Uncle Rupert's story to tickle or pinch.

"A high plain was home to the nomadic Pale, a ruthless and barbaric people who dabbled in a wild magic powered by the blood of their victims. Even the simplest of the Pale's horsed warriors dreamed of stealing away the beautiful girls of the Valley People, as the Pale's own daughters were haggard and ugly from the unnatural magic their fathers made."

The old man's voice dipped toward the sinister from the airy tone with which he'd described the idyllic world. With a sour smile to himself Kyle heard how the storyteller manipulated his audience with word and glance and sleight of tone. Kyle wouldn't let it capture him this time, no matter how seductive Rupert's tale. Kyle had seen a bit of the world beyond Potter's Flowage and the Nelson clan now. In less than two weeks he'd have to pack up for his final year of college at Madison. Home, he called that sag-floored room in a lower on Dayton, the smell of unwashed socks and stale beer more fitting than the tamaracks of the Black River, in a disquieting sort of way.

He needed to go. He could feel his annoyance growing at Rupert's allure, his attraction to the old man irrational, considering none of his stories held anything new for Kyle. They were more lies. He should just go. Or at least adjust the volume.

"Denalku's first thoughts and last went to his people, his heart true. No one in his Clan went hungry or lived with injustice. He heard all comers, no matter how lowly a laborer against however rich a landlord. In his far travels he collected gifts he portioned out to his subjects, gifts that had special powers when bestowed by Denalku. Magic."

Kyle clenched his eyes shut, trying to pinpoint what it was in the story or storytelling that wheedled under his skin. It felt too real and strange to be just fantasies told to family come up from Madison and Milwaukee for a weekend of camping in the Nelson's back yard, the adults upstairs scarfing down beer and the beer-battered filets of fish caught that morning, playing euchre and retelling the same stories they retold each time they gathered at the Nelsons. It had grown thin, now that the world was larger. Get up, Kyle, get up and go upstairs and end it now, he needed to do that, just stand up to Rupert and show him how he could see right through him.

"Oh and the magic!" Rupert said in that undertone of his: mocking, yet not; wistful, yet not; threatening, yet not. His hand would reach out for his water glass full of wine. Kyle heard Uncle Rupert's lips smack together and the clink as the glass resettled on the coaster. Kyle didn't need to open his eyes to know the rest of Rupert's audience hadn't noticed. They would be riveted on the man's craggy face and rheumy eyes, seeing neither. They wouldn't notice the way the spittle collected in the corners of Rupert's mouth when he spoke, only washed away by the wine that stained lips and the bulbous end of his nose magenta.

"Denalku's wizards used his gifts of magic to correct the ills of a world without the conveniences and medicine of this one. And, they needed their natural magic to fend off the Pale."

Kyle let his feet slap to the floor and sat up. He felt the instant's chill as Rupert's gaze touched him. A bushy, dark brow cocked as one near-black-irised eye widened at him. Denise lost her balance against the chair arm, but merely leaned somewhere else, as if she hadn't noticed Kyle at all. What power Rupert exerted over them!

Kyle stared at his uncle, again bobbing his head to a tune he couldn't hear.

Rupert appeared to suppress a smile as if he knew Kyle's defiance was only a ruse.

"Like any tale of those who have, and those who have not, some jealous wizards wanted to control all the magic, including that of Denalku. They joined the Pale to take the most powerful magic of all." The man stared at Kyle as if no others sat in his audience. "That magic was shape shifting. Oh, they didn't call it that," he nodded to an unseen nephew's muttered question. "They called it 'Traveling.' The magic let Denalku jump through a portal to other worlds, swimming along the gods' stream through the universe, to where he gathered magic items he gave to his wizards. A great power, indeed. Imagine what treasures one might find, the many worlds one could haunt to slip away with the least trinket, or the greatest: say a bazooka, a phaser or a tactical nuclear weapon."

The children giggled at that. Even when he was as small as the youngest, Kyle never laughed around Uncle Rupert, only cringed, inwardly, as if soiled by coming near a man who smelled so of unwashed clothing and wine. Yet he always came back for more, as if drawn by the very magic that ruled Metatha. That he had once believed such nonsense! That he had let his parents push him toward Rupert when the questions were hard!

"Of course, there's a downfall. Can't have a tragic tale without one. And the reason, as it so often is, was balance of power. Denalku controlled the wizards' tools from the least of gems and powders and crystals to medicines or learning. They had a cozy peace all right: the Valley People's rulers—the Reign—grew rich, the wizards, the educators, grew weak and the people didn't know any better. They didn't know that such government control would make them ripe for invasion by the—"

"Time for bed!" Kyle's sister called down the stairs to the tangle of children.

Kyle took that moment to wrench free of his chair and dart up the stairs two at a time, escaping the whining protests of those demanding Rupert be allowed to finish his tale. The story had grown stale and angled toward the political again.

Eventually, given another glass of wine, Rupert would wax over the ills of gun control, how the entire U.S. lay open to invasion by the

United Nations and list the government conspiracies to defraud the people, including cover ups of alien visitors.

Whatever spell Rupert cast over Kyle-the-child had unraveled since Kyle had left Potter's Flowage. Once, Rupert claimed he had taught Kyle everything he needed to know, public education be damned. Rupert spoke to him then in the gibberish he claimed was the language of the wise, a tongue Kyle grasped at eagerly as a child, delighting in the secrecy of his own special code. The words translated themselves in Rupert's stories: Metatha, the place of many paths, Kylik, the light son. Kyle still hadn't lived down trying to claim Metathan as a foreign language on his entrance application for college. He had to take four semesters of German because Rupert told him he had Metathan and didn't need high school foreign language credits. And his parents had simply looked away, said it was *Rupert's* decision, not theirs to make.

Kyle let the screen door slam as he stumbled out into a cool night. Behind, his aunts, sisters and mother called young children to bed, shaking out sleeping bags for the youngest while older children chased each other through the back yard with dim flashlights, whooping as if their loud racket could beat back the pitch black of night in the forest. Light beams briefly limned bats or the ghostly reach of trees, night creatures bounding into hiding in the thick of aspen or maple or remnant pine, the greenery lost in forest broken only by a patchwork of logging roads, ATV trails and swamp.

By now, Rupert had joined the adults in the kitchen, watching their game of euchre in silence, reserving judgment on the play as his hand moved mechanically to have more wine fill his water glass. Kyle's parents would defer to Uncle Rupert, the others ignore him.

So strange, this family Kyle called his. He didn't belong: not among the wide-eyed children drawn into Rupert's fantasies, and not among the adults rehashing each embarrassing event of their past as if it were some laurel they wore proudly, topping it off by deferring to Rupert, the largest embarrassment of them all. For Kyle.

In the dark vastness of west-central Wisconsin, the night hugged Kyle, something real, something dark and living here in the midst of state and county forest, military and tribal lands. Tamarack-stained Black River tributaries backed up behind earthen dams, the waters glittering darkly from just a few yards distant. Frogs or crickets sent up a shrill cadence into the night, the occasional owl or whip-poor-will adding punctuation. He caught the briefest chemical whiff of pesticides from the cranberry marshes just around the curve of Potter's Flowage, and in the distance a campground cast campfires skyward in flurries of sparks and flame-lit smoke, the occasional voice or firecracker barely touching the blanket of night. A late moon pulled from the flowage surface, giving a measure of substance to the night. A low flock of geese winged across its face, silent, oblivious to the Nelson home backed up against forest and flowage, its windows casting gold pools onto the black water, the brown cedar siding giving the house a sense of a giant tree trunk carved into a home.

This place was in his soul, a terrible, deep beauty in the wildness around him. But he felt like an observer simply enchanted by its face. He wanted to fit, but he didn't truly belong. One day his mother told him that, just out of nowhere, when he'd been riding her about how he'd found Rupert passed out in his own wine-red vomit and why did they make him hang around the besotted dirtbag.

"Don't be so judging," she said. "You don't know where you came from."

No punch had ever taken the wind from him like his mother's words had. He wasn't a Nelson. She didn't come out and say so, not then. But he felt it. Was that why nowhere ever felt right? Even in Madison he felt singular, out of step, despite being surrounded by thousands of people, as if he were visiting and might as well not unpack his bags.

He knew he should chide himself for falling prey to the dark mood, but the night drew him, the strangeness of Rupert and his tales, and the niggling feeling of tension that something was about to change forever. His last year of school and then graduation, certainly that was it.

A rectangle of lamplight briefly invaded his world, stretching a long slash over the yard. Then the stench of stale cigar smoke and red wine told him Uncle Rupert approached. He tried to fight down the urge to cringe as he turned up his music. Rage in the music pounded his ears like a mad heartbeat.

Rupert handed Kyle a cold, dew-slick can of Leinies. Kyle didn't even look at Rupert as he took it. In the past, Kyle had claimed beer to be his political statement against the drinking age and made his statement every weekend since he was eighteen. Rupert encouraged him, claiming that if he was a man in every other way and old enough to die for his country, Kyle had a right to an ale. Rupert his advocate. An ale, he called it. Kyle smiled privately, certain one day he would convince himself that his motives had been so much higher than a way to numb the boredom and feel less like an outsider in his own world. The self-pity thing again. Why did Rupert always trigger it?

Rupert yanked the ear buds from his ears, shattering an answer half-formed.

"You're restless to be away," Rupert said.

Kyle grunted and took a few steps toward the glassy flowage into which the occasional stump jutted, darker than the water, suggesting some mystery far beneath. Rupert followed.

"It's time. You've learned what I can teach you."

Kyle turned to stare at the silhouette, hunched and grizzled and smelling of wine, missing only the shopping cart full of castoffs to show his disengagement from reality.

"You've come of age. In Metatha it would have come sooner. This world coddles its young. But I think you've finally recognized the lessons I've taught you."

"You taught me what?" Kyle couldn't keep the sneer out of his tone.

"What you need to know. To swim."

"Swim," Kyle echoed. "Cut back on the wine, Rupert." Kyle jabbed his thumb at the glass as Uncle Rupert took a deep drink. "You're beginning to move into your fairy tales."

"Mock me at your peril, boy."

Kyle stared sullenly at his elder, then opened his throat and drained his beer, scrunched up the can and tossed it back toward the house, only an unconscious hesitation keeping him from hitting Rupert with it. Maybe he should just head home to Madison tonight. Rupert's childish games felt sinister, like the way a dirty old man might smile with too much pleasure at the little girl sitting in his lap—

"Even your insubordination proves it's time. Time was you couldn't resist the words of a wyseer."

Kyle let out a derisive snort.

"You know you don't belong here," Rupert continued.

Kyle gave Rupert one of his most scathing looks. It wasn't like Rupert read his thoughts as much as planted them. Dark-haired and dark-eyed like Rupert, Kyle didn't look the role of the fair-headed Norwegian-German Nelson family. Before that day his mother had snapped back after his angry critique of Rupert, they always claimed he was just a genetic throwback. His sisters teased about some mysterious lumberjack. Finally, his mother told him he'd been adopted. It wasn't a big deal; he had no complaints. It could have explained why he stuck out in the Nelson clan, or in classrooms like the Native Americans or the migrants. But why did he still feel so out of step in a university town with representatives from so many of the world's cultures? His family didn't see it. They said nothing of dark moods that made Kyle wonder what bad blood he'd inherited. But the true lies, the betrayal came unmasked just this summer. He hadn't even been adopted, more like borrowed, somehow, from Rupert. In exchange, the Nelson's came to own this home, Kyle like some prize hog that paid the rent. His mother insisted that Rupert was a benefactor, an elder, someone to be honored. But Kyle rejected that. He couldn't picture Rupert in any way but passed out in his old sprung chair in the cottage behind the Nelson house, wine stains on his clothes.

"We're of the same kind, you and me," Rupert said, again seeming to rummage through Kyle's thoughts and forcing him to again look at the old man.

"Oh, then I can look forward to my future as a demented wino?"

"Is that a way to speak of your own kind—Metathan?"

"I can't believe we're having this conversation. This is so stupid."

"Why, we even look alike. *Na he pata.*"

"'We speak the same'? Not likely." Kyle translated the phrase mentally with far better recall than he had for German. "Don't you get it, Rupert? We're nothing alike. I don't need a play world anymore. There's a real world out there that's far more interesting, someplace where I'm going to make a difference. You, you're stuck here like some old tree stump waiting for the flowage to drain, sitting around complaining about the circumstance and not doing a damned thing about it. I can't wait to get as far away from here as I can. I'd rather live somewhere like Madison, where there's more than two theaters in town and 'ethnic food' doesn't mean pizza. Have you ever been to a city larger than Black River Falls? Have you ever even been out of Wisconsin? I don't see us much alike at all."

"I traveled farther than you can imagine. You know why I don't leave."

"You still expect some weird miracle out of the river? You're so full of—"

"We're kindred spirits, Kyle. Very much so. This place is the Traveling point. It leads home. To my home, yours, ours. That's why we're here. It's why I bought this land, and why I convinced your parents to care for you. I was a much more persuasive fellow in my youth."

"And you've never quite explained that to me either. Just what bomb is Mom going to drop next? That you're my real father?"

"No, gods no," Rupert said with what might have been a snort of amusement. "You're my work. That's all you've ever been. A piece of work."

"Work. Like you ever lifted a finger but to raise your glass for more wine—"

Rupert's chin thrust at him from the dark. "I had my work. You. You're my work of art, Kyle. I come to ask but one favor, one small favor, and you disdain me for the lifetime of companionship I've given you … lifetimes. Where there's magic, time passes swiftly, more than a month for every day here, more than a year for every fortnight, generations for every year. I've worked what small magic this world will tolerate to see to your needs, giving you a home, keeping you healthy and fed. I am utterly alone, as you. Yet you can't see that for your selfishness."

Kyle swallowed hard. There was something different in Rupert's stance, a pleading to be understood, not merely heard. A truer sorrow. He was falling into the man's fantasy, co-dependent.

"Alone in a house full of children?" Kyle scoffed.

"And your excuse? At least I know the place from which I came." Rupert sat on the splitting stump, settling his wine carefully on a patch of lawn. "So many times I swam to this river. Years passed in Metatha while I labored here but months. The world changed, the gods more forgotten with each return home. Now and then a Reign fetched me home for a few months or a year. One time I met a youngster who fit my mood better than my own son. I became his mentor. He learned from me more eagerly than Arlin, more eagerly than you. And when my protégé became ruler, Denalku, he, too, sent me here. In the end, I was generations older than my wife, and eventually she and my son far older than I. Then Denalku didn't return. No one came. I knew war had broken out with the Pale. And the people, wyseers, even Reign, had rebelled against Denalku. I'd even … helped defend my chieftain. I waited to be called home in service of my people, knowing minutes were hours, hours were days. But the river remained as dark and smooth as the night. I didn't want to think about why they hadn't come. I didn't want to think about what might have happened to my wife and son. I was so certain someone had to come, as I am the link. Yet no one came. But you."

Kyle felt something about the dark flowage calling to him, taunting him. Why did he let Rupert do this to him?

"What do you want from me, Rupert?" Kyle turned from the glittering water to find his uncle with shoulders bent, as he looked up from beneath dark brows.

"We are of one people, Kyle."

"Related, you always tell me that. Then how are we related?"

"Not related, not by blood, I don't think. But by … race I guess it would be. The only two of our race here. We must go home. It's been too long. We must go home. But I need you to take us there. That's what you've been training for; what I've been waiting for."

Kyle heard some deception in Rupert's tone, as if this was another of the many games he had played on Kyle through the years, his own private entertainment found in messing with Kyle's head. He shook himself for listening and daring to believe the unfounded nonsense

Rupert spouted about Metatha. He wanted to shove the old man into the flowage, be rid of him, at least wash away the foul stink of him. He knew he couldn't. As much as he wanted to dismiss this disgusting creature and his lies, Uncle Rupert was, well, family. Someone you had to care about despite the way he pushed all your buttons. Someone you—he couldn't quite think in terms of love—maybe in terms of, he'd miss Uncle Rupert if he died. Maybe he needed to feel a little more pity for a man so desperately out of synch with reality.

Rupert pulled from his jacket pocket another can of beer and handed it to Kyle. "You hate me because you fear me. You know I tell you the truth."

Kyle turned back to the water. The can sweated into his hands like the dew settling on the grass around him. In the far distance, deep booms echoed from Fort McCoy's bombing range where weekend warriors waged their mock battles, oblivious to the campers chatting quietly around their campfires, the lone honk of the occasional goose overhead and flutter of bat wing.

Rupert did actually work a little, at Fort McCoy, in civilian maintenance. He claimed some past as a soldier, though no one ever brought up which war or which campaign or how he had served, but it seemed to explain where his money came from. Rupert didn't seem to fit Vietnam, and was too young for World War II or Korea. Wouldn't war have taken him away from the flowage he must watch? Then again, maybe Rupert's fantasies were the results of some battlefield trauma, or his claim to time in service another of his fanciful tales. Next he might claim he was an alien delivered by UFOs and spend the next ten years trying to convince Kyle to believe that tale as well. Was he as crazy as Rupert to listen to any of it?

"You're well off the mark, Kyle," Rupert said softly. "When the first of the moon rises, find me here. It'll be a good time, when you are expected to be heading back to school and won't be missed. I need your help—"

"My help at what? Watching you lose your sanity? Maybe you should see someone, Uncle—"

"Just be here, Kyle. You'll understand."

Rupert gripped Kyle's elbow, peering up at him with his dark expression before his silhouette slipped back into the house. Kyle shivered. He had no reason to fear Uncle Rupert, yet he did, as if he touched something dark and cold that might yet tow him beneath the surface of the flowage.

CHAPTER TWO

Rupert studied the lure he tied to his line. A weedless silver spoon, perfect for the snaggy waters of the flowage, glimmered in the white glare of a propane lantern he'd set on the bank of Potter's Flowage. Moths flitted around the lamp as frog voices thrummed from nearby inlets. Rupert turned the spoon over and over. In his hand, it took on the aspect of a silver leaf fluttering to the ground.

Suddenly, instead of the dark water and the glaring lamp he recalled a lush valley. A tiny spring he and Denalku wriggled up through bubbled from the base of a sandstone bluff that rose red and furious from the head of the valley, blazing in the early rays of dawn on Shesta. Birds chattered. In the distance came the squawk of domestic fowl, and nearer grazed a herd of shaggy bison-like beasts. A gangly-legged creature, man-like, but unclothed save for a coating of his own hair, prodded the grazing animals with the twig end of a tree branch, sending them homeward with a few clicks of his tongue.

Denalku clapped his hands together. The man looked up, then swiftly dropped to his knees. The chieftain gave Ruperion a satisfied smile as he approached the kneeling Shestan. He took from his soggy robe a small box, then set a trembling hand on the man's head. The Shestan gazed upward with wide eyes, cattle forgotten, to look upon a god from the sacred spring that had yielded many a Traveler seeking the power of this world's herbs and powdered horn from its cattle.

"We are pleased by Shesta's devotion," Denalku said.

Both Metathans knew the Shestan couldn't understand a word of their language, if he even understood the Metathan pronunciation of the Shestan's own word for this world.

"We have a gift for you, a way for you to honor your gods. *Na he pata*." With this honored greeting between men of the same tribe, Denalku gifted the furry Shestans.

Denalku flipped a small pebble from his thumb. It blazed out, then dissolved into a tiny silver leaf that fluttered down into the grass beside the Shestan. It was the marker they always used in this world, proof of greater power. The silvery leaf image engraved on the ebony box mocked the Shestans' devotion to the Travelers.

The Shestan took the box as Denalku pantomimed how the Shestan should pour the contents of the vial within, still labeled with biohazard symbols, into a misting device also contained in the box, then shake the contents over each member of the tiny village as a blessing from the gods. Breathe deeply of the gods' healing essence, he implored through his motions. Slowly the Shestan backed away, head bowed in deference.

"He bears that box as if the greatest of treasures," Ruperion said as the Shestan hurried over the hill toward his village.

"Perhaps for them it will be."

Ruperion narrowed his gaze on his erstwhile pupil.

"Ruperion, we don't know what afterworld his people seek. Perhaps we have sent them somewhere better. Maybe they will be born to another world, a better one. They might next become Metathan, all these worlds are connected—"

"His luck, he'd be born in the Pale and you would assault him again with your evil—"

"I think that's enough judgment from you."

"Great One, what if here the Anthrax spores are as benign as the talking boxes from Earth that needed power we don't have to make them work? Yet in Metatha it could kill everyone; it could be more powerful. It could be contagious or spread. It could change into just about anything and pass from the Pale to our own people and all the cattle or every tree including the manfish—"

"You'd come up with excuses until the Pale were on our very doorstep—"

"Why not just make the fair fight?"

"We'd lose a fair fight! Do you think I don't know what my people think of me? They would desert me before fight for me. I am willing to risk this for the greater good."

Denalku's tone carried a power Ruperion had taught him. Ruperion felt genuine fear, low in his gut. How far could he push before Denalku would realize he no longer needed a personal wyseer? Did Denalku know that in many ways he wielded a greater and stronger wyseery?

"You wyseers and your sciences," Denalku continued. "And you, always theorizing. I'm a man of action."

Ruperion said nothing as they waited beside the Shestan's sacred spring.

"Besides," Denalku mused as the day lengthened. "If we're their gods, perhaps it's our right to do with the Shestans as we wish."

Ruperion stared at his chieftain. "You don't think our gods made the Shestans as well, Great One? What if our ability to change the worlds we visit betrays the gods' intent?"

"Oh, don't be a fool. Look at how simple they are. Clearly the gods thought them a lesser being and placed them here for us to use as we see fit, as they did the cattle and trees and stone of Metatha."

Ruperion felt the breaths shorten up in him and found it difficult to swallow. Travel wasn't a godly gift, but a theft, a wyseery. And now this. What had he done? If only he hadn't discovered the U.S. military, had never let Denalku abandon him on Earth for days—weeks, months—to explore and learn the languages and ways of alien peoples while years passed in his own home on Metatha, this the curse for meddling with the very ban he'd created.

It was he who had first Traveled and he who had banned it to all but the Reign. It took years to recover from the spells that opened the portals into the womb of the universe. And more to recover from the effort to lock them again, the key given to a Reign bearing a Travel stone who fetched from other worlds the trinkets the wyseers needed for their work. He meant well: Reign were banned from being wyseers. The Travel ban balanced the powers, ending an era when wyseers built personal arsenals to control their rulers. It had been a tortured world that drove him to the act of meddling with the gods' own portals. A worthy end to his efforts.

Then Ruperion made a wyseer of a Reign. Hadn't Ruperion been the first to argue, so long ago, at the corruptibility of power?

As the hours of Shesta passed, mere minutes to Metatha, Ruperion kept his sense of a vigil to himself, praying that here the disease would be benign, perhaps even beneficial, or at the worst no more troublesome than algae in a pond.

When at last they dared crest the distant hill as dusk shadowed the world, they saw a smoldering fire. No one stirred the fire for the Shestan communal meal. No one lingered by the village spring, laughing as children finger-painted with the red mud. A child wailed somewhere, then slowly wheezed to silence. Only the fowl continued their clatter.

"We should check to be sure they are not merely asleep or suffering from mild symptoms that will soon pass," Denalku said, taking a few steps down the hillside. He stopped, looking up at Ruperion, who hadn't moved.

"It may be in the air or contagious, Great One. I'm going no closer. I see clearly from here." Ruperion couldn't take his gaze from the little village, the curl of smoke rising so pleasantly, and the glint from the silver leaf resting atop the tiny, death-bearing ebony box beside the fire.

"Is this the way it works on Earth?"

Ruperion shrugged. "Maybe. Maybe faster here. Just as the pink quartzite I bring from Earth's Baraboo Hills means nothing to those in Baraboo, but is a powerful magic to us, for all we know this disease is more lethal or less in another world. They may recover, or linger near death for weeks only to succumb to starvation or neglect. We don't understand Traveling well enough to know what we do."

That last he meant as a rebuke. Denalku brushed it aside, striding by him back to the spring, forcing Ruperion to trot like a puppy to keep up with the man who had once followed him thus. He didn't even have time to grasp a breath, and barely an instant to touch his Chieftain before Denalku had dived back through the spring.

They emerged in a shallow pool a short distance from the city. The small wood surrounding the secluded pool gave off the chatter of dozens of tree rats, another mistake brought from a far world. Shedal awaited them again, along with a unit of Denalku's personal guard and a carriage.

Denalku scrubbed himself with the edge of the soft blanket Shedal held, shivering violently, his skin a mad red as if whatever madness his mind had created spread outward. How did he fend off the Traveling sickness that left Ruperion so disoriented he could barely keep his feet? Was this another manifestation of Denalku's growing mastery of wyseery?

"It worked," Denalku was telling Shedal.

"None too soon, Great One," Shedal said. "The Pale mass on the plain above the valley. Your subjects are restive and many away from their labors today, and wyseers and Reign are absent in numbers too large to be random."

"Send my gift to the Pale." Denalku said around a grin that might have been a sneer. "Have a false `traitor' offer it to the Pale, claiming it's a Traveling wyseery if they breathe deeply of its essence."

Shedal nodded and sped away on a lone horse as Denalku and Ruperion, surrounded by the high Chieftain's mounted guard, rode in the comfort of a carriage back to the palace city. No buses, no cars here. They were a primitive people, scavenging from other lands like the Earth crow that stole shiny things for the mere act of collecting them. What power did those shiny things bestow upon the bird?

Ruperion knew he shouldn't let his mind wander in Travel sickness. It left him vulnerable. Yet, if he didn't, the only thing he could focus upon was what they were about to unleash, in their own world. How much time had passed on Earth? But an hour? Could he find a way to return to Dugway and steal antibiotics to thwart the disease before they realized someone had walked off with two vials of anthrax? He had an anchor stone here—he hadn't been a total fool to put bans on so powerful a wyseery without a way to undo it. He'd used an artifact from Earth's own past to bind the Traveling stone Denalku cherished. Perhaps he could take Leta and Arlin with him, ensconce them in his Wisconsin cottage until he was certain no threat remained from Denalku—

Ruperion looked out the window of the carriage to see the sun reflecting from the gilded peaks of his home nestled among manfish trees high on the hill overlooking the valley and palace. The anchor stone was there, among his Travel logs, his store of powerful trinkets gathered from the hundreds of worlds he'd found so far, and the strongest artifacts that he held back from Denalku's portionings.

"Are we certain this is a safe thing to do?" Ruperion whispered to himself, hoping Denalku would hear, think. "What if it spreads to our own people? What if it lingers for eons in a place where people will encounter it again and again? There's talk the soils of Dugway are rich with latent anthrax that have killed flocks of sheep—"

Denalku glared at him. The carriage had come to a halt in the courtyard beside the palace. The river flowing languidly by them glittered darkly with shadows thrown by the high valley sides. The river disappeared to the east through a narrow notch where it then tumbled over a scarp to the ocean. There, fishing fleets would be sailing in with their catch—he could simply float—

"You are becoming a liability, Rupert," Denalku said in a tone that made Ruperion go chill, yanking him into the moment with the stress on a name the wyseer adopted in his Earth travels. Denalku took him by the arm, guiding him to the edge of the river and away from the guards. "Perhaps we would be better off if you were to leave for a while, gather wyseery somewhere out of the way to be Portioned to the faithful after all this is settled."

"I need to rest, Denalku. We have been to two worlds in two days! I'm Travel sick and dear Leta and Arlin have seen me but a week this whole year! Arlin's older than I am now, and—"

"I will retrieve you when the time is right. With this unrest, the rumor of a Traveling wyseer could trigger rebellion. We don't need people fearing a return to the dark days atop an invasion by the Pale! Shedal says rumors are rampant about you, that you haven't aged a day—"

"I wouldn't trust Shedal, Lord. I wouldn't doubt he's organizing rebellion in your very house. Don't his partner and daughter serve you?"

Denalku silenced him with a gesture that snapped Ruperion's tongue to the roof of his mouth with a wyseery stronger than Ruperion, ancient master, could easily counter.

"My mates are none of your affair. It is beneath you to speculate on the Queen's Consort and cast blame at my trusted servants! Is this some petty fear that I will ask Leta to join my house? She is well past child-bearing. Do not fear what you cannot understand."

Ruperion wanted to spout his denial but Denalku's spell held.

"It will be safer for you if no one associates you with what is about to happen."

Ruperion couldn't even protest before he felt Denalku's hand on him—and the splash of river water closing over his head. Denalku had pushed him, with more than just his hand, a hand holding the tiny Traveling stone Ruperion had hidden in the look of white quartz, when its true face was a dark thing of unknown origin. Dark, like the deeds done with it.

Ruperion breathed deep in protest to find his lungs filled with the musty flavor of tamarack-stained Potter's Flowage and the sweet pesticides from nearby cranberry bogs. He almost screamed his rage as he surfaced among the snags and reeds, too exhausted to more than flail to the safety of the shore.

For days he glared at each surfacing fish, watched each ripple from beaver or muskrat or water spider, each passing boat wake in the hope Denalku returned to lead him home. In Metatha time fled. Had he destroyed all of Metatha? Would Denalku arrive demanding an antidote the wyseer never dared seek? Would he expect greater and greater arsenals? Where would he draw the line? It should have been before Shesta. Perhaps this would be Ruperion's punishment for mentoring such a demon: He would forever sit here in this world of dullards blind to the magic surrounding them, waiting for a dead man to retrieve him home.

Rupert startled. A large moth burned on the lantern mantel, then dropped to the bottom of the lamp with a snap and a puff of smoke. He looked out over the dark flowage. Nothing surfaced. No bubbles rose from an arriving Traveler. It had been forever. Did the Valeuta still exist? Had the Pale consumed them? He looked down at the tiny silver lure in his hand and realized that he had clenched it in his fist. With a scowl at himself he ripped the barb from the flesh of his palm and cast into the dark night. The first of the moon approached. Then all the waiting would be over.

CHAPTER THREE

The last week before Kyle would pack up his rust-puckered Ford Escort and drive to Madison for the semester sped by. Rupert seldom troubled him. At least, relative to how often Rupert appeared out of nowhere with some oddment or other or some proclamation to make or obscure lesson to impart, this week he seemed scarce. Kyle tried to wipe away that last odd encounter with speculation at how much wine the old man had consumed. It left Kyle no more comfortable. Rupert wanted something from him. He stated it clearly: He needed Kyle's help to go home. What would be home to a delusional man? And how would he get there?

As another dusk crept over Potter's Flowage, Kyle wandered along the shoreline among reeds and sedges, tickseed and jewelweed, sneaking up on the leopard frogs and turtles to see how close he could come before they'd dart into the water. The turtles splashed in an ungainly urgency, the frogs leapt effortlessly and surely far enough out to taunt the bass and muskie. Mostly, water snakes scurried from the shore ahead of him to startle anything he hoped to see and sent the few leaves and tufts of cattail seed into the gentle, swirling flow.

"About time you showed up." Rupert's voice assaulted him from the bank so suddenly Kyle almost slipped into the mucky water.

"What?"

"I asked you to meet me here at the first of the moon." Rupert gestured toward the last sliver of moon in the twilit sky sinking into the west after the sun. "It's time to go home."

"Don't remember it," Kyle said with a nonchalant shrug he didn't feel. He felt like running. "And home appears to be around the bay—"

Kyle's arm jerked out in a gesture toward the house only a hundred yards distant across the water, but now seeming miles away.

"There's something I want you to have," Rupert said suddenly, in a tone so light and airy Kyle took an involuntary step back. Rupert held out a pecan-sized white stone. "It's to remind you of me," Rupert said easily as he dropped it in Kyle's palm. "This is your last year at school. I wanted to send you off with a memento. It's vested with all my hopes for you. I really am proud of you, you know."

Kyle swallowed down the tiny sense of guilt that leaped up at him. He'd become so cruel to Rupert, who really did dote on him. If the man just weren't so pathetic. Kyle nodded at the stone in his hand, noted its seeming flawless surface and dropped it in his pocket. Rupert was smiling at him, something that raised the hairs on Kyle's neck. Surely he'd just blundered right into whatever Rupert planned.

"I need a small favor. I dropped a pillbox in the water here when I was fishing and I hoped you'd fetch it to me." Rupert pointed toward a deep spot just off shore. Here no tree stumps grasped for the sky. Before Valley Power dammed Potter's Creek, the bank he stood upon had been a ridge overlooking a deep cut where the millrace powered a sawmill. A whole village had disappeared down there in the tea-stained murk of tree trunks rotting as they stood.

"It's better than thirty-foot here, Uncle Rupert."

"I must have it. It's something special to me. A memento Leta and Arlin gave me."

Kyle gave him a measuring glance. "What are you up to now? This is some ploy to get me to do something I don't want to do, again." In the back of his mind he heard Rupert's gravelly voice on a hushed night, speaking of the many times he swam to the flowage, of his thoughts of home and family gone forever.

"*Na he pata*," Rupert said with a smile.

"We speak the same." What else could that phrase mean to him that Rupert grinned so oddly?

"There's snags all over down there. It's dark. You're not even funny."

"You've never refused a demand of mine before, Kyle. You are, indeed, ready if you can resist a subtle magic."

"So you expect me to just jump in at your command?"

"You would have in the past," Rupert said with a wistful sigh. "I need you. We need each other. You can swim alone. I can't swim without you; the ban is on me, even though I changed the marker. Once it was black. It was a wild magic that uncolored it. Who knows what's become the control."

"Uncle Rupert, I'm sorry, I think you need help. I have a friend at school interning at a counseling—"

"You aren't a Nelson. You know that. You know I'm more like you than not. You know I've been here since the beginning. You know your parents defer in all decisions about you to me. How can you ignore everything I taught you, things your reason must show you? How can a man who claims college so enlightened him so quickly dismiss the unknown? There's magic in the water—"

"There's stumps and the bones of an old mill town—"

"Just as there are effigy and burial mounds down there. What power did those confer to the people here before you? The water can carry you many places, mean many things, be a portal to something beyond your knowledge. Remember the creation tales? The universe is a bubbled place in a womb full of life about to become. It's through the water that we go to Metatha. They are bound together, each world linked with the water of the god womb. My road home is right there." Rupert pointed out over the languid flowage.

Kyle took a swipe at a cluster of cattails, sending tufts of white over the dusk-dark water as Rupert stared at him with his disquieting gaze. The cool of evening raised tendrils of mist from the flowage. Frogs whirred out sudden and loud and a heron spread six feet of wing in flight.

"I wouldn't dismiss everything you say if any of it made any sense," Kyle said. He turned to leave.

"I know something of your true parents." Rupert blurted the statement, stopping Kyle mid-step.

"You would seem desperate, now, Uncle Rupert."

Rupert pulled a small bundle from a clump of dogwood on the bank beside him. He held up a cloak of rich green, but tattered and worn. A glimmer of gold sewn onto the hem would be a family clan marker; he remembered that tale.

"Your mother once wore this cloak," Rupert said softly. He touched a turquoise pin in the shape of a Navajo lizard clipped to the collar. "She was Reign. From the bloodstains on this cloak, wrapped about you, the soiling of new birth and injuries, it would seem you survived a battle. I knew the girl to whom Denalku presented this pin. She would have been near him. Remember the Pale? They were massing for war when I left. Did they succeed? Instead of the High Chieftain coming as promised, a tiny babe rose up through the bubbles one morn: A babe that brought with him the key to the portal home. Instead of ever looking again upon my own child, my own partner, I had only you. Generations have passed in these twenty-one years. Did the Reign survive? Have they evolved as this world, swiftly? Did the Reign or the Pale discard clannish tradition in favor of democracy? Have they had a cold war or arms race or space race? Have they gone in search of the worlds to which they once Traveled through a lost magic?" Rupert was trembling a little, and that terrified Kyle more than anything the old man had ever said or done before.

"A small stone gripped in the palm of a babe, that's what brought you here," Rupert continued. "You can take me back with you, but we must see the nature of that world first; we must be careful. See, wyseers are both good and bad. They can give people good things: medicine, security, readings of the future. As well they can be evil. They can twist wyseery by twisting nature. People, whoever came to succeed Metatha, say, may not perceive me as a good thing."

Kyle didn't immediately reply. One-half of him thought that Rupert had finally gone off the deep end. But Rupert had seeded this ground for years. Lunch went sour in Kyle's belly.

"So like I'm some long-lost prince to return home, is that what you're claiming?" Kyle asked, trying to keep the sarcasm out of his tone.

"Gods forbid," Rupert said with a snort. "Reign are merely a clan and caste. The High Chieftain selected his successors from among his kin, based upon merit, usually. Weren't you listening all these years? There are all levels of petty nobility among the Reign. Likely you're less important than the least of goatherds: at least they know something of the land they live in. If the Pale won the battle, then they rule. Who knows what the intervening years brought? I only know that someone sought to send at least one Reign away with the tool to return, a tool I couldn't use without a Reign, one old enough and mature enough to do what I need. Your parents wanted you safe, Kyle. I have tried to do that for you. I've tried to open your mind to the kinds of things—"

"This is cruel, Rupert. Don't you see that? It's hard enough getting over that weird sense of being discarded. Even though someone else wanted me, it's hard wondering why, and what things would have been like, always wondering. Were they just young? Were they on drugs? Were they abusers? Did they go to jail? Were they just that irresponsible? Did my father know I existed? Did her parents insist? Did they die? It's not an easy thing to get past, wondering all these things, answering the question of why you feel different, wondering why my parents saw fit to lie to me about me, about you. Now you come along and build some fantasy. It's a Navajo scarf pin; probably the cloak came from some Renaissance Faire. You're trying to screw me up with all your lies. It's just cruel, Rupert. It's *cruel*."

Kyle took a step, but Rupert blocked his path. "Listen to me, Kyle I need you. A simple thing!"

"You always call this exile. Why do you think that? What awful thing do you think you did that deserves exile?"

"You don't understand. I never asked for this. This is where I am—"

Kyle threw his hands up in dismissal and tried to dart around him. Rupert grabbed for him, missed. Kyle lost his balance. He felt the slightest pressure against his side that sent him off his feet to plunge into the dark waters of Potter's Flowage with the white stone still in his pocket.

CHAPTER FOUR

Kyle gasped as dark, ice-cold spring water closed over his head. He contorted, his mouth opening to fill with a bitter taste that oddly refreshed him, as if he breathed. Yet, no water reached his lungs. It assaulted him like a childhood nightmare of being tossed adrift, wailing, dragged downward by something—

He kicked for the surface, but the move propelled him sideways and down. What if he became tangled in some old stump or treetop? Kyle kicked again, angling deeper. Nothing like his feet moved him. He couldn't see his hands. Yet he could see through the dark water, if he really saw, rather sensed.

Startled, he drew a breath. Cold water rushed into him. More kicks propelled him deeper, farther, into a murky world that seemed familiar, unfamiliar, and at the same time nothing like Potter's Flowage.

Finally, instead of kicking he slithered upward. At last he broke the surface to find sky. The air thumped with the pulse of wings rising from the surface. For a second the air burned him, the sun on his skin seared. He flailed, his arms splayed out, limp. Panic seized him as he flopped, limbs unresponsive. The feeling fled in an instant when his legs kicked free of the cold paralysis that had gripped him and the blazing sun became something warm and almost familiar.

Treading water, he shook the wet hair from his eyes. His mouth fell open and he almost sank again, too stunned to swim.

Kyle Nelson dog paddled, not in a musty Black River flowage at dusk, but in a warm sun-gilt sea. He tasted the brine on his tongue and deep in his throat as if he'd drunk of it, breathed of it, exhaled it. What looked like sea birds disturbed by his wild splashing whirled skyward. A light rain of feathers still fell from their flight.

A gentle swell and salt water buoyed him as a strong current drew him shoreward, where stark black cliffs, stained by the white streaks of a rookery, reached from the sea. Weathered trees fringed the tops of columnar pillars of stone behind which rose a distant snow-capped peak. The waves swept over a black-sand shore clearly built by volcanism.

Where was Rupert? Where was this?

Not Metatha.

Surely he remained snagged in some old tree—perhaps even the moldering mill works in the bottom of the flowage—and now his dying mind created this pleasant possibility to shield him from painful drowning.

Or he'd swum right into Rupert's tales.

He felt giddy and foolish to believe anything his eyes revealed.

"We aren't in Wisconsin anymore, Toto," he whispered to himself, so stunned, his own attempt at humor annoyed him.

Even if Metatha, it didn't seem quite like Rupert's Metatha. No giant Metathan fishing armada covered the sea with multi-hued boats, their stone-weighted nets clattering on decks. No flags whipped from the bluffs to signal ships into port. No lithe shell divers leapt hundreds of feet into the sea. He saw none of the towers and rooftops of a city peeking above the crest. No swarm of children played "net the fish" on docks that stretched out into the bay.

Only an empty shoreline greeted him and the multi-hued swirl of fowl crisscrossing the sky, bobbing in the waves or resettling in his wake to chatter angrily amongst themselves.

Once he'd trusted Rupert, hungrily sought a sense of belonging to some greater purpose or culture, an exile from a lost world. It explained so many feelings the younger Kyle had felt. Then common sense—if not science—proved Rupert false, one more betrayal. Yet, here he swam in a warm sea when Rupert should be chortling from a marshy bank.

But Rupert's Metatha had existed hundreds of years in the past, twenty-one generations, or so he said. Had the Pale and Reign fought to their mutual extinction? Or had Kyle come upon some desolate shore far from habitation? Was this even Metatha, if anywhere? If the stone truly brought him here, how come he didn't merely pop back into Potter's Flowage? Why hadn't he come up beside the sprawling palace Rupert had described so many times? Could he even go home at all? Supposedly each Metathan puddle led to a different world, yet none of Rupert's tales began in the sea.

Kyle's head throbbed. His limbs felt leaden as he let the swells tow him shoreward until sea grass swirling in a low tide brushed against him. Numb. Just numb. If he could just think—but an odd exhaustion, a heaviness crept into his mind even as it turned his limbs to rubber.

When he reached the black-sand beach, he crawled above the waterline and collapsed. His whole body trembled. He knew he should hide first, or be sure this was a safe place. He couldn't even think to recall if Rupert had described any predators on Metatha, other than the Pale. Unable to move, he sank into the sand. Something in the sound of the ocean, in the warm, black shore, drew him as if into comforting arms.

When he opened his eyes he knew he had slept. The sun had moved beyond the towering black cliffs to slant at the sea, leaving him in a cool shadow. A tide had come in, threatening to wash him from a narrow shelf of sand that would afford no protection were the swells to grow. No dream then. He shivered, feeling sunburned, the salt and sand on his skin itching as gooseflesh took him, his still-damp T-shirt and jeans no comfort. Around him he found only a few boulders weathered from the cliffs above, and a host of silvery driftwood that broke the line of dark beach—some of it wedged high up in the rocks, with girths at least twelve feet in diameter. He examined one such monster, running his hand across irregular rings, years, centuries, if trees were trees everywhere. Had this tree grown and fallen in the course of Kyle's own lifetime? He swallowed hard. He needed to work through that, or maybe not think at all.

His legs trembled again and he sat, hugging his knees to his chest to stare out at the eastern horizon. It could be Earth, yet not. The sky appeared to him almost darker on the edges as if twilight approached from all directions, with several star-like points already appearing in the eastern horizon, bright and near though sunlight remained in the western sky. The whole world seemed to somehow cant away from him, quivery—

He retched the briny taste from his gut, feeling no better, only shakier.

"Get a grip, Nelson," he muttered as he stood again, his body protesting. He stumbled north along what appeared to be a wider stretch of beach. The black sand yielded beneath him as if he walked through a mire and often he waded through the surf at narrow points, plodding what seemed like only a hundred yards in an hour of labor. Something about this world, or traveling to it, swiftly had him in a sweat and pulled the breath from him in gasps.

He had never been athletic. A decent softball or soccer player maybe, but he didn't have the farmer build of most of his friends. He'd stayed on the lean side, much to the annoyance of his older sisters. Still, he shouldn't feel this exhausted by just walking along a beach.

Dusk came swiftly and soon after, darkness fell. The sand beneath his sodden sneakers gave way to sea-washed black stone, grading from pebbles to palm-sized, near-flat ovals like hamburger patties. The comparison made his stomach growl. He remembered Rupert's testy remarks about time; perhaps the splash from his fall was just reaching shore in his own world and thus less than an hour had passed since he'd stuffed himself with pizza while the rest of the Nelson clan went out for fish. Here, most of a day had passed. He shook his head at the thoughts, detached, not wanting to believe any of it. Yet, here he was.

As night overtook him, he'd have had no sense of the world around him without the brilliant stars. The dark sea purled surf on one side, the black cliffs rose on the other. Black stone stretched away beneath him. He felt so alone. Not the lonely he could feel among a crowd of Nelsons, but isolated, like the last man on Earth, an eternal shadow moving through eternal darkness.

He hesitated, wondering if he dare go on. If he dived back into the sea, what would happen? Would the white stone take him to Potter's Flowage, only to find Rupert there with his questions and demands? What could he report: a stark shoreline, no more. Besides, the more he paced along the base of these interminable cliffs, the more he wanted to see what lay above, where he'd glimpsed that distant snow-capped mountain. Did the gilded palace that Rupert spoke of, with its lofty halls and green-robed gentry stand beside the river he'd described, just over the ridge, anachronistic bits of other worlds decorating its walls and the streets of the city? What snippets of other worlds might he see? Would there be family to welcome him, wondering and amazed that he had come to them after so many generations?

The more he let his curiosity toy with him, the more he wanted to let all his thoughts spill out at Rupert in a rush of apology for his disbelief. He wanted to know more. How many of Rupert's tales were tales? What of other worlds? Were there people there, or creatures? Was it a Star Wars universe of intelligent oddity, or a Star Trek world of bumpy-headed humanoids? A giddiness filled him, of wonder and fear, adrenaline pounding through his veins. He needed to see beyond the next curve of shore, reach the cliff top and the mountain vista beyond. Kyle walked on, ignoring the way the stones bruised his feet through his shoes.

A moon pulled up from the sea, a blue and oddly misshapen creature much pock-marked and far too close for comfort. Kyle paused in his trek to stare. Soon after, something more like Earth's moon emerged, more distant, with its own tiny yellow satellite in tow, the latter racing about the bright moon in a path Kyle could almost mark. The Guardians, Rupert had called them: Danat, the grandfather and old guard moon grown slow and dim with age—like this blue beast?; Kylik, the light son who followed his father—sure and keen as a sword; and Siph, the grandson, a mere shadow of the father he tagged behind, the warrior yet to be made.

This indeed was Metatha. He hadn't pictured the moons this way. Not with Danat seeming so close, an illusion that made it appear as if it might scrape the top of the cliff as it passed. It seemed to take ages to draw near. Then Kyle's heart leapt in his chest and a tiny thrill of fear raced through him as, nearing, the moon seemed to race at him like a canyon wall on a white-water river. Gazing up gave him that carnival-ride sense of the world spinning, as if he lay on his back watching clouds pass overhead. Nor had he imagined Kylik so blazing, like an eclipsed sun shedding a dim day-like light, and Siph appeared to zip across the face of Kylik as the larger moon crept to the cliff face and disappeared beyond, losing its race with Danat.

Gawking at the sky, barely watching where his feet took him, he felt the tug of something flitting about his face. In a panic, he swung his hands in the dim light, briefly making contact with something soft yet mobile. It flitted away only to return and hover like a hummingbird, now and then coming closer. At last it snagged a lock of his hair, yanked with more strength than he would have imagined for its size, and sped away.

It felt like a short night, dawn arriving strange and sudden. Rupert had never mentioned it, but certainly another world wouldn't work on a twenty-four-hour clock. He stumbled on over the stones, their clatter beneath his feet lost in the morning's high tide swirling about his ankles. He clung with one hand to the cliff wall, wondering if he would thus walk the circumference of a continent because he could find nowhere to climb the cliffs. Or would he collapse soon, desperate for water and food?

When first he noticed the rolling thunder, he thought it a trick of wind or wave. The sun, something less bright than he imagined, had been up for a short time when he rounded a bend and stopped in awe. A broad river dropped from the cliffs to the sea in a pounding roar, impassable. There he saw the first sign that someone other than fowl had lived in this world.

Not merely a staircase, a work of monumental proportion zigzagged across the cliff face beside the falls, reaching skyward some five hundred feet before disappearing above the cliff.

No marina awaited at the bottom of the falls. Nothing grew here but lichen and barnacles and the depth of the driftwood. The world remained as oddly unpeopled as before, but now with the eerie sense of emptiness in a place that shouldn't be. Rupert left in a time of war—

how could Kyle have so disbelieved everything Rupert told him? With what arrogance had he dismissed this fellow Traveler?

He had a brief image of the man's rheumy eyes flashing in firelight, the wine-purple spittle gathering at the corners of his mouth as he spoke of a special world only good children could know.

He pulled the white stone from his pocket. Kyle nearly stumbled, stunned to find no white stone, but an almond-sized black stone as glassy as obsidian. His heart climbed up into his throat. His hand began to tremble. He gripped the stone in his palm, forcing himself to carefully return it to his pocket before he dropped it in the surf.

Sudden and keen he recalled the boggy scent of Potter's Flowage. Not even during that first night alone in Madison had he so missed not just the scent of home, but even the glutter of idling boat engines, the chunk of a canoe striking a submerged stump, and the spit and bubble of fish in the deep fryer. He may never have fit in, but it was still home.

Now the magic that brought him here had changed. What if he could never return and Rupert couldn't retrieve him? Where had Rupert got off thinking he could do this without Kyle's consent? But then, he hadn't believed the old sot when he did ask for Kyle's help. Maybe all these years when he'd been so out of step his body had been crying out for his birth world. What if he could never go home? He deserved at least the choice!

He took a deep breath, another, and tried to control the way his thoughts raced through him out of control. It didn't mean the magic wouldn't work.

Magic! Why hadn't Rupert mentioned this little oddity of stones and color shifting? Rupert, who should be here himself. This was Rupert's dream, Rupert's home. Though maybe Kyle's, too. It was all too much to think about. If only he could clear his head.

Nearing the stairs up the cliff face, he found moss-slick steps collecting the mist blowing from the falls. The water had the clean scent of fresh, but he didn't dare drink from it until he could see from where the river flowed, letting just the mist rest on his tongue the way it had plastered his hair to his forehead in moments. He could have wrung out his shirt and his jeans remained salt-stiff and clammy. He shivered, feeling the power of the falls thundering up through his feet, beating the air as if to steal his breath away.

Now he saw that fittings remained where a railing had once bounded the stairs. He gripped damp and crumbled steps that were stained white, despite the mist, where birds had turned them into nesting shelves. As he climbed the steep cliff face he thought surely he'd fall into that thunder of water, or break on the rocks below. Each moment he expected some predator to sting or bite his groping fingers. He almost lost his grip several times as he spooked a bird from its nest and the damp, ammonia-pungent rookery left his eyes watery and vision unclear.

When at last he reached the top, he only slowly crept above the last stair, imagining a village or collection of farms stretched out along the river.

His breath caught in his throat. A lake spread away at his feet, its surface a-flutter with waterfowl of varying sizes and colors, and the sweeping shoreline of a lush valley. Red rock cliffs rose on either side, again in the steep columns of cooled lava. More than two miles distant, the valley head sported another large waterfall, and beyond, snowy mountains jut into the horizon. Near at hand a jumble of stone filled a notch that split the diamond-hard columns of lava through which the river flowed, damming it to form the lake.

The steps opened onto a crumbled platform in an almost overgrown clearing, which quickly gave way to thick brush and a forest of multi-hued trees. Some sort of animal path edged the lakeshore, often disappearing. The calm lake drew him, icy to the touch, his presence sending a host of waterfowl paddling away with irritated clucks, quacks and hisses, some of them easily larger than a grown man, other fowl so small they wouldn't fill a child's hand.

Risking the nasty intestinal parasite he was sure he'd acquire, he drank deeply of acidic water that trickled down the shore to seep into the lake.

If anyone still lived in Metatha, certainly they would live in this valley. At least their houses would line the bluffs. He imagined looking out each morning on such a view, sunlight rushing across the valley between clouds, the greens seeming ever so much greener than anything that could grow—rainforest lush, yet northern forest dry. He had stumbled into Eden. An oat-like grass reached well above his waist in clearings beside his path. Trees shook multi-hued leaves in a breeze that didn't touch the lake. Auburns, greens, silvers, intermixed in a variegated fringe. One tree species, jutting above the canopy, sported giant grey-green leaves and bore a gold seed the size of a grapefruit.

A slash of yellow fluttered before his eyes. He jumped back, nearly stumbling in the tangled undergrowth. A bird darted in to sample a drop of sweat on his forehead before backing away.

It struck him that he heard only bird-chatter and the bright flutter of wings. No insect or rodent or hint of people troubled this Eden. The closer he looked the more he noted how the foliage seemed to undulate with birds, most of which seemed fitted to the plant upon which it fed, including a green-gold iridescent species swarming the giant golden seeds. Multitudes of green birds stirred the grass. Others competed over giant flowers, plumage the bright pink of the bloom, tail jutting from the flower like stamen and pistil as they shoved one another aside. They seemed to occupy every niche that other creatures filled in Kyle's own world.

Island evolution, he decided, like the Galapagos finches they talked about in Freshman geology.

Something about that struck him, that he should remember from Rupert's stories. But no coherent thought could compete with all that he took in as if it were newly painted or freshly made for him to view. It couldn't be only birds—something had made the hesitant trail he'd walked.

He decided these must be the lands of the Valley People—the Valeutans, Rupert had called them. The Pale lived from a broad basin of high desert and grassland ringed by mountains. Rupert's people came from a thriving city beside a river, fleets of fishing boats dotting the seas nearby. How many valleys would he need to search before he found Rupert's people? And why had they abandoned this valley and the stairs to the sea?

He scanned the valley's length. The high falls at the head of the valley obscured what lay above. He needed a sense of where in Rupert's world he stood.

Kyle trudged along the tangled lakeshore trail fighting down the light-headedness of hunger and whatever it was about Metatha or his journey that made him feel so weak and disoriented.

His attention swung up to the trees with their gold seed. It was more a fruit he realized when he saw the way the seed dripped some sticky nectar that engrossed a dingy ground bird so that he almost trampled the creatures before they moved out of his way.

He tripped. His knees took the blow from a crumbling stone curb that ran from the lake and up into the colorful forest spreading across the valley sides. The stone curb hedged cobbled pavement, now the food for roots that ran right into the deep, cold lake. Around him hummocks of vegetation took on the shapes of crumbled buildings beside which grew the giant gold-fruit trees. Everything spread downhill to the edge of the vast lake.

Kyle struggled up the valley side for a better view and there, at last, with a sinking feeling of loss he couldn't quite justify, he saw Rupert's city.

Beneath the surface of the icy lake and its complement of waterfowl he clearly discerned the remains of a city drowned. Whether because of some calamity, or deliberately, Rupert's river had been dammed at the notch to swallow the valley. Far out toward the middle, shoals formed by what must be turrets or towers close to the surface. What he had before thought to be tree stumps or rock ledges were roof crests and wall tops.

As he stared down at the lake from the shade of a towering gold-fruit tree, he saw again Rupert's intense dark gaze, his mulish insistence that he must return home to Metatha. Beside the flowage, at moonset, Rupert had radiated the excitement of a child about to open a present. The old man had waited forever, generations, to come home to his people, and they were gone. No one had been here for lifetimes, possibly twenty-one lifetimes.

What tragedy befell this city on the day of Kyle's birth? Had his parents really walked this place?... This place. His heartbeat coursed in his temples. Was this the home he'd been ripped from, the reason nowhere felt right?

A chunk of gold fruit, whittled free by birds, plunked him on the head. As he retrieved the discarded rind, its citrus-like aroma assailed him and his stomach let out a long growl. Emboldened, he brushed aside a flitter of birds and tugged a gold-fruit free of the tree. The rind felt soft like an orange, but thinner. It yielded to the pressure of his finger to squirt him in the eye with something that looked, smelled and stung like a cross between an orange and a watermelon. Several brownish birds scurried from the undergrowth, one already picking at the fallen rind, the other darting in to catch the juice running down Kyle's arm to drip from his elbow.

Kyle touched his tongue to the salmon-colored fruit, waiting for the fateful moment when his breath would seize up on him or his skin begin to tingle or his heart stop. His mouth watered for more and he gave in, ignoring the scavenging birds as he sated himself on the tangy fruit.

The pale Metathan sun had moved toward the distant mountain peaks before he had eaten his fill. A scattering of gold-fruit rinds about him drew a confusion of birds so numerous the ground seemed to writhe.

He checked the stone in his pocket again. Still black, shiny, it told him nothing. Did he now return to Rupert to tell him his world was gone? He was so tired. Should he go home, sleep, and plan his return? But this was just one valley … A vast distance separated him from the nearest mountain peak he'd seen. He needed to come back with something. Perhaps the people had moved somewhere up beyond the waterfall at the valley head. The sun's slanted rays glowed from the mist of the distant cascade, taunting him with the mystery of what lay beyond, the source of the cold river that had swallowed the city, like Potter's Mill somewhere beneath the surface of Potter's Flowage all those years. Rupert deserved some better explanation for his long wait, a peace offering from his disbelieving protégé.

"Just do it," he muttered to himself. "You know you want to. It's not like you'd fly all the way to Tokyo just to see the airport."

The path that led away toward the upper end of the valley appeared to have once served as a major artery west. As it left the crumbled city behind, fewer gold-fruit trees reached through the canopy. Kyle gathered as much fruit as he could tie into his t-shirt and slung it over one shoulder before striking out for whatever lay beyond Rupert's valley.

Either distance deceived, or the groggy sense he'd felt since he'd arrived, combined with exhaustion, slowed him. At dusk, he had only just reached the foot of the giant falls on the west end of the lake. The view behind—the glitter of stars reflecting from the lake, the strange blue-blackness of the sky and the reddish valley sides—stole his breath. He wished he could just soak it in slowly, like a Saturday morning fishing for bass in the Black River backwaters as the mist rose into the sun. But he didn't dare treat this place so casually. He needed to find a safe place to sleep. So far he'd only given a few hairs to the local fauna. But something else might be hankering for his blood.

The path zig-zagged across the cliff toward the head of the falls, which dropped from a height even greater than the falls to the sea. From this higher elevation at the base of the falls, he could clearly discern the submerged city that once filled the entire valley. Traces of its edges crawled out the other side of the lake, and the hint of roads crested the valley sides to some purpose north or south that perhaps only Rupert could tell him.

He sat for a moment on a crumbling wall that had once girded the road up the scarp.

When he opened his eyes from his unintended sleep, the sight of Danat's blue and craggy face seeming so close—its mirror in the lake racing toward his feet—he almost fell backwards into the boiling water at the base of the falls. As Kylik pulled above the horizon, Kyle wondered how long he'd slept, what time was here. He hurried to rouse himself and climb the looping road to the unknown beyond.

He was crossing a long loop in the road near its crest, noting how the shadows played along the cliffs to reveal wind-hollowed caves, when he saw a glimmer of light.

He froze. Not moonlight flickering from water or leaf, he clearly discerned the warm yellow glow of a lamp. The lamp dipped, swung, neared. It took a course adjacent the path he followed yet below the crest of the scarp he hoped to top. In Kylik's light he could now see it was a well-worn path. Should he follow it? Should he hide?

"*Ki' ktal nethra pata tathral?*" The demand came from behind him as another lamp emerged suddenly. It took Kyle an instant to realize he knew the words. Or at least he thought he did. "Who are you to walk the same road" he imagined at first, then remembered that the inflection on "*pata*" could change its meaning to "traveler." Who was he to walk the traveler's road. Hadn't Rupert used that odd inflection in his last, "*Na he pata,*" moments before tipping Kyle into Potter's Flowage?

Another lamp emerged to his right and left, and the one that had been adjacent now swung before him, lighting only barely the shape of someone slightly shorter than Kyle. The speaker again made his query. The Traveler's road. Rupert referred to the magic as Traveling. He tried to shake loose all the strangeness rushing him, his giddy fear, the odd detachment and exhaustion he'd felt since arriving, the oddity of all Rupert's tales coming to life.

"*Na he pata,*" Kyle said aloud around the breath seizing up inside him, surprised he could even remember to utter Rupert's favorite line, one that doubled as a greeting.

People. He'd found people. He couldn't feel more disoriented if he had suddenly found himself walking in the world and meeting up with the characters of any other fairy tale he'd been told as a child.

The stance of those around him softened slightly. Remembering Rupert's instruction, he held his hands out, palm up, to reveal the sticky juice of gold fruit and the bloody scrapes of his climb up the scarp.

The figure before him held up a light to reveal himself a man of some forty years. He had dark hair, like Kyle's but flecked with grey. His stature was bent, though his expression indicated no weariness with the world. The lamplight glittered from eyes as dark and glassy as Rupert's. The man echoed Kyle's greeting.

"Stranger, we watched you follow the Traveler's road. We watched you honor the manfish. What draws you here? Where are you going?" the man asked.

Manfish. That didn't translate right, certainly. Metathan had always seemed a pictorial language, not unlike German, in which the description of something might somehow be contained in the compounding of its words.

Manfish. How could he explain when he didn't know who these people were or into what he had stumbled, nor even whether he was in danger?

"I am a stranger," he admitted, palms still up in what he was pretty sure was a gesture of non-aggression. "I have lost my way. I fell into the sea and was washed to this shore."

His questioner glanced outward beyond the ring of light thrown by the lanterns.

"It is well then that we find you," the man said. "We are, perhaps, better prepared to lead you back to your road."

The man held out his hands, though one still gripped a tiny lantern, then bowed until his cheeks touched his forearms. "*Atathal Rehatna*," he said, introducing himself as Atatha—some diminutive of road—from Red Bridge, or Ledge.

"Kyle Nelson, from Wisconsin," Kyle offered, wondering how his hosts would take this oddity. Thus far they had done nothing threatening. Kyle doubted he could defend himself against so many, especially with only a pocketknife.

Atatha threw a sharp glance at someone else Kyle couldn't make out in the dim light.

"Kyle Nelson, you will be guest in my home, humble as it is," Atatha said. "Kylikset nears and the Traveler's road is not safe in the dark beyond this point. You may wish news before you proceed on your way."

Kyle nodded at what sounded sensible, just as he realized that something in the scent of the burning lamps had changed. They gave off a sweet smell like incense. It made him light-headed, giddy. He felt himself swaying on feet that hadn't been all that sturdy to begin with.

"Forgive me, I feel … off," Kyle managed, unable to find the word in this tongue to describe the way he really felt.

"We take you somewhere safe. It is better you do not know the path." The words came from a woman. He could only nod dumbly as his knees buckled. Arms were there to keep him from keeling face first into the rocky path.

He was at their mercy, carried by unseen hands, yet he felt comforted. Friend, or foe, people populated this world. People who spoke in a language he knew. He let his imagination wander through dreams in which birds carried him high above the valley.

CHAPTER FIVE

A rasp and snap like a turning pepper mill roused him. It intruded on Kyle's sleep like the strong odor making his nose twitch and the coarse fabric itching his skin. He forced an eye open to discover he rested on a mat in a low-ceilinged, smoky cavern open to the day on one side. His jeans and t-shirt hung from a dowel just inside the cave opening. A small fire burned at the mouth where sunlight made a silhouette of a stooped figure working mortar and pestle.

He pulled aside a blanket to find himself dressed in a knee-length tunic sewn from a burlap-like material. A rope belt gathered the tunic at his waist and supported an empty purse-like pouch. Bare legs glared back at him. He gazed about in sudden panic, then realized the few things he'd carried in his pockets, including pocketknife, keys and sodden wallet, had been carefully set upon a small stone ledge jutting from the cave wall near his clothing. The black Traveling stone glittered in the sunlight, beyond his reach.

He tried to pull up his knees to rise. A small grunt escaped him as muscles and joints protested, and drew the attention of the man at the cave mouth.

"Traveling is not easy on the body, they say," the man said, the words taking a long moment to sort into meaning, as if he must decipher poor English around a bad accent. Atatha the man had named himself in the dark near the top of the waterfall, what, last night?

"Traveling?" he asked as he struggled to gather his thoughts. Certainly, they could have done him harm by now if they meant to. What did they know or surmise about him?

Atatha worked at his mortar and pestle in silence, a glance from the corner of Atatha's eye reminding Kyle keenly of Rupert.

"Forgive me." Kyle again made the palm up gesture Rupert had taught him. "I forget courtesy in my confusion."

Atatha tapped his chest then flit his hand away as if to simulate the flap of a bird wing or the swim of a fish.

"It is not so kind to put the Traveler to sleep to make a guest of him. The headache and stomach-sick should pass soon." Atatha smiled suddenly to greet a slight figure briefly framed at the cave mouth. As she ducked within and saw Kyle, the new arrival, too, made the strange gesture from her chest to swim away, before she paced to a flattened boulder cluttered with a collection of lidded pots, spoons, knives, mallets, bowls and other cookware. She carefully kept her gaze averted.

"Jia, greet our guest," Atatha stated.

She turned, the elfin features of a girl or young woman catching the light, though she moved with more grace and control than he expected in one who appeared so young. She bowed, arms outstretched, long dark hair falling over them to reveal blue and green feathers bound into an occasional braid.

"Traveler Kyle Nelson from Wisconsin, may your Travels be profitable. We speak the same."

"Just Kyle is fine."

"Jia is my *etlith*," Atatha offered as Jia studied him with some combination of awe and skepticism not unlike his own look on this world. Etlith seemed to have its root in three or four different words. Kyle decided it meant something of a disciple or student.

"Her parents sent her to me because the manfish dreams said she would be ours, and her parents follow the *Fidrel*. We are pleased the Traveler came first to the Fidrel."

Manfish again. Fidrel, something to do with follower or faithful? Kyle shook his head. "Forgive me, I'm not sure I'm understanding. Are you a priest?"

Atatha smiled and studied Kyle from beneath his brows, reminding him of Rupert when he played coy. "I am Fidrel," Atatha stated as Jia offered a steaming bowl to Kyle.

He recognized seaweed, a few floating seeds of the oat grass he'd seen, and chunks of some sort of seafood in a thick soup.

"Is this manfish?" he asked as he tested the stew.

Jia gave a derisive snort. Atatha cleared his throat sharply. Hastily, Jia bowed.

"Forgive me, Kyle," she whispered. Again her hand made that strange motion from her chest.

"Perhaps the lore goes by another name in Kyle's land," Atatha said carefully. "He may even call his gods elsewise. Please forgive Jia. The excitement of your arrival clearly impairs her judgment."

Kyle weighed each word he heard against what he thought they meant. "It is my own fault," he said. "I am new to this ... shore. I arrived just two days ago, and climbed the stairs to the lake and submerged city."

"We call the city Ta'atit," Atatha said.

Kyle puzzled over that only a moment. A place of hidden treasure.

"I confess I do not know where I am. I fear I will never find my way home. It was all an accident. I fell ... from a ship." No, I was pushed by an ancient wizard who spent twenty-one years manipulating me, he thought, then stopped himself abruptly. What if these people could do magic, as Rupert claimed, and read his mind?

Atatha nodded at his mortar and pestle while Jia's gaze narrowed on him a little, her hand in the little pouch hanging from her belt appearing to work some object there.

"You came among us, Kyle, and that is very good. If you had continued on, well, I cannot speak to your safety," Atatha said. "The manfish revealed itself in you."

"Why would my safety be at risk? What happened to Ta'atit? What is a manfish? Why have you brought me here?" Kyle didn't mean to sound so desperate and angry, but as the soup struck his stomach he began to feel uneasy again, that odd floating sensation that had assailed him on the stony beach.

Atatha turned back to his work, his mouth slowly arching toward a frown.

Jia gave Kyle a chunk of heavy bread that had a strong taste of citrus and spice. He leaned back against the cavern wall as she squatted before him, her earnest face seeming too wise for her apparent age, nothing like the giggling nieces and cousins Kyle had left behind. Jia, like Atatha, wore garb similar to that in which he'd been dressed—a variety of feathers and multi-hued quills worked into them in differing patterns—though both had a heavier dark over cloak, soft and more painstakingly woven, like the green cloak Rupert had shown him. Tiny details woven into the fabric were lost in deep soiling that remained despite being scrubbed until threadbare.

Then he realized that Jia's frame appeared thinner than would seem healthy, her dark hair dull. Had he eaten their entire morning meal himself?

"Ta'atit we lost in war, many lives ago," Jia said. "That story is widely known even beyond this valley. We were conquered, and because of that we live now, thus." She gestured at the low cave with its crude furnishings, most of which were carved from the rock, hung from dowels driven into the walls, or appeared thrown together from rushes and branches without benefit of plane or saw. "The manfish, that is a tool of divining. It brings dreams to those who need them, and marks those who will be apprenticed to a mentor, like me. You tasted of it yourself. And carried several with you."

"The gold fruit is this manfish? What an odd name for it."

Jia smiled. "When you halve the manfish, you see in the center a blood-red figure against the pink pulp background, in the shape of a man's upper body with a fish tail. This figure is the Traveler, key to Fidrel beliefs."

He'd dined from sacred trees. What next, would he clean his feet on some sacred icon? Piss in a sacred pool?

"And why do we bring you into our home?" Atatha asked as he rose from beside the fire. "To honor you, the Traveler. To keep you safe. To learn what you are. We have waited for you for hundreds of years, but we don't know whether you are benevolent or malign." Atatha smiled. "Who could believe a Reign yet lived? The end of so much suffering could be at hand. This the council ponders as we speak. Much time has passed, indeed, since you left Metatha."

Kyle felt something cold up his spine. He should have left aside his questions, not given away how much like a fish out of water he was. He almost groaned aloud at his own pun.

"What makes you certain I'm Reign?" After all, Rupert Traveled and he wasn't Reign.

Atatha gave him a smile that again made him think of Rupert, though less sinister. Had he just given something away?

The man took up a hunk of driftwood and with his knife flicked a chunk of wood away to form a small hollow, into which he spooned the paste he had been making in his mortar. He glanced up now and then to motion with his head at some passerby peering curiously in through the cave entrance to catch a glimpse of Kyle.

"Once the Valeuta lived in the great city that is now Ta'atit," Atatha said. "Travel drew our conquerors, and they destroyed the Reign, the only caste that could Travel. We lost our leaders and our prosperity — earned from Travel. We are occupied. We are prisoners. Our enemies dismiss the bans on unnatural wyseery and suppress our people. It is why the Fidrel toil here, preserving the lore for the day a Traveler comes again as the lore foretells. You are a Traveler. Therefore, you are Reign. Our enemies must not discover you."

Kyle felt the jagged wall of the cave against his back, something firm and real to keep him from losing his balance and sinking through the floor. His mind raced to plug the stories Rupert had told into the world in which he now sat. They drew so many conclusions about him, so quickly. He certainly didn't look that much different from them, except for his clothing. Just how much had Rupert neglected to tell him about this world?

"This must be very unsettling for you, Kyle," Jia said softly. "The lore says time in other worlds may run faster or slower. It must have crept by to return a man so young who speaks with the accent of the old tongue. How did Ta'atit appear in your day? We tell tales of streets with flower-draped lamps lit for festivals —"

Kyle shook his head hard and gripped his knee tightly to his chest as the dull throb of a headache pounded his skull again.

"I think we have given Kyle much to think about. Perhaps too much," Atatha said in an instructor's voice. "Remember, he is fresh from Traveling and we have used him hard with these wyseer's potions. He may need days yet to recover. We do not want to make so honored a guest feel unwelcome."

The older man held out his hand to help Kyle to feet, which did, indeed, feel unstable beneath him as he was led to the sunlit ledge where the tiny fire worked on chunks of driftwood.

From this vantage, Kyle saw the waterfall at the head of the long valley he had trudged through. The cliffs looked out over the vast lake from the shore opposite where he'd walked. These were the red columns of lava he had seen, the caves carved in a softer rock that had settled atop it. The distant snow-capped mountains hid behind a haze, but the dark lake below sharply mirrored the surrounding valley walls, underlain by the shadowy city.

Closer, a narrow ledge followed the contour of the cliff wall, looping to reveal around another bend other caves from which small trails of smoke rose. Here and there an occasional Fidrel worked at some task, or lingered with others to study the opening to Atatha's cave with speculation. Below the cliff the detritus of generations disappeared into a dark forest that from this height appeared like a lawn at their feet. He felt giddy and unsteady, letting Atatha's slight tug lower him to his knees without hesitation.

"It takes some time for visitors to get over the distance down," Atatha said. "Most come here from Overmount—" He gestured beyond the valley wall across from them. "—as young children. They adjust much more quickly than their elders who must retrain their instincts."

"You aren't born here?" Kyle asked when the silence felt too long.

Jia sat cross-legged on the other side of the fire and gestured at the far side of the valley. "A few are, naturally," she said. "But most Valeutans live in Overmount. They may farm or fish the rivers and gather from the lands with some exceptions. A few have even been allowed to become artisans. The Fidrel are chosen from among them."

"So you must give up much to come here," Kyle stated, looking at the girl's pinched features, her dark eyes too deep for one who appeared so young. But the curve of her body suggested a young woman, not the child he had thought at first.

"Give up?" Jia looked around her. "Traveler, this home belongs to Atathal Rehatna. I brought with me only a mind to be trained. He gives up his home and his wisdom. My family can visit me. I have not given up—"

Atatha's bare movement of one finger silenced her. "I think the Traveler assumes that those in Overmount live better than we. In that assumption, of course, he is correct, since we are prisoners, and those in Overmount live a freer life. We exist on their charity. In exchange, we train their children in the lore of wyseers. Again, please forgive Jia's imprudence. It is, after all, exciting to have you among us."

Kyle sat back a little. The Fidrel were wizards. Rupert had called the educated class of the Valley—no, Valeuta they named themselves, wyseers.

"I didn't mean to insult," Kyle muttered, the scrutiny of the Fidrel openly staring all along the ledge made him feel like a bug on a pin, or maybe a monkey in a zoo, his every moment analyzed and plugged into some tale carried on for generations. He'd always been a bit of a monkey. But this place was supposed to be where he belonged.

"We do not assume the Traveler knows what has occurred since he left, though you do know more of us than you would admit."

"What happens now?" Kyle asked. "I need to find my way home."

"Why did you come if not to return home?" Jia returned.

Kyle frowned. Home? It should be Rupert here, speaking to his own people, eagerly hearing the news of centuries. Yet he had groomed Kyle to do this task alone, unsure he'd be welcomed. Why, when clearly the Traveler answered Valeutan prayers?

"We await the decision of Isra and the council," Atatha said. "I am a member of that council, but have the honor of seeing to your needs while the council decides on issues of security. We fear your rumor will reach our enemies." Atatha scanned the ledge path; his glance alone sent two curious observers on their way. "Please understand, it is important to learn what we can from you, keep you from harm, and determine what portents your arrival may mean. The lore is closely bound with the Traveler."

"It's why we are here," Jia said. "Oh, the elders and our mentors always talk of the lore as if there were more to it. There really isn't. The sole reason the Fidrel exist is to prepare for the return of the Traveler. You're here. Now we must ready for battle—"

Atatha's hand moved in a sharp gesture that instantly brought a silence so biting Kyle felt its edge like a knife to his throat, the word so sharp it stuck in his ears. Battle. What did they expect of him?

"It is easy for the young to second-guess the wisdom of those who go before them," Atatha said, his voice like cold steel. "Each new generation thinks itself the first to contemplate life's issues, without regard for the precedents for why one might not follow the most attractive path."

Jia's eyes had gone wide, but she wasn't expected to respond. Kyle cringed at the rebuke he heard in Atatha's tone.

"I don't know that I can help you. I—" Kyle began.

Atatha's glance tore from the view outside to look up at Kyle sharply. Jia sucked in a deep breath as her attention turned to something on the ledge road. Kyle glimpsed a group of fair-headed men wearing bold red coats, all riding what appeared to be almost skeletal horses along the ledge road. They paused, most of them dismounting to enter the first of the caves.

"That did not take long." Atatha grimaced as he handed Kyle the spoon-shaped piece of driftwood he'd been working, with its paste tamped into one end as if into the bowl of a pipe. Atatha swiftly threaded a thin wick into the hollow opposite end and touched a burning twig to it. As it smoldered, Kyle wondered whether he was supposed to smoke it.

"Jia, now," Atatha said sharply.

Kyle wanted to look up at the wyseer to see what put such panic behind his words. He couldn't pull his gaze from the wooden spoon, which now sent up a tiny spiral of smoke that had all of his attention. Kyle expected to see the wick fizzle out when it came to the confined end of the pipe. Instead, it sizzled on contact with the wood, burning through the wood swiftly in a line that raced for the paste in the bowl end. He sensed the smell, deep in his lungs, like menthol, yet with the overbearing citrus of manfish. His lungs seemed to open, to welcome a familiar smell that drew his attention. He realized that the fire, Atatha and Jia, the sunlight on the ledge, the green valley, all had blurred into a slash of bright color, centered on the smoldering driftwood spoon. Surely the breeze would topple him from the ledge, but in this odd moment of fancy, he imagined the tree tops cushioning his fall, a soft green bed that would hold him up.

A hand gripped his arm. Had he stumbled too near the ledge? He couldn't take his gaze from the spoon, but now it flared, blazed, bright orange as if with fire, then—almost—he thought he saw the red figure of a manfish dancing in the center of the flames, or maybe it was a bent figure … smoking a pipe?… more like some Earth symbol he recalled but couldn't name. Some hallucinogen then, and he couldn't fight the intense, simultaneous, euphoria and fear.

Suddenly darkness stretched away from him, black as the beach he'd swum to, looming as the cliffs that rose above him, impenetrable as the obsidian stone that might take him home. He tried to feel for his pocket, but it wasn't there. He wanted to reach for the niche above his head that held the contents of his pockets, but found nothing but empty space. He thought he heard sharp voices, then Jia's, in his ear, close.

"Silence, Kyle."

He jerked back, realizing that she'd slapped him. He wanted to object, but couldn't form words. Her small hand pressed against his mouth.

"They come. We can't let them find you." Urgency. He focused on her wide eyes staring out from somewhere in the shadows at the back of the cave. He heard angry voices, distant, near the cave mouth. Atatha spoke, his tone placating. Then another in a dialect Kyle found at first difficult to understand: it swam in and out of his thoughts as if he heard it from under water.

"We know there is a stranger among you," a voice stated clearly. "Why would Atatha, an elder wyseer, not be at a council of the Fidrel?"

Kyle almost gasped as a tall, fair-headed man with steely grey eyes passed within inches of him, trailed by a dark-headed man who looked like every other Valeutan he'd ever met. Kyle identified the latter as the speaker, and likely a wyseer. He carried a walking stick with a chunk of polished stone bound to it, and draped from a belt that cinched his red cloak were a profusion of bulging pouches. The man emanated the scent of herbs and sorcery, a perception that didn't seem at all odd to Kyle.

"There are no strangers here. Only me and my etlith. I have been ill and was not needed on the council today—" Atatha began humbly from the mouth of his cavern.

"We know he's here!" another man bellowed from the cave mouth.

Kyle almost shouted when a cudgel swung around to strike Atatha in the side of the head. The Fidrel toppled to his knees and sagged to one side, revealing a face erupting in blood. Kyle strained to move, but Jia's hand gripped like iron.

Something crashed. A clutter of cookware shattered on the cave floor, lidded pots busting open to reveal a variety of herbs, powders, oils and extracts. Another crash, and a shelf's contents had been swept away. A crude stool flew against a wall with a crack. The red-cloaked wyseer picked among the clutter, tearing apart sleeping mats and blankets, smashing pots with the heel of his stick, for the sheer destruction, as he searched. Atatha still mumbled denial from the cavern floor.

"So Atatha, you have been collecting forbidden herbs and trinkets again," the wyseer said, emptying a pouch full of pebbles. "You test our tolerance. One of these days you will miss your head." The wyseer glanced around the cave, his gaze seeming to come to rest on Kyle. "Ah!"

Kyle tried unsuccessfully to ball his fists as the wyseer approached, knowing he was about to be unmasked. Instead, Jia shrieked. The pressure on Kyle's arm released. She lurched away; he saw her held up from beneath her arms, her face even with the red-cloaked wyseer. Kyle wanted to push his way between them. His limbs failed to respond. The cavern canted to one side, but he didn't know if he'd fallen without her support.

"Destroy it all," the wyseer said. "Resistance, contraband essences. Clearly punishment is all they understand."

A man raised his tunic and grunted over the cistern in the corner, another kicked the bedding into the pile of foodstuffs and herbs, then urinated on the whole. Kyle briefly wondered where his things were. He only knew he clutched the burning wooden spoon.

The wyseer shook Jia. Her arms and legs flopped like a rag doll. "Where is he. I can turn you over to the Chieftain—or his armies—if you do not cooperate."

He must focus! Jia and Atatha were suffering to protect him. He must stop this! But the pain as the spoon scorched his palm made the cavern seem distant. The wyseer slowly scanned the cavern, peering into each shadow. His gaze touched Kyle, then slipped away. Kyle couldn't move. He must! The wyseer dropped Jia and shoved her toward one of the fair-headed soldiers. The soldiers laughed, each pushing her toward another, the girl unable to regain her balance but to fall against another and another. They boasted of the wonders she'd learn in pleasing them. One ripped the green robe from her shoulders. Another ripped the belt from her tunic and grabbed for her breasts. She shrieked her denial. Then someone shoved too hard. She tripped over the clutter on the floor, fell and struck her head against the stone that had served as their kitchen. She lay still in a sprawl. One man hiked up his tunic and moved to straddle her. Kyle lurched against whatever hallucination he experienced.

"Hadro," the wyseer gestured at the man. "No time. We must find the Traveler and keep him away from water." Hadro let his tunic fall. "Besides, you certainly aren't going to make an impression on the dead." The wyseer added his boot to Hadro's rear to encourage the man to move along as he tossed the torn robe at Jia's still figure.

The fire spit and steamed as a man urinated on it, and Atatha sprawled beside it.

What kind of world had he come to, swum to, Traveled to? Who had betrayed the Fidrel, and the Traveler the Fidrel believed in? Did he need to fear treachery from even the friendly faces here? Jia and Atatha bled into the dusty cavern floor, because of him and whatever unfounded hope they had in him. And he had done nothing to stop it.

Moments later, it seemed, the assailants were gone. Kyle smelled burning flesh, and distantly knew it was his. He must go to them. Were they dead? What had happened to his stone? He must do something. Where were the soldiers? What had become of the other Fidrel, the council? He must do something. What had Atatha done to him with this burning wooden spoon?

With an act of will that he thought might rip him apart he forced his fingers open, letting the driftwood spoon fall from his hand. He lurched up to his knees, stunned as the world came suddenly, swiftly, back to him. Everything remained overturned and in a jumble, the smell of urine pungent in the fire.

He reached for Jia, gasping at the touch of her. The spoon had burned its shape into his palm in an ugly weal that already blistered and bled. The pulse in her neck beat strong, contrary to the claim of the red-cloaked wyseer. He tried to rouse her with a shake of her shoulder. She groaned and cried out, seizing up into a little ball a moment, before she opened her eyes and blinked at him, wincing as if even the dim light of the cave burned them.

He parted the dark hair on her head to examine the lump and cut where she'd smashed her temple.

"They're gone," he whispered, unable to find his voice.

She barely nodded as her hand explored the lump. He scrambled through the clutter to Atatha's side. The man looked up at him from one eye the other swollen shut already, the side of his head swathed in blood. For an instant, Kyle feared he looked on the man's death stare, then realized the gaze followed him.

"I am so sorry," Kyle said as he tried to find a clean patch of fabric to staunch the flow of blood. He realized his own clothes were tucked into his rope belt. He quickly ripped his T-shirt into rags.

"Jia?" Atatha swallowed hard, his one eye watery.

"Hit her head. She is all right."

Kyle peeled the soiled tunic from the man's back, revealing the markers of past beatings that bent a man of no great age. Kyle stared, feeling a strange surge of blood as if during the assault his veins had frozen and now thawed in a rush. What kind of world had the Metatha of Rupert's tales become?

A shadow filled the doorway. For an instant Kyle almost panicked. Then two Fidrel wyseers resolved. A young man rushed to Jia's side, a somber-faced woman bearing clean water and healing herbs swiftly assessed Atatha's wounds.

"Is the Traveler injured?" the woman asked in a low voice, as if waiting for Kyle's permission to move. He could hear the young man asking Jia questions, Jia's answers lost in the sound of the wind echoing in Kyle's ears and the staccato beat of his heart.

Kyle's hand throbbed mercilessly, and his tongue felt thick in his mouth, but he muttered no to the woman's repeated query.

She swept toward the back of the cave, as if searching the clutter for some usable herb. Instead, she bent to pick up the charred driftwood spoon. She studied it a moment, sniffed it. Her glance found Kyle and she approached him as if he were a dangerous animal poised beside Atatha.

She held out her hands, dipping her head in an abbreviated bow that sent gold-feather-bound hair over her arms and strings of pearls in her hair and at her throat clattering.

"I am Isra, head of the Fidrel Council," she said as she squatted before him, holding out the charred remnant of the spoon. He remembered to hold out his hands in greeting, dipping his head a little. She pulled a leaf-wrapped shell from a pouch at her side, spreading the salve it contained over the burn in the palm of his hand.

"Atatha proved himself today, thinking so quickly to protect you. He justified my trust in him." She gestured with the driftwood spoon toward the wyseer. Then she wrapped Kyle's hand with layers of green herbs and the large leaves from a manfish tree, her fingers trembling and charged.

"What of Atatha—" Kyle began in a hoarse voice.

Her head dipped in acknowledgment. "He is gravely injured, indeed. But first we must tend to you."

Kyle was ready to protest, but she had already begun to unpack her herbs to minister to Atatha.

"Why did they do this?" Kyle asked. "Who were they? Why did they want me?"

He heard Jia mumble something to the other Fidrel as he emptied the soiled cistern.

Isra sighed deeply. "Where you come from, are there deep beliefs? Are there moon gods as some of the Pale believe, or animated spirits who guard the dead, as many in Overmount believe?"

Kyle shrugged a little. "Sure, people believe in different gods."

"Well, the Fidrel exist for the return of a Traveler. You. Yes, you are the Traveler." She raised a brow at him as if his attempt at protest would appear a lie. "We liked the old system of balances: of rule, and labor and wyseery. Our conquerors have long been comfortable thinking you no more than an unrealized prophecy. It makes them uncomfortable if the Fidrel have hope. The lore conflicts about you: whether you would be Reign, or wyseer. Some feared the most evil wyseer of our lore, himself, would return. You are too young to be him. That should rest many fears, but not all. Simply, you are the hope we believed in for hundreds of years. Thus, you are precious."

It was Rupert who belonged here to be looked upon as if some sort of messiah.

"There is a mistake—" Kyle began, but Isra shook her head, smiling.

"The ilyath works only for Reign." She gestured at his burned hand with the charred driftwood. "It's an old lore. Atatha took a chance trying it without knowing if it would work. He gave you a special gift. See, while the ilyath burned in your hand, no one could see you unless he held a wyseer's seeing stone, a rare wyseery. They could touch you; you could be injured. But they must first find you to harm you. The casting of the ilyath can be confusing and disorienting. But now that burn is a spell you carry with you always. You need only touch flame to the scar and you will remain unseen until you cool your hand."

"That was a spell? It made ... I could not see clearly. I saw strange images, dancing manfish, a darkness—" He paused at Isra's unguarded surprise.

"The lore tells of wyseers 'borrowing' off of the ilyath's power," she mused. "Visions are recorded as a potential part of the experience for a wyseer, though I know of no lore of vision for Reign. Nor of an ability to discard the ilyath by one's own will. Atatha risked having an addled stranger at the Pale's mercy. His luck for you was better than for himself."

"They were the Pale?"

The Pale conquered then, as Rupert feared. He felt so weary he thought he might just slide down into a puddle on the floor. Now, he decided, would be a good time to go home and break the bad news. This was no home to which Rupert would want to return. And this might indeed be the world he was born to, but he certainly didn't belong here.

"Who else?" Isra returned. "You are their greatest fear. You underestimate the novelty of your arrival. It has been five hundred years since a Traveler came to Ta'atit. How old are you in the place from which you came?"

"Twenty-one."

"And here, five hundred. Unless more Reign escaped unaccounted for, I believe, now, the council will agree the most plausible of the tales makes you the child of Kyla—Ah, you know the tale."

Kyle realized his startled glance had given him away.

Isra remained silent a moment. "The council has not finished its deliberations and I must take my leave. It is not safe for you to remain here, and there will be much work to make Atatha's home livable again. Others will care for Atatha; he should not be moved yet. Jia and Wilnath are Atatha's etlith, they can serve in Atatha's stead—"

"Then," Kyle said, his words slurring with his weariness, "The Pale were satisfied to look no further?"

"They will return." Isra's voice went so soft it became the echo of wind in the eaves of the cave. "To the Pale we are game in a hunt that never ends. If we behave suspiciously it is justification to punish us. They need that justification to keep the Valeuta from rebelling in defense of their wyseers. But punishment is a justifiable reason for selling a young girl off at Waymeet, or beheading an elder wyseer who has been caught too many times with the tools of wyseery in his home. They will be back. There is nowhere else for us to go, and they know we would never let them find you."

Kyle glanced across the cavern to where Jia rested her head on her knees, watching them, her face puffy on one side.

"Wilnath," Isra called to the young Fidrel who had begun to clean the worst defilements. The younger wyseer, a muscular man who looked as if he'd be more at home logging a woodlot in the Jackson County Forest, quickly dropped his task to come to Isra's bidding like a puppy to its master. Kyle knew so little of these people! Wilnath swiftly made the motion from his chest, and bobbed his head over his arms when Isra introduced him to the Traveler.

"Wilnath of Highpoint is among our younger wyseers," Isra explained. "Atatha took him in and he served as an adept before Jia joined them. Wilnath and Jia will ensure your safety until we have a decision on this matter."

Kyle frowned. He sensed a decision could be made that he might find unacceptable. But a swift glance around the cave told him he would need to follow the Fidrel a while yet, until he knew for certain into what he had fallen ... been pushed. Rupert *had* pushed him.

"Wise Isra, should we not all prepare to go into hiding? The Traveler is here—" Wilnath began.

Isra silenced him with a sharp gesture. Instead of contrition, the young wyseer's gaze narrowed on his leader, his mouth forming a tight line. Despite the expanded protest his expression still made, Wilnath's words were gracious as he turned to Kyle.

"It is my honor, Traveler," Wilnath said with another bow, his large frame dwarfing Isra and Jia, his features so much lighter and his sandy hair at odds with the other Fidrel. Wilnath's glance cut sidelong to the council leader. "Perhaps we shall go to *Hindlain*."

Kyle quickly translated this new place "behind the veil," but Isra had again slashed her hand away from her, almost striking Wilnath.

"You know my feelings on this, Wilnath," Isra stated. "Can you not be trusted to carry out the simple duties assigned you by the council?"

Wilnath stepped back as if from a blow. Jia lifted her head from her knees, ready to dart away.

"My apologies, Wise Isra," Wilnath said with a bow. "Please blame fear for the Traveler as my failing. I will take him to the collapsed cavern. You will find us awaiting your wishes."

Wilnath gestured for Kyle to follow as he helped Jia to unsteady feet. Between the two of them, they supported the adept as they slipped out onto the ledge, leaving behind the stench of Atatha's befouled cave as they climbed up and away from the path a little onto a crumbly slope. Here the scrub clinging to the loose soil and the occasional jut of boulders from above sheltered them from view of the valley, ledge and other Fidrel caves as they made their way east.

"I sense I just totally missed an argument," Kyle said to the uneasy silence of his companions.

Wilnath looked up from his study of each step Jia took with a quick glance, then his face cracked into a lopsided grin.

"Such arguments are subtle, but yes, Traveler, you witnessed my undressing. Isra's threat needs no restatement. We will go, as I said, to a cavern abandoned when it collapsed to heavy rain. It's a small place, but away from the bustle of the other caverns and perhaps safer. I will not, however, completely forsake Hindlain as an option." This last seemed to be spoken for Jia's benefit. Wilnath gave her lithe figure a little hug and she looked up at him with bright eyes, eager, resigned.

Kyle stumbled, almost falling. Even after Wilnath caught the Traveler's arm to steady him, Kyle felt as if he continued to tumble. He'd become the center of something far greater than he could imagine. People were willing to die for him. There were plots he'd fallen into far deeper than he could fathom just yet. He would need to be prepared, at the least, to flee home—that at least even the Pale feared he would try. His stone! In a sudden panic he tried to turn back, sending a skitter of loose rock away from his feet.

"Please, Kyle Nelson, our way goes on," Wilnath insisted, reaching for Kyle so quickly that Jia stumbled almost to her knees on the rocky path.

"I left behind my things—"

"We will see to your needs for now. We can fetch them after dark, perhaps. It is not worth the risk now. Isra will send someone with food and other needs. We will ask that your belongings be brought then."

Jia squeezed Kyle's arm, a familiar gesture of assurance.

With a longing look back, a sense of loss Kyle didn't dare explain, they rounded a curve in the cliff side and plunged into the cool shadows of forest, a seeming curtain that cut him off from his only escape.

CHAPTER SIX

By the time Kyle had helped Wilnath clear a place for a small cook fire and their sleeping mats, Kyle was ready to sleep standing in a corner if he must. He said nothing as each scoop of the cavern's sandy soil wore through the poultice wrapped around his hand, at last raising blood. The giddiness returned, the world around him canting from side to side and the faint westering light shining down through the trees around the cavern seeming bright and jittery.

Jia watched them from just inside the cavern mouth, stripping the bark from firewood to make kindling as Wilnath had commanded with a gesture. What kind of discipline ordered this world? Who had left those imprints on Atatha's back, a mentor? He couldn't imagine the kind of power Isra might wield that could silence the kind of emotion—was it anger?—he sensed just beneath Wilnath's friendly exterior. Jia, too, seemed to emanate it, a sense of anticipation, of eagerness, of barely controlled excitement.

By evening, when the long shadows from the forest that concealed this cavern—like it didn't the other Fidrel abodes where cookfires had long ago consumed the forest—Kyle and Wilnath had cleared a sizable section of the cavern floor. Cozy compared to Atatha's, it would shelter from wind or rain and unfriendly eyes. The light from the fire pit they dug in the back corner hid behind a curtain hung at the entrance and a portion of the caved in roof. Isra's adept arrived with blankets, mats, and a pot ready for the fire. The young man merely stared mutely at Kyle, before nodding to Wilnath's instructions and scurrying away into the twilight.

Wilnath removed the cover from the pot and grinned. "Stewed blue! A feast to honor our guest." He tapped his chest, his hand slithering away.

Kyle peered over the pot rim to see the shape of a plucked, uncooked fowl, breast up, surrounded by broth, seaweed and a few floating objects that might be Metathan vegetables amongst the now-familiar oat grass kernels. The pot gave off a pungent scent of spice and the bird's musky odor. He couldn't help grinning, his stomach growling in anticipation, if not a little disappointment that it would likely be hours before it was cooked.

"Isra took the trouble to have someone snare a blue for you. They are a feast bird, not given to everyday," Wilnath said, then tapped his chest again, and again his hand swam away.

"What's this," Kyle asked, repeating the gesture.

Jia emitted a small snort of amusement. "Kyle, it's your sign," she said. "'Traveler be praised.' That would probably be a close translation. You just did yourself an honor."

"Jia, you mock him!"

"Oh, Brother, you would think him a god! He is a stranger to the Fidrel. Think if you were suddenly thrown into the market at Waymeet. Would you know how much the Pale ask for each item for sale, or what curses their gods wield, or what each trinket they wear might symbolize?"

Wilnath's expression remained wary as he settled the pot into the coals of the fire.

Jia pointed to the blue quills sewn into the waist of her tunic. "These were from the blue we feasted upon for my joining day with the Fidrel." Her fingers lingered over the yellow feathers that had been threaded in between. "I caught a manfish bird and made a wyseery of it. That proved my skills to be named adept." She gestured at the silver and black feathers lining the mouth of the pouch hanging from Wilnath's belt, and the black and white quills that had been braided into his rope belt. "Wilnath ascended to full wyseer a few years after I came to join Atatha. When you move among the Fidrel, you will see how we stand in the caste by these markers. Council members, like

Atatha, have shells among their adornments. And Isra wears sea beads, and golden feathers in her hair, to show her rank as our leader."

Kyle reached out to touch one of Jia's feather-adorned braids. "And these feathers mean?" he asked.

"That Jia is vain," Wilnath said. "She hopes some handsome young man, perhaps someone particularly notable and exotic, will see how beautifully she dresses her hair."

Jia had flushed, but her grin was genuine and fond. She slapped Wilnath's hand away as he tried to tweak a feathered braid.

"Sister, I'm sure Kyloreign knows these things and needs no fickle adept to tell him."

"Shows what you know, wyseer," she taunted. "If you recalled your lore better, you'd know the Traveler left before the Withering. And of course the Traveler wouldn't know of the Fidrel, as they weren't needed until after we lost the Traveler, and it is a Fidrel tradition to so mark this caste. So there. And you a wyseer. You'd let an adept disprove you."

Wilnath's smile hinted that he might have let her show him up on purpose. Kyle leaned back against the cavern wall, tucking his blanket around his knees and feeling the warmth of the fire on his cheeks, the rich scent of food in the air and almost felt a sense of homecoming. He almost imagined his nieces and nephews squabbling over tent space and sleeping bags. His guard began to slip; they weren't so different from him, almost.

"You're siblings, but you look so little alike," Kyle muttered, feeling as if sleep would win and the food have to wait. "If anything, Wilnath looks more like a Pale—" He stopped when he realized that Wilnath's grin had faded. "No offense intended," he apologized as Wilnath frowned to himself and stirred up the fire under the pot.

"We're siblings because we are part of Atatha's family. It isn't by blood," Jia explained. "Wilnath—" she coaxed, calling his name again when he wouldn't look up.

"No apology needed, Kyloreign," Wilnath said softly. "The Pale blood of my forbears shows in me, yes, but not because my mother wished such a child. And my father would have just as well killed me for being born. I came among the Fidrel as a mercy, an infant, that I would be raised by them as a servant, if not a wyseer, because I was unwanted in the home where the Pale had so ill taken my mother. I don't even know those people. Atatha raised me."

"My apologies." Kyle felt the blood rising in him again. His gaze locked on the bruise working its way down Jia's face. "Why do your people let them treat you this way?"

"We are occupied—" Jia began.

"You told me that. But you also said that was five hundred years ago. In my world, five hundred years wipes away such distinctions. Fifty years will wipe away some of them. You behave as if your war was just last year."

"Does everyone in your world believe the same things and their views never collide?" Wilnath asked.

Kyle chewed his lip. "Of course there are exceptions."

"And how long have the wars gone on in the places of exception?"

"Yet it isn't as if the educated are prisoners—or, at least, it's rare. They aren't beaten for collecting a few herbs and pebbles!"

"The few herbs and pebbles the Pale found in Atatha's home weren't of the most innocent sort," said Jia with a smile. "We do, somewhat, test the limits of our imprisonment. Is your world free of hardship? We wonder why the center of the universe seems destined to have a harder lot than other worlds."

"Some parts of the world have it worse than others. In my part, people come and go as they like and are not treated so violently. Even those with few means have some protection."

"One need not be destitute to face undeserved hardship," Jia said. "My sister in Overmount died because the Pale would not allow us to use simple herbs that could have saved her. My grandmother starved to death. An uncle in Highpoint died of a beating. The manfish chose me, but I also chose it, because I believe in the Fidrel."

"You accept oppression, then."

"Oh, no, Kyloreign, we do not. We awaited you," Jia said. "Kyloreign. That's the name we've had for you since before you named yourself Kyle! Kyloreign. You are what we awaited. You are our call to arms." Her hand made that gesture as he mentally translated the name: reign of light.

Wilnath shushed her gently. "There is only so much we dare say so soon. We will see how Isra and the council decide. If they make the wrong choice—Either way, Traveler, you are the tidings of change."

"I'm not sure I like the idea of a council deciding for me, and me not able to speak up for myself."

Something in Wilnath's tone had made the hair on Kyle's arms stir. He found himself too easily slipping into the language and idioms of a place he'd never been. He needed caution, but he had so many questions!

"You are an unknown, Kyle," Jia said softly. "No one knows what happened in the last days of Denalku. Some wyseers believe a Reign remained Traveling when Ta'atit flooded. But the Seven Writs witness Denalku's head on the pike of a Pale warrior and later adorning the abode of the Pale Chieftain. Denalku hoarded power. Why would he let others use the Traveling stone when he could have escaped himself?"

"Besides, you are too young to have been an adult of Denalku's time, even if your speech and manners place you in the past," Wilnath said. "It is said that one must be an adult to initiate travel."

"Two of the Writs say an evil wyseer was unwittingly exiled with the stone, safely locking away the power of Travel."

"Those are the tales the Pale like to believe, and which the *Methiliim* encourage," Wilnath said as he stabbed at the coals beneath the stewing fowl.

Kyle tried to translate Methiliim but found himself being spun into declensions that made no sense.

"The Writ of Tabed suggests the Traveler will be the offspring of another world," Wilnath went on. "Scholars rejected that prophecy: the ban is a powerful spell; the lore claims it prevents even those with one non-Reign parent from Traveling."

"One Writ even claims that in his last act, Denalku destroyed the stone. That one is universally doubted. Denalku was far too vain to destroy his precious tools of wyseery," Jia said with a matter-of-fact tone as if she had known the Chieftain herself. Kyle recognized the tone as one Rupert disdained when he heard it from Kyle: "College knowledge," the old man opined, "so certain, you are, that you know all the ways of the world."

Kyle frowned. Who had a better sense of history, the wyseer who witnessed it, twenty-one years removed, or those five hundred years removed?

"The Fisher's Writ says Chamberlain Shedal cut Denalku's child from the body of Shedal's daughter, Kyla, and cast the child and the stone into the sea to send the power to another world where it could never be used against Metatha again. Shedal would have initiated the travel, thus bypassing the need for the child to be an adult." Wilnath glanced out through the doorway, his voice lowering as if he feared the night might overhear him.

"The Fisher's Writ recorded evidence for its theory: a girl's body found in the flooded valley, one who looked much like Kyla, but with no robe or marking," Jia said, equally circumspect as she peered out around the cave mouth at the dark. "A child had been cut from her womb. Chamberlain Shedal was found dead beside the river, covered in more blood than could be his own, though he may have been marked by battle. Yet, no battle had come to that part of the city."

"In many ways, even the Fidrel—though our mission is otherwise—have hoped no such threat as the Traveling stone would ever be seen here again," Wilnath admitted. "I think that was Isra's wish. I fear Atatha concurs. Our council is unwilling to act upon the primary tenets of our faith, solely, I imagine, because they never expected the Traveler to return. We have had many generations to build complacency."

Kyle's heart beat in his throat. "You mentioned evil wyseers," Kyle said. "Were they Pale?"

Wilnath hesitated, looking to Jia. "Wyseers who served the Pale invoked blood and sacrifice to alter natural laws. They now name themselves Methiliim. The products of those spells are aberrant," said Wilnath.

"Once Valeutan wyseers *were* evil," said Jia. "*We* brought the unnatural into this world, unchecked power, horrors from other worlds, not mercy. The factional fighting almost destroyed the Clan. It's said *we* attempted to manipulate the gods as if Travel wasn't a total abomination to begin with."

"The Pale occupation saved us. Valeutans rallied to them to stop the atrocities our own leaders performed," Wilnath added.

"But the Pale are your enemy," Kyle said.

"They continued to occupy us and destroyed more than evil wyseery—they destroyed the Reign, an entire caste of people murdered, and outlawed wyseery that didn't serve them. They destroyed our lore, our people and made of us a servant caste," Wilnath said. "And all this because of one wyseer, a favorite of Denalku's, and his wyseery was the most aberrant of all. He appears through too many generations of tales to trust all the lore about him. But even the Writs blame only that wyseer for the near destruction of Metatha."

Unbidden came the image of Rupert's glare. He pictured his uncle stockpiling weapons pilfered during his work at Fort McCoy to stave off some imagined UN invasion. How many times had he suggested that the Traveler scavenged weapons of mass destruction? Wouldn't a wyseer of those factional times be that kind of an unhinged lunatic? Had Rupert's desire to return been that innocent if he needed to send a point man?

He realized his mouth had fallen open.

"We don't imagine you as an evil wyseer, Kyle," Jia assured him. "Atatha's test spared you the worst doubts the council had."

Kyle stared into the coals. He could see a glint of speculation behind the reverence in Wilnath's expression. How quickly would doubt resurface when they finally asked the question: how did a babe survive Travel to another world, learn Metathan language and customs and know enough to return? Where was his stone?

CHAPTER SEVEN

Through that night, Kyle slept fitfully. A buzz of voices swirled around him, in and out of the cave, wandering through his dreams, hovering over him now and then to study the monkey boy washed upon a beach. Each time he opened his eyes someone watched. Wilnath or Jia always reassured him and with the whiff of some scent or another he would sink back into sleep, his stomach grumbling to the aroma of basted blue.

When finally the dawn of his fourth Metathan day arrived, he woke to find himself alone in the cave, the stewing blue reheating on a stoked fire. He turned at the sound of hushed voices near the mouth of the cave, the figures watchful as they glanced along the rim trail now and then. He recognized Wilnath and Jia with two others, catching the occasional word, including the elusive "Hindlain" that had brought Isra's wrath when Wilnath uttered it before, and the hint that the Pale had continued to search for him among the Fidrel.

He roused himself to an elbow to find his jeans and the remains of his T-shirt neatly folded beside him, his wallet, keys and pocketknife perched on top. No stone. He looked up in panic. Wilnath and Jia glanced at one another, then made some sign to their two visitors, who slipped away into the blaze of morning washing the cave entrance.

"The pot will be warm soon," Jia assured him, busying herself checking the progress of the fire. "See, Wil, I told you the scent of food would rouse any man from sleep, no matter who he is."

"There you go again, making light of the Traveler," Wilnath said. "He may be tolerant, but there are many among the Fidrel, including

Isra and Atatha, who had better not hear you speaking with such familiarity and disrespect."

Jia grinned and winked at Kyle in a gesture that felt both friendly and false. "To the Fidrel, familiarity *is* disrespect. That's why we take our adepts from Overmount. We certainly wouldn't want to become familiar with one another."

Wilnath frowned at her. Kyle couldn't shake himself awake enough to understand the oddity of the exchange.

"Isra's adept brought your things last night after you slept," Wilnath said, gesturing at Kyle's belongings. "The council still hasn't adjourned and you are no safer today. Jia's to stay with you. I must report to the council."

"Report what?"

"Oh, did the Traveler perform any wyseery during the night?" Jia said with a nervous giggle. "Did he shapeshift into an evil wyseer or somehow reveal in his sleep that he wears a glamour to cover his ancient face. That sort of thing."

"Jia." Wilnath's warning came out a weary sigh. Wilnath made the Traveler's sign and rolled his eyes. "Perhaps something of that nature. I'll have nothing to report." He swung his worn robe over his shoulders and swept out into the bright of day.

Kyle thought he caught the glimpse of another Fidrel resolving from the pines to join him, and the movement of another shadow taking its place.

Kyle spent the day in waiting: waiting for someone to decide his fate, waiting to learn what might help him find his way home, waiting for the strange feeling of "otherness" to leave him, waiting to return to Atatha's so he could search for his black stone. If he asked about the stone, would they keep it from him? Did they already have it? Such thoughts made his stomach sour on the leftover blue and speak to Jia more sharply than he meant to.

Mostly she left him alone, nursing her headache and waiting almost as impatiently as he, now and then speaking in whispers with this young wyseer or that. If he based all of his knowledge of the Fidrel on just those who came by this cavern, he would think none of them much older than himself. A few times he caught an angry word or two in the conversations, always the mysterious Hindlain would come up, and Jia angry that they hadn't found it, for the instructions were quite clear they should. At times they made Kyle think of a coffee shop full of activists planning civil disobedience. At home, they'd all be messaging each other on social media, not gathering to whisper in the doorways. But Jia only responded to Kyle's questions with a surly shrug.

He startled to find night had fallen as he dozed beside the cavern's entrance. The moment took him unawares, as if he had finally broken free of the lethargy that followed his swim to Metatha, and the after effects of the ilyath. Had he been watching the birds swirling over the lake far below? He couldn't recall.

"It takes time to recover," Isra said from the shadows deeper within the cave. He tried to remember when she'd arrived but had no recollection of much of the day. She swept a handful of some sort of pungent herb from a chopping board into the pot over the fire. She regarded him with dark eyes not as cold as Rupert's, not as skeptical as the other Fidrel's, not as awestruck as Wilnath's, nor as wondering as Jia's. Had they been conversing? Or did she see the awareness rushing him, the realization that he lived, that he sat here in a tiny cavern overlooking the drowned city of his birth in a land so alien from his own?

Isra added a piece of driftwood under the cool side of the cookpot, then joined him near the cave entrance. Her glance barely touched Jia where she slept, then swept the rim trail. To live like this, forever, like mice fearing the hawk swirling overhead, it brought a shiver up his spine. Where was the hawk? What had become of his black stone?

An overcast night had settled over the valley and the darkness swallowed the firelight, and all the small fires farther west along the ledge. He missed the moons. Stiffening muscles protested each movement, soft flesh resisting the stony ground. He caught himself glancing at Jia, then the rim trail. He knew Isra watched him.

When he met her gaze again, he thought he would fall into it. Vaguely, he realized she had pinched some herb between her fingers, something fragrant like oregano, but not. Sleep crept on him just slow enough for him to realize she brought it—what tools these wyseers managed so simply!—but fast enough to give him only a moment to consider how completely the Fidrel controlled him, as Rupert had managed him for so many years. Had they always thus manipulated the Reign, and Denalku had merely been the first to challenge their power? The contrary thought lunged at him, then became lost in a dream in which he and his sisters cavorted on the shores of Potter's Flowage, swinging from a rope looped over a withered limb to splash into the dark, cool waters of the flowage.

Morning found him curled up alone beside the fire, a dark green cloak spread over him. The valley glowed below, vibrant green against the cliff sides, the lake reflecting the red and black stone. It was the kind of view he could awake to every morning. He noticed Jia studying him with a bemused expression from the shade of a twisted tree that grew close to the entrance.

"What are you looking at? Come to see the monkey?" he demanded when her regard began to creep under his skin.

"I look upon Kyloreign," Jia replied lightly, her eyebrows meeting over a pair of black and purple eyes. "Moon key? What is that?"

"Fat lot of good it does you," he said, ignoring her question. Her forehead screwed up as she tried to figure out an untranslatable idiom. "You prayed for your Traveler. What do you get? Me. I have no answers. I have nothing."

Jia didn't laugh, though her eyes crinkled up with humor. "We weren't expecting a wyseer, Kyle. Do you see the significance in your name? Kylik is the light son who follows his father, Danat, one of the Guardians. He hosts Siph, the progeny of the future. Your name even hearkens to the promise you are, the hope that you are. No one expects miracles of you. We don't know what to expect. You're like a lost moon come home: Something that belongs and finally returns to its rightful place. Order restored."

Kyle stared at her, his glance falling again to the shapeless garb that only added to the illusion that she couldn't be more than eleven. How old was she, really?

"We work for the day the Pale rule us no more," Jia went on, ignoring his scrutiny. "That's what makes the Fidrel. It's what drives the Pale to search for you throughout the valley. They fear you, which makes you a power. You are a power to us. You will help us."

"How?" Kyle asked. "You prayed for a Traveler for five hundred years, yet what possible difference do I make, that your people couldn't have done at any time in all those years?"

Jia shrugged and looked at him sidelong. "The council will decide. Isra speaks well for you. That's good. They will question you, try to understand how you came to be here, what tool you used to swim between worlds. They will explore it, likely, and see if it's something we need a Reign to accomplish, and then perhaps—"

"Where in this scenario does Kyle get to go home?" he asked softly, wondering a little at how strongly that desire to see Potter's Flowage, his family, even his goofy college roommates, had emerged.

"Kyle, you've come home. This is your home."

"This isn't my home, Jia. Neither is Ta'atit. My home is Potter's Flowage. My parents are there, my sisters and their kids, my aunts and uncles and cousins. My friends. You have a family in Overmount while you study here. I have my family at Potter's Flowage, while I study in Madison. I have to be back in Madison soon or I'll fail—"

"You're training to be a wyseer?" Her eyes went wide and she took a small step back.

"Yeah, right, Jia," he said with a roll of his eyes. "I'm going to be a wyseer of literature. There's no wyseery in my world."

"What a sad and boring place then."

"Not at all! We just don't need it. We make our dreams happen with hard work and innovation." He had to struggle to find a Metathan word for "innovation."

"You have Technology. The lore says wagons fly like birds. Words float in the air. There's a lot of wyseery that must stay in your world or other worlds. It's too large for a Traveler to carry or missing some element that nulls it here. Like the talking boxes that never worked no matter what the wyseers tried on them. All they got was a sound like wind and a flickering grey-white light. Other wyseery, though, is wondrous: tiny nuggets that relieve pain—"

"That's all science."

"There's one world with a special oil crucial to the strongest wyseery. Another world is all made of minerals that do great things," Jia said. "It's from such a place that many of the stones come. What kind of place did you visit?"

As the sun tracked along the valley, Kyle told Jia about growing up beside Potter's Flowage. Prodded by Jia's questions he highlighted each facet of his life and school, all of which enthralled her: the magic of his car taking him so far so fast. There was the magic of television and the science fiction shows that postulated travel to other worlds in ships, not with stones, and electronic games, radio, microwave ovens, and even flashlights. There was the oddity of a world where anyone could obtain a wyseer's education.

Through Jia's eyes, he lived in a magical world, one where everyone spent their time looking to be entertained and at their leisure. She waved away his layman's description of electricity or combustion as scientific principles, each item seen instead as a wyseery that could be transplanted to Metatha. Kyle couldn't help but wonder at a people who were so adamant that magic ran the world.

Danat raced toward them from the horizon before Wilnath sent word that Atatha wished to see them. They found the older Wyseer sitting up beside the fire, nibbling on a bit of bread. His mouth had a sour turn Kyle hadn't seen before. The dark eye not swollen shut measured the Traveler, then warmed on his etlith.

"Jia, what have you done today?" Atatha demanded.

"I have learned about a far world where wyseery is everywhere but goes unrecognized," she replied easily. "In that world, everyone expects to have their every moment filled with entertainment as if there were a play or a game of chance that never ends."

"It is wise to learn what you can from every encounter." Atatha let his gaze fall on Kyle. "I hope Jia and Wilnath have made the Traveler comfortable in his homecoming, not merely plied him with a rush of questions when we have plenty of time in the coming months to learn from his Travels."

"Um, there seems to be a misunderstanding," Kyle said, beginning to squirm under a scrutiny that eerily reminded him of Rupert. "I'm a tourist, not a resident. My home is the world I came from. Everything

I know is back there. If I don't return, my parents will worry. They have no way of knowing where I've gone."

"Reign parents?" Atatha asked, his tone suddenly sharp.

"They adopted me."

"How will you get home?"

Kyle shrugged. "I carried a white stone when I arrived here. It became black. I have not seen it since the Pale came."

"How did you come by the stone?"

"It was given to me."

"By whom?"

"My uncle, who found me in the river the day I was born." Kyle felt a light sweat break out beneath the coarse tunic he wore. He knew by Atatha's expression that he'd said too much. Atatha's brows joined as the man slowly rose to his feet. "It interested me because I was clutching it when I was found," Kyle added quickly.

"Hmm," Atatha's expression lost even its pretense of friendliness. "How did an infant come to grow up speaking a dead dialect? Is this the native tongue where you were raised? If so, how is it that you don't know the words for common things? How is it you knew the proper greetings to give? How did you know words and gestures not used since the end of Denalku Reign? What evil wyseery is this?"

"Atatha, he's not evil." Jia pushed her way between Kyle and the wyseer. "If he meant us harm he could have done it by now."

Kyle swallowed hard. What would happen if the Fidrel who sheltered him made him their enemy? Who would protect him from the Pale until he could find his way home?

"Even Isra knows he cannot be Ruperion," Jia said. "He's too young. He's clearly Reign, the ilyath proved that, and Ruperion was not Reign. There's no doubt in the lore or the Writs."

"I do not need my etlith explaining lore to me!" Atatha returned.

"They have such great wyseery in his world. They can walk from here to Waymeet at Danat's pace. They can make their dreams appear in a vision box. We could learn so many things from him, and clearly in his home he has many tools of great power, yet he brought no wyseery here to harm us. Why are you being so unkind to the Traveler?

The Traveler! The one to mark it all, Atatha. It begins with him, the end of all … this!"

Atatha patted Jia's hand, a brief gesture of fatherly warmth a moment before turning his dark gaze back to Kyle. "I do not suggest that Kyle is evil, or even dangerous. I suggest that perhaps his parents are, or his uncle. Perhaps Kyle is merely a tool designed to make the link they could not."

Kyle's throat had tightened so that he couldn't swallow.

"If you are a threat to us, Kyle, the least you can do is warn us after we have given our blood to protect you," Atatha said as he settled back down beside the fire. "The Pale continue to search our homes, destroy our work and hurt our people. We don't begrudge such sacrifice for the Traveler; the Traveler is why we exist. But to have the Traveler be our undoing—"

Kyle sighed and squatted so he could look Atatha more surely in the eye. "He can't Travel."

"Who?" Jia blinked at him, as if seeing a truth she hadn't wanted to see.

"My uncle, Rupert."

"Ruperion!"

Atatha shushed Jia so Kyle could continue.

"He taught me as a child. Then I stopped believing his stories about Metatha. I think he really just wants to come home. He talks of nothing else but glorious Metatha and the family he knows died hundreds of years ago. I fell, or he pushed me into the water while the stone was in my pocket. He wants to know what this place is so many generations after he left his own family behind."

"Can he Travel while you're here?" Atatha demanded.

"He needs a Reign to bring him over."

Atatha nodded slowly. "You can't go back, Kyle. The risk is too great."

Kyle shook his head. They couldn't deny him that! He'd merely dive into the stream, or the well … but what had become of his stone? Had Atatha taken it?

"That's cruel," Jia protested.

"Jia, he just admitted that *Ruperion* is his guide! It is the will of the council, and ours is not the right to disregard that will. He will live among the Fidrel and we will learn from him—"

"He's just an old man, addled by ... bad drink. He wouldn't hurt—"

"Perhaps he is such in a world without wyseery," Atatha said. "But his power here would be great indeed. We cannot, will not, risk it."

He felt the throb in his temple again, and an old ache deep inside him. He thought of his mother, holding his hand as her young son told her about a magical world from Uncle Rupert's stories, and how he thought he must have come from there because it sounded so much more wonderful than Potter's Flowage and its boring sameness. The kitchen had emanated the bitter odor of beer brats steeping in the crockpot, coals from the grill sending the scent of mesquite into the house; the whole family gathered outside on the spongy lawn, their voices echoing through still forest and bog. She had told him then that their paths had crossed on a special journey and that she didn't know where he'd been born. Then she had cried, the only time she'd ever done so in front of him. He saw that moment, now, so clear, so starkly, he almost thought he smelled brats and musty cedar paneling. Rupert had convinced him he didn't belong in his parents' home, but now, more than ever, he knew he did. They had lied to him, not to betray him, but to keep him. The wondrous and magical world Rupert described didn't exist.

"Isra sees potential in you, Kyle Nelson," Atatha said, shattering the image of the Nelson kitchen. "Your ilyath visions are something unusual. Perhaps the manfish will show us that you should be a wyseer. You can train—"

"I thought the trouble with Denalku was that he was both wyseer and Reign—" Kyle began.

"The Reign are no longer in power. There is no significance to a caste that only exists in you, but that it can bypass a device meant to keep wyseers out. You *can* still Travel. You can help us rebuild what we lost."

"We need not remain prisoners of the Pale," Jia agreed with a bob of her head. "We can take back our dignity and regain our freedom."

How they had all laughed at Rupert's tales of a wizard facing swordsmen with a bazooka. Just what kind of magic had the Travelers sought?

"This isn't right," Kyle muttered.

This was what Rupert had groomed him for, then, to continue a war across centuries and worlds. He heard Jia echo his words with a question mark. But he ignored her. Two steps took Kyle out into the cool dark of night over the valley.

"Kyle!" He heard Jia's voice rise up, Atatha's response lost in the light wind blowing up from below.

He didn't care where his feet took him. He strode along the narrow ledge, fighting the dangerous urge to run along the trail. They'd betrayed him, all of them, even that smiling image of his mother that let Rupert manipulate him. His feet led him down a sparse trail to the lakeshore opposite where he had first realized he stood in the midst of a dead city. Danat obliterated all other reflections on the lake—a broken pattern that swam among the sleeping forms of waterfowl—then Kylik chased after, giving the half-light of day to the cliffs above. The son of the first guardian, the promise …

He reached the shore and stared across. If he dived in, would he go home? Would that end it? The water appeared so dark. What lay beneath the surface, grasping weeds, a maze of buildings, dead trees?

He thought he heard Jia call his name, softly. Night birds stirred all around him. Several fluttered close to his ears to sample bits of hair and cloth. Others fled from underfoot as he settled on a rock beside the vast lake.

He couldn't talk to her now. He had trusted them, trusted Atatha, even Isra. He'd watched the man take a cudgel to the head for him. Clearly not for Kyle the person, but only because they could use him, scavengers who find a treasure washed upon the beach. They kept him under their spells to manipulate him, demanding he trust them but he didn't get that trust in return. He'd had a vain thought today as he chattered with Jia, looking out over this Edenic valley, that he could feel a sense of comfort here. His entire branch of the family tree had been obliterated by the Pale. He should feel angry and want to help their cause. But it wasn't real.

Jia stopped calling for him and he remained, sitting on the rock. He knew he wasn't alone. Somewhere above him Fidrel kept watch. To protect him? To keep him from escaping? To prevent him from doing them harm? He thought he made out their silhouettes against the rocky walls and now and then heard over the whisper of breeze and mutter of sleeping fowl their feet shifting on the rough stone.

Late in the night when the three moons had long receded beyond the mountains and a few clouds dimmed the stars, he touched a toe to the water. Cold. Very cold. He tested the depth with a stick. It might be four feet or so. He stared up at the cliff a long moment. It had that glow of starlight, an eerie half-light that even the dark in this world could take on. The cave mouths above sat judgment, dark disapproving eyes. He turned his back on the cliffs and before he could convince himself of his foolishness, he ran for the water, cannonballing into it.

Icy, it sloshed together above his head, the sound a rush into his ears. The strange sensation didn't come. He gasped a little at the cold, the water pouring into his mouth, deadly, cold. He struggled for the surface, coughing water. He'd jumped too far, in over his head. His foot clipped something solid that certainly wasn't bottom, likely some battlement or roof edge that might snag him. It took him several moments to swim to the shallows and slog ashore to his boulder. Many minutes passed before he had coughed the acidic water out of his lungs.

He couldn't go home. He sank to the damp ground, his back against the rock, and stared out at the dark lake that had taken on the color of Potter's Flowage. Somewhere back home, Rupert would be passing his fifth hour in vigil on the shores of the flowage. The house would be dark by now, everyone back from the Friday fish fry, the children asleep in tents, or in sleeping bags in the basement family room where the fire had burned low—likely dreaming the stories Rupert had told them. Upstairs, his sisters might be giggling like children as they tried to squeeze into bunkbeds with their husbands. He wanted to go home.

Kyle woke to something jabbing him in the ribs. He blinked his eyes open to find Jia swimming in a bright sun, holding out the long stick with which he'd tested the water.

"You could have bathed up there," she said, gesturing with her head toward the ledge. "I thought you needed your stone to get home."

"I do," he muttered. "Apparently. I can't find it."

"Atatha has it. He's had it since the Pale came."

"Why didn't he tell me?" Kyle demanded. "Why didn't you? It's mine. It isn't his to keep."

"It wasn't my role to tell you. And, you never asked. The council hasn't concluded yet. At least he didn't hand it over to Isra."

Kyle scowled and yanked the stick from her hand when she prodded him again. He tossed it in the water.

"Surly does not become you, Kyle."

"They have no right to draw any conclusions without consulting me. I know what I want and where I belong." His voice maintained an even ice that made Jia's jaw jut out at him.

"You belong here," she stated. "You're the Traveler. It's foretold. It's written. There's nothing you can do about it so you might as well just accept it and make the best of it. Clearly we need to entertain you. If you don't have so much time to brood, maybe you won't be so insufferable—"

"Is that how you speak to the Traveler?" he demanded.

Her eyes widened and she hesitated a moment, then, watching him warily she tested a small smile as if uncertain, still, whether he jested with her.

"I'm assigned to keep you out of trouble until the council adjourns. The cavern we were in has been compromised so we'll just go out under their noses to keep out of the Pale's way. If we could just find Hindlain—" She shook her head, leaving the thought unexpressed. She tugged his arm, leading him along an overgrown path to where they could cross the river before it gathered in the lake. The curiosity in him won—or did she apply some magic that drew him to follow her even when his heart was up on the ridge, likely tucked into the old wyseer's pockets?

Jia led him across a series of stepping stones, then around a giant slab that had at one time been atop one cliff or the other, and through a maze of ruins. When they rounded a tall moss-covered tower that had weathered away to a shell, again the lushness of Ta'atit's overgrown streets greeted him. The manfish trees loomed over all, a florid display of bird plumage.

"There's no bugs here," Kyle said.

"Bugs?"

"Um, flying pests."

"There's plenty of birds," she replied as she plucked the odd feather from the trail and dropped it into her pouch, or collected nuts or a particularly good throwing stone.

"Pests, I mean, that bite, suck your blood, leave behind welts."

Jia managed to both look up at him, and down her nose at him at the same time. "You're very lucky that you came ashore here, Kyle. In Overmount we have the blood moon, when the young of the blood birds hatch. They're only a bother in their fledging season. All other times they live off other birds. But when they fledge, they're so ravenous they take all they can find. If a herder is not alert, he may leave his fattening fowl out during the blood moon and wake the next morn to find all his fowl picked clean to the bone. If not his own self."

"You're making that up," Kyle said as he followed her along the path.

"No I'm not." She glanced back at him with that coy smile of hers and kept going.

"Uh-huh. Well, we have furry birds that can turn you into a blood-sucking bird if they bite you. They drink you dry to make you dead, but still alive, in thrall to them, forced to drink the blood of others to survive."

"You're making that up," she returned, tossing the rind of a spent manfish at him. He batted it back at her. She stopped then, so that he almost bumped into her. "You have to be serious now. We have work to attend to."

"Work?"

"And we need to be wary. The Pale still seek you and we're outside our bounds. To be caught in Ta'atit—Many of the ruins contain remnants of wyseery, even after years of Pale looting, and Fidrel scavenging, and many things we found beneath the waters. A lot of our wyseery comes from the things we find here. The Pale discover anything remotely wyseerish in our homes and they will use it as an excuse to kill us."

"They bother with excuses?"

Jia gave a little snort. "Sure, they would be pleased to sacrifice the last Fidrel. But the Valeutans look to the Fidrel for their spiritual guidance, their link to the gods and the beyond. The Pale wish to give Valeutans no excuse to revolt in our defense."

She scanned the city, as if seeing through the thickets and inside the ruins, sifting shadows for her enemy.

"Their search for you destroyed many years of work, including a few pages of one of the original Writs, though, of course, we've hidden copies. So we come here to replace those things we need: Atatha found the means to make the ilyath here, from the scraps of lore among the garbage of ancient wyseers. We're going to search an old site where we've found things in the past and see if we can find stones similar to your Traveling stone, and I have been seeking a pink stone mentioned in one of the Writs."

Jia led him up the valley side to a cluster of particularly tall manfish trees that threw a deep shade at feet cluttered with the leavings of ancient dwellers, a place not so overgrown as the rest of the city.

"Just look through there, slowly," Jia said, gesturing at a brush-covered pile of rubble a few feet from where she squatted to peer into the dirt, picking at it with a stick. "You never know what you'll find in garbage. I found my white stone here, the one I saw in the manfish. We've already gone through that pile, but now that we know what to look for …" She left the statement hanging—her admission to having deceived him.

"I don't understand the role of the manfish," Kyle said as he picked through the rubble, finding a few shards that might have been pottery, a few stones that appeared unnatural, but not pink as she needed, nor obsidian or white as he needed.

"Since before traveling began, we tested our young to know who is gifted with the makings of a wyseer. Since the occupation, some few of bad heart choose to follow the Pale for an easier life and become Methiliim. Others, most, the Fidrel. I was born to parents who favor the Fidrel. No matter our faction, all begin tasting of the manfish in their third or fourth year. Those who dream the right dream apprentice a wyseer who mentors them."

"Dream the right dream?"

He found a small pendant, perhaps an amulet, that hinted of turquoise coloring beneath years of soiling. The stone had been set in some kind of metal. As he cleaned away the soiling he discovered an image like a stylized manfish blowing into something like a flute. He held it up for her. Jia shrugged, shook her head. It reminded Kyle of Kokopelli, the flautist of southwestern petroglyphs. Then he remembered the image he'd seen as the ilyath pulled him into what Jia named a manfish dream. He worked at the metal back of the pendant. Soil chipped away to reveal "sterl," the rest lost in corrosion. It had to be a treasure purloined from Earth. He caught a whiff of the boggy backwaters of Potter's Flowage as the piece linked him to home. Kyle tucked the pendant in the pouch he wore and continued to rummage through what little hadn't struck the Fidrel as magical.

"It was my third manfish year, when I was ten," Jia was saying as homesickness tugged at Kyle's thoughts. "I saw the path, and I've been with Atatha more than six years now. I am Fidrel because I believe the Valeutans need to be strong again. You, you're the path I dreamed."

"The path?" he asked, distracted.

"Well, for everyone the vision is different. I saw what Atatha interprets to be a path. I saw black sand stretching ahead of me, as far as I could see. The sand appeared smooth, damp. I sought something. I knew that. I kept thinking that I sought something dark, like the sand I walked upon. I couldn't find it. It was as dark as if night lay down upon the sand and left behind his coat.

"The surf beside me was silent. No wind stirred nor gull called. It was absolutely silent. The sand became fine pebble, like the seeds of night, tiny buttons from night's coat. Almost sand, but loose, I had trouble walking through it. Then the pebbles became black stone, sea-scoured and smooth. I stumbled many times, my knees bloody, my hands and feet bruised. Then night fell upon me, darker even. Not even starlight could reveal the surf in this total darkness. I had come seeking something as dark as the night. Instead, I saw before me on the beach a white stone. It gave me hope. It is power. I know this."

Kyle realized her story almost relived his walk on the Metathan shore. Surely she had walked there before. But she had dreamed his stone. He *was* her path. It didn't comfort him.

"So you worship a stone, too?" he asked.

She gave him a sidelong glance. "You of all people should see a link between visions of stones and Traveling." She gave him a sour look to realize he was teasing. "No one else has had a dream like mine. Others have dreamt of the stone, but mine is special. I dreamt I sought a black stone but found a white stone. That isn't in the lore. To see if I was true of sight, Atatha brought me here to the ruins and told me to seek what I would like. I came to this very house, a powerful wyseer's indeed to have five manfish trees in the yard. And sitting right there as perfect and strange as could be, was the white stone."

Jia pulled from her pouch a perfect, almond-sized white stone, like the one Kyle had received from Rupert that day. Only Kyle's had become obsidian.

Kyle stared at what he could swear was his stone, the stone he had used to come here. He looked up at her again when she gestured that he examine it.

It felt the same, the weight, the texture, its creamy glow. Not chert, more like quartzite.

"This is mine," he said, looking at it in wonder. But she was shaking her head.

Hundreds of birds rose suddenly from the trees below.

Jia jumped to her feet and peered down at the valley end. "Do you remember how to use the ilyath?"

"I need fire," Isra said. "What is it?"

"The Pale come."

She appeared so calm. His heart labored to imagine again the way he'd seen her through his haze of ilyath, the Pale warrior Hadro tossing her about like a rag doll. She was already hurrying along a trail under the eaves higher up on the ridge, gesturing for him to follow her. He hurried after.

Her feet moved sure and quick on the stony path. Kyle stumbled several times, biting back exclamations each time, or not ducking in time to avoid being whapped in the face by a branch. Now and then, through the trees, he saw the squad of crimson-garbed Pale following the shore on this side of the lake. They watched ahead and the ridges. No one watched behind, clearly Jia's ploy as they raced to a point even with the shallow river crossing. He struggled not to breathe hard as they crept down the slope behind the Pale, then dashed across their trail.

"Hey!" The shout went up so loud, Kyle thought it had been shouted into his ear.

Jia looked back at the Pale and stumbled to a halt, Kyle almost ramming into her. A wyseer in the party held up a staff with a pyramid-shaped prism atop it like those sold in New Age stores in Madison or on the cover of a Pink Floyd album.

"Run, Jia, it's just a prism. It can't hurt us—" Kyle began. A flare of light burst from the staff, aimed at Jia. Kyle pushed her toward the cover of ruins jutting up beside their path. A sharp pain ripped across his shoulder blades as he took the fire that would have struck Jia in the eyes. He felt the burn, like the ilyath, deep and penetrating.

Jia darted around the shell of a building, splashing through the shallows toward the stepping stones and boulders in the river and the cover of the hillside opposite. Kyle hurried after her.

Just as he rounded the ruin, he heard a bow twang. He dived for cover, too late. He felt the arrow's bite just as he belly-flopped onto the lake. He expected to feel the stone blocks of ruins in the lake smash into his chest. Instead, a sharp pain ripped through his side from head to toe. He sank, slithering downward among the ruins, fearing more arrows. The water remained cold and clear as he sliced through it like a fish. He dared a breath, tasting the acid in lungs that weren't his, knowing he swam again, the manfish.

The pain persisted as he moved, broken like a minnow hooked through the back. He knew an arrow stuck from some part of him but he couldn't tell any longer what part of him that might be, nor see more of himself than the occasional silvery flash of a lower extremity. Jia's white stone, the one still gripped in his palm—melded to his side—must have made him a fish. He could make out the ruins of the lake. He remained in Metatha; he took a deep breath of the water, comforted that he could Travel, but that he could come back to ensure Jia reached safety.

The water around him dimmed the deeper he went. He expected soon to encounter the ruins of the palace. Instead, he brushed against a moldering stump.

No! He panicked. The water had gone musty. What time raced by in Jia's world? Did she escape? Did the Pale find her? Did they race along the rim trail clubbing those in their way?

He struggled to the surface. A cramp in his side ripped through him. He forced a breath that burned with the scent of bog. He grasped a stump, trying to stop the wheeze in his breath. Deep and moonless night lay over the water, but he knew home by its smell.

He'd wanted to be here, but not by leaving Jia in danger! He wanted to know the door was open, but choose his own time for coming and going.

On the opposite shore, a dim lantern marked Rupert waiting vigil for him. He'd been gone, how long? Almost six days, about six hours, sometime between two and pre-dawn.

He reached for shore. The pain ripped through him and he gasped. The frogs fell silent.

"Kyle?" Rupert's voice carried across the narrow expanse.

Kyle remained silent, crawling through the reeds as snakes, turtles and frogs scattered. He grasped his side where the arrow had struck him, penetrating a bit more than an inch—an arrow that he tugged free to find not merely blood but *scale*. As he moved, the coarse tunic scraped the burn on his back. How bad?

Would the Pale come in a vengeance, sell Jia into slavery, or worse? Atatha couldn't survive another beating. When Kyle failed to surface, would the Pale assume him dead, or would they be certain a Traveler had been among them and intensify their persecution? How could Rupert, *Ruperion*, have done this!

Kyle stumbled along the shore path toward the home he longed for just last night. Less than an hour ago. He could see Rupert on the opposite shore, staring into the night as if expecting Kyle to swim to him for help. Ruperion, the evil wyseer, they claimed, who had tried to destroy Metatha. What did he really know about him? A drunk—guilty conscience for the tens of thousands he'd killed?

Kyle slipped into the house without turning on any lights until he reached his room. There, he used a flashlight to strip out of the coarse tunic, throw on jeans and toss a coin jar and Jia's white stone into the bag he'd packed for school. He paused, emptying the pouch onto his dresser. He sorted through for his water-soaked wallet and keys, leaving all else. He'd escaped Metatha, but what had he caused by being seen? Rupert might try to make him go back, to lead the wyseer there. Hours would have passed, almost a day by now. Would it be dark yet? He might slip back to check on Jia. But then, they were determined to keep him from returning home, mostly out of fear he would return with Rupert. He had to get away from Rupert. He'd tricked him into going to Metatha once. He could do it again. He couldn't let Rupert—

He could see the flashlight play across his bedroom window. Rupert was coming. He hurried through the house, going for the side door. Before he could slip out, Rupert blocked his way. The old man flipped on the light, almost blinding him.

"Kyle!" Rupert grabbed for Kyle's arm.

Kyle shook him off, holding up in warning the blood-sheathed hand that had held the arrow, and been marked by the ilyath.

"You must tell me!"

"You can't go back. You're the evil they fear," Kyle said, pushing past the wyseer to hurry to his car. "You lied to me. People have been beaten; likely will die because of me, because I believed you. You were using me!"

Kyle felt the heat rising in him, his throat locking up.

"Kyle, you're hurt. Let me help you! Tell me what you found!"

Kyle slammed the car door to shut out Rupert's protest, locked it and released the clutch to roll down the driveway before Rupert could reach him, almost running the man down in the driveway as the engine turned over and he jumped on the accelerator. He didn't know what to do. How much time had elapsed? Twenty minutes? So most of a day.

Each breath gripped him in the side he grasped with one hand, hoping to hold the blood back. He knew he needed help. Stitches at the minimum. How deep had the arrow penetrated? To organs? Was he dying? How much of the boggy water had entered the wound? Who could he possibly go to that wouldn't demand to know what had happened to him? He had to get away from Rupert. He needed to be somewhere he could think.

He couldn't even wonder at his own irrational need to reject Rupert's help. He just knew, as if Atatha were in his head warning him away from his parents as though they couldn't be trusted, that they were in league with Rupert. And Rupert, he must escape Rupert.

As he struck paved highway and sped toward the Interstate, he felt the first twinges of the weakness that had assailed him when he first reached Metatha. Travel sickness, Atatha had called it: the faint, the weariness, the nausea, now compounded by injury and his certainty Jia would die because of him. He didn't dare pull over. At this hour, only truckers and a few lone travelers were out. He sped into a night so dark no tiny moon of his could light it. As if the night had left behind its cloak.

CHAPTER EIGHT

Rupert stared after Kyle, long after the night noises had returned. He knew Travel sickness crept upon Kyle. Someone had marked him with the ilyath, so he had come from a dangerous world. That was blood he'd seen on Kyle's hands.

He thought he glimpsed a face in the window as he finally turned back to the house. Betty Nelson met him at the door. She stared down at a bloody footprint on the yellowed linoleum.

"Rupert, *this* you have to explain," she said softly. "You may have brought him here, but he's my *son*."

Rupert shook his head and pushed past her to Kyle's room. A bloody, wet tunic lay on the floor. Betty followed him, protesting, only to fall silent at the sight of the tunic, more like a burlap seed sack. Was this prison garb? Had he been beaten or harmed for his strangeness? He had the ilyath mark. Someone had to protect him from … something. Rupert should have prepared him better, not just pushed him.

"Damn it, Rupert, explain this to me!" Betty yanked him by the arm, the good woman who had taken in his child showed a face he'd never seen: the mother that would defend to the death her cub.

"I'll go after him," Rupert said, sorting through the objects on Kyle's dresser. "He'll be all right." Rupert spied a familiar shape and his heart skipped. He swallowed hard as a trembling hand cradled the Kokopelli he'd used to craft the Traveling spells, the anchor stone that had sat on his desk hundreds of years ago.

He could return now!

How had Kyle come by it? And what made Kyle so angry, and afraid of him?

"I won't stand for this, Rupert. There's blood everywhere! He clearly needs a hospital. What's going on? Is this something to do with those survivalists you drink with? You're not taking my son into that foolishness."

Betty's face held a genuine rage he'd never seen before and, for the first time, he realized that it mattered.

"Answer me, Rupert!"

Silence.

"I'm calling the police," she said with a finality that cut through Rupert's hesitation. He dropped the Kokopelli in his pocket and grabbed Betty's hand as she spun toward the door.

"You have to trust me," Rupert said. "You've never had reason not to. The police would be a bad idea. I don't *know* what happened. All I know is whatever happened frightened him so that he's afraid to talk about it. You wouldn't want him to get in trouble would you? Let me talk to him, get some answers. Believe me, Betty, I couldn't harm him to save myself."

Rupert left Betty standing in her son's room, sobbing silently as Rupert left to gather his tackle box full of wyseer's tools. What could have turned Kyle's skepticism so quickly to hate, or doubt, or fear of him?

By the time Rupert had packed up the old pickup truck he'd been driving for the last twenty years—never wanting to waste his money on something he'd leave behind one day—dawn was beginning to streak the sky. He could see the shadow of Betty looming in the kitchen window, watching him with red eyes and worry lines on her brow. So much she'd given to him with her heart, so many questions she'd let lie. She harbored and nurtured his dreams for him, kept them safe. And Rupert had repaid with more of the evil of Travel. This time he was the poison that took a mother's child.

CHAPTER NINE

Jia hid among thick brush on the far side of the lake, ignoring birds that plucked at strands of hair in her face. Any moment Kyle should pop up from hiding, or emerge along the bank.

He didn't.

Each moment the lake's surface remained glassy her heart pounded harder. As if her blood poured out of her, she felt empty, weak, faint—with fear? The Pale searched for them on the far bank, sending skyward clouds of birds to darken the afternoon. Had Kyle drowned? Had he swum to another world? He had her white stone! She almost sensed it, felt it pressed into her palm, smelled the musty scent of a bog—

She shook her head at the odd turn of thought. She didn't dare hide here waiting much longer. When the Pale exhausted their search along the lakeshore, they would seek among the Fidrel. She needed to warn her people. She couldn't draw breath deep enough to find the calm she needed. All her training in self-control shouldn't fail her at so inferior a test! She silently urged Kyle to stay away from his uncle, to return to her because she needed him. They needed him. It was why they lived, breathed: to end this Pale tyranny. He could bring that!

She slipped up the steep trail to the ridge path, hugging the shadows thrown by stubby trees. He traveled with her white stone, not the black one Atatha had taken from him. She wanted to sort it out, but her heart pounded too hard yet, throbbed behind her eyes, made the vibrant greens of forest and bird leap in her vision. A brilliant purple slysucker circled her, his bright yellow tail a searing slash of color striking her in the eye. She almost stumbled. It must be fear, or awe. Kyloreign had saved her life. Now he was gone.

At last, Jia staggered into Atatha's tiny cave, gripping her side as a stitch stole even her stamina from her. It was a ripping pain that almost made her stumble. She stopped short: A dozen wyseers stared at her.

Isra rose from her seat. From his mat beside the cool fire, Atatha's gaze narrowed on Jia. She had disrupted a meeting of the council, right here in Atatha's cave of all places.

"Kyle … gone." Jia gasped, trying to pull breath around the stitch. "Pale."

"The Pale have him?" Isra asked as other Fidrel gathered to press into the tiny cave behind her, young adepts like her, old wyseers, those who saw her running up the path from the lake.

Jia shook her head, accepting the ladle of water offered her. "The Pale came on us," she explained as the catch in her side eased. "A wyseer threw glass fire and their warriors shot arrows. I know the glass fire and at least one arrow struck Kyle. He fell into the lake and didn't resurface. The Pale search the valley. When they don't find him, they'll be looking here for me."

A buzz of voices rose behind her as more and more wyseers and their etlith arrived to catch the import of her tale.

"Everything we have dreamed, all these years," a council member muttered from near the back of the cave. Jia noted tears in the eyes of another, people whose names she knew but in this historic moment couldn't remember. She had lost the Traveler!

"We must hide before the Pale come," Jia urged Isra as she at last regained her breath.

"We have never run to hide from them before," Atatha said, scowling.

"But he's the sign. Now there's no need to wait for a decision on *him*, he's gone. The Traveler returned, the marker to go to Hindlain—" Jia sputtered, the words tumbling from her mouth before she could recall them. She saw Wilnath on the edge of the crowd, stiffen and turn quickly to whisper to another young wyseer.

"We needed the Traveler, not just the marker of his existence," Atatha said, his words muffled to her ears.

The floor canted beneath her, the faces all seeming to repeat, ripple, glittering dark eyes like stars on the edge of the dark. It took a force of will to return to the present.

"Kyle was right to disdain us," she said. "We spent generations waiting for him and him alone. All this time we could have fought back. We could have preserved the lore of our Clan without becoming such pitiful creatures at the mercy of the Pale."

Many in the growing crowd murmured their agreement.

"Jia, you don't understand." Isra's words were meant to soothe the restive crowd. "We have nothing comparable to their power. You yourself saw the glass fire, you say. The Methiliim practice a dark wyseery of the kind we can never condone." She held up a hand draped in sea beads, reminding all of her rank. "We will never find another Reign. Perhaps in the past the wyseers might have brought his body back and reanimated it, perhaps even taken some bit of his flesh and made it whole again in someone else. We haven't that power. We must resign ourselves, at last, to defeat."

"He's not dead. He swam away!" Jia almost shrieked it, the echoes of her anger almost overwhelmed by the buzz of wyseers pressing in behind her. She felt each breath on her back, the pound of each heartbeat like the pound of the Pale riding to destroy them.

"You are distraught, Jia," Atatha said. "We all were enamored of the Traveler's glamour. You are almost a wyseer yourself, plenty old enough to overcome this—"

"You're the ones not thinking," Jia returned, knowing her insubordination may cost her life. "Are you so ready for defeat that you won't believe me when I tell you he lives—"

"He can't Travel," Atatha reminded her, offering Jia the black stone he had taken.

It felt glassy and warm as if Kyle still gripped it in his pocket with the desperation of one who knew himself trapped.

"No body rose to the surface," she said, speaking to the dark thing in her palm, like a button from night's cloak. "The Pale beat along the shores, prodded among the ruins. No body rose. I swear I saw the flash of a fish slip away into the deeps." She looked up to find Atatha's dark gaze. "He had my white stone, Atatha! The stone I dreamt in my manfish dream!"

Atatha leaned back as the host of wyseers and adepts murmured among themselves, exclamation growing. Atatha's face had gone red.

Isra held up a hand to silence the crowd in the cave. "So, your stone was true and we merely needed one who could pass the bans."

"You indeed are an adept of promise, Jia, that you saw so truly," Atatha said. "But he wanted to go home. Once in his world, he won't return. Likely he cast the white stone far from him. We have lost him."

"What of Ruperion?" someone asked from the rear of the cave.

Isra scowled. "If Kyle returned to his own world, and his uncle is indeed Ruperion, then we have much to fear."

"We knew this would come," Atatha said, patting Jia's hand. She yanked free of him.

"We knew that if we were going to fight the Pale we would have to abandon the caverns. We haven't yet. If we had, this wouldn't have happened," Jia said to a murmur of agreement from several older adepts behind her. "This is what we trained for from the beginning—"

"Jia, you forget to whom you speak," Atatha warned.

"Of course it's difficult to understand, Jia," Isra said. "To see everything we have believed in end so swiftly."

"You aren't thinking!" Jia shrieked; the room seemed to melt around her. "The Traveler asked why in five hundred years we never fought for ourselves. Why can't we hone our own powers and fight back? He wondered why we scavenge instead of invent. We don't even try to help ourselves! We can call up the Valeutans. We have Hindlain. Why aren't we there? The Pale will be here soon and this time they have cause."

Murmurs and even challenges rose louder among those gathered behind her. How dare she, an adept, speak so to the council!

Isra merely looked on her with pity. "Jia, the way you propose will lead to our demise far faster. You seem to think that young wyseers haven't always chafed at this way and suggested it was time to take to Hindlain. Even in my youth, we asked the same questions." Isra raised her bead-draped hands to hush the crowd. "You dare a great deal to suggest the council cannot rule with more wisdom than an adept of a mere sixteen years. What you propose goes against all that the Fidrel believe in. Would you suggest that you can face the Pale? What dark tools would you raise? Will you sacrifice some poor creature to give you the power to make a spell larger than yourself?"

Jia swallowed hard. Isra suggested treason. How far dared she go? Kyle was alive. She knew it. The Pale would conclude their search of Ta'atit soon. The council should be ordering people to scatter and reconvene in Hindlain. They merely stared at her: some stormbird harping its warning as if no one could see the lightning in the hills.

"What is your counsel, wise Isra?" Jia asked softly.

"The Pale will come. They will search. They will find nothing. A few people will be beaten. In the end the Pale will leave and all will be as before. We can live on in peace, in our quiet study."

Several council members frowned, including Atatha who stared at the cold fire. No one spoke against Isra.

"Wise One," Jia said, "if all our claims for existence were to prepare for the return of Kyloreign to again serve the people with the good powers of other lands, what esoteric purpose will that study now serve with no hope of the Traveler's return? And if the Traveler does return, shouldn't we be preserving ourselves for him? What if it is Ruperion who comes? And if no one, why do we remain here serving no purpose to our Clan?"

Isra stiffened, then held up her hand to halt Atatha's attempt to apologize for Jia. She glared down at Jia.

"It is not the purpose of this council to answer to an adept. Describe for me, Jia, your lengthy years of work that can justify your wisdom to order the ways of this council?"

"Wise One, it is not wisdom, but a desire to live that makes me speak. I chose the Fidrel to plan for Kyloreign's return, to plan for an end to suffering and servitude. To suggest we continue to submit when the main tenet of our faith is proven—Your own daughter was sold at Waymeet—"

"Jia!" Atatha warned, but it was too late.

"My daughter made her sacrifice as do all the Fidrel. Our ways were set five hundred years ago. Do you think the people of those times thought that we would wait so long for the Traveler? We are weaker now than we were then, and the Pale stronger."

Jia realized suddenly that Isra wasn't speaking to her, but to the doubtful wyseers pressed into the cave entrance, many of them warily eyeing the ledge trail. Isra was asserting her will and losing. What had Jia done?

Jia turned away, still clutching the black stone as if she could drive it into her palm, melt it into her soul and disappear into some far world. She pushed through the crowd to escape the cave. She heard Atatha's voice raised in defense, claiming Jia hadn't been right since the blow to her head during the Pale's last assault. Jia wanted to spit something sour from her mouth. Why *had* the Fidrel waited all these generations? If it was to use the Traveler to collect the evils from other worlds, then they would be no better than the Pale to hold him against his will. Did they expect Kyle to spend his life swimming from world to world to collect trinkets for the Fidrel simply because the Fidrel honored him? Even the Fidrel must admit the very Travel they prayed for was an aberrant wyseery that twisted the will of the gods. Kyle was but a catalyst, she decided. Perhaps he had served his purpose, to demonstrate the futility in waiting for some savior from the past to return and teach them how to take care of themselves. They could have learned more. They should be taking care of themselves this very instant!

Jia strode toward the tiny stream that crossed the ridge path, staggering a little in the bright of late afternoon, feeling faint to see the fringe of trees so far below. She needed to cool her face. Somehow Kyle had shaken her composure, had made of her a rebel and malcontent. As she knelt over a pool in the stream, seeing reflected defiance still bright in her eyes, she wondered if she had just doomed herself forever. The council could easily banish her back to Overmount, a failed promise shipped home to parents much poorer for having supported her study. The Fidrel could make the rest of her days one of challenge, or could force her to take a penance quest that well might risk her life. It could be one even more dangerous than the initiate's rites when she had to sneak into a Pale camp to steal a token from a wyseer's pouch. She'd been caught then, but had so startled her captor with the powder she flung in his eyes she'd escaped. Penance would be harder, even more dangerous.

She startled at a tug on her sleeve. She looked up into the glare of late sun to find the silhouette of Wilnath.

"Have you come to haul me to my judgment?"

Wilnath crouched beside her, shaking his head. "You spoke well and wisely, Sister," he said. "We knew this might happen. Your wise words brought us even more support. We must preserve the Clan, as we promised. Sister, truly you have grown to earn a wyseer's fare."

Jia flushed, inclining her head at the compliment. "So, Wil, have they named my punishment?"

Wilnath smiled a little, a lopsided sort of grin that reminded her of when they had been siblings playing in a wyseer's house. "The truth can't be punished. The time has come for the Fidrel to recognize our true founding principle: to help the Valeutans, to preserve our Clan. We're going to Hindlain as we should have all along. We said that we would launch our battle when the Traveler returned. Nothing in the lore said the Traveler must be here to see it through."

"Isra conceded then?"

Wilnath stood, holding out his hand. "A representative will tell Isra and the council that we flee before the coming Pale and will fight back for the good of the Valeutans. We expect her to resist. She will likely cite the need for a Traveler to bring us other-world wyseery. We'll inform her that we are breaking from the Fidrel and will fight, as our oaths require. I thought we numbered a third. Now I'd say more than half."

It happened so fast! Was this all it took? What if they were wrong? Could they stay true, and fight, without outside wyseery? She bobbed her head. Her hair flowed across her outstretched arms, the light on her skin striking her odd.

"Gather your things. We don't have much time."

Jia hurried home, finding Atatha alone, propped up beside the fire. From the cluster of milling wyseers outside of Isra's cave, Jia knew the council had moved there after her outburst.

"You disgraced me," he said.

A pang of guilt twisted up inside her at the rebuke, but she continued on with her mission, skirting where he sat beside the fire to gather the few oddments that she had brought with her from Overmount.

"So, disgraced," she muttered as she stuffed a sack with her belongings. "What will the council sentence me to, prison? Random assault? Poverty? Hmm, nothing new there—"

"The council reconvened elsewhere after I was dismissed. I don't know what sentence they will invoke."

"Dismissed!" Jia paused as she rolled up her sleeping mat and blanket, still feeling that giddiness that had made her speak out before the council. That strange otherness, as if, as if—"It isn't your fault that I have an opinion. I spoke up, not you."

"You know your mentor is responsible for you until you become a wyseer. And as your mentor I spoke in your defense. As close as you are to that naming, I wish we could have waited a bit longer before you discovered your opinion."

She eyed her mentor, detecting a sour humor she didn't expect to find.

"Come with us, Atatha. I couldn't bear to watch the Pale beat you into the dust again. We deserve better than that."

"And always each succeeding generation thinks itself the first to forge the trail. Don't you think when I was young I, too, chafed at the way we are forced to play this game? We spoke of resistance, of hiding, of how the old were so reticent."

"But when you were young, the Traveler was an unproven prophecy. The time is now. If Isra declines to follow us, as we're sure she'll do, we will go without her blessing. From hiding we'll do what the Fidrel were always meant to do: preserve the ways of the Valeutans."

"Do you and your faction realize there will be retaliations on the easiest targets to find: the Valeutans you're pledging to protect?"

"But our lore acknowledges that the Traveler may be no peace-bringer, might not even be friendly. It makes no mention of any special thing about the Traveler but that he comes. How can we deny what is so clearly stated in our faith? We must do as we preach. I think Isra is very happy that he went away, because things can stay predictable, if unpleasant. The adepts and younger wyseers still remember the manfish dreams and the hope we saw in the Fidrel. We came here not to join a long tradition of do-nothings, but to help our people."

"Well-spoken, if perhaps a bit idealistic." Atatha gave her a sad smile. A shadow wearing Wilnath's shape paused in the cave opening.

"It's time, Jia. Isra declined. And scouts report that the Pale are gathering. We think they may make a major strike in the morning," he said.

"Atatha, please." Jia held out her hand. Atatha glanced out at Wilnath. A file of wyseers and adepts slipped by Wilnath to hurry east along the ridge path, away from the direction the Pale would come. The rebels, a few elders among them, toted light packs, eyes bright with hope, jaws set with determination, many already serving as warriors setting up defensive positions and hiding traces of their trail.

"I think you'll need some of this old wisdom, but I'm not yet well. The Pale will be upon you too soon. I doubt I can travel so far at the pace you must keep. I will stand among the rearguard."

"Wil!" Jia called, pulling Atatha to wobbly feet. In a moment, Wilnath had tapped another young man and the two supported Atatha between them. Jia stuffed a bag with the wyseers's gear and food and thrust a blanket into Atatha's hands.

"You'll need a naysayer among you, to hold a check on your foolish exuberance," Atatha was telling Wilnath in a curmudgeonly tone that made Jia want to smile.

As they joined the retreat, Jia looked back along the ridge trail to see Isra staring after them. Her dark hair settled like a shroud about her shoulders as she made a barring sign at the backs of so many of the young wyseers fostered by the Fidrel, the faithful, those who awaited the return of Kyloreign. The light glittered up from her sea beads. What were the Fidrel now, but the old, the bent, who would now bow before the Pale? Jia squinted, thinking she spied the distant flash of crimson and cringing deep within.

She turned her back on the Fidrel, and for the last time, she turned her back on the Pale.

CHAPTER TEN

The day had long fled and Danat loomed directly overhead, chased by Kylik, before they reached the top of the great stair down to the sea. Instead of the stairs, the exiled Fidrel took a hidden path along the northern side of the great waterfall. Stumbling in the dark, Jia felt as if she had already swum to another world. All sound drowned by the thunder of water, she stared out at the strange luminescent sea beneath the moons, wondering how it had appeared to Kyle, how he had seen pocked and wizened Danat scraping along the horizon and wondering at what place he had come to. Wilnath nudged her and she realized she had stopped moving, caught up in the mist, feeling as if a light breeze might send her easily wafting down into the white foam like no more than a hint of fog. Sharp stone beneath her feet roused her from the sense of vision, the sense it all came from something she had seen in a manfish dream, though this had never been in her dreams. This morning she had laughed beside Kyle as they told each other stories of blood birds. This noon she had watched the dreams of her people slip beneath the surface of the lake. This afternoon she dared to challenge the council of wise who had guided her people for more generations than she had years. And this night she stepped most fully into exile as she followed the ghostly silhouettes of her fellow idealists into Hindlain.

Long ago the southern stair had led from Ta'atit to a marina that served fishing boats. The boats had withered away to bleached bones and at last were gone with the expertise to build them and navigate the great sea. The Fidrel had discovered a cavern behind the waterfall where roiling water undercut softer rock beneath the hard upper layers. Ages of wyseers broadened and widened the cavern until they made it high and safe, looming several hundred feet above the sea, yet several hundred feet below the cliff tops. Here they had amassed those most powerful tools of wyseery they didn't dare take to the Ridge where the Pale might find them. From here the exiles would carry out the prophecy of Kyloreign, if they remained unbetrayed.

Jia paused as the last of the exiled Fidrel surveyed their trail to ensure they'd left no mark of their passage, then slipped behind the waterfall. The last of Kylik's light shimmered white through the wall of water thundering before her, the mist plastering her clothes to her body. Something in all of this felt so surreal, as if she weren't truly herself, as if some part of her—the practical side that would bid her not wander so fancifully, not speak so flippantly to her elders, not move so boldly to embrace the unknown—had been lost this afternoon when the Pale came upon her.

She looked over her shoulder to where torches and a fire had been lit, far back and away from the dripping roof and rolling mist. There she could see that Wilnath had settled Atatha on a rush mat. Her mentor studied her from a distance and she knew he saw the strangeness in her and at last with the insight of one who is a wyseer and no longer an adept, she knew what it was that had strayed into or out of her this day.

Kyle had swum to another world with her stone, a piece of her, the thing the manfish had shown her so long ago. He had bound her to him. Perhaps, she hoped, she had thus bound him to her.

As Kylik at last moved on over the submerged valley beyond the scarp, the waterfall fell dim and dark. She went first to Atatha, who took her hands and stared up at her, his one unmarked eye measuring her mood. She thought for a moment that he could see into her very soul.

"You have stepped into a great role and erase the disgrace," Atatha said. "You make me proud."

Jia shook her head. "I only hope that Isra or some other poor fool remaining doesn't lead them to Hindlain in hopes of stopping our 'foolishness.'"

"No," Wilnath said as he came close, checking the health of his former mentor as easily as he seemed to measure Jia's own state. "They will continue in their way, and we will go on as *Kylalnethra* long after anyone knows that the name has more to do with the disciples of one who was named Kyle, rather than those who worship the light. Kyle is the catalyst. Kyle said we should defend ourselves and count on no one else. And that is what we shall do."

Atatha inclined his head slightly, a tacit agreement.

Jia glanced around the cavern. Perhaps a few more than one hundred worked to assess their food supplies, mark off sleeping areas, communal areas and latrines. So many were young. All but the very youngest of the adepts had abandoned their mentors and among the wyseers, few had worn wyseer robes for more than five years. Atatha had the longest tenure among them and already an adept had been assigned to take his things from among Jia's and set them up in a privileged corner of the cavern, usurping Jia's role. She frowned. Wilnath followed her gaze and grinned that lopsided grin of his.

"There are more important tasks for you, Jia, than waiting on your mentor. Beginning tomorrow we must learn to defend ourselves. We must learn what it means to be Kylalnethra. You are too wise to get off with the simple tasks of an adept. It is time you become a novice. We'll have need of you."

Jia glanced at Atatha, who nodded slowly. Jia felt a warm glow work its way up from deep inside. Yet she shivered, feeling again that strange other sense, that odd feeling that a part of her had passed beyond this world.

She rubbed her side and frowned, staring down into the sandy cavern floor. The more she concentrated, the more she had that sense of distance from herself, as if she looked upon herself from afar, through the waterfall perhaps. A glitter of silver passed before her eyes.

"Jia!"

She heard Wilnath's voice close beside her ear, thought she felt his hand beneath her elbow, and sensed her legs had become rubbery beneath her. She fell a great distance, yet never reached the ground. She couldn't shake the strangeness of this moment, as if water buoyed her, or air, as if she looked through refracted water in a bolder light and darker night, breathed a musty odor with a hint of rot.

Wilnath again called her name, more urgently. She blinked and looked up at him, finding several wyseers gathered around her. Somehow she had come to lie on a mat on the sandy floor on her back. One hand gripped her side, the other Atatha held. In a fleet instant she recognized the scent of the sourweed paste Atatha had placed beneath her tongue. She swallowed and felt herself regain a measure of the solid world around her.

"How much time has passed since Kyle Traveled?" she asked herself.

"A day, perhaps," Wilnath said. "You've slept through the night. We feared for you. You suffered convulsions, Jia."

"In his world that is but an hour," she said, focusing on Atatha. "I think he's seriously hurt." Her mentor's one good eye closed to a slit.

"Your concern has you overwrought, perhaps," Wilnath said.

Jia tried to shake her head but that sent little sparks of light before her eyes.

"Kyle carries a very powerful wyseery," Atatha said. "He carries the white stone that was Jia's manfish dream, a stone she found among the clutter of Ta'atit and likely a stone once used to make great power. It is also a stone of opposition to the Travel stone, a path foretold in a dream. And it may have helped him Travel home. If, indeed, Kyle went home. He reentered at a different traveling point than when he arrived. If he knows nothing of Travel, he may have exited in a completely different world."

"I feel as if he's beside me, yet I can't see him. I feel ... I don't know how to describe this."

"You will need to fight the urge to slip away or it could bring you harm," Atatha said. "I don't know what will happen, but you appear no better for having it get the best of you. Perhaps a combination of focusing exercises and willpower will help. Yet, too, this may be a tool."

"You're thinking that Kyle feels the same connection?" Wilnath asked.

"If so, Jia will draw him back to us. The power of a Traveler wouldn't be a bad thing."

"Let us hope, then, that Kyle survives to return, without his uncle," he said. "No matter what his claim of innocence: no one, not Pale, not Valeutan, will tolerate Ruperion walking this world. Even if it means killing the Traveler to prevent him from Traveling."

Within herself, Jia struggled to find the sensation of Kyle, to send thoughts that would make him flee his uncle, to flee anyone who might prevent him from returning to help her, unsure if she could do such a thing. She was the link that could draw the Traveler back. And as such, she might well destroy him.

CHAPTER ELEVEN

Kyle shifted with a groan, reaching for the wastebasket. Nothing remained in him to purge, yet still his body convulsed, just to remind him that something had pierced his side, that something had burned his back and that he wished he could just die to make the throb in his head go away.

He'd sprawled on the floor of his room in the lower flat he shared with his two roommates. Upstairs a board creaked as someone moved back and forth across the same spot with a grating regularity that made him want to throw up again. Dust bunnies hovered under the bed. They swirled on the hardwood floor with each breath he took. Grit stuck to the side of his sweat-slicked face. He couldn't move. He hadn't felt anything like this when he traveled to Metatha. He'd been disoriented and exhausted, but nothing like this.

Then again, he hadn't had an arrow sticking out of him—one with *scales* attached to it—or been burned by … magic. That's what Rupert would tell him it was; Jia would call it wyseery. Jia. He saw her running, fleeing the red-cloaked Pale who rode misshapen creatures that vaguely resembled shaggy ponies, their gear making him think of some tapestry of a Mongol invasion.

He couldn't recall the two-hour drive home to Madison. He had only a brief limned memory of stumbling through the door as if drunk, overturning a lamp and falling across the couch before he made it to his room, only to miss the bed and hit the floor like a sack of cement.

Eyes half open, he stared at the underside of his bed. Cobwebs filigreed the wooden slats and old-fashioned spring set. A hazy sense of somehow not having both of his feet planted in the same time and place intensified as Jia and Metatha and his need to escape … escape something, someone—

He groaned to himself and shut his eyes. He bobbed in a light sea swell, but he could see Rupert sorting through the clutter on his own dresser back home. The old wyseer picked up the turquoise and silver pendant Kyle had found in Ta'atit the morning before. The little image like Kokopelli, like the manfish, danced before Kyle's eyes as Rupert held it up in triumph, his features appearing demonic as he roared that now he would finish off Metatha.

His eyes flew open and he almost retched. What if he'd left something behind Rupert could use to return to Metatha? His imagination turned Rupert's gaze on him and again he felt the stab of something striking him hard in the side.

He realized he'd groaned aloud again when his bedroom door creaked open.

"Kyle? Hey, man, is that you? You tie one on or what? Christ, it stinks! You puke?"

"Ripp?" Kyle couldn't move to see which roommate spoke from the doorway. A spill of yellow light fell into the room. Morning or night? How many days passed in Metatha? "I'm sick."

With the snap of the light switch fire ripped across Kyle's eyes.

"Holy shit," Ripp said. "What the hell happened to you? You get in a fight? What's the other guy look like?"

"Yeah. Help me out, will ya?"

"Did you call the police?" Ripp tugged at Kyle's T-shirt. The cotton stuck to the wound. He yelped and opened his eyes to find the beige T-shirt dark with a crust of blood down his whole right side. The burn on his back from the wizard's magic prism had seeped, too, shedding skin as it pulled away.

"No cops, 'K, Ripp? I don't want to get into it—"

"You come in with a knife wound, you know they have to call the police." Ripp sat back on his haunches and peered at him as if seeing someone he didn't know. "Maybe I should call 9-1-1. You look awful."

Kyle tried to pull himself up to sitting. The room spun on him as he shook his head no.

"You're just going to have to deal, y'know?" Ripp's voice trembled as he tossed the T-shirt into the wastebasket.

"No. It's complicated. Is Jacko back?" Kyle asked, referring to his other roommate, Jack O'Malley, as Ripp made feeble attempts to help him sit up.

"He left a message on the answering machine. He'll be flying in tomorrow."

"Is he still seeing Kim?"

"Aw, man, Kyle … She's not a real doctor yet and she isn't even into that kind of medicine."

"All I need is some stitches, maybe some antibiotics."

"Yeah, and giving them to you is probably illegal. I'll call her, but there's no guarantee she'll help."

"'S'all I'm asking." Kyle closed his eyes against the light, again that sense of urgency. Flee! They were there to stop him, stop him from… He thought Ripp had left, then felt a blanket draped over him. He realized he was shivering but he didn't know for how long or if it was even Ripp who put a pillow under his head and took away the stinking wastebasket. Instead, he saw Jia, her eyes too large and dark for her face, her features too elfin for her age, as she peered, desperate, into a glassy black lake in search of the silvery glint of the Traveler.

Fire ripped up his side, yanking him out of a place where the moldering stumps had given way to crumbling ruin. He had been running, the Pale were riding along the cut, earlier than expected. The intelligence was bad! He needed to reach his position to signal the assault. He swore, forcing eyes open to see Ripp, pale, bent over his side. Kyle lay on the bed now.

Kyle grabbed Ripp's arm. "What the hell—"

Ripp shook him off, gesturing with his head at the half-empty bottle of rubbing alcohol on the bed. "Kim says you really need a doctor, get an x-ray or something, make sure you didn't slice into something important. I don't know why I'm doing this. She said rubbing alcohol to sterilize. Stitch with sterilized fishing line. I think six-pound test'll work. Lots of aspirin, till your ears ring. She still thinks you might've nicked something that could cause, um, peritonitis or something like that. Even if there's no damaged organs, since it's a puncture wound, you could get all kinds of infection. Cleaned up it doesn't look as bad, but it's still pretty deep."

Ripp's forehead glistened, slick, and his blue eyes seemed oddly dark in a face so pale as he pulled line through the two lips of torn skin. Kyle barely felt the sting and tug for the burning alcohol in the wound.

"Dan, I can't believe you're doing this," Kyle said.

"Yeah, well, you owe me. If I ever get in trouble 'cuz of this I'm going to pull these stitches out through your teeth. This had better be a good story."

"You won't believe it."

Kyle closed his eyes again, uncertain he should. Each time he closed his eyes he saw Rupert laughing at him as he rode rapine over Jia's people, toting an assault rifle or bazooka on his shoulder, carefully laying mines along the Ridge trail. That or he saw Jia, seeming thinner and more haggard each time. How many hours had passed? For each hour a day, each day almost a month. Had it been two days, three? Had she survived the Pale attack? Did the Fidrel now suffer some unspeakable fate because of him?

He woke to find Ripp lightly shaking his shoulder. Kyle opened his eyes but he couldn't speak. He felt as if he'd swallowed a wad of cotton.

"It's like this, you're still sick, worse, I think," Ripp was saying. "And your uncle has been calling your phone constantly, your mom two or three times, your dad once, three sisters. What is it with your family? Then your uncle shows up here and I told him you weren't here, even though your car—full of blood and puke, by the way and stinking to high heaven—is sitting in the driveway—"

Kyle grabbed his arm. Ripp wasn't even looking at him.

"What are you getting at?"

"I don't know what I can do anymore, Kyle. You've even pissed yourself, you're so sick. You need a hospital."

"I can't tell anyone how this happened. They'd call my family, my uncle. I don't want him getting near me."

"What's the deal, Kyle? C'mon, whatever it is, it isn't worth dying for. School's started. I can't be here for you all the time. Jacko helps, but he gets weird about things."

Kyle tried to focus, shaking his head. Even when he was awake, he felt as if he were somewhere else. "How long?"

"It's been a week, man. You've got a high fever. Kim says it can cause brain damage. Remember when Erickson got mono? That fever just fried him. Had to drop out. If he'd just gone to see health services they could have diagnosed ..."

"Take me to health services, then. We don't need to tell them anything, just that I have a high fever, like mono."

"They're going to smell the pus on you."

"They'll give me antibiotics. And whatever you do, don't let my uncle get to me."

There was such a long silence, Kyle thought maybe he'd fallen asleep. What did he sound like, a raving lunatic? Maybe he should just call his parents. But that idea was quickly shouted down. Why? he wondered briefly. What made him not trust his parents? Rupert would know what to do, but, no, that idea too seemed wrong. All of it was wrong. He had to go back to Metatha.

Ripp appeared again, nodding, holding out a pair of jeans and a shirt. A week. That worked out to about seven months. The Kokopelli on his dresser, Rupert could Travel with that. How did he know that? What would Rupert do? What had happened in Metatha? Had the Pale wiped out the Valeutans, the Fidrel? It couldn't have happened yet.

He felt Jia. She was begging him to return and help her. That there was a war raging and they were suffering. At least that's what her eyes told him, somehow, and that he must flee before Ruperion came. He sensed. He knew. She was there, in him. He thrust his hand into his pocket. Empty. There, on his dresser, next to his keys and wallet, the nut-sized stone. He grabbed it and pushed it into the pocket of jeans that fit him far too loosely.

It took both Jacko and Ripp to get him to the car. He barely heard anything around him. Was that Kim in the background saying they should just take him to the hospital and let him deal later with the consequences, that saving his life was the first thing they should be thinking about and they could all get in trouble if he was in trouble?

Kyle looked up to find Jacko putting a hand on his head to help him into the front seat of the car, then Ripp was there fastening a seatbelt. These were friends. These were people who cared about him. Not like Rupert. He looked up, and there through the glare of the sun on the street he could swear he saw Rupert leaning against a parked car, staring, glaring.

"That's the guy that's been hanging around claiming to be your uncle," Ripp was whispering into his ear. "I'd like to call the cops on that one."

Then he wasn't in Jia's world. He still needed Kyle for something. What, the white stone? Or did he just need a Reign? Why was he afraid of him?

"Run the bastard down," Kyle muttered, but he wasn't sure if anyone heard him, or when he even said it. The next thing he knew he was in a hospital with an IV in his arm and someone — maybe a cop, the man was turned away from him — bedside asking Ripp questions while Ripp wrung his hands. What was he supposed to tell them? The Pale had come after him, an unprovoked attack. They were using magic and arrows. Get them with a hate crime.

How many hours now? How many days? He could see Jia. She was there, waiting for him, counting on him, needing him! He saw a bloody streak on her forehead. She crouched in undergrowth, overlooking a moons-dark clearing. He heard the rip of nervous breaths, felt the strain of eyes peering into the dark desperately trying to mark a shadow against shadows.

"You're bleeding," the words came in Metathan, the voice familiar. Wilnath?

"Grazed is all," Jia whispered, her words filling Kyle's head as if he spoke them. "There." Through Jia's eyes he saw her hand point through the brush at a barely discernible shadow. In moments the clearing was a shifting landscape of dark figures and their swirling cloaks. Several appeared to be Pale wyseers. They oversaw Pale soldiers manhandling a ... cauldron into place. He knew it meant blood from somewhere would be poured into the pot, incantations spoken, power invoked. To what end?

"He's with me," Jia muttered. She looked at her companion. Wilnath appeared more pinched than Kyle remembered, his eyes shadowed and his mouth in a sour turn.

"You need to be alert. Distraction now could kill you. Make him go away."

He fought it. He had to. He needed to understand what was happening.

Jia made a motion. Quick movement. At least a dozen companions. As one, arrows raced among the shadows just as Kylik disappeared behind clouds. At that instant, Jia and her whole squad slipped back and around as some wyseerish light blazed in the clearing behind them. Shouts rose up. He felt the ripping breaths, the adrenalin pounding through veins. Branches whacked into his, no, her face.

They halted. "Marks?" Jia asked amidst a gasp for breath. Voices sounded softly. "Eight," she said, repeating the total number of arrows that reached their target. "That's not nearly good enough! Only two Methiliim!"

A flash ripped through the forest they hid in, someplace hot and stuffy that—three men had fallen. Wyseer's fire.

"Scatter!" Wilnath hissed. Hands grabbed for fallen. Wilnath and Jia took up a young man whose expression was a grimace of fear and pain.

Another blast ripped the forest behind them. He felt Jia's involuntary cringe. Those behind her gathered up the fallen again. Half her unit were injured. A blast felled a tree before them. They dodged a flutter of kindling and green leaves that clung to their sweaty bodies.

"Scatter to the hideouts," Jia's words ripped out as a hiss among the crash of underbrush. "Leave the wounded there and circle back on the pursuit."

"It's glass fire!" someone said. "Arrows are nothing."

"Kill the wyseer with your arrow and there won't be glass fire!" He sensed Jia's desperation in the angry words as she left Wilnath to take their burden on alone. He watched as she carefully slipped among the trees while the crashing passage of escaping Valeutans grew distant. The silence felt deep, complete, her every movement studied.

There, in a brief patch of moonlight, a shadow moved. She gripped something in her hand and Kyle knew it was his own traveling stone she called on for strength as she crept up behind her target. She leaped. He saw then the flash of a knife in her other hand. The Pale soldier turned at the last moment. Her knife harmlessly grazing his collarbone. He shrugged her aside and whipped around with a sword. She ducked the swing, losing her balance. He came at her. She kicked and his sword came free. She tried to press her advantage. But before she could scramble free of him something—a log? a cudgel? a foot?—swung toward her head.

Kyle gasped. She was gone.

She needed help. Would they kill her? Was she held prisoner? Sold off to slavery? Had she overcome? The moments ticked by so swiftly. They needed him because he was Valeutan. Could he return? He had her white stone. He crossed the first time with a black stone, but it had looked white. But the Kokopelli still taunted him from his dresser. Jia stared out of the dresser mirror at him with her black eyes, the hollows deep in each cheek, the dark hair limp and dank and … there was the smell of wyseery in the air. How did he know that? Someone, fair-haired, stood behind her, holding her up, encouraging her. Pale? Wilnath.

"Kyle, it's time to go."

"I'm so tired, Rupert," Kyle muttered, then opened his eyes wide to see that, indeed, Rupert had him alone in a hospital room. Rupert appeared more disheveled than usual and there was a strange glint in his eye.

"Ruperion," Kyle muttered.

"Ah, that is a warning. Just as well I didn't go first, eh?"

"So you're really an evil wizard that's— How could you have done this to me? They say you murdered thousands, destroyed a culture, were the ultimate aberration. And here all these years my parents deferred to you like some privileged elder. How could you?"

Kyle realized that whether it was the antibiotic or the IV, he felt better than he had since the moment he'd reappeared, gasping, in

Potter's Flowage. And angrier. Was it Rupert's doing? The old man really did look awful.

"You're delirious, Kyle. I'll have them release you to my custody and we'll get things set straight."

"I'll refuse. I don't trust you."

"You have to. After all these years are you so ready to believe anything said about me? You should know from your college knowledge the victor writes one history, the conquered writes another."

"And you told me there are good wyseers and bad, and just maybe you were one of those bad ones? They say you and Denalku, the one you always claimed was so benevolent, were so awful that the people sided with the Pale to throw you out. You were so awful they tried to wipe out all trace of your culture."

"Well, I think both sides of the story are exaggerated just a bit."

"How long has it been?"

"Since you came back? Ten days and some hours in change."

"God. Almost a year."

"All these years you didn't believe me. Now what do you think, huh? Your Uncle Rupert didn't need some shrink to tell him what for, huh? You thought you were so bright and college educated. What did you know of the world? *Worlds!*"

"So you were right. And destroyed a people. You don't get it, Rupert, the Pale won. The Reign were destroyed. There's *nothing* left but little clusters of wizards fighting amongst themselves. The Fidrel count on the return of the Traveler to escape their occupation. But the Pale have their own boatload of slimebag wizards out to destroy any of the Valeutans that dare to think of their freedom. It's as if these people don't realize five hundred years have gone by. They're *still* in the same battle. And you dumped me in the middle of that, unprepared for any of it, and I probably caused a war or something."

Rupert studied him, his face a mask. "You certainly weren't unprepared. You knew the language, the history as best I could account for. You were as prepared as you possibly could be. I'd have never sent you unawares. Remember, I *am* the Traveler. I know the risks of what one can do, accidentally, by stepping into another world. I waited until you were mature, of age—"

"They beat them because of me!" the words gasped out. "The Pale got wind that the Traveler had returned. Atatha took a cudgel to the head. Jia, just an etlith, they would have sold her into slavery … She looks like an older Denise, just this little girl and they beat her because of me! It was a Pale arrow in my side, and some magic from a Pale wizard's prism that burned my back."

"So, blood wyseery," Rupert said, softly. "They still use it. That was the abomination we resisted. It takes great horrors to create strong magic without the tools of wyseery. But the Valeutan wyseers, we couldn't face those who turned from art to blood without stronger and stronger wyseery, and the only place we could find it was Traveling. And then, well, bad decisions were made in desperation, people in power who shouldn't have been. The wizards were always scheming against each other. If there hadn't been Travel bans it would have been dozens of petty wars, and we would have been looking at relying on mercenary wizardry to defend ourselves. But they haven't had Travel in so long. I thought they might overcome that great mistake."

Rupert's gaze narrowed a little on his pupil. "The only thing I didn't prepare you well for was the act of Travel." Rupert nodded toward Kyle's hand, scarred by the burning spoon. "And I certainly didn't expect whatever danger they thought to protect you from with the ilyath."

"It's not the world you left."

"You come home with me, we'll talk about this and then—"

"No," Kyle stated. Immediately he had an image of the conniving Ruperion again, dissonant, urgent.

"The police have some questions for you Kyle. They don't know what to make of your wound and aren't too happy with any of the answers your roommates have. You're going to have to come up with something that satisfies them. They've postulated everything from a sour drug deal to a bar brawl. Since there is no other injured party you might get off. But you still have some explaining to do. Your parents are worried sick."

Kyle wanted to wipe the smug look from Rupert's face. "Can't you just leave them alone? It's been five hundred years. Do you really think that they'll accept you? You certainly can't just want to go home, it isn't the home you knew, Rupert. The city you told us about is now named Ta'atit."

"Hidden treasure?"

"Under about fifty feet of water."

Rupert scowled as he paced to a window looking out on Lake Mendota. Without seeing it, Kyle could picture it, a vast, deep, cold water. It called to him, across city blocks, through stone walls. If he dived deep, swam to the very bottom, would it take him back to Metatha? Rupert always claimed that Potter's Flowage was the portal. But if he went back, would they take the white stone too? Could he just go back to help undo the wrongs Rupert had done, stop this strange link with Jia, then come home to his family and school? What if he went to the wrong world?

"I'm not clear on that," Kyle said aloud. "If Potter's Flowage is the portal, okay, but I came up in a sea on Metatha, but I left in a lake. Why did I return to the same place?"

Rupert roused himself from some reverie. "How long did you remain submerged and how far did you swim? If you dived into Potter's Flowage, or any water on Earth, you should have come up on the shores of the city when you arrived. If you were startled, maybe you surfaced too soon. The river beside the city is the true portal there. If you stayed in too long, maybe you came up in the ocean because it is more 'downstream.' It's varying points in Metatha that will take you places, each spring and pond and river leading to a different world. Earth doesn't have the Travel magic. Earth has only one portal, that which leads through Potter's Flowage to Metatha, no matter what water on Earth you enter. That's the way the gods connected the universe, through Metatha. That's what holds it all together, the universal sea."

Kyle sat up in his bed. Cards and flowers had arrived for him. From whom? The people he had claimed at some point didn't matter to him? What fool had he been to make such claims? He belonged here more than he ever belonged in Rupert's world. But Jia's world, that was something else. He could see her, thinking about him. Suddenly she clutched her side. She looked out at him with those pained dark eyes, as if she challenged him to return to her...

"Kyle?"

He looked around him. Rupert had gone. Ripp stood at the foot of his bed, wringing his hands again.

"Don't be pissed at me, man. We thought you were gonna die. They said you could have. There was all this infection and your fever was so high." Kyle realized suddenly it wasn't a hospital, but his own bedroom in the flat on Dayton.

"How'd I get here?"

"You don't remember? You checked out of the hospital. Your uncle wanted to take you home but you refused. Said you had classes. Not that you've been."

"How long?"

"It's been? What are you, a timekeeper?" Ripp shook his head. "It's been two weeks. You're gonna have to skip the semester. You aren't going to be able to make it all up. Your parents already put in a hardship refund request for you. You signed the paperwork. Don't you remember?"

Kyle forced himself up. Why did he have such moments of lucidity, only to disappear for days as if he really wasn't in his own world?

Something resonated. He wasn't in his own world. How was it he could see Jia so clearly, that he could hear her heartbeat, feel the touch of her breath, even when he knew he looked upon a dream? Did days blend together for her as well? Or, since her time passed faster, did a blink of instant pass when in his own world a week had gone by? He had bound her to him with her white stone, she with her manfish dreams. He had no choice. He would never undo this strange ... time warp was what it felt like it must be ... if he didn't go back.

"Am I better?" he asked when he thought Ripp's forehead would crease to the center of his skull.

"Only low-grade fever. All the sleep you get seems to be helping. Your wounds weren't healing because of the infection but they're beginning to now. You'd nicked a bit of intestine. The weird one is the burn on your hand. That just sort of stays there and won't heal. You gonna tell us what this is all about?"

Kyle studied his hand. It wasn't a serious wound, just an irritating case of peeling and scabbing. If he touched his hand to heat … Would it even work in a world without magic?

He had to escape. Was Rupert hanging about waiting for Kyle to take him back to Metatha? Kyle had to go back, if for no other reason than to sever the bond that took him out of his reality with such annoying frequency. He was drawn to a place that had crawled into his soul and wouldn't let him rest. Rupert knew it would happen. Is this how the old man had felt all these years?

He couldn't let the old wyseer use him. But then, he couldn't believe Rupert could be so awful. Maybe he'd seen the error of his ways. Maybe it had been like some horrible act during war. But each time he even thought of giving Rupert the benefit of the doubt, something inside him told him not to risk it, that he must always regard Rupert as a dangerous enemy.

"Hey, you know, I feel pretty cool. I'd like to try walking down to the Terrace, get some fresh air. Maybe that'll make things stay in focus better. Maybe throw a bag of popcorn at the ducks."

Ripp grinned. "Only if you stay away from the beer lines. But you're sure you're up to it? You don't want to relapse or anything."

"I think I just need to put things behind me, distract myself, you know." Ripp was nodding, with the happy expression of one who sees a crisis receding. "Ripp, I don't know how to tell you how much I appreciate what you've done for me. It's more than I meant to ask."

"Well, payback time'll come."

"I may take off for a couple of days, get my act together, y'know? Work some family things out, that kind of thing. Don't worry about me if I disappear, 'K?"

Ripp gave him that guarded expression, but then shrugged. "Whatever. As long as the rent's paid. Just be careful. I'd hate to think I'd wasted my fine stitching."

If Kyle could just hold the grin. If he could stop the room from swimming back into an image of Jia. There. He could hold that. He ignored the humming in his ears, the strange sense of otherness flooding him as he accepted his jacket and tucked his wallet, keys and the stone in his pocket. He focused on an image of Lake Mendota's waves lapping up against the Terrace frontage. He would fight this. He could fight this. He must fight this. Jia waited. He could think no further than returning to Metatha.

A brief thought insinuated itself: perhaps he should talk to Rupert first, answer some questions, get some guidance. The Fidrel had controlled him so much. Something inside him slapped that idea down so fast he utterly rejected it. No Rupert. He must do this alone. The Traveler would go home.

CHAPTER TWELVE

Rupert muttered to himself, going over words he might remember, might not. So much time had passed, so much wine, so many other cares that had his memories bound up like a fat fly in a spider web. He couldn't seem to jiggle loose, might as well give up, yet he must to help Kyle, whether the fool wanted it or not.

Rupert sifted through the discards of Kyle's life that he had assembled on the kitchen table in the Nelson house. A gum wad in its wrapper; a Popsicle stick stained red and chewed to fiber on one end; hair plucked from a brush; backwash in the bottom of a soda can; a toothbrush rolled up in a dirty sock; the pus-stained T-shirt scavenged from the flat on Dayton and the bloody tunic Kyle had worn in Metatha: all were things Kyle would never have left lying about if he remembered Rupert's lessons. When wyseers were about, leave nothing of yourself that could betray you, not even your garbage. That had been one of the first things he'd taught him, so quickly forgotten.

Rupert pretended not to notice Betty's raised-brow scrutiny as she topped off his wine. He didn't touch it. He needed a clear head. He'd been the greatest of wyseers, once. He'd been the Undoer, who deconstructed best his enemy's evil spells. Once a rebel wyseer threw up a mountain in the path of the Valeutans, using his blood wyseery, his slap to the faces of the gods. Ruperion the Undoer had thrown it down so that it became the deepest lake in the land.

It had been Ruperion, most powerful of wyseers who committed the ultimate in unnatural wyseery. He it was who had with the first and last power stone opened the gates to Travel, the first portal, taking him here, to Earth, to this second home. It was for the gods to control the gates, the universe. But Ruperion the great Undoer had undone the goddish wyseery that held the universe together, yet apart. If he could undo time, that would be a worthy effort, so they could return Metatha to before Travel, before they had forgotten their lore.

He rolled everything up inside the tunic. Again sorted through the words he must recall correctly as he fingered the pendant Kyle had so innocently delivered to him. A sharp memory took him back to a day so many ages back when he scavenged the odd silver and turquoise piece. It was a stylized version of the Navajo flautist Kokopelli, a fertility symbol that reminded him profoundly of the manfish. He'd lifted it from a roadside vendor in Nevada during a long-ago search for the technology to annihilate the Pale. What a fool he'd been! The worst kind, he had thought himself wise simply because he had seen far worlds beyond others' imaginings, while Earth, a world technologically superior to Metatha, still debated whether life could exist beyond its self-centered sphere. And Rupert had let himself think that simply because Earth remained ignorant, that he would easily master the technology of fools. He knew better now.

He wondered, sometimes, why Metatha hadn't been shattered to bits earlier. What if he *had* managed to bring some weapon of mass destruction home, only to find that Metathan magic magnified its power? No one understood the Traveler's portals. Metatha was the center of the universe, what if by destroying Metatha, and her portals, he had ended all the worlds linked to it?

Rupert let his breath out as his hand stroked the smooth turquoise. So long ago that had been, maybe twenty-nine or thirty Earth years, perhaps seven hundred Metathan years back. What might Metatha have accomplished in those seven hundred years if, instead of magic and scavenged tools, he had returned with knowledge?

He shook himself, turning his attention to arranging a ring of stones and candles. Each stone bore power or symbolism that meant little on Earth, but everything in Metathan wyseery. He contemplated a powerful spell to cross worlds, when he hadn't even practiced a sleight of hand more complex than plucking an egg from a child's ear or spell stronger than planting a suggestive thought in decades. The spell he now devised must be so strong it would draw a little magic from Metatha to Earth, and there was no better place on the planet to do that than this kitchen beside Potter's Flowage.

He'd settled a dozen votive candles atop his powerful stones. Each votive perched precariously and threatened to teeter off as he carefully lit them one by one. The pink Baraboo quartzite was special, one of the most powerful he'd ever brought home to Metatha, and special to Wisconsin. He made it his power stone. He once tried to explain the power stone concept to Kyle as something similar to yeast, which, when fed properly, could turn a small amount of dough into many loaves. The pyrite he figured symbolized his fool's mission, though it possessed a stabilizing power on Metatha, a much-needed commodity for keeping spells alive. The red granite, plentiful in Wisconsin, he made his anchor stone to keep him from being torn loose from his own reality, as Kyle clearly had been. And so, each special stone or mineral bore some measure of meaning or service to his spell, his little white votives like prayers for the dead.

At last he lit the candle atop a stone wickedly diverse. Soft metals, hard crystals, gold, mica and quartz glittered from one stone in the candle light, reflecting like the stars of so many worlds to which he must bind himself. For this was a spell to link him to Kyle, a way to track and find him. The final stone opened the doors to all the worlds with the simple addition of the Kokopelli pendant. And Kyle had brought it to him. He'd bound his backdoor around the banning of Travel into a pendant where none would expect to find it, but only someone from Earth would recognize it for its source.

As the votives burned, wax dripping down to conceal the stones supporting them, Rupert wrapped the bundle of Kyle's things in burdock leaves, spitting upon each layer, until he bound it all with woven nettle he'd collected from the shores of Potter's Flowage. He passed the bundle around his flaming circle, pausing over each stone to let the candle slightly singe the leaves until they began to dry and brown, before moving on.

Betty remained silent, staring, perhaps incredulous, perhaps finally seeing him for the mad man he was, perhaps fearing she'd trusted her son's safety to a fool.

Perhaps a fool but not one to let some snot-nosed college boy slip away from a wyseer of Rupert's magnitude.

"Hidden paths be shown, Travelers bound," he began, the incantation lurching out of him, uncertain, as if he'd never cast a spell before, and in Metathan, so even stranger to Betty's ears. She clutched at the cross around her neck as he continued, as if she'd let the devil into her home. Perhaps she had.

He pressed the Kokopelli into the soft wax coating of each stone. When he at last touched the pendant to the gold and quartz, he felt a jolt through his fingers as if he'd touched a live wire. Kyle flooded him, ripped into him, angrily asserting his needs, his confusion.

Seeing through Kyle's eyes, Rupert gazed upon a vast waterscape that eventually resolved into Madison's Lake Mendota. A chop had blown up, the first uncertain waves before a squall line moving across the lake.

No Kyle. You're not ready. You're not strong enough.

Kyle hesitated a moment. He looked down at a small white stone in his hand. Rupert sensed resistance distinctly not Kyle's, not so much stronger, as more compelling.

Trust me, Kyle. I can help you.

"I want to, but I can't."

Though the words were spoken miles away, they resonated in Rupert's ears as if they filled the room.

You must let me help you!

Again he sensed he fought a battle with someone more persuasive for Kyle's will.

"I need to understand. I need to fix what I broke."

Kyle was striding down the stone pier, walking now into the wind of the coming storm, into the spray of waves washing up over the pier. Autumn had come, cool and swift, yet Kyle ignored it. He stared into the darkly green-grey water, into the boiling foam of whitecaps, and dived.

Rupert felt the horrible pull, a drag against him, as if he was towed along on the Traveler's journey with Kyle. But Rupert was the wyseer, the master of his spell. He knew what to expect, and with the facility of a master, he sat back from his work.

Rupert opened his eyes with a sigh. Betty watched him carefully through the flicker of candles. Her hands gripped the wine bottle she'd brought for him.

He swept up his glass and emptied it before he could meet her gaze.

"Kyle went somewhere difficult for me to reach. Much could happen to him before I arrive. I think it's safe to assume they won't kill him on purpose. He's too important. But he could be done great harm by those who don't know what they're doing."

Betty shook her head, her mouth taking that hard turn he'd seen that night Kyle had fled the house, bleeding. It seemed ages ago, but a mere few weeks.

"Rupert, I'm tired of your lies, or evasions, or whatever it is that's going on," Betty said evenly. "You may have brought Kyle into our lives, paid some to ensure his care, but we raised him and made him our son. You don't have the right to take him away, not now, not after so many years. I want answers, clear answers, and I want them now. I will not put up with this any longer."

Rupert studied her for a long moment. In the back of his head, as always, Metathan time raced by, a clock set to the beat of a hummingbird's wings.

"I'm going to tell you a story, Betty. You've heard bits and pieces of it over the years. It's the story I tell the children. And as hard as it is going to be for you to hear it, believe it, you must. Kyle is part of that story. I haven't told you for the same reasons Kyle didn't believe me. It takes a young person to understand things too strange to believe. But I *am* going to tell you, now, because I do know what it is to fear for the life of your child. And I fear for Kyle, too, like my own son. But I haven't much time. Hours have already passed since Kyle made a foolish decision. The longer we wait, the harder it will be to find him. When I'm done with this story, I'm going to do something I haven't done in twenty-one years. I'm going to go home."

With that, Rupert leaned forward in his chair, staring intently at Betty across the table. The flicker of candlelight barely lit the kitchen and his animated face as he told the stories he'd always told, but now for an incredulous adult, and with the real weight of a life in the balance.

CHAPTER THIRTEEN

A hot wind whipped the streets of Waymeet. Unlike the wind on the grasslands outside the low city wall, moving like a sigh across the ground, here it raised grit into the air. It added a deep rust to approaching sunset and boxed the ears. It snaked through narrow alleys and market stalls, around wellmeet, shelf gardens and Palif Talik Atannen's bare, dusty feet. The ivory mantle he wore belted over his hide trousers, and only partially concealing the intricate histories tattooed on his chest, billowed, while the wind lifted his rusty beard to reveal a neck unknown to the sun. A strong gust tugged at the woven-grass temple roof set high above an altar and fire ring, slithering beneath the open sides, and threatening to topple the lashed poles that supported the structure. It was a crude place of worship for the High Chieftain's own palif, but for Talik, it was the very humility of this shelter that brought it close to the gods.

The palif circled the clutch of acolytes gathered in his temple. The youths looked upon him as if they witnessed a wonder that might at any moment perform another miracle as one of the gods' chosen.

Palif Talik squinted against the ashes slithering up out of the cold fire pit, turned his back on the wind and hunched toward his pupils so that his words could find their ears. He knew that halfway through his lesson the winds would die with sunset and then the gods they worshipped would light the cooler and calmer night. He made a swift gesture and the half dozen students straightened in anticipation of his words, the wind lifting their fair toplocks to snap in their eyes and reveal the shorn backs of their heads. Six sets of pale eyes locked on him. He kissed a hide scroll painted in the same rich hues as his chest and barely unrolled it, preferring to keep the memorized text safe from the tugging wind.

"Like the thunder that shakes Mount Achlim came the riders of the Pale, your fathers' fathers' fathers mastering all that they encountered," Talik said.

Most of them but twelve or thirteen cycles, with many years of schooling ahead of them, the acolytes hadn't heard the story as many hundreds of times as Talik had read it in the ten years since he'd first donned a palif's mantle. Yet the newness had worn from the stories for even these youngsters. To hold their attention, Talik matched the cadence of his words to the drum of horse hooves on the prairie, tried to bring the story of their past to life.

"The dust billowed skyward and the clods of dirt shot up beneath their steeds' hooves, darkening the day behind them. Their great beasts snorted. Their rich trappings raised a shrill and wild jangle that struck fear in the hearts of all those who opposed the Pale, for they bore the strength of Danat, the eldest, whom they had honored since Time's beginning."

As he spoke of Danat, Talik grasped his cherished moonscape dangling from the belt at his waist. Metatha's three moons, depicted in gems, were captured in a stone of some mysterious origin. The side of the stone that gripped the blue gem representing Danat had been worn smooth by the caress of his fingers, and the fingers of his mentor before him and his before that. It was one of the greater powers a palif carried. In this simple vestment of service, Palif Talik could touch the whole history of his people, and his calling. It made a tremble resonate through his voice with the strength of Danat the grandfather.

He scanned the words so painstakingly formed on the scroll, feeling the jarring gait of the beasts beneath him, smelling the salty sweat that flung from their sides, the whip of manes stinging his face. He must first imagine the Pale steeds, creatures that had not existed since the First Withering. The abominations ridden by the Methiliim were bred of dark wyseery that merely mocked the magnificent creatures depicted on his scroll.

A murmur rose among his pupils and he turned to see a clutch of crimson-garbed Methiliim crowding under the eaves of Danat's Temple. It took him a moment to realize the wyseers wrestled a young woman toward the altar, her black hair bound up in braids wound with colorful feathers and a dark green cloak, better suited to cool valleys beside the sea, flung open to reveal course sackcloth for clothing. The image stung him in an unhealed wound and a memory of Martrena reared up. For a moment it was Martrena's arm snaking out to strike one of her captors.

"What is the meaning of this?" Talik demanded as they slung their burden against the rock base of the altar, stunning her to stillness. No one answered or even acknowledged him, not only a dishonor to his office and temple, but bold in the face of a man built more like a warrior than a priest. Torches around the altar burst into flame, seemingly without motive, then flickered untouched by the wind. They dared wield their vile magic in this sacred place!

"You will not desecrate this altar of Danat!" Talik shouted. "These children need not see your abominable ways!"

Five Methiliim wyseers turned their wooden gazes on him, their bloody red robes swirling large around them. One straightened, his dark eyes impenetrable beneath his unnatural dark brows, a true throwback to his crude Valeutan roots. He strode up to Palif Talik as if the land he walked upon were dedicated to him, not the gods that made Metatha. The corner of his mouth had begun to curl into a sardonic snarl and he raised his prismed staff in a tacit threat that instead of freezing Talik with fear, made his blood boil.

"What prattle, little priest? You think to halt the sanctioned work of the Methiliim?"

Talik searched his memory for the name of the man, which popped up as suddenly as he spat it out. "Tarcatha." He gestured with his scroll toward the small cauldron one Methiliim wyseer had settled beside the altar. "You will not waste here what is only given to Danat to feed the sacred springs. You dare take it for yourself for your dark arts." Talik sensed the acolytes huddling up behind him, as if they could disappear in the shadow of his palif robe.

Tarcatha's glance sent the sacred scroll flying from Talik's grasp to scatter before the wind, an acolyte racing to catch up with it before it could be defiled further.

"You dare mock the Palifiim!" Talik's voice rose with his rage into a bellow. The woman, no longer struggling, regarded him with dark Valeutan eyes so like Martrena's.

"Perhaps you should have given blood for treason beside your little slave girl," Tarcatha said. "The High Chieftain should review your service and join you with your treacherous mate."

Talik had to choke back a roar of rage, but before he could respond, two of Tarcatha's wyseers had gripped his arms. His tongue locked to the roof of his mouth by some wyseer's trick. He flung a wild glance at the acolytes witnessing this sacrilege of the house of Danat. To his relief, he saw his niece Danathea shepherding the other five acolytes away, the girl's face twisted with a grief of her own.

Talik went limp, forcing the Methiliim to drag him through the streets of Waymeet like a Valeutan slave being led to the cauldron. The words welled up in him behind his frozen tongue, his rage stripping him of reason as he wished Withering upon these aberrations and their blood rituals. The populace dropped their burdens to stare. Let them mark the day the Methiliim dared to lay hands on a palif!

The potential power in a small pouch on his belt beside the moonscape tempted him. He wished his hands free to grasp the vial of heavy gray grit peppered with tiny white fragments, but such a power served best a purpose more noble than saving his own pride. Danat knew the injustice being done and would remember. In the hundreds of years of blood wyseery corrupting the Pale, the wyseers had always known their place. But now Methiliim dared, dared, strike at the heart of the Pale soul!

The tall doors to the Atannate, the palace of the Chieftains of Atannen for the span of seventy-five rulers, yawned before him. Airy stone passages that opened upon gardens fed by fountains from sacred springs usually invited him to linger and walk slowly, contemplating the long history of his line before him. Now he only had a swift glimpse of palace guards astonished at the sight of the High Chieftain's own palif, before he was thrown at last to his knees, with no fanfare and a great deal of disdain, at the foot of his grandfather's throne.

"What is the meaning of this!" High Chieftain Wakthral Atannen demanded of Tarcatha, his tone less assured and more hesitant than Talik expected. "It is treason to bring harm to an Atannen and palif."

"It is Talik Atannen, Great One, who commits the treason," Tarcatha sneered.

"You will call him Palif. Whatever your charge, only I can unname the teachers of the moons."

Tarcatha made a half-hearted gesture of deference to the High Chieftain of the Pale, then nudged Talik's back with his foot so that the palif's head snapped back. "The palif interfered with the works of the Methiliim, works that you, yourself, sanctioned." He nudged Talik again, almost tipping him on his face.

"I gave no sanction to molest the Palifiim," Wakthral said quietly, his gaze on Talik as Tarcatha's foot again nudged the palif.

"He disrupted a sacred ritual, the sacrifice of a Valeutan Fidrel!" Tarcatha's words crowed up into the rafters to mock them all.

"Is this true, daughter-son?" Wakthral asked.

Talik struggled to protest, but his dry tongue remained frozen to the roof of his mouth.

"Give him his voice!" Wakthral ordered harshly. "What other liberties would you take if you dare silence the voice of the gods in men?"

With an abstract wave of Tarcatha's hand, Talik felt his tongue drop into place. He swallowed hard, shaking loose those gripping him as if they were flies, his strong arms could easily have flung them across the room, but such violence was the way of blood wyseers, not a priest of Danat.

"Wise Grandfather, they omit that they intended to shed the blood of their sacrifice on Danat's altar."

Wakthral blanched, then studied the floor at his feet, remaining silent as his mouth worked something sour.

"Blood given to Danat's altar is sacred, pledged to Danat! It comes not from the living, the hale or the non-believer, but from those who have lived long lives in honor of Danat. Sacred blood must be desiccated and fed to the sacred springs, not boiled in a cauldron to create abominations that only serve to make these vile wyseers more powerful, more cruel, masters of their leaders."

"Careful, daughter-son," Wakthral said. "You tread very close to treason."

Tarcatha began to sputter a retort.

"No, it is my turn," Talik said with a silencing gesture that swished through the air. "I have said nothing but praise for your greatness, Grandfather. This is not treason to defend the very truths for which the Palifiim serve! The Pale are conquerors! Yet we bow before Valeutan wyseers?" He jerked his hand toward Tarcatha's dark demeanor.

"We do not bow before any wyseer," Wakthral replied. "You do not know all the needs of our realm. You are a spiritual guide, not a man of politic and defense. The wise men bring me counsel that I have chosen to follow—"

"Wise men! They are murderers! Their counsel is about power, the very power that brought the Withering to our people! They make of the High Chieftain a horsehair doll—"

"Enough!" Wakthral shouted as guards leapt to flank Talik. "You are thinking of Martrena. That is the source of your rash talk."

The name hit Talik like snow to the face, stopping his racing thoughts. He reached for the treasures dangling from his belt. Before he could respond, the High Chieftain went on in a softer tone.

"I told you it was too soon for you to return to the temple. But if you ever listened to me, you wouldn't have taken a mate against my wishes. A palif has no business thinking of earthly pleasures, much less bringing the enemy into his home. In the end, she broke your trust and your heart, as I told you she would. Her unfortunate death—"

"Murder, Grandfather. She was murdered for being revolted by these awful deeds, not for taking any action."

"No one is above my law. I warned you that her first loyalty would always be to the blood, as yours should have been. Her death taught you nothing." Wakthral let out a long breath. "We live in a different time, Talik. The teachings of the gods are important, but it is more important to protect our people from real threats, first. You teach old ways, dusty memories of our people's past. They are important, but not as important as keeping the Traveler out of the hands of the Fidrel."

"Grandfather, have you forgotten your gods?" Talik asked softly.

"Never, daughter-son. But we are no longer a wandering people. Your teachings put fanciful dreams in children's heads, lauding a past, when we must be strong for the future and the unknown."

"Would it hurt if a few children grew to love the grasslands and desired to live a simpler and truer life in honor of their gods?"

"You want a bunch of wandering minstrels? Or will you be bird herders?" Tarcatha scoffed.

Talik didn't rise to the bait. He suddenly felt emptied, as if he watched his temple burning up in the fires of his enemies. He felt a familiar numbness overtaking him.

"Why must they desecrate the altars of Danat? Why can't they do their hideous deeds on their own sacred ground?" Talik asked, hearing a plaintive note in his voice that he resented.

"Because it is the very power of Danat's Temple that strengthens their rites."

Then Wakthral had known. Talik realized it with a sense of dismay and fear, a disappointment in his leader so deep that perhaps he deserved to be labeled treasonous.

"Then it is the degree of desecration to life and soul that gives power to their dark wyseery. And this is a path you have willingly chosen to follow?" Talik's words held more bitterness and scorn than he meant to use.

"I think it is time for you to find yourself, Talik," Wakthral said with the soft finality of a death sentence. "Perhaps it is something you should have done immediately after Martrena's death. You must overcome the bitterness in your heart before you can be trusted to teach and carry out the duties of palif and advisor to the High Chieftain."

"You are banishing me?" Talik blinked hard. How could this be happening?

"A palif names a Realing banishment?" Tarcatha scoffed. "Now there's a sentiment that'll bring the repentant population to temple."

"Indeed, you need some time to meditate on your faith," Wakthral said.

"It leaves you without a palif, it silences the gods' voice in this house!" Talik protested, stopping when he caught a glance that passed between his grandfather and Tarcatha.

"I lived many years before you took to your robes, daughter-son, I can find a palif in need. I certainly foresee no need."

"But it is in the unforeseen that you most need your palif," Talik replied.

Wakthral threw a dismissing gesture in the air and almost instantly Talik felt the hands of the palace guard on him, gently leading him away toward his rooms near the High Chieftain's chambers. He felt the angry knot of a child wrongly rebuked by a parent, but yet more. There had been more to this event. He could see it, needed to think about it. It had all come so suddenly. Why would his grandfather demand a Realing? That was the realm of the Palifiim, a drastic measure against those who disrupted the spiritual community, and such an order came after lengthy consultations, negotiations, second and third chances. His grandfather certainly couldn't believe his confidante, his personal spiritual advisor, could ever think of treason, could ever be so hopelessly dangerous to him that he must be removed from society.

Something about it all seemed too odd, the insincerity, the quick decision, the complicity with sacrilege. Why would the High Chieftain and the Methiliim need to silence him?

They had planned this. They had known he would rage at them and give them excuses to denounce him. Why else would they choose his temple, but to commit the most heinous of sacrileges, one against the Atannate itself? Talik felt the color rising in his face. A throat cleared behind him, reminding him that guards waited for him to pack his things for his Realing, his journey to find his inner self in the wildlands of Metatha, a place still vast and empty, and dangerous, so many years after the Withering. A palif sentenced to a Realing by his High Chieftain, he could be disgraced no more if he were stripped of his vestments and paraded naked through the streets.

He let his robe fall upon the bed and looked around his room, struggling to regain his measure of control. Like his crude temple, his rooms were simple and austere in contrast to the fine trappings that surrounded him all of his life. Shadows clung to corners, the furnishings dark and colorless, so unlike the bright and vibrant home Martrena had made. He slipped into a loose white woven shirt that hung halfway to his knees, concealing the tattoos on his barrel of a chest. He hooked his belt up then, slipping his few treasures into his purse, adding a sheath and knife, and struggling to tug boots over feet that seldom saw covering. In no time he'd wound up a blanket and a few other needs into a hide and slung it over his shoulder.

"Quite the huntsman I must look now," he muttered to the guard who appraised him with a sour twist of his mouth.

"You mind yourself, Palif," the man said in a low voice not meant to carry. "Watch your back. You may appear a big brute of a man when you set aside your robes, but we know where your heart is. And you do have enemies. And they've already bled their own hearts into their cauldrons."

Talik gave the guard a sharp, sidelong glance. "Then it's as I feared," he muttered.

Another guard stuck his head in before the man could respond. "Palif, the kitchens will have a pack ready for you."

"Fare well. May you not Travel far," the first guard said, giving him a half-executed bow before slipping away.

The newcomer fell in step with Talik as he guided him to the kitchens through the back ways used by palace servants. They would be slipping him out the rear of the palace then, so no one would know what had happened to him. What lies would be told to explain today's happenings? Indeed, people would notice the missing palif, and his temple converted to dark wyseery. What would it do to the faith of his acolytes? And what of his poor niece Danathea? First she lost the only mother she'd known, and now the only father.

His thoughts raced, yet settled nowhere. He was simply too stunned to consider events logically as his boots echoed around him. In an hour he'd gone from the most respected of Palifiim to a man disgraced, his temple debased. Numbness spread as he moved closer to the dream world he'd wandered in before, a place dark and alien where he'd become lost in the wake of Martrena's death. At midday she had been teasing him and Danathea, flicking water from a bucket pulled up beside the well as they shared their meal at wellmeet. By sunset she had been named a traitor and her life had been bled into the Methiliim's cauldrons. Treason. She had said nothing that hadn't been muttered daily by hundreds of others as the Methiliim took greater and greater liberties with the chieftain's leave. The only difference, Martrena had been born to an enemy. It hadn't made sense then; it still didn't make sense. What had she said? It had been there, at wellmeet.

"Palif?" The guard was holding open the massive door to the kitchens, the heavy scent of oils and fats assailed him and a racket of activity made him recoil.

What did the Methiliim fear from him? He was Palif, not the Traveler, not a wyseer, no one of consequence, except for the role he played in guiding the High Chieftain on his spiritual and moral path, and thus setting an example for the city. He went cold at the hint of a half-formed thought. But it was too much, now, too much to think about. His world had crashed in upon him. He had nowhere to turn with his grandfather against him.

He barely acknowledged the water gourds and satchel of provisions thrust into his hands, a familiar pat on his back, a strong squeeze of his shoulder, though he had no sense of who might be giving him these wishes. He kept struggling to link the day's events and they didn't make sense.

When he felt a cold wind in his face he looked up suddenly, finally pushing aside his stupor to find himself outside the wall, facing the night, with not even a thought of where he would go.

He looked back over his shoulder at the warm evening lights of Waymeet lighting the sky and glittering above the wall. He sensed, more than saw, what must certainly be a Methiliim wyseer ensuring he had indeed left.

He took one hesitant step, feeling oddly as if he were stepping into a cool bath. When Martrena died, he'd lost his future. He had lost his ability to see himself a day ahead, a season ahead, to even imagine anything beyond the needs of the immediate moment. He'd begun to emerge, walking his students through the discovery of their past and their gods. He had Danathea and his grandfather to guide, reasons to rise each day. And now, again, he was a man without a future. With no greater certainty he at last strode into the night.

CHAPTER FOURTEEN

The soft sigh wove in and out of his dreams. It was a sound he knew must be an ocean, though he knew only of oceans from tales. A fleet of ships—they must be ships, they looked so like the images from ancient scrolls—their colored sails full of wind, their rigging laced with colorful ribbons, sailed over a wind-tossed sea of grass. From the grass in the bow wake bolted steeds so magnificent and fine they must be those of the ancient Pale. Their trappings jangled in their flight as the ships bore down upon them, their riders shaking sabers that glinted with the bright fire of Kylik.

Suddenly, all wheeled around to stare as shouts of horror rose from the ships, which had begun to founder in the grass, some already listing. The sailors scrambled up the rigging, now and then one losing his grip and falling, silently, into the grass. About to raise their arms in triumph the horsemen instead screamed as their beasts, too, sank earthward into the grasslands, their throats open in wrenching wails of denial, their mounts' teeth gnashing at the wind.

Finally, only one man stood on the prairie, the others gone deep beneath the soil. He stood there in a palif's ivory robe, arms upraised and beseeching of the craggy face of Danat, which moved on across the sky unseeing. And as Talik opened his eyes, he realized the man in the midst of the grassy sea, alone, had been him.

He sat up quickly, finding the sighing prairie around Waymeet rising above him. A tiny patch of it had flattened beneath his too-small blanket. It took him a long moment to register his surroundings, and then the injustice struck him like a fist in the gut and he leaped to his feet, almost stumbling back to his knees as stiff joints failed him.

In the dark, sometime after moonset, he'd left the road a short distance behind to seek the concealment of the prairie and sleep had come almost as soon as his head touched the ground. He realized now that he was lucky he hadn't stumbled right into a stream that lazed but a few yards distant, its companionable chuckle promising a cool place to wash the dust from the road. A rustle close behind him brought him around, reaching for the knife at his side.

"It's me, Uncle." Danathea stepped from behind a curtain of grass bearing a basket full of waterweed still dripping from the river. For the first time he noticed that a bulkier pack lay beside his own in the grass.

"Danathea what is this foolishness!"

"You are all I have, Uncle. Would you have me packed off and silenced among the Palifiim, or made a prisoner in the palace for my thoughts? What they did to you was wrong. I was there! I saw it. It was wrong! And admitting that, would I be next?"

Talik gave her an indulgent smile and sank into the grass again, letting his head come to rest in his hand, elbow propped on his knee. "This is a Realing, Danathea. I'm supposed to be alone so I can see the error of my thoughts."

"Oh, Uncle, even I know this isn't a Realing." She hesitated as his brow shot up at her tone. She folded her hands and lightly bowed, the wind lifting up the toplock to reveal the shaved back of her head. "You taught us the rules of the Realing in our first or second year. If the Palifiim council didn't order it, it isn't a Realing. Respectfully, Uncle, you were banished."

Talik didn't respond. The finality of the sentence caught in his throat. He had even flung that challenge at his chieftain.

"Did the High Chieftain name an end to your sentence? No, because they don't expect you to return. Methil Tarcatha wanted you out, and so you're gone, Uncle. They had Methiliim watching you, one followed at least until moonset. I imagine he has orders to ensure you can never return. After you were taken away, other wyseers tore apart the temple and sacrificed the Fidrel, before the High Chieftain had even commanded the Realing."

Talik leaned back, stunned. Had his grandfather intended he be killed, or did Tarcatha take such liberties because he was fearless?

"I would like to believe Grandfather had no idea such orders were issued," he said softly.

"I saved what I could," Danathea continued as if he hadn't uttered yet another treacherous thought. "And Palifiim came quickly to gather us up. I slipped away. I watched the palace and saw you out the gate to the Hot Springs Road. I gathered what I could and ran to catch up. I don't know how you intend to survive in the wilderness, Uncle Talik, but you didn't even hear me or your wyseer shadow and I was on your heel most of the night."

Talik shook his head at her, forced to give her a smile despite the horrible emptiness he felt inside, and her presumptuous tone. She had been shaking out the waterweed as she spoke and now rummaged in her bag for seasoning and two small wooden bowls, then through Talik's pack for a handful of ground nuts and seeds and salted prairie fowl that she crumbled atop the waterweed. She idly shooed away the occasional flitterbird hoping to snitch part of their meal.

At last, Danathea took a taste from her bowl and shrugged, handing the other to Talik. "It could do with a little egg," she mumbled, "but the prairie fowl isn't a bad substitute."

As he ate, he discovered he was ravenous. The numbness had begun to fade.

"I hadn't thought about surviving," Talik mused. "Truth, I hadn't thought about anything, not even which way to go. It all took me by surprise."

"Then it's well I followed," Danathea said as she emptied both packs and repacked them more efficiently. "Hot Springs Road isn't a poor choice. Perhaps a little time in the baths beside Misty Lake will ease your spirits and help you decide what to do."

"You sound more like a palif than an acolyte," Talik teased. "When did you grow so much common sense? Perhaps you chose the wrong calling."

"It must be the influence of my mentor," she demurred. But he knew she'd taken on many roles since Martrena's murder.

Talik spied some of his temple scrolls and his anchoring altar stone in among the necessities she'd had more time to consider. She followed his gaze and held up the solid, white, water-carved stone. "You may not return to Waymeet, but that doesn't mean you will never again need an altar."

Talik swallowed hard as he stared at the blinding white stone held in her sun-browned hand. It still hadn't sunk in: he had no temple. He had no calling, nor faith of his clan. He had no home, no mate, no family. He stood utterly alone and homeless, but for Danathea. As she scrubbed at the bowls with rough grass, Talik tugged the braid ring from her toplock.

She reached up and felt her hair. He knew the strange sensation of release she must feel, one he remembered well when his own braid ring had been cut away on his ascension to the Palifiim, the odd itch of hair growing over his neck after years of shaved stubble.

"Have I done wrong, Uncle?" she whispered, her eyes as wide as he'd ever seen them.

"We are hiding. An acolyte wandering in the wildlands without her palif? That raises questions. We are simply travelers, searching yet, searching." He didn't really know what they sought, but he sensed the journey would shatter his foundations. "The toplock marks a child in training. By the time we again find an altar you will be finished with your training."

She simply nodded, choking back tears. It was her turn to realize just what she left behind.

By the time they stowed their gear and adjusted their packs for a long journey on foot, then refreshed themselves in the shallow creek, morning had advanced toward mid-day. Talik pondered one of the scrolls, a map of Metatha encircled by horses and the symbols of the three moons.

"The Hot Springs Road?" Danathea prodded softly.

Something he needed to do was struggling to get his attention. If he just thought a little harder, perhaps it would rise up and he could grasp it. But his thoughts still churned through him like a carriage careering through the mire. As he stared at the map, instead of the green strokes that depicted the prairie around Waymeet, he saw a palif, arms upraised to beseech an unseeing god.

"What do you think they feared of me?" he mumbled to himself.

"Perhaps a nice walk will help us ponder it," Danathea stated, craning to try to see over the grasslands as if she could mark those on the road. Only once this morning had they heard anything: a laden wagon heading south to Waymeet with flocks of prairie fowl rising skyward before it. She rested a hand on his shoulder. "We don't know what happened to the wyseer last night. He may still be seeking you. Could they mark you in some wyseer's way that would lead them to you? It might be a good idea to get ourselves lost in the Misty Peaks."

"Hmmph, without your braid lock you already presume too much. You're only thinking of a long soak in the hot springs," Talik grumbled, but let her pull him to his feet.

Danathea peeked out onto the road that led from Waymeet to Misty Lake through a plain that slowly rose onto an arid plateau before swiftly falling to the vast lake at the mountain's feet. They could see no movement along the road, though a slight curve far ahead signaled where the road descended to the fords of the Great River. Barges, waterfowlers and the fishing fleet could all be lingering near the crossing to note their passage, the ferryman naming those who crossed to the Methiliim, for a price.

Talik tried to shake away such ridiculous thoughts. Of what importance could he possibly be that the Methiliim felt any need to track him or hunt him down if their sole desire was simply to get rid of him? What was it they feared from him?

As they made their way along the road, Talik's feet already beginning to blister in the unaccustomed shoes, Danathea now and then complaining of cramps in her calves, the dream kept reappearing as he scanned the vast prairie. The way the wind swept across it made him think of waves racing to distant shores. He half imagined the distant mountain peaks as sails rising out of the horizon. He had seen some great symbolic battle between the Valeuta and the Pale, both of them in their strengths of old. He'd seen no wyseers in this battle and the light of Kylik, not Danat fell on them. Yet, both had failed. The dream meant something. It must.

The broad expanse of the Great River had carved a deep canyon in the prairie, a rift that suddenly yawned out of the plateau with a dizzying suddenness and depth. Far below, the road zigzagged to a ferry that fought roiling waters urgently seeking a far sea. The surface of the river, which ran a milky white despite the distance from Mount Achlim's snowy sides, and the many springs that fed it, fluttered with myriad waterfowl that almost obscured its surface. In any given moment, the surface rippled as fowl slipped beneath the opaque waters to miraculously emerge with silvery trophies. Others nibbled at the greenery from quieter, clearer waters along sand spits and inside shoals. It almost appeared one could walk across the river on the backs of so many birds. But then there were the boats. Broad-prowed barges with sails set to fill with wind—partly blown upstream, partly towed by those twisted imitations of withered horses—waved at those barges speeding downstream, guided by broad-shouldered oarsmen who fought the tumbling waters.

The ferryman gave them only a cursory glance, jerking his head toward the landing where they would await the ferry's return. As they passed, the ferryman suddenly peered at Talik, as if reminded of something and about to shout it out. The man as quickly looked away. Talik's cheeks burned. It was true. The Methiliim sought him. But why? Talik glanced at Danathea. From the set of her mouth and the quick look she gave him, he knew he hadn't imagined the ferryman's scrutiny.

Ducks paddled angrily away in the ferry's wake as a wheel hauled the vessel along a cable to the far shore. Danathea nudged him and pointed to the decks. Fresh mud from the wheels of the wagon that had passed this morning had been overlain by the recent traffic of at least three sets of hooves, the last of which must have passed north if the ferry sat on the northern shore. Talik kicked at one spot with his boot and noted that the mud remained discolored where it adhered to the ferry, not yet dry. Quite fresh.

"Perhaps the Hot Springs Road is a little too open for us," Talik muttered as he and Danathea trudged up the long loops of the road to the north of the ferry. The ferryman's eyes bored into their backs as if he pondered the value of a net full of fish.

"Across the prairie, on foot?" Danathea's words puffed out from the exertion as they took another loop in the road.

"Certainly I'd prefer to stay at the rests, if for no other reason a comfortable bed and a good roasted fowl. But if we're trying to avoid wyseers we would have had to avoid the rests anyway. We'll have to make do with what supplies we have and hope we can snare something more nourishing than waterweed."

Talik pulled out his map and studied it as he trudged upward. The symbols marked a desolate land too arid to support even herdsmen. Once the horses of the Pale had galloped across these plains, their hooves a thunder that echoed from the mountain peaks. The mutants that survived the Withering, those beasts wouldn't know thunder if a storm rolled upon them.

"The river loops north toward Misty Lake. We can follow the river to a close point."

"And when we get there?"

"I have no idea."

Danathea paused as they reached the lip of the valley and peered over his shoulder at the map, her breath still coming in small gasps.

"Maybe there's a place where we can cross the river again and just follow the Ta'atit road. It follows the river, too, and would make the travel a little easier," Danathea said, her finger tracing a winding line on the south bank of the river.

"I think it would make them just a bit more worried if they caught sight of me on the Ta'atit road," Talik said softly.

"I'm still not clear on all this, Uncle. What are they afraid of? Did you do something?"

"Of course I did something. I took Martrena as my mate."

"Simply because she was Valeutan? That seems a slight reason to spend so much effort on banishing the High Chieftain's palif."

"Well, Martrena wasn't your average Valeutan."

"I found her a wise mother to me, Uncle." Danathea's composure wavered for only a moment. It was too soon. It had been too soon for him, and this child no better. Martrena had been a mother to Danathea since she'd been selected as an acolyte when she was but seven cycles old, an orphan in the chieftain's house lost among the multitudes.

"You who have always spoken ill of the Valeutans who unleashed the Withering, I always wondered why you, why—"

"Why I went against my convictions?" Talik volunteered, as the red rose in her cheeks.

Talik paused on the road as the river became just the hint of bird racket somewhere among the waving grasses. He could see nothing on the road, nothing on the horizon. He took a deep breath and slipped through the skein of grass nudging up against the road. Immediately the world closed down to but an arm's length around them, the grass pulling at their feet, scratching their faces, tugging at their stamina as if they waded through knee-deep water. Now and then, fowl rose with a clamor, but most simply moved away.

"Why did you marry her against the High Chieftain's wishes?"

"Because I loved her," Talik said, trudging ahead, his glance back enough to silence her next question. Not now. Not yet.

The force of the prairie against them drove them closer and closer to the edge of the Great River in search of a respite on the wind-swept rim from the deep tangle of grass. To Talik's relief, the land sloped lower, the river broadening and calming as it left the steep uplands around Waymeet. Here they might hope to scramble down to the shores and steal a fish from a bird, or snatch up a duck. As they put distance between them and the ferry and Waymeet, the barge traffic thinned as dusk neared and boatmen tied up at the river rests. At long last Talik allowed them to halt for the evening, sheltering in a dell where a small stream joined the Great River. Talik carefully tended a fire fed with twisted grass logs that barely burned with enough heat to roast the two ducklings they snared. Wrapped in waterweed and stuffed with eggs and grains, the fowl tasted like a feast and Talik had to feel a little satisfied with his survival skills thus far.

Once they'd doused their fire and resigned themselves to the annoying flutter of birds hovering about them, Talik curled up in his blanket and in moments had fallen fast asleep.

Martrena walked along a beach of black stone and sand. A green robe billowed out behind her in a tempest wind. Rotting manfish rolled in the surf, sucking at her feet. The dancing manfish in the fruit withered in browning pulp. Here and there along the black beach appeared white flecks like the shattered fragments of his altar stone, tiny razor chips that cut away the flesh of her feet and ankles, leaving behind her a trail of bloody footsteps. She plucked one shard from the beach and it cut her hand, the blood, splashing upon the beach, her robe, filling the ocean and turning the manfish rinds to powder. Birds in the bloody sea floated dead in the waves, others rained from the sky to splat the stone, starved in a Withering like no other.

Martrena held out her red-dripped hand to him. He saw his own white-robed arm reach for her, fingers almost touching. Then she too floated among the carcasses in the bloody red seas. The light of the moons glistened darkly from its surface, the winds calmed, the night birds and surf silenced. In this silence so deafening he suddenly heard a wail; it came from deep inside his soul and burst from his throat to awaken him.

"Uncle!" Danathea shook him. He sat up quickly, staring around a moon-washed landscape. Grass sighed, the scritch of birds among their blades like a soft music.

"A way to reason must be found," he muttered. "This is a wyseer's dream."

"What do you mean? Have the Methiliim cast some spell upon your sleep?"

Talik shook his head. "No, no. This is more. This goes deeper. This is something that cries out from the very soul of Metatha."

He was painfully awake now. His thoughts raced. His heart pounded. He dug in his pack for a chunk of bitterroot and chewed on it, feeling the rush of wakefulness.

"My banishment is about Martrena, yes, I think. But more. She was murdered to silence me. I think they assumed she was the source of my pressure on the High Chieftain to stop the killings. Oh, so much blood has been shed, Danathea. It's foolishness. We have become no better than the Valeutans we conquered so long ago. We have become them. We now prey on others with unnatural means. All these blood sacrifices to gain more and more power. The wyseers are the wrong. All of them, I think. They thought her a spy among us. They intercepted a letter to her father that mentioned how the Methiliim had become obsessed with their blood rites, and Travel." The words seeped out of him around the juicy bitterroot, thoughts forming as they emerged. He saw again an image of himself alone in the prairie, arms upraised to his disinterested god, the prairie bleeding from the battle.

"Uncle, it came so suddenly, not like they were suspicious of her," Danathea said softly.

"I've gone over it so many times. So many, many times: Her last words at the wellmeet. Remember, we were laughing there. There were people all around as the three of us ate our mid-day meal. Then she said it, I think, the thing that doomed us all, as innocent a thing as could be said."

"I don't remember anything profound," Danathea's face had screwed up in confusion as she stared into her hands at a small flitterbird trying to remove a thread from her blouse. "We were talking about, hmm, the way that girl was flirting with—"

"Remember, just then, Methiliim passed on the street. Remember that?"

"They had a Fidrel, I think. Green robe, right?"

"And Martrena said, 'They are so urgent in their attacks! Twelve Fidrel in as many weeks. You'd think they had bagged a Traveler in their hunt.'"

Danathea looked up at him sharply. "She did say that. And I wondered at the conclusion. I meant to ask you about it, but I never had the chance."

"We must see a wyseer about this."

"Methiliim!"

"No, Fidrel."

"Why?"

He could feel Danathea staring at him.

"Martrena, she, she had some little knowledge of the Fidrel. But she came to be disillusioned. When I met Martrena I was so young and full of myself. She was searching for what she believed in this world. She came to Waymeet as a slave, but she sought me out at my temple. She was searching for the gods all people once worshipped, forgotten by her people and ours. She said she'd become disgusted by the Fidrel's search for a Traveler to solve their problems, and the poverty of her people, and the devotion to wyseery of the Methiliim. She said she wondered if Danat turned his back on the Valeutans because they turned their backs first. Martrena was a wise woman. I wanted to hate her because her people brought the Withering. But Martrena, she didn't bring the Withering. She was a searcher for the truth and the right ways of things, as I am. She was a rebel. She left her people to come here, but she never really left her people. She hoped instead to show them a different way."

"But what does all this mean, Uncle? Why were you banished? She's gone now."

"I spoke of conciliation to the High Chieftain, and against the search for the Traveler. Rumors claim he came among the Fidrel, forming a schism in their ranks. Martrena knew this. She remained in touch with her father. She saw her people being slaughtered, their blood given to some dark purpose. And then she said those words, those fateful words."

Danathea was shaking her head.

"What it all means, why I am having these dreams, I don't know. Perhaps the gods see me as the voice of reason for pleading to the High Chieftain against the foolishness of Travel. But I have my suspicions."

"And you suspect?" Danathea prodded.

"The Methiliim have the Traveler."

CHAPTER FIFTEEN

Kyle leaned hard on Wilnath's arm, the cold water dripping into puddles around his feet as he shivered violently, fearing he'd sink into the puddle. He closed his eyes, feeling the pump of water through his lungs, the metallic flavor of a glittering sea rushing him, its eely beasts slithering up from the seabed to lay claim to new prey foundering by…

At last he felt a heavy green mantle thrown over his shoulders.

"This has to stop Wil," Jia said from somewhere behind him where she adjusted the mantle. "He never recovers enough."

"What did you find, Traveler?" Wilnath asked breathlessly as if Jia hadn't spoken. The shivering abated as Kyle huddled in the robe. His breath took in the crisp sea air of the cliffs north of Hindlain while fowl resettled in the spring pond green with waterweed.

"I found no surface. Only … only." He recalled the terror that arced through his gut as glowing beasts with fangs longer than his hand lunged from the dark depths. "Eels, hungry eels."

Wilnath nodded as if not surprised. "Eel oil from that world is powerful, very powerful. So they still exist. Very good. The lore says the right dose mixed with a fixant—"

Kyle lost track of Wilnath's words as they became a rush of nonsense, Metathan words like bubbles rising up beside him, the deep clicks, booms and whistles of sea beasts discussing their prey.

"Wil, he needs rest."

"We must catch up, Jia. They are generations ahead of us with their blood wyseery."

"Then we're no better than the Methiliim and their blood rites. They sacrifice Valeutans, we sacrifice the Traveler."

"We've drawn no blood, Jia, it's a foolish exaggeration." Wilnath's hand gave the air a dismissive swipe. "He volunteered! He returned! He knew our need."

"We forced him! And don't tell me we didn't. I know what thoughts I planted."

Through half-lidded eyes, Kyle could see them facing one another, Jia holding the white stone out that had drawn him back to her, Wilnath's head shaking, his mouth set in that stubborn way that all knew meant it wasn't open for discussion. Kyle's hand was empty. He knew that Wilnath had quickly retrieved the Traveling stone for safe keeping … no, to keep him prisoner.

Jia's dark hair willowed around her, its feathered tresses taking wing. She had grown into a woman while he foundered in Madison. She'd always been persuasive, and certain, but she didn't hesitate now. She was no adept, and though a novice, she had become a leader. In the more than a year that had passed in his absence, she hadn't simply become a wyseer. Now she wore a battle knife at her belt and the scars to show she'd had cause to use it.

They had been watching Ta'atit for his return. They knew better than Kyle when it would happen. Jia told them, "The Traveler comes," and the Kylalnethra were there before the first bubbles rose from the dark lake. They plucked him from the moonlit surface before the startled fowl roused from their sleep. Jia had looked at him, weak and Travel sick, as she checked the healing injury in his side that had brought him from the water with a stitch.

Would he always be at the mercy of those not Travel sick who awaited him on the other side? Certainly they could find some wyseery that could heal him of it, or perhaps they found it better to let him succumb, keep him always weak, always dependent so they could manipulate him as they desired. He didn't like the turn of his thoughts, a familiar direction, a place the fatigue took him readily.

Jia had known so much about him, better skilled at reading that strange bond across worlds. And now, her stone restored, and his kept safely out of his reach, he missed that sense of belonging somewhere. He was alone, a singular entity in this world. A tool.

"Do you think you could retrieve one?" Wil asked him, suddenly close as he pulled Kyle to his feet. Kyle immediately lost his balance, both of them almost tumbling back into the pond with the stone to pull them through.

"Wil, no," Jia said.

"Our need is great, Kyle," Wil was saying as he regained his balance. "They redouble their efforts. They decimated the Ridge last week and two nights past while you were still Traveling, they raided an Overmount settlement. Five dead, dozens taken as slaves and likely already bled for their foul rituals. Without your help, our children, the innocents, are slaves to serve a dark wyseer."

"Enough!" Kyle threw off the mantle and Wil's crooning entreaties.

He caught Jia's stark expression of concern. She'd worn that face when he returned, her mix of joy and fear. What had she seen as she wandered through his head? She barely spoke to him now, avoided him the way she had once followed him, with diligence. He would see her leading away a party of Valeutan werran who fought beside the wyseers. She would give him a nod to his regard, and be gone without a word.

"But Traveler," Wil was calling after him, his hand fluttering with his salute to the Traveler.

"Spare me your honor," Kyle managed around the gag of rusty seawater that wanted to roar out of his gills. He shook himself, trying to step out of the delirium, but he was too much the manfish to— Not manfish, man!

"Kyle," Jia began as Wil placed a comforting hand on his shoulder.

"You mock me with your honor. You want me to pity a slavery you never tried to escape. I'm a slave, new-made, by you. But how dare I be pissed off about you abusing me?"

He heard venom in his tone that he didn't know he had. It roared out of him. A red haze before his eyes seemed to make a glow around them. Heat welled up where he had been so cold before. The very land around him seemed to burst out in flame, writhing with the glowing eels, glittering from their venomous fangs as they spun about him in a feeding frenzy.

"Kyle! Oh, Kyle."

Jia's horrified expression drew him back to the cold, stark cliff top beside a spring pond, a few ragged trees clinging against the wind. All the fowl had fled the pond. And now he saw Wil, sitting on the ground, stunned, studying the blistered hand that had dared to grasp Kyloreign's shoulder.

What had he done?

"I told you, Wil," Jia said softly. "Isra and Atatha both thought he had a wyseer's making to him. He had the manfish dreams, the way the ilyath worked on him."

"And who trained him?" There was that slightest and familiar hint of suspicion in Wil's tone, and Kyle knew immediately Wil was thinking of Rupert.

"We did. We've honed him. Now his body took over the defense his mind was too weary to launch."

Wilnath stood slowly. "Is that what you think?" he asked softly. "That we've enslaved you?"

Kyle gave him a sullen stare, trying to sort out what had just happened. "What's a slave? Someone kept in bondage for the purpose of doing someone else's bidding?"

"You are not bound," Wilnath said.

Kyle gestured at the small pouch where Wilnath kept the Traveling stone. "Then you tell me what you think bondage means. When you lived on the Ridge with Isra, you certainly were bound. You expect me to sacrifice my life to your pursuit of power. And what is it I'm to receive in return? Oh, your honor." He made the little salute to himself with his hand. "That's right. That makes it all worthwhile, doesn't it?"

Stiffly, trying not to stumble on his rubbery legs, Kyle turned his back on them and picked his way back along the trail toward Hindlain. He mechanically followed the secretive ways he'd learned, the soft step, the sweeping reconnaissance. His ears pricked for sounds, his senses attuned to the birds, the wind, Metatha. And indeed he felt honed to a sharp edge.

What had he done? He'd been angry before. But nothing like this had ever happened. Somehow with just his rage he'd burned Wilnath.

As he descended into the more forested slopes that would take him back to Hindlain, the cold sea wind died and he warmed from the exertion. Now weariness rushed him, so powerful it almost overwhelmed him. He stumbled over a tree root, skidding down the trail a dozen feet before he regained his footing. He dragged himself to his feet, gripping tree branches, clinging to rock, his breaths wailing out of him as he strove to move on. He shouldn't keep moving. It was dangerous here where the Pale might happen upon him any moment and he so addled with Travel sickness that the sounds of the forest had simply become a hum in his head.

What foolishness had he listened to when he returned? He came back without even listening to Rupert, who begged him to let him help. Jia had done that, had used their bond to deny him even the comfort of healing, to steal him away from the trust of his family, from Rupert … he felt the heat in him again, that anger that made the world redden around him. What was this?

He stumbled to a halt at the top of a steep descent where he might easily turn a knee if he wasn't careful. He crawled beneath the base of a rock outcropping. The memory ached within him of the forested valleys of home, and the chimney rocks rising up out of the plain.

He retched. Iron-red water from the world of eels poured its alien nature into the soils of Metatha. What if some devastating bacteria or parasite had hitched a ride? These people didn't know with what foolishness they dabbled! What was it that Rupert had brought back that had made the Withering? It took most of the small mammals, leaving only twisted mutants behind, and killed three-fourths of Metathans. And now Kyloreign was simply walking in the footsteps of Denalku and Ruperion, returning from far worlds with the tools of destruction, not the wyseery for healing that Atatha and Jia had once told him was the noble goal of the Fidrel.

It had been a month, maybe more. What, little more than a day back home? And in that time he had traveled to six worlds, with repeated trips to five of them. First he went to find out if the worlds existed as the lore said it did. Indeed, this particular spring pond had led to the watery world of eels. And it had been a quiet forest pond that led to a world that must be Shesta. And each time Wil or Atatha or whatever Kylalnethra held his stone would note the important artifacts of wyseery that he must fetch from that world, and off again they would send him.

It took days to recover from one journey. Sometimes he Traveled three times in three days, without a rest. Eels today, or whenever it was he had departed, the time skipped about in such a strange manner he didn't know how it had gotten to be summer so quickly. Yesterday had been his third trip to Shesta. Before that, before that … he felt himself sinking away. The ground pulling him downward more strongly than the Earth ever could. The hum was so loud in his ears.

Somehow he needed to stop this wild ride. He had hoped deference toward him would be the trick, but clearly that was only a formality, the oddity of him. They had no intention of listening to anything he had to say on the subject. He'd been wrong to think he could solve this. Now that they had some of their most powerful tools, the field was evened a little. He should find a way to steal away, leap into the lake behind Hindlain and just, finally, go home.

Even that solution felt like an alien urge. Besides, he was too weak to stand, much less do battle with a wyseer, a friend, to steal back his stone, then run for the lake before they could stop him. And Wil had been a friend. Or he thought he had. And Jia. Now he wasn't so sure. You didn't use your friends to death.

The ground reached up, comforting. It tucked the mantle tighter about him. It eased some liquid past his lips, warming, enervating. He opened his eyes, briefly, to see Jia bent over him, checking him for injury. She whispered a sharp order and he knew Wil leapt to answer it, likely now realizing how sorely they had used their prized tool.

"Wil's fetching help to carry you back to Hindlain," Jia said when she saw his regard. "You're just freezing here. You shouldn't have run off so addled with the Travel sickness."

"Yes, do mend me so you can drop me in some other pool. Will I next come up in a geyser where my flesh will boil away while I fetch some crucial mineral that makes a spell more lethal? Or would you have me find a world of sea monsters to do battle with just to see if they're still there, maybe slip back all bloody and gnawed with a scale that might put a hard edge on your knives."

Jia bit her lip and didn't respond for long moments. The ground reached for him again, the dark swarming him as his eyes slid shut.

"I'm sorry, Kyle. I didn't think … well, I did, but I didn't. I wouldn't have you used like this, ever. It's wrong. You were supposed to be our catalyst, not our Denalku."

He managed a weak snort of derision, more like a puff of air through his lips. The sea roared in his ears, thundered over the falls of Hindlain, the manfish dancing in the flames of red behind his eyes.

"I'm sure Denalku decided when and where he should Travel. I doubt anyone held his stone hostage."

With that, Kyle let the waves crash over him, roll him in the surf of black rock, batter his body against the stone, piling him up around the driftwood along the shore. He felt like the empty husk of desiccated manfish fruit floating on the waves, bobbing, aimless. And at last he let the tide take him.

CHAPTER SIXTEEN

The down-stuffed mat in the small curtained niche made it all feel unarguable. He was comfortable. Nothing else mattered as he listened to the natter of great matters, a drone that lulled him back toward sleep like frog song on Potter's Flowage. He'd slept, for days from what he could tell. Or was it hours? Time had become so relative to where he stood at the moment that he had no sense of it, except that it moved too swiftly when he needed it slow, or too slowly when he needed it fast. He understood now so many of Rupert's most irritating rants. He wished he could tell him what a fool he'd been. But then, Rupert knew.

A throat cleared and Kyle's head jerked up sharply from where it had settled down onto his arm. Jia had stopped speaking and the eyes of the council were on him. He quickly propped himself up on one elbow again. Atatha wore that forbidding scowl that so reminded him of Rupert, and Wilnath's mouth hung open, finally listening it appeared, as he mulled through Jia's words. They weren't Jia's words, more, Kyle's arguments.

They couldn't go on like this. They had to plan their independence from the Pale with logic and foresight, not with happenstance raids and sending the only Reign they had off to dangerous worlds to collect bric-a-brac. Jia delivered it with far less heat than he had. He almost chuckled at himself. And that strange red haze, that was something else they had heard about.

"You understand that Travel is imperative for us?" Tiva, a wyseer of some indeterminate age perhaps ten years younger than Atatha, was the first to break the silence.

"I do not," Kyle returned.

"The Fidrel existed solely to—"

"To preserve the ways of the Valeutans and prepare for the Traveler's return," Kyle finished. "Not to return to the days of Denalku and Ruperion. Remember, the ban on wyseer Travel began precisely for the reasons I've been Traveling: to build an arsenal stronger than the next wyseer."

Dakul, a wyseer who had served with Atatha on Isra's council, shook his head as he waited for Kyle to finish, a deference that made Kyle's ears go hot. How insulted would Tiva be for his interruption? She frowned into her hands now. It was so easy to make an enemy here by violating some protocol that escaped him. It was likely why Rupert would rage at him so for his impertinence. To interrupt or naysay an elder? Among the Fidrel it could mean death and banishment. Among the Kylalnethra it was yet to be seen.

"The wyseer's wars were petty rivalries, Traveler," Dakul said softly, his hands open in his lap as he looked on Kyle with an almost reverence that made Kyle's skin crawl. "This is two sides in a battle."

"Granted, Wise One," Kyle returned. "But we condemn them for unnatural magic, and they can make the same argument. It was something unnatural to Metatha that brought the Withering. It was unnatural introductions from other worlds that displaced the plants and animals that belonged here. You tell me the mere act of Traveling is unnatural: it opens gates the gods chose to leave closed. Metatha, a world of many paths, could better be a portal of knowledge."

Atatha leaned forward and peered at him. "You've mentioned this before, Kyle. What kind of knowledge is more powerful than the knowledge to make wyseery?"

"How about using Metatha's own natural plants and minerals to create the medicines to keep your people healthy? Or breed a better mount than those ravaged beasts that survived the Withering. Or improve living conditions so you can spend more time in the pursuit of knowledge."

"We have these things now in wyseery," Tiva said with a dismissive wave of her hand.

"Wise One, not really," Kyle replied, holding his hands out in what he hoped was apology. "If you have the cure for a disease, and your enemy doesn't, then you have a powerful tool for peace. If you create something that improves the lives of the common Valeutan, you make yourself indispensable to them."

"Gaining that knowledge takes time, Kyloreign," Atatha said. "The Fidrel did gather knowledge, for many years. Granted, it was mostly knowledge of wyseery and the lore of wyseery. It is a noble goal, and perhaps one we should work toward. But it doesn't have a place in a battle to save ourselves. When the Kylalnethra left the Ridge, we declared battle. We must fight that battle in the only way we can, with the tools we have."

Atatha glanced pointedly at the black stone lying on a scrap of cloth beside his mat, a place of honor to which they all deferred. They worshipped a stone, despite Jia's denial.

"With respect, Atatha, you didn't have a Traveler for the last five hundred years. And when I am dead, you will be without a Traveler again. You wasted the last five hundred years. Putting it off any longer only dooms you to fail. What if the next time I Travel I surface on a planet that has lost its atmosphere, or its sun has exploded and the world has been baked or torn to pieces?"

"You can't surface where there is no water," Tiva said.

"Then hot springs, or a sun-boiled sea or the belly of a whale. Then what? I and the stone are gone again. You can't place all your hopes in me."

"I agree, Kyle," Jia said evenly. "But while you were away we did try it the hard way. Werran and Kylalnethra lost their lives, and accomplished nothing."

"That's because you spent five hundred years studying Travel instead of learning how to defend yourselves. You didn't accomplish nothing. The Valeutan people are organized. You have the werran, you have someone besides Kylalnethra to call up for battle. But it isn't enough. I understand the dilemma. I really do," he said quietly. "But I am the only one who knows what is happening inside of me. You are killing me. It's that simple."

Atatha looked up at him sharply. Others stared into their hands.

"I can't swim from world to world like I'm taking a walk along the Ridge popping my head into my neighbor's cave. It rips me apart, molecule by molecule, changes my nature, then reassembles me somewhere else, all in a few flicks of a manfish tail. According to your own tales, I am Traveling in the womb water of the universe, unmade."

"How often could you Travel safely?" Dakul asked.

Kyle knew the question would come. They knew they'd pushed him too hard. But even Kyle didn't know how long he could do it. Something that had at first been exciting, exploring worlds unseen by any other human, he now dreaded.

"Once a month," he said, never taking his gaze off of Dakul. A pshaw escaped Tiva. Atatha sat slowly back. Wil's mouth could hang no farther open.

"What it would force us to do is study before we send the Traveler," Jia said, leaning forward. "We haven't been thinking. We can't just drop him into a puddle to see if something still exists. We must send him where we really need him to go, with a plan in mind that if the place is as it was in the past, then he can retrieve the items most needed."

"It would take forever," Wilnath said in almost a whisper. "There are hundreds of portals."

"It has taken forever, Wil," Kyle said. "If I had never returned—"

"But you did!" Wilnath protested.

A slap of hands greeted the interruption. Outrage shone in Atatha's and Dakul's eyes as Tiva gave Wilnath a disapproving gaze.

"My apologies, Kyloreign, for my exuberance. What I'm saying is, you are here. So 'what if I wasn't' is moot. You are here. And you are a tool. It's not kind to you personally, but certainly you must see things in the larger perspective, the greater need. It's like saying, don't plant by the sun because one day it might be gone, or don't set your time by the moons, because one day they may collide. Kyloreign is here now.

You were the catalyst for our struggle for freedom. And you are the means by which we will attain it."

"At all costs, Wil?" Kyle asked, feeling the anger welling up in him at the audacity of it. "I am simply a tool to be used, and once broken, discarded? Is that how you would like to be viewed, Wil? Isn't it that disregard for your life and rights what you hate about your bondage?"

"I don't mean disrespect, Kyloreign. But if I were given the opportunity to lay down my life for my people, I would readily do it."

"But you aren't stupid about it, are you? You don't just shout out to a passing band of Pale wyseers, 'Here I am, ready to die for my people.' Without planning or reason, you've thrown away a perfectly good tool. You also forget: this isn't my battle."

"But we are of the same blood," Tiva said. "It was your people the Pale murdered, your parents. You are the last Reign."

"I might have been born to Reign, but they weren't my parents, people who raised me. On Earth, your ancestors could come from anywhere. It's who you are now, and where you live now, what you believe now, and who you call your family that decides loyalties. The ones who hold grudges and don't move on are those who break the peace. I feel for you and your people. But you have to see your part in your plight. You can't expect one, mortal man to come in and fix it for you. I have another life. I'm here because I want to do what's right and just, and to help genuine friends. But you need a better argument to convince me to throw my life away. I've lived among you all together only a few weeks. I have no sense of blood duty. I care. I truly do care. I hate to see injustice of any kind. But you can't expect me to give my life for your 'cause' simply because you think I should, and you dreamed I would."

The silence crawled around him, raising the hairs on his arms, though he knew it only to be the humid mist from the falls coming in with a change of the watch. And the silence, too, was in his head as the caverns were abuzz with the daily living of more than one hundred people. They must understand. They assumed too much from him.

"So, we reach an impasse," Atatha said at last. "I have heard many of these arguments before, when Kyle first arrived among the Fidrel. Then it was a matter of understanding what the meaning of the

Traveler's arrival portended. We did things without regard for his fears because we didn't know his nature. We grappled with the hoped-for-but-never-expected miracle. I don't know when we leapt from recognizing the Traveler as the culmination of the Fidrel mission, and becoming manipulators of Travel wyseery and a desire to err as did our forebears. I don't recall a point where we asked Kyle. We simply took the wyseery from him in those first hours among us. The parallels Jia drew to how the Pale treat slaves is well taken. But our needs are great. Yet, we must respect what you have given willingly despite our treatment of you, and recognize that if we kill you with our needs, we are no further ahead. I'm troubled, too, by how the Travel sickness grew in you, and the strange manifestation of unbidden wyseery in an untrained Reign is something even more miraculous to ponder. Did the one come from the other? Did the Travel disease, or some encounter of another world do this to you? You have failed to use this skill on command, and it is clearly a wild wyseery, making it dangerous. What power will you next reveal, wild and uncontrolled, when next you're, as you say, 'pissed off'?"

The silence became unbearable. Kyle was on the verge of giving in simply to end the strange scrutiny when Tiva cleared her throat.

"The idea of setting priorities is a wise step," Tiva offered. "It is basic, and oddly not considered. I think we are still wearing the robes of scholars who grasp for all information, and not of warriors who must set realistic goals. We must identify those artifacts and worlds that are most important to us."

"We have also approached Travel itself with little forethought," said Dakul. "There are potential dangers, and we can't expect the Traveler to know what artifacts we seek unless we take the time to teach him. Since that time may not always be available, perhaps he should Travel accompanied by a wyseer who knows what we seek and can help defend him."

"In a way, I've already Traveled with Kyle. I seek the honor," Jia said softly.

They went on as if they hadn't heard her, making decisions for him again, perhaps improving his lot. Still, he was no better than a personal shopper—less. The personal shopper wasn't likely to be killed for his efforts.

"Kyle is quite correct about one aspect of our people. We are short sighted," Atatha said. "We have a long memory for the past, and we work hard on that memory, so hard we don't think ahead. That must change. We will begin planning for alternatives to wyseery. Not that it will happen in our lifetimes, but perhaps in a generation or two when our role might also be keepers of the knowledge of alternatives to wyseery as well. And when we have that list of priorities, we will stop. Indeed, we do not want to bring on another Withering."

"The council is in agreement?" Tiva asked. All of them nodded but Kyle. "The council has spoken and it is done."

"What is done?" Kyle asked under his breath.

"Not enough, but something," Jia said softly.

CHAPTER SEVENTEEN

His hand tingled as if asleep, though he'd merely touched the flame of a small brand to the mark of the ilyath. And with Jia's nod, he knew that he'd disappeared to those who didn't carry a seeing stone. Barul, a Valeutan from Overmount who, like dozens of other young men and women had rallied to the Kylalnethra as fighters, stared slack-jawed at the place where Kyle stood, a note of near panic in his expression.

"I'm still here, Barul," Kyle said softly, the young man startling at his words. "It's wyseery. I'll be right beside you."

"But Traveler, how can a simple werran find you to protect you? What if you come between a Pale and our knives?" Barul spoke to space, his head cocked as if unsure where Kyle might be as he scanned the thick woods for a shadow of Kyle there.

"It's my responsibility to stay out of your way," Kyle said. "This is the safest way for me to observe, and not be captured."

At last, Jia gave the signal. Three dozen wyseers and werran donned dark hoods and cloaks, their skin smudged with charred wood. They slipped one by one from behind the hollow of forest they had camped in a day west of Hindlain above the north shore of Ta'atit. He heard the occasional rustle nearby, but in the dark of a cloudy night they had become one with the shadows.

On cat's paws, they moved through forest, with such practiced stealth that they barely roused a bird. Far below, where the Great River had submerged Ta'atit, no glimmer could he see. The lake had become a darker shadow of slumbering fowl. They climbed steadily, avoiding each other's path and careful not to leave a sign of their passing, not even a bent twig. The smoke from the Ridge invited him to the cozy caves of the Fidrel below, their numbers dwindled, their purpose uncertain. Some roasting fowl forced a growl from his gut, loud in the quiet night. At last they descended toward the falls at the west end of Lake Ta'atit, the roar a steady drum roll to hide their passage as they marched into the mist. Jia paused and held up her fist. He sensed an instant halt in the movements around him as if a faucet had been suddenly closed.

Jia gestured, one hand right, the other left. They split into two units, one following Wilnath, the other staying with Jia. As he passed, Wilnath, armed with the seeing stone that unmasked Kyle, laid a familiar hand on Kyle's shoulder, his face unreadable beneath his hood.

Kyle caught up to Jia. Now he could see the Pale encampment beside the Ta'atit road below them. A small fire had died back to embers, barely revealing those slumbering beside it. Somewhere, he knew, a sentry would be posted, and if his hunch was correct, a Pale wyseer slept in the tent pitched in the soft grass beside the road. Kyle thought he counted at least twenty, assuming only one wyseer slept in the tent, and only one sentry had been posted. A twig snapped. All tensed, but then Jia gestured toward the noise. A darker shadow moved from the shrubs beside the road where a Pale had relieved himself. The sentry stared up at the slope above the road, as if he sensed their presence, seeing them without recognition. Did he feel them watching him? Had he heard or smelled something unnatural above the dew of the falls and the distant rumble? Did it occur to him he might die tonight?

Jia shook her head as she stared down. He realized as she pointed them out that anyone attempting to cross the treeless slope below them would be easily marked against the light-colored ground cover, without even boulders or bushes to conceal them. Would Wilnath see their vulnerability? Jia turned and looked at Kyle, shaking her head. If they lost the element of surprise, the soldiers sleeping around the fire could be on their feet and ready to do battle in moments. They carried swords, and bows, and their racket would certainly wake the wyseer within.

It wasn't his battle. Yet, as he saw Jia signing her directions, he knew that it would be too costly. He couldn't stand by and watch his companions walk into a slaughter. They had to have the element of surprise. He swallowed hard and tapped Jia on the shoulder, and pointed from himself to the sentry. Jia shook her head, dismissive. Before he could talk himself out of it, he stood and brushed between her and Barul, his invisible presence almost drawing a squawk of surprise from the werran. Jia grasped the edge of the green robe he wore.

"No, Kyle, it's too dangerous," she breathed, her words barely carrying to him through the mist.

"You can't lose the surprise."

As he sidled down the slope, each step taking forever as he tested the security of the footing, willing each stone to hold firm, each blade of grass to stillness, he suddenly realized he had no idea what he hoped to accomplish. He had no weapon. He had no intention of killing anyone so a knife would do him no good anyway. He wasn't a warrior, much less knowledgeable about martial arts or how to knock out one's opponent. Even his preferred sports avoided contact.

Several times the sentry turned toward him, as if sensing his approach. At one point he froze for several minutes as the sentry stared directly at him. Those around the fire coughed and turned now and then, restless in their sleep. Did they feel the danger sneaking up on them? Would dawn come before he could reach his destination? At last, he reached the level ground of the road and closed on the sentry.

The squawk of a blood bird made the sentry turn away from Kyle and stare into the night on the other side of the road. Kyle had watched Wilnath create that particular spell. A signal. In one swift move, he swept up a curb stone from beside the road, took a long step, then slapped one hand over the sentry's mouth. Kyle brought the stone down on the man's temple with a sickening thump that brought the bile up in Kyle's throat. The man's weight sagged into him, and he eased him to the ground carefully, only to watch in horror as a passing shadow slashed a knife across the man's throat.

Kyle stared as blood pulsed out, a dark black pool in the road eased toward his feet, gasping bubbles, a choking cough. It took him a moment to realize the night had become noisy as shadows swept upon the camp and roused soldiers came to their feet with a roar.

"Methil Sethina!" a shout arose, the soldiers calling the wyseer to their aid.

Swords swept long hunting knives aside. The tent erupted in flames. He saw two dark figures battling with guards at the entrance to the burning tent. One ducked to dodge a sword that caught the edge of cloak and revealed Wilnath's sandy hair in the firelight. His face set and grim, he didn't flinch, merely sidled and stabbed. The slight figure beside him he knew was Jia, and suddenly she was upon her foe, and came away with a bloody knife.

She ripped up the sword from her fallen opponent, almost pulled down by its weight, to knock aside Methil Sethina's staff winging toward her head. Jia planted her feet apart and whipped up her hands, something glimmering between two fingers and a blaze of light shot from her hand into the eyes of Sethina, framed by the flames that licked at her crimson cloak. Flames caught up in the Pale wyseer's hair, but she ignored it, her lips moving as she held out her staff again, the bright stone at its tip sending a blast toward Jia. Jia ducked, and the flame rolled into the night, fizzling into sparks near the dead sentry. Jia brought around the sword. Sethina fended her off with a brush of her arm.

Kyle couldn't believe the woman hadn't fallen to the searing heat yet. But then he could see the shimmer of some field that distorted the flames like a mirage. She protected herself from the flames, and used them to keep her enemies at bay, as Jia continually dodged back from the heat, the sweat making rivulets on her coal-streaked face.

Wilnath and other Kylalnethra gathered now. Their weapons bounced from her. Their wyseery seemed merely to fizzle as it neared her. Kyle heard a low laugh, something dire and mirthless that came from the Pale wyseer.

"It is really quite flattering, so many little children trying to play at wyseery," she said. "It is, you know, the blood of Fidrel that keeps me safe."

Wilnath bowled into her feet, but he fell back as if burned by her, steam rolling up from his clothes. Kyle took a step forward as Barul rushed to tamp at it, unsuccessfully. Wilnath peeled away the black cloak, which continued to burn as if acid ate into it, and furiously rubbed at a spot on his arm that continued to smolder.

Jia hadn't taken her eyes off the woman, but Kyle could see Jia's lips moving, her hands open and cupped upward, the white stone in one palm, a powerful chunk of quartzite in the other. Methil Sethina suddenly seemed to notice her, and pause long enough to decide if she was concerned.

It was too late. Jia brought her hands together and in the ghosting wake of the flash, Kyle saw that the shimmering around Sethina had given way to smoke, the flames on her cloak erupting in fury. Whatever wyseery Jia had called upon bowed her head and bent her shoulders. He took another step. Sethina's mouth opened, her staff coming around in an arc at Jia's head. Barul brought up the sword lying beside Jia, the staff shattering on it. Then with an angry bellow, he jammed the weapon into Sethina's chest.

The sudden silence roared in Kyle's ears. The sentry was dead. The flames in the tent had subsided. The fallen lay all over the road and in the ditches beside it. The only sound he heard above the constant rumble of the falls was the slight clink of weaponry as the dead were stripped of swords, knives and other gear. Others dragged the bodies to the river's edge and sent them on their way over the falls. Supplies were broken into, and Jia slipped into the pocket of her robes the crystal stone from the head of Methil Sethina's staff as all traces of the traveling party of the Pale disappeared into the river or the packs of the Valeutans.

They had fared well, Kyle realized. The two with the most serious injuries would survive. Stealth had paid. With the wyseer's death, the magic that had struck Wilnath stopped burning, though it had left a hole in his hand.

"Has anyone seen Kyle?" Jia asked in a tired voice.

"He's there, before you," said Wilnath.

Kyle paused as he helped another man drag the dead sentry to the river while Barul and another washed the blood from the road. "Sister, did you lose your seeing stone, or are you unwell?"

Kyle plunged his hand into the river, knowing from the gasp beside him that he had undone the ilyath.

"Ah, there he is," she said. Before he knew he had moved, Kyle was beside her as her legs gave way.

"And you were thinking you're up to Traveling?" he said as lightly as he could.

"This is what we've been trying to tell you," said Wilnath as he bent to look into Jia's eyes. "They are just too powerful. All of us to one of her and look what it took. All you've seen before is the small feats of wyseery like the ilyath. Defeating a blood-made ward, that's a tall order for a wyseer stocked with nothing but a few stones and trinkets from far worlds."

"It should have been Wil, or someone more experienced," Jia said as Kyle led her toward the hillside. "Knowing how to do something and actually carrying it off, two different things."

"There's another party around here somewhere," he heard a man telling Wilnath as they trudged back up into the forests above the road. "One of their soldiers tried to escape with orders to fetch, I missed the name, but it sounded like he was going to call for help somewhere close enough that help would come."

As if to punctuate the assertion, they heard the sound of an arrow striking a tree.

"Scatter!" Wilnath hissed.

Shadows disappeared in moments. Kyle supported Jia, but she led him, urging him upward with the pressure of her hand on his back. He heard the clink as someone carrying a bundle of Pale swords stumbled in the dark.

As they reached the top of the ridge above the road, Jia fell. When he pulled her to her feet he could see in the dim light growing in the east a red-cloaked wyseer striding through the encampment beside the road below, turning, turning, pausing now and then to study some spot the Kylalnethra had concealed. He peered down at the place where the sentry's blood had been washed away with river water.

"Come on!" Kyle nudged Jia to her feet. She merely nodded, now leading him by the hand up the forested slopes.

To the east, shouts broke out, the ring of metal on stone. Jia paused, taking her knife from her belt. She looked up at Kyle in the dim light.

"Mark what I do. It's something you can learn," she said as she muttered the words he recognized as a series of almost-nonsense "making" words that were often a part of the Fidrel wyseery. Then she tapped the knife to the ground. To his amazement, the knife disappeared, though he could tell from her grip that she still held it in her hand.

She jerked her head to one side and Kyle realized that a tow-headed man was trying to creep across the slope level with them. Even in the gloom of dawn, they could tell they hadn't yet been seen though some sound must have given them away. The man's quiver hung empty at his back, a bow slung behind him. Kyle slowly eased behind the cover of boulders that had fallen free of a rock ledge and pulled Jia after him. As she made to follow, her foot slipped and sent a small stone rolling downhill through the litter of leaves.

The Pale soldier froze, reaching for a knife as he approached that place a few feet downhill of them where Jia had slipped. Kyle thought his breaths would rip from him soon if the soldier moved any more slowly, clearly thinking himself unnoted. Each moment the gloom lifted until Kyle feared the dawn would reveal them. Their pursuer was almost even with them and slightly downhill. Kyle could almost reach out to touch the man. If he looked to his right he would see them.

Kyle silently plucked a sliver of stone from the base of the boulder and carefully lobbed over the soldier's head so that it would fall among the trees farther downslope near another outcropping and boulder field.

The soldier turned to face the noise, crouching slightly. Kyle leapt in an awkward tackle, knocking the sturdier man down with an oomph. Before Kyle could recover from his own stunning fall, the soldier had rolled and planted himself on Kyle's chest. He grasped him by the ears, lifting Kyle's head and smashing it down against the ground.

Kyle thought his head would explode, a blaze left his vision blurred and dim. He struggled but couldn't budge the soldier's weight from his chest as pain bloomed through his head. Again, he felt his ears tugging upward, pain shooting down his neck.

Suddenly a flash stunned him and he realized it came not from within his head, but from uphill. Jia had spent the last of her will on a fireball that struck the Pale soldier in the chest. Kyle's head flopped back down with a smack as the soldier's weight shifted downhill. Jia had fallen to her knees, her face ashen in the pale light of dawn.

Kyle stumbled to his feet and immediately fell again. The soldier shook himself, then charged uphill for Jia. Kyle grasped for the passing legs but failed to trip him. The soldier struck Jia with the force of his weight smashing her against the rock. A bellow ripped out of him as Jia's hidden knife suddenly appeared again, wedged in the soldier's side.

What if the racket brought Pale reinforcements? He didn't dare call for help from the rest of the scattered Valeutans. The soldier swiftly yanked the knife from his side as if brushing away a sliver and turned it on Jia. She hadn't moved. Her eyes were closed. The knife in the soldier's hand arched back, about to descend on Jia.

Kyle lunged, grabbing the soldier's arm, feeling himself still propelled downward toward Jia's chest with the knife, his strength no match for the soldier's. His vision went red. A flash blinded him. He fell heavily, already sinking into the ground and the comforting dark. The Pale would capture them now, bleed them for some ritual, what foolishness had he shared?

CHAPTER EIGHTEEN

With a languorous arch of his back, he rose in a swirl of bubbles, not rushing, picking carefully, watching, watching. There loomed a wall, another, with a turret atop it. Here a courtyard spread deep and dark before a rampart reared up again. Now and then some arching neck and sharp beak would dart beneath the surface at him, startled by the outline he made. Experience was a thing one didn't forget so easily. And he knew to be wary. At last he sensed the sheltering overhang of brush and rose to the surface in the shallow of its shade.

Ruperion took a deep breath of Metatha, remembering so clearly the scents of his home that he almost choked on the alien scent of this place. No bakeries lined the Wideway in this time. No open market hawked fish and cattle, produce and the wovens with their pungent dyes. The hazy smoke of cookfires and smokehouses had become simply a whiff of memory. No snufflers worked among the thick brush, nor tree rats chattered from the overhanging limbs.

The deep weariness of Travel sickness struck him suddenly in the gut and he retched up a good quart of brackish water mixed with stale wine. The stench of damp fowl and their acrid droppings overwhelmed the scent of over ripe manfish. The odor clung to his mouth. The red columns flanking the lake still rose, though the forest above them had thinned. But no city, no fast river, nothing else familiar said home to him. Manfish trees stood tall in the canopy as ever they had, but no livestock lowed on pastured hillsides, no stags or rams stood out on the high bluffs, no biting flies hovered near the water, no turtles or frogs dived for safety at his arrival. Only fish and fowl seemed to inhabit this world.

A broad lake overspread his home. Ta'atit, Kyle had called it. And paddling above it floated a sea of squawking, flapping, preening, diving, mating birds of all size, shape and color. And as he marveled at the vast flock, he reared back, stunned by a small yellow-green bird that darted right up to his face and plucked a damp hair that dangled between his eyes.

His senses reeled. It had been more than twenty years since he'd Traveled. He had never warned Kyle about the sickness and wondered if maybe he had forgotten how hard it could be. Now age crept upon him and years of wine and Friday night fish fries left him too weak to pull himself from the water. How frightening this moment of weakness must have been for Kyle, as it made his own heart labor to realize he wasn't even sure who or what might be his enemy and he couldn't protect himself if he did. Had wisdom failed when he had so coldly shoved his charge into the void?

He studied the sky. Soon sunset would bring the moons he had longed for each night Earth's solitary satellite rose so distant and cold. Would they still be the moons he'd known, or would they, too, show him an alien face? In moons' light he'd be ready to venture out and see what legacy he'd left upon the land.

Huddling under the cover of the brushy bank, he sifted through the clutter in the wyseer's pouch he wore at his belt. He'd brought many powerful tools with him, but would Metathans have refined their wyseery in all these years? Did they have countermeasures, antidotes, or the equivalent of seeing stones to show through every sleight of hand and illusion, to reveal him wherever he hid? He hefted the quartz and gold stone, his power stone. It still bore the wax stain that bound him to Kyle. Instantly he had a sense of him, strong, not muted like the long road through the portal. He gripped the stone hard, turning inward to feel Kyle's needs, sense his dismay, to protect him as only his Uncle Rupert could. He could see the places Kyle walked, feeling the sense of Travel sickness lingering about him.

"Be strong." He told the image in his head, and dropped the stone back in his bag.

He awoke to the faint blue light of Danat overhead, and the silhouettes of fowl nattering in their sleep. He gingerly slipped from his shelter and walked the dark streets of his home. In the midst of the Wideway, which now rolled down into the unseen depths of the lake, he surveyed the crumbling ruin of all that he had known. It wasn't until he had climbed to the cluster of manfish trees that had marked the yard of his sprawling home that he allowed himself to lean against a tree and weep. So many years he had quenched his grief with wine, drowning the questions with each sip, wondering what fates had met family, friends, and what horrors he had left in the hands of Denalku. A sob ripped up through him that he barely suppressed, hating this weakness in a world he had mastered.

More strange birds rustled about him as he held back the depth of his dismay. Had Leta and Arlin died of the anthrax he had turned over to a madman, the disease more fatal and more cruel where none could resist it? Or did the horsemen of the Pale ravage them, string them up, behead them, flay them? Did Denalku, unhappy with his servant, have them sent away as slaves, or brought into his house where certainly they would have been killed? Did they die of old age? Did his son have children? He tried to picture them, see her trimming the herbs in the dooryard, see his son clambering limb to limb up the trees, but it was like trying to remember a snapshot. No landmark remained, and his memory had become so fragmented, fleeting. After so many years, he doubted even their bones remained.

He kicked at the pile of detritus that generations of wyseers had pawed through, including Kyle, in search of fragments of wyseery. But in the political climate of Denalku's reign, even Denalku's mentor never felt so confident of his security. Outside the high window of his study, the crotch of a manfish tree had stood just beyond easy reach. Now, Rupert struggled to haul a body gone soft and stiff, from branch to branch, until he could reach up one hand to feel the niche of hiding place in a tree gone massive and near to its end. His hand brushed against something solid and squared wedged in the crotch of a branch. He had to work it free, then at last he gripped a weathered softstone box and dropped from the tree, almost falling when a knee gave way beneath him. It was still there, locked with his word, its powers and tinctures intact and the most powerful of stones, including one very special stone.

It didn't look like much, this sliver of pink quartzite he'd found in the Baraboo Hills on some long-ago foray in search of Earth's magical treasures. He could almost sense its power as he held it. It could create power. It and others like it had held open the portals, the first there in the river that led to Potter's Flowage. No one, not even the long dead chieftains before Denalku, knew what wyseery Ruperion used to first Travel, then hold open the portals, what he had done to mock the gods.

Suddenly he looked up, peering at the far slopes of the mountains above Lake Ta'atit. Dawn remained distant, yet the sky had taken on a glow, giving a hint of the red cliffs and columns reaching high above the lake. Something happened there. Something powerful in the hills on the west end of the lake not far from the falls. He reached for the power stone that bound him to Kyle and dropped it, stifling a yelp at the shock. A flash ripped the night and a thunderclap followed a moment later, stirring the fowl on the lake into a chatter and fluff of disgust. He sensed the slightest added weariness, a weakness the stirring of Travel wyseery could force from him as its maker. Kyle had been at the center of that explosion.

A sound, that noise of intentional quiet, pricked his ears and he crouched instinctively. With a breath of thought he pulled himself within the shadows of approaching dawn, the magic not rusted or lost, simply reawakening in his memories. Easily he picked them out, though they might think themselves secretive. A line of green-robed figures crept among the trees above a trail that emerged from the gloom of dawn. His heart thumped hard. They looked like Reign robes! A hand went up and several froze in their tracks. He sensed a gaze crossing him, but they didn't seek him in the gloom. They sought the crimson-garbed party just below on the lakeside trail. Red-robed figures, some clearly soldiers, others emanating wyseery, rode twisted apparitions that might have been horses, moving slowly as they peered up into the forested streets of Ta'atit.

A whistle of arrows sped toward the crimson party. A crimson-cloaked wyseer flicked a finger and the arrows burst into flames and fizzled to ash before falling as feathers at their feet. The three wyseers among them tipped prism-capped staffs toward their foes, who scattered for the trees as the soldiers nocked arrows. A blaze of light ripped into the woods. It sucked the breath from the world around Rupert and he almost gasped aloud at the hideous display of a god-forbidden power.

From the wood, came a clatter of stones shaken together in a hollowed wooden tube. He knew the weapon well. The taut skin of a drum sealed each end, held in place by the dried and woven fibers of manfish peel. The ground rumbled, the horse-like creatures shifting nervously but too cloddish to feel fright. Trees lashed about overhead, branches falling among them. Rocks fell from the tumbled structures still standing amidst the vines. Several of the shifting rocks almost seemed to take wing as they bounced free of the grasping ground and sprang for the heads of the riders.

The stones bounded back from some protective force that split several stones and turned one to a powdery dust. One of the soldiers fell from his mount to the ground, a sliver of stone that had somehow passed the barrier buried in his eye. The other soldiers shifted nervously as they noted their fallen, the woods and the wyseers bringing their staffs around.

He caught movement from the corner of his eye. A dark-haired runner sprinted away from the group upslope. An arrow caught him in the back and he fell silently.

Stock still, only his eyes moving within the cocoon of shadow he'd woven about himself, Rupert watched something he had dreaded, something he remembered from a past so far distant that worlds had come and gone since then: Battle fought among wyseers. This path led to waste and ruin. It had spawned the whole system of castes and the bans on Travel. The wyseer wars had leveled mountains, shifting earth and stone, marching trees over precipices and damning the Great River to drown Ta'atit. The wyseers had thought only of their own ends, not how the world groaned at the assault, or how farmers must survive on wyseery-wasted lands, or how families must mourn dead innocents.

This way lay ruin. He had been there before. And he knew: Kyle was in the middle of it.

What had he done? He'd thought he helped his world when he opened the portals. He made them difficult to pass when he saw how they were misused. Then he had poisoned his world, piece by piece until finally he had turned the bane of another world upon poor Shesta, and by giving it to a madman, on his own beloved Metatha. And now, he did it again, sending Kyle only stirred up the old wyseer wars, certainly. It must stop. It must be undone. Ruperion was the master undoer.

As the wyseers' battle moved downslope and east, Rupert pulled the shadow more tightly about himself and crept to the fallen man, clearly Valeutan by his features. The man lay in the litter of leaf and the crumbled stone of a once-proud city, sobbing into the dirt he certainly expected he would soon become.

Rupert lay a hand on the arrow and the man went instantly silent, a resigned eye turned skyward like a beached fish, as if he expected a final blow.

"Who do you serve? To where were you running?" Rupert asked gently in the Metathan tongue, hearing it in this world like music after twenty years of racket. The man pursed his lips. "Do you serve the Pale? Your answer will decide your fate. I could, perhaps, save your life."

"I don't care if you kill me now. I'll never serve the Pale against my people."

"We speak the same," Rupert said, knowing that in some ways it wasn't true. He almost had to struggle to understand words. The dialect had shifted westward in his long absence, with tones of the Pale speech, and other affectations that felt unfamiliar. Had he sent Kyle to a world he should know, speaking a foreign tongue?

The man let out a small gasp as Rupert neatly tugged the arrow from his back, then sprinkled a few grains of sand into the wound. The flow of blood became a trickle. He chewed a paste of leaves and stuffed it into the hole the arrow had left, then lay another patch of leaves over all, using a shred of the man's tunic to hold it in place.

"There, it should heal in a day or so. You can move now. Let me get a look at you."

Hesitantly, the man rolled, eyeing Rupert as he let the shadow fall back to reveal himself.

"What wyseery is this? It was a fatal wound. I couldn't move my legs. I—"

"You are called?"

"Davath. Who—"

"Very well, Davath. We must find shelter until you have healed enough to travel," Rupert said, searching until he found a shadowy line of brush overhanging an old stone wall. Rupert helped the young man to his feet and supported his hesitant weight as they moved under cover just as the dawn broke free to light the hillsides. Rupert hesitated a long moment, feeling that familiar sun on him, the way it fired the northern cliffs red. The tumult of the wyseer's battle, however it had fared, had faded away and quiet had returned. The fowl on the lake roused for the day, flocks wheeling together and heading out to sea, others heading inland.

He turned to find Davath gazing up at him in fear. Rupert reached down and lifted the wooden disk worn around Davath's neck on some sort of thin string. A finely carved image depicted the three moons, but with Kylik a blazing light with the manfish at its center.

"You speak strangely," Davath said as Rupert let the disc drop. "As Kyloreign did. You—" Davath's eyes widened.

"Yes, I am him," Rupert said. "And yet not. You do not know who I am. But it would seem you have my mercy, and have your life, so could I be all that you fear?"

"Perhaps," Davath said. "I don't know yet why you spared me. Maybe you hope to use me as a tool in your arsenal against Metatha."

Rupert grinned a little at that, and gave him the speculative look that used to send the young ones scurrying with a shriek of fear.

"Oh, I do not doubt you will be useful to me," he said, then chuckled at the way Davath blanched. "But it may be a mutual using. I intend no harm to Metatha. It is my home. Instead, I come to right wrongs."

Rupert reached for the pouch at Davath's belt, the man quickly grabbed for it, but too late to keep Rupert from snatching it free.

"What would send so brave a man fleeing from battle?" Rupert said softly as he opened the pouch. He poured out a handful of stones, herbs, amulets and the obviously fresh powdered horn of Shesta. He narrowed his gaze on the man. "You are not a wyseer."

"I'm a werran for the Kylalnethra."

Rupert stiffened at the name. "Yet you carry with you wyseer's potions."

"When the odds are long, you do not risk handing to the enemy the means to your end."

"In other words, were they to see the Shestan horn, they would know you indeed have a Traveler in your midst, gathering for you the tools to fight them."

Davath's eyes had widened as Rupert spoke, but now he wrapped himself in his arms. "I didn't say that."

Rupert nodded slowly. "Yes, you did. It is well you ran, though I dare say your wyseers would be better off with their potions than without them. You misunderstand me. I am not your enemy."

Rupert settled down beside Davath, ignoring the way his stomach growled. "You are going to tell me some stories, Davath. He reached into Davath's pouch and placed the tiniest few grains of Shestan horn on the end of his finger and held it up for Davath's inspection. The young werran leaned forward, closer, closer, closer, until if he blinked his lashes would brush the horn dust from Rupert's finger. At that moment, Rupert blew on his finger and Davath leaned back, his eyes slightly glazed. He looked at Rupert, his mouth falling open.

"Let us start with Kyle," Rupert said softly.

He could see some last inward struggle. Then words fell from the man-like water fighting free of a dam. Only now and then did Rupert need to prod him with more questions, or explanations, or to hold up his finger to again deepen the spell that bound Davath to him. And as the day wore on, his frown deepened to a scowl. Waste and ruin: that was where it was heading. And Kyle, Kyle was the cyclone at its center.

CHAPTER NINETEEN

The red cliffs rose from the dark lake so stark and sudden that Danathea let out an unwilling gasp. Talik's head jerked up, his mouth working to form a smile out of a scowl he thought he'd worn forever. There had been that long trudge through deep prairie—only to meet the forbidding and barren remnants of volcanic ruin the closer they came to Misty Lake. Then came a desperate passage on a river raft. Then treacherous swamps when the river grew too swift. Talik felt worn to a desperation that made him fear for his sanity. Now, at last, they were near. But it gave him little comfort. What would here mean?

Their first sight of Lake Ta'atit left them still a half-day's travel away. But it felt like the end after almost a month's journey. It might have taken them a bit over a week if they could have taken the Ta'atit road. Their initial successes at provisioning weren't so easily repeated and their forage often left them picking apart shellfish or living from seeds, berries and unsatisfying greens.

Now, as they slogged through marshes perched on a plateau that trickled toward the Great Falls, each parting of the scrub revealing another view of the stark lands of the Valeuta, he had to admit that his experience had indeed been a Realing. He may not have found a greater devotion to his gods. In fact, he probably had more doubts than ever. But he sensed Martrena closer to him than since that day beside the well, perhaps even closer than her living being because he knew she was within him, guiding him in some plan of her own.

Danathea stopped abruptly, Talik almost ramming into her before he noticed her peering along a road that blocked their path.

"Rim Road," Talik said with a nod, pulling out his worn map of Metatha. "South it intersects with the Ta'atit Road, the Overmount Road and at last finds the Prairie Road in the foothills of the southern mountains. It used to end at the Ta'atit Road. That's why it doesn't appear on this map. The road was extended north to the haunts of the Fidrel."

He studied the darkening sky as Danathea stared north as if she were about to enter the lands of her most mortal enemy.

"We wait until nightfall and we go on."

"Will they trust us, Uncle? I'm still not sure why we're here."

"You just regret missing the hot springs," he said absently. "As for trust, I certainly doubt they'll trust us. You must be prepared to go unseen. If something were to happen to me, you must be ready to hide yourself. You've practiced it, but a true test is to walk unseen among wyseers. We are easily marked here."

"That's what worries me."

"Whether they trust us isn't as much of an issue as whether they will listen to us."

"I still don't understand how the Fidrel can be of any help. Your issue is with the High Chieftain."

"And that issue has everything to do with the Fidrel," he replied with a dismissing wave of his hand.

He wasn't ready to discuss it. He needed to meditate, to stare at the way the water pooled around his feet, hear the sigh of the reeds and the clack and clatter of birds, the beating flurry of wing as a raptor dived into a small flock of birds stripping the seeds from the reeds. Soon he must place himself at the mercy of an enemy. Soon he must go against all the ways of his people and ask for the help of an enemy against his own. Soon he would cross a line from which he could never retreat.

And soon he must break a man's heart.

They had walked so far that the moons lit the road with an eerie and brilliant light when Talik was brought up short by a soft word in a language so accented it took him a moment to recognize it as Martrena's dialect.

"Who walks this road?" the query came again, with more urgency.

"Fidrel?" he asked of the person who had hailed him, suddenly fearful that he had stumbled upon those who guarded the passes where the Fidrel were permitted to dwell.

"Who else would live here?" the accented voice returned with a note that could be humor, could be bitterness.

"We speak the same. I am Palif Talik Atannen, late of the Atannate of High Chief Wakthral Atannen. I would speak to Isra, or her appointee." Talik swallowed hard, fearing that his words would ring with the wrong authority, appear presumptive, not express, as he hoped, his worthiness of an audience. He turned his palms upward to show he bore no weapon.

"And?" the voice asked as if he'd named himself a barge poler on the Great River.

"And?" Talik echoed.

"Your companion has a name as well? Or would you have us believe it is the High Chieftain beside you?"

Danathea let out a little snort. Talik cleared his throat to silence her. "Danathea, my niece, is an acolyte of the Palifiim."

Talik squinted as a lantern threw light upon them briefly, before swiftly being hidden again.

"You don't look like a palif," the man returned.

"I have my reasons." Talik heard low voices in the shadow near his questioner.

"Isra will speak with you," the man said, sounding somewhat surprised. "Our people will lead you. Please do not give them reason to doubt you are on a peaceful mission."

Talik bowed his head slightly, as two women clad in the green robes of the Fidrel took him by the arms, another offering Danathea his hand.

He blinked hard, his eyes watering as he ducked within a cave entrance and a blaze of lanterns met his eyes. At least a dozen Fidrel, all of them clearly elders stood in a semi-circle before him, one woman, draped in white beads, stood slightly forward from the group. She stared at him with no pretense of friendliness, then bowed curtly and introduced herself as Isra.

"Why have you come here, Palif?" Isra asked. She appeared tired. They all did. He could see they lived in poverty deeper than he had imagined.

"I came seeking wisdom, and bearing news of a lost daughter."

"And what wisdom could the Fidrel possibly offer the Palif of the Atannate?"

"I search for a way to reason. The Methiliim, it would appear, may have grander designs than mere wyseery to serve the people. They would appear to have an urgency that has the streets of Waymeet running in Valeutan blood. Soon they will run out of Valeutans to feed their cauldrons and will turn to the Palifiim, the Chieftain's house, the people of the Pale, perhaps their own. It has gone too far."

"And the Palifiim now turn to the Fidrel. We're to help them, when never they raised a voice in our defense?"

"The Palifiim do not come to you, Wise Isra, I do. I have been banished from the High Chieftain's house by Methil Tarcatha, who would move the High Chieftain's lips for him. I was guilty of asking for restraint, that blood should not be wasted on unwholesome acts against nature, but only given to Danat from those who die a natural death. I warned that turning our eyes so far from Danat as to allow them to foul the altars of Danat's temples, to let them rule in the place of the High Chieftain, was wrong."

The barest hint of a smile ran fleet on Isra's lips, though her eyes showed a deeper humor that remained. "And you suffered only banishment for your impertinence?"

Talik gave her a weak smile. "Only because my grandfather, the High Chieftain, is fond of me. I was his personal palif. His favorite grandchild. Yet, he banished me from my house, ripped me from all that I knew, murdered my mate, allowed the desecration of my temple, and witting, or unwitting, let the Methiliim plot my demise."

"What are you asking from us?" a man asked from the gathered elders.

"The question needing to be asked is, why," Talik said. "The Methiliim find me a threat to them. They murdered my Martrena," he nodded at a small gasp of recognition. Many in this room would know the name. "They feared my conciliatory words. They feared my power with my grandfather. What else did they fear? As I journeyed I had profound visions that require a wyseer's reading. I think the message in them is clear. I could be wrong. I read it as time to turn from Danat, to Kylik. It is a time to turn from the past and move forward, or we will see all our peoples drowned in blood. My visions are of another Withering, of all that is sacred to all of us. And there's one thing more, it is a suspicion that, well, I think they may have the Traveler."

Talik ignored the murmur from the back of the cavern, concentrating on Isra, who studied him closely.

At last she turned and looked at those gathered.

"He must speak with Atatha," one man said. "The Traveler is their business."

"Is this a sign, perhaps, that it is time?" another queried.

"Perhaps the time comes for the Fidrel to embrace the Kylalnethra," another said softly.

"If it is your will, I will take him to the Kylalnethra, and Atatha, and perhaps we can speak," Isra said softly.

Talik didn't understand the grave nodding of heads, almost a resignation, looks of fear cast amongst them. He remembered hearing of a schism amongst the Fidrel, and that one faction had been troubling the Methiliim, but that the Fidrel were the ones being captured and killed to feed the blood fires.

"Did the Methiliim grant you leave to seek the Fidrel?" Isra asked innocently, though Talik was acutely aware he was being scrutinized, closely.

"I think the Methiliim are disappointed they weren't able to find me on the Hot Springs Road and kill me as they intended. We avoided the roads. I don't think they expect to find me traveling with my niece, so I hope I'm not attracting their attention."

"If I didn't recognize the name, have some knowledge of your story, I wouldn't imagine you a palif, to look at you."

Danathea tried to hide a smile behind a cough. He nudged her and gave her a sharp look. "I do rather look more the warrior. My heart has always been as a servant to Danat. It is a deep loss to me that I understand these dreams are guiding me elsewhere."

It was only moments before a young adept had arrived to present Isra with a cloak against the night, and a pack that she slipped easily over one shoulder.

"I am taking you to a place that, we hope, remains hidden from the Pale. Yet, we would lead, unbidden, one of our enemy there. And it isn't all that certain that I will be welcome and trusted. But the concerns you raise are better understood there. They would know of the fate of the Traveler, and might need to heed any visions or warnings. And then, of course, there is the matter of Martrena. I must ask you to trust us, and allow us to blindfold you and your niece. The lives of our people force us to this indignity. Please forgive us."

Talik inclined his head slightly. "I regret that the years have not improved our relations. We are all Metathan. We all speak the same."

A hood slipped over his head, gently tugged shut with a drawstring. Suddenly, he felt closed off from the world. Words faded to the murmur of a brook. The darkness was so total he had no sense of light through the cloth, which didn't feel that heavy on his face. Yet he had no trouble breathing. He keenly sensed himself, his breaths, his heart beat, the gurgle of hunger in his belly, but nothing more but the slight movement of propulsion, perhaps an arm guided his. Perhaps he was lying down, or being carried, or maybe he simply floated above the ground being pulled along like a raft on a stream. He had the strangest sense of being everywhere, and nowhere, with the world a far thing that concerned him little. And as he floated upward, distant from the world, far from its cares, he saw the brilliant light of Kylik pulling itself from a glimmering sea as old blue-faced Danat slowly ground overhead, unnoticed. He watched Kylikrise in a strange slowed and silent reality, each wave seeming to pull another small piece of Kylik skyward, the night growing by miniscule degrees brighter and brighter, and Talik felt as if all time moved thus, and he in no hurry to move on from this vista.

At some point, he had the distinct sense that wyseery brought the vision, the sensation. The realization startled him, though on making the connection he felt stunned that he had so naturally accepted a vision. It made him want to retch. The ground seemed to shiver beneath his feet. He felt so misused. How dare they suggest a simple blindfold then use wyseery on him without his leave! He went to rip the hood off his head, but found it wasn't there. His eyes were closed.

He opened them to find blinding light, his ears suddenly full of pounding thunder that rumbled through the ground at his feet. The light dimmed to torchlight scattered throughout a deep cavern. As he slowly took in his real position in the world, uncertain for a moment if this was part of the vision, he realized he was propped against a sweating cavern wall, cushioned pillows beneath him and a warm blanket over his shoulders. Isra and several other wyseers sat on cushions around him.

"Danathea?" he asked, not seeing her as his eyes watered furiously in the dim light.

"Your niece sleeps beside you. Should we wake her, or would you like to speak with us privately? Please forgive the manner of your arrival. These are dangerous times. Were I to ask your leave to put you at our mercy, would you have willingly submitted?" Isra's tone was gentle. He heard strain in her voice and noted the set features of the other wyseers. He wondered what he'd awakened too late to hear.

Talik straightened a little and tried to regain his composure. He nodded that the hood should be removed from Danathea's head as well. In moments, she sat up and blinked at him. He wanted to know if she had the same strange journey. But now wasn't the time to explore the wilds of the mind.

"I did not share your … news. I merely told them you had dreams that needed interpreting and information to share that matters to all of us," Isra said. She gestured. "These are several of the members of the Kylalnethra council. Two of their number, Wilnath and Jia are … not here at this time. Here are Tiva, Dakul and, Atatha."

Talik stared at Atatha. The man was gnarled and bent, not so much with age, as Talik could see, but with a wearing existence. The man's features had a familiar cast about the eyes. Talik swallowed hard, pulling from deep within his training for the calmest voice he could find. He hadn't considered how he would do this. What could he say?

"Atatha, it is with deepest fondness and love that your daughter spoke of you. And thus, it is with profound sorrow that I bear the news of your daughter's murder," Talik said quietly as Atatha visibly arched, then sagged, his face portraying no emotion. "She was a wise and loving woman, mother to my niece, and she drove the hatred from my soul. She came to me troubled by the beating you had suffered, the murder of her mother, and as a slave of the Pale she came in search of the gods all people once worshipped, forgotten now. She was murdered, perhaps to strike at me, perhaps because they thought her the source of my talk of restraint, perhaps because they thought her a spy. At her hearing, they produced a letter to you, intercepted, that talked about the Methiliim and their violent and offensive rites, and their obsession with … Travel. Truly, her worst offense against the Pale was a true heart."

He saw Isra touch Atatha's hand. He simply stared, rocking a little as his mouth worked as if he chewed on a response too great to be swallowed. Talik felt Danathea's hand on him, and realized he was trembling, his hands clenched into white-knuckled fists.

Dakul cleared his throat uneasily. "You say it was murder? How so?"

"We do have process and law," Talik said, trying to keep the bitterness from his tone, failing. Danathea gripped his arm harder. "Martrena wasn't given that. She was named a traitor, given no defense, and was bled into the cauldrons of the Methiliim."

Atatha's breath came like a gasp. He held it a long minute, before letting out a sigh so deep that it seemed capable of shifting the rock walls of the cavern.

"Thank you, Talik, son I am first meeting. Martrena wrote of you and I came to think I knew of you, and that you were indeed honorable in your own fashion. I forgave her for not returning, knowing the hard life of the Fidrel might very well shorten her life. If one does not believe in the tenets of the Fidrel, one has no business remaining among them." Atatha turned his glance briefly on Isra, and Talik had a sense again of an unfinished conversation. "It is why I, too, turned from the dark years of our past. I will grieve in my way, but first let us hear why you have come. It certainly wasn't to bring me news that could have been more simply dispatched by messenger. And Martrena is but one of many Fidrel who have given their blood to the Pale."

Talik glanced at Danathea, who was gripping his arm hard and staring at him. "Yes, Danathea, she was a wyseer. I told you she knew them, rejected them and her home. She helped me see the wrong in the ways of the Methiliim. And though she professed no affiliation to the Fidrel at all when I petitioned for her freedom, she was indeed a wyseer, of a very different sort. She didn't practice blood arts like the Methiliim. And she didn't prepare for the return of the Traveler as the Fidrel. She simply sought solutions to the everyday life, her wyseery a help to her and others much as an acolyte aids a palif. So, indeed, Grandfather and Tarcatha may have a case when they say my acts were treasonous. I took no simple Valeutan as my mate."

Talik then turned to the council and spoke, slowly at first, of his experience, his dreams, Martrena's last days, her fears. He spoke without pretense, with nothing hidden. He knew better than to hide truth from a wyseer, but he needed them to know all if they were to understand the depth of his fear.

"So, you believe they have the Traveler," Isra said quietly as Talik ended his tale.

"I don't know. I've heard rumors that at first I doubted. But Martrena's words that day, she was right. They have become so urgent. I don't know what special mission they are building for, but they let blood at an astounding rate, taking over temples to Danat to gain strength from their sacrilege. In the past such bloodletting might occur one in two or three seasons. Now it is weekly. And they had never dared to cross the line of the Palifiim. It's as if they perceive a need for wyseery that exceeds anything ever known. Yet any talk of the Traveler or the Fidrel is greeted with great suspicion. Why was I so important, so key a threat? They know I had a strong influence over my grandfather. They know I bear the banners of history, including the time of the Withering—"

"Banners of history?" Tiva interrupted.

"If one is deemed a master of a branch or feature of knowledge, he bears his wisdom, so to speak, for the world to see. There is only ever one master at a time, the teacher of young and old. I *am* Metatha's history, personified, among the Pale. If one would answer to the past, as we must daily if we are to learn from it, then one must consult with the Master."

He carefully undid the ties on his blouse, to reveal the richly colored tattoos that interlaced much of his body with the history of Metatha. The gathered wyseers gazed with unabashed wonder at the lacery of Pale horsemen, smoking volcanoes, wars and famines, Valeutan ships, battling wyseers, and portals yielding oddities from far worlds. In tiny, intricately drawn images he wore the world's tale.

"Why would anyone banish the Master of History, unless the hope was to take a page from that history and instead of learn from it, repeat it?" Talik asked.

Tiva boldly pointed to a small figure in the center of his breastbone. It was of a green-robed Reign, pressing a small white stone into the hand of a robe-wrapped infant and about to cast it into water lapping up stone steps of a palace. At the Reign's feet was a blooded woman, womb slit open, her dead eyes gazing upon a Pale swordsman as a black hand of death, greater than all of them reached for them. Dancing in the open gash of the woman's womb was the manfish, and in the water where the babe was being cast was a symbol that denoted the portal to Earth.

"Among the Palifiim, there is no question what happened to the Traveler," Talik said quietly. "We were witnesses. It is why the threat has always been real to us. We had Denalku. But nowhere could the chieftain's wyseer, or the Traveling stone, be found. We knew that a Reign had been sent to Earth, and how time would pass on Earth. The Methiliim await the return of the Traveler most urgently because now would be the time of his return. Now such a babe would have reached maturity."

"This isn't anything new," said Tiva, sitting back and making a dismissive gesture. "The Pale have been seeking the Traveler here for more than a year. We know that. They know that. It doesn't explain anything."

"It does appear to show a level of assumption that surprises me," Dakul said. "Could it be that what they have been working on with their blood rites is a way to bring the Traveler to them, control him, perhaps even usurp the wyseery of the Traveling stone for themselves?"

"That's a lot of assumption," Tiva returned.

"But Palif Talik is quite right. What could be gained by the banishment and murder of the Master of History? There are no trained replacements," Atatha said. "Is it simply to control the Atannate? That isn't to our benefit, certainly. And I do see a great deal in the visions. It is the people, and a palif who survive the battle in the grasslands. It is another Withering of a global scale he sees in his second vision, and a closing of the portals."

"Atatha, do the Pale have the Traveler?" Isra asked, staring at him intently. "I have come to you today, not just to bring this man and his tales, but to tell you that the Fidrel Council have at last decided that it is time … time for us all to, as Talik says, embrace the future, rather than the past. The last we knew, he had returned to his own world. You must tell me, do they have the Traveler?"

Atatha looked from Tiva to Dakul, then gazed at Talik as he answered Isra. "Kyle is with Jia and Wilnath on a raid of a Pale encampment in retaliation for a Pale attack on Overmount and the Ridge."

"He's back!" Isra's eyes glittered, her hands clenched in her lap.

"We drew him back. It was wyseery. It was a cruel trick."

"How could you let Kyloreign risk being lost again?" Isra demanded. "What foolishness is this!"

"Welcome back, Isra," Atatha said with a sour note. "I have missed your calls to reason. But he went guarded by the ilyath, with werran assigned to protect him, and his own convictions that he would not lift a hand against another in a battle that isn't his. See, the battle isn't his. We may think it is, because we reason that he is Metathan and owes this to his people. But he is no more Metathan than the trinkets the Traveler seeks on other worlds. We can see even the Pale know: the moment he drew his first breath, it was the waters of a portal. His birth cries were first heard in a world that raised him. That is where his loyalties lie. We asked Kyle for inexcusable sacrifices. He had no idea what we face here. We have always filtered what we tell him. He rebelled. He almost died of our misuse of him. So, we sent him along to observe, so he would have a sense of why we use him so."

Talik glanced briefly at Danathea, seeing comprehension in her eyes and gratified by it.

"Kyle," Talik said. "Kylalnethra. I understand now. Kylik. This adds a new dimension to my visions, does it not?"

"It does indeed, Palif," Atatha said. "Turn from Danat to Kylik, and in the same way, it is turn from the old ways to the new. Kyle isn't simply a Traveler who marks a point in the lore of the Fidrel." Now Talik sensed Atatha's words were aimed at Isra again, could see it in her posture. "The Traveler was a catalyst for us, but also a symbol that it is time for us to progress as other worlds do. In five hundred years of subjection, Valeutans sat by and waited. The leaders, us, kept to our studies, waiting, waiting, offering only more study, no new thoughts, no solutions. Kyloreign is more than catalyst. He's almost a personification of Kylik. It is time to move ahead and learn to take care of ourselves, as the son must one day replace his father."

"You were the one who cautioned against allowing Kyloreign to be venerated and trusted when first he arrived. Now you equate him to a god. You surprise me, Atatha," Isra said.

"I did not say he *is* Kylik, I said he is almost a personification of Kylik. There is a great difference."

"The Traveler is a young man, but wise?" Talik asked, waiting for Atatha's nod. "Where did so young a man come by so great a wisdom? And what of Ruperion? Did he return with the Traveler?"

Atatha and Isra exchanged glances.

"Would that we'd had you here when the Traveler first found us, Talik," Tiva said.

"We believe Ruperion is unable to Travel," Atatha said. "We manipulated Kyle into not trusting Ruperion, who apparently raised him and certainly Kyle reflects his training. But he's a good young man who cares about Valeutans, and justice. But this isn't his battle. And he's right, we must change our ways, or be doomed to another Withering. He's warned us many times that we put so much faith in him, and he's the last Reign. What will we do when he is gone? Your words come all too clear to the Kylalnethra."

"Where are they? When are they due?" Isra asked.

"They should have returned by now," Dakul said. "They are two days overdue."

"So, the Pale may, indeed, have the Traveler," Isra said softly. "And Talik's dream was perhaps prophecy."

"Let us hope not," Talik said, staring into himself, watching the way each breath moved the babe in his banner closer to the water.

CHAPTER TWENTY

When Kyle opened his eyes he couldn't place himself. A warm breeze tossed the treetops overhead, as low and golden sunlight dappled the forest floor. He expected to hear the rap of a woodpecker or the whine of a chainsaw or perhaps the hum of dragonflies battling among the reeds beside the flowage. He felt something lying in the open palm of his hand. Had he dozed while fishing beside Potter's Flowage, his bobber now wedged in an old stump as a perch furiously circled beneath the surface to foul his line?

He tried to sit up. An ache roared through him as his head pounded. Everything came to him in a blazing flash. He looked around quickly. Jia lay unmoved beside the rock outcrop. The low sunlight revealed that while she remained ashen she still breathed. He turned to find what lay in his hand: the soldier's lifeless wrist, Jia's knife still gripped in the cold hand.

Kyle flung himself to his knees to retch as his head throbbed and the world canted about him. He'd seen magic, but it hadn't been the Pale wyseer. Certainly it couldn't have been Jia. He could discern no mark on the man.

What had he done? Had he done this? What was happening to him? Killed a man. It was self-defense, but this wasn't his battle, it was wrong.

He retched again, then scrambled to Jia's side. He found a pulse but couldn't rouse her. He didn't dare call out for help in the silent forest. He tucked her knife in the sheath at her side, and slipped the soldier's knife, lost in the clutter of Kyle's initial assault, in his own belt. He staggered to his feet with Jia's slight figure in his arms and trudged up the mountain.

The sun had risen well past mid-day before he stumbled to the edge of the hollow where they'd camped the night before. He heard a sentry's whistle, and in moments, Wilnath, his hand swathed in a poultice, had swept Jia off somewhere out of sight. Kyle looked up, startled, to realize that Barul had a hand on his arm, leading him toward a small cleft beneath a shelf of rock where an adept treated four wounded and Wilnath already peered into Jia's pale features.

"We searched for you and found no trace. We feared the worst," Barul said as he helped Kyle onto a soft mat stuffed with leaves.

"We didn't get far," Kyle said, his voice coming hoarse and so low he wasn't sure he'd even spoken.

Wilnath held up Jia's bloody knife, and gave Kyle a quizzical look. "I don't see a wound on her."

"Smashed against a boulder, might be internal," Kyle muttered, then yelped as something suddenly stung, then burned on his scalp. He felt the warmth of blood running down his neck and tried to swipe the offense away, only to find his bloody hand gripped by an adept armed with a bone needle.

"The wound needs to be cleaned and closed, Traveler," the adept said with a bob of his head. "And you've bruised your brain. I think you will be fine, but we must tend you."

"What else could be her ailment?" Wilnath appeared before him so suddenly, his hands on Kyle's face keeping him from rearing back into the adept. He realized it had been a gentle gesture. He clenched his eyes shut tight then opened them again, finding his concentration slipping and skipping again, like those lost days in Madison.

"Wyseery I think, that … No, that was me. No." He closed his eyes and tried to concentrate. There, he saw it all again. "Some blaze of light struck him, I think. He fell on her. She never woke … I'm afraid the rest of it, I…." Kyle stared at nothing a long moment while an image sorted itself out before he met Wilnath's gaze. "I must have killed him. I don't know how. He tried to stab Jia, but I … I don't know what happened. There wasn't a mark on him, either."

"Do you think it was … like before?" Wilnath asked softly.

Kyle tried to nod, but the adept and Barul held his head steady. "But no burn. I thought it could be from their wyseer. Oh, man, did I really kill him?" A tremor ran through his limbs, a shiver that roared up through him. He wanted to retch again.

"If you had not, Jia would be dead and you their prisoner," Wilnath said firmly. "There was another wyseer? He fought with you?"

"No, on the road. We didn't get far. Jia couldn't make it. There were five or six soldiers with him. I heard some fighting in the woods. Then this one came on with an empty quiver."

"We lost two more wounded," Wilnath said with a nod. "The gods are watching over us that we suffered no deaths. You carried her all this way, injured as you are?"

"What, you want me to leave her behind?" Kyle returned more sharply than he intended.

"Well," Wilnath said around a grin. "When she was younger I would have wholeheartedly said yes. It must have been an overwhelming struggle to bring her here alone. I'm indebted to you."

"To tell you the truth, Wil, I don't think I can remember it."

"Rest, Traveler. When the sun falls behind the peak we'll set out for Hindlain. Our fallen will slow us, but Jia needs more than we can do for her here. And we need to return you to a safe haven."

The few hours they waited for the sun to fall low seem to plod by. Kyle's head throbbed too intensely for sleep, but he was too groggy to think, much less sit up or eat. Finally, as the shadows grew long on the eastern slopes, they packed up and left the hollow. The hike over broken hills and through scragged woods left him again in a daze. He refused to be carried like the other wounded, imagining the awful swinging of a litter would be worse than being bed-spin drunk, and likely to bring back the dry heaves that made his guts ache. But the hike left him so light-headed and weak Barul had taken his arm and led him to keep him from stumbling.

Wil, too, appeared less than sturdy. Perhaps there was more poison in Methil Sethina's bite than they had imagined. He muttered something of the like to Barul, uncertain even what words he'd chosen. Barul's eyebrows knit briefly before he spoke a soft word to a companion, who moved ahead to speak with Wil. Had he spoken truly? Prophetically? Or was the passing of the message to Wil simply more deference to the Traveler?

As they trudged through the gloom of nightfall darkened by heavy clouds rolling in from the sea, Kyle wondered if the Kylalnethra could even dare to face the Pale without stronger wyseery. But it took no effort to recall Uncle Rupert teasing the Nelson clan about Travelers hauling home bazookas and shoulder missiles among their loot. In what way was Travel, the very thing he did, any better than blood wyseery? The bottom line was Metathans would die. His only comfort, and fear, was that they would never send him to Earth for tools, at least, not yet.

CHAPTER TWENTY-ONE

The thunder of Hindlain's falls had never felt so welcoming, despite the way it seemed to feed the throb in his head. The cold mist enveloped them like a breath of homecoming. Kyle stumbled, catching himself before a tumble would have sent him plummeting hundreds of feet to the rocky shore below, likely pulling Jia and Barul with him.

He glanced at Barul, finding the man's pale face wet with mist, his eyes wide as he waited for Kyle to right himself. For a slip of a young woman, Jia was a slack burden that only grew more weighty with each hillside they trudged across.

They continued along the trail, two werran rearguard cleansing the path of any sign they had passed. At last, they slipped around the curtain of water.

He could barely hear the gasp and a shout of alarm over the thunderous falls. The blaze of the torch-lit cave sent his head pounding harder. He stared down at his feet until his eyes adjusted, noting that somewhere he had lost his shoes and he had somehow trudged along on bruised and bloody feet.

"Kyle! Where's Wilnath?"

He recognized Tiva's voice and looked up to find instead that Isra stood before him. The cave took a cant to one side and he almost lost his balance. Someone pressed him onto a stool and set the cool liquid to his lips that he knew would help bring clarity.

"Where's Wilnath?" Tiva asked again.

"Pinned down, four dells over. We feared discovery as we tried to retreat. He's trying to lead them off the trail, but we needed to get Jia to safety and … "

"And?" Isra prompted.

"And, me. We didn't want me to fall in their hands. Wil's injured. It's a poisonous wound, something from Methil Sethina's wyseery burned him."

"Sethina!" Tiva spat the word like an oath.

"Who has the stone?" Isra demanded.

"I do," Kyle stated, feeling an old anger rekindled.

"That seems a foolish risk. How can you let him—" Isra began as she turned to Tiva.

"How can they not and be any better than the Pale?" Kyle interrupted, ignoring the way Isra flared at his rudeness.

"It's not at all the same." Isra sputtered, but Tiva had touched her shoulder.

"We do not treat the Traveler with such disrespect, Isra. If you will not honor those we honor, you are not welcome to witness matters involving Kyloreign."

Isra's mouth fell open a little then she nodded curtly to Tiva.

"Forgive me, Traveler. I forget my place, and yours."

Kyle gave her a spare nod, distracted by Atatha's appearance and that of the sandy-haired bear of a figure behind him. Barul trotted along speaking quietly and urgently into Atatha's inclined ear, pointing at the back of his head as he spoke. It didn't surprise Kyle when Atatha unceremoniously pulled Kyle's head forward to look at the bloody knot and stitches.

Kyle sucked in a breath at a closer view of the sandy-haired man who might have been a brother to the Pale soldier he'd killed above the Ta'atit Road. Tattoos peaked from beneath his tunic, a trio of moons dangling from his fingers like rosary beads, and a young girl dogged his steps with an expression both more wise and more solemn than he expected. The man studied him as he rubbed an unruly beard with the moons dangling and flashing in the torchlight.

"Um, Atatha, I don't know if you've noticed, these people are Pale." He winced a little as Atatha pressed against the knot, then pulled Kyle's head up to look him in the eye.

"Yes, I noticed," Atatha said as he let light fall in Kyle's eyes, then shaded them.

"And Isra's here."

"Yes, I noticed that, too. She arrived with the Pale, Palif Talik Atannen."

"Like the High Chieftain of the Pale Atannen?"

"You paid attention, Kyle. The very. This is his grandson, mate to my daughter."

"You have a daughter?"

"I had a daughter. I lived a long life before you came along to complicate it, Kyloreign. A most boring and unsatisfactory life, but one nonetheless." Atatha stood. "He will survive, though he will need bed rest until his brain heals."

"Are you well, Atatha?" Kyle whispered as he took in Atatha's sour expression beneath eyes deeply shadowed. "You don't appear your jolly self."

Atatha dismissed his concern with a wave of his hand. He sprouted the hint of smile as he helped Kyle to his feet. "I can't recall ever being … jolly."

Too weary to protest, Kyle allowed himself to be led to his bed, the commotion of the cavern a distant hum as reinforcements prepared to rush to Wilnath's aid. Furtive murmurs nearby came from those charged to see to his needs. Low conversation from near Atatha's niche sent only the occasional word his way. He knew Barul retold their tale. He knew others hovered over Jia. At last he slept, finding the thin mat comfortable after several days in cold and stony camps.

A sudden and impending silence drew him to open his eyes and turn to find the Pale man sitting beside him just as the bloom of headache returned. He closed his eyes, the images from the man's half-bared, tattooed chest leaving behind their ghosts, especially one that leapt at him with the certainty of truth.

"How is it you have the alleged legend of my birthday tattooed on your chest, when even the Fidrel argued over how I could have come to be?" Kyle asked softly.

"I am Palif, and Master of History. It's my job to know all there is to know of history and those things that matter to the Palifiim."

Kyle struggled a moment to sort through the Pale's heavy accent.

"Travel has been the root of many of Metatha's troubles," the palif continued. "It binds the history of our world and even usurped the worship of Danat. Thus Travel is important to an historian. When at last our people overthrew the evil Denalku we found the journals, records and histories of Valeutan abuses of Metatha, and we came across Chamberlain Shedal cutting his grandchild from his daughter's womb to throw it into rising Lake Ta'atit."

Kyle watched as Talik traced an image in the tattoo with a reverence that seemed to bring silence to the caverns.

"Shedal's might have been just one more barbaric atrocity in a war of great atrocities, if it weren't for the stone in the babe's grip. As the babe sank in its swaddle of Reign cloak, the flails of a fish were seen. It was a moment that has lived in speculation and mystery in the generations since. Such a powerful last statement, don't you think? Was it Shedal hoping to rescue a friend on the other side of the portal? Or to send his grandson to safety? Or to lock away this dangerous tool in the only way he knew how? Why his grandson and not himself? We will never know these things. But we do know much."

"I wish Shedal had never had that moment then," Kyle muttered.

"Oh, I disagree, Kyloreign," Talik said easily in a gentle voice that belied the man's build. "In truth, the Pale reached an impasse that would have happened with or without you. The Methiliim have repeated the history of the Valeutans: the power of wyseery has driven Danat from their leaders' hearts and they cannot gain enough power to sate themselves. I fear they are no longer satisfied to be the servants of leaders. Without Kyloreign, there would be no one to resist them. The Fidrel were weak, ineffective and unprepared," Talik gave a conciliatory nod toward Isra and council members who had gathered as Talik spoke. "But the Kylalnethra, that is a different story."

"Catalyst Kyle, that's me," Kyle muttered sourly. "But you're one of them. Why are you here?"

Talik stiffened, looking nothing like the kindly servant of Danat he had appeared a moment before. His pale eyes went steely and with that tattooed barrel of a chest and beard, he looked more like a lumberjack spoiling for a brawl.

"One of them? The Pale? Yes, guilty. Methiliim? Not even close. They are wyseers, mostly of Valeutan ancestry, dedicated to power and I am a palif dedicated to the gods. They murdered my mate, Atatha's daughter. They desecrated my temple, destroyed my credibility before my Chief and saw me banished to where they hoped I would die. They did not do this because I was a servant to them, certainly. But because I sounded a voice of reason against them."

"I'm still not clear on the threat you posed," Tiva said.

"Neither am I, to be truthful. I suspect they feared I was a Fidrel spy, or sympathizer, or that I would somehow raise the populace against them, or turn my grandfather's ear."

"Maybe it's because you knew the history," Kyle said.

"Yes," Talik said slowly. "But what in history did I know that threatens them?"

"Maybe what Rupert—Ruperion—knew," Kyle replied, recalling those summer nights beside the fire as Rupert gathered the young to hear his stories. "He talked about a watery void and the creation of the moons where guardian gods rested while they watched over Metatha. He told how the pre-born and the dead passed through the void until at last they live upon Metatha among the gods, and take their final swim home to Danat. He spoke of how an unnatural and arrogant wyseery opened the portals, though he never claimed responsibility. He's the one who opened the portals and explored each world. And he's the one who found the wyseery and made the bans. Rupert was Travel. Is this history recorded in the journals the Pale found?"

Talik nodded. "But they weren't complete. And it was quite clear that Ruperion easily violated the very bans he created."

"Exactly," Kyle said. "You would probably recognize attempts to bypass the bans and likely you have a record of what the wyseers collected from each portal."

"What are you getting at, Kyle?" Isra asked, leaning forward. He could see she knew exactly where he was taking them and feared him going there.

"The bans can be undone," Kyle said.

Isra leaned back. Talik was nodding. He knew.

"Rupert, Ruperion, once said he wished he hadn't created the bans because it wasn't enough. He never said any of it directly. It was always twisted up in stories, but I see it now. He was the great undoer who had left one thing undone. He regretted not simply closing the portals to the most dangerous worlds forever. He could do it. He'd opened them. He could close them. I asked him why, when so many hundreds of years had gone by in Metatha, why did he hover over the portal, never leaving for long, as if afraid he'd miss something. If he was just waiting for me to grow up, he wouldn't have needed to watch the portal the way he did. Unless he thought someone was bound to figure it out and would come through one day. Was it because he'd left a record? Is that what the Methiliim have done? Figured it out? Clearly they need me if Travel is their interest. Or maybe they don't. They haven't been that aggressive about finding or keeping me if I'm the only tool. Those were killing shots that were fired at me and Jia and they knew very well whom they sought. Maybe they simply want me dead so that Travel wyseery is not part of the even playing field. They don't want the competition."

Kyle could feel their eyes on him. It all seemed so clear to him as if he'd needed a knock on his head to knit together all of Rupert's stories at last.

"It would explain my dreams," Talik said softly. "The devastation of a Withering so clearly seemed to be related to Travel, and blood."

"But what remained in your vision was Kylik," Atatha said. "That's something, too. You saw a cleansing. Your vision in the grasslands was of an ordinary man standing there, not wyseers."

"But in the other vision, the rotting manfish, Martrena stood on the black beach, the blood falling and filling the ocean. You know she was Fidrel. That vision showed destruction of the Fidrel and the Methiliim unchecked."

"I don't know what vision you had," Kyle said, picking his words as if he were dancing around an essay on a lit exam. "But if it is the black beach I dreamed about, I have a sense that dream has more to do with a search, and less to do with an outcome. It might not be the *death* of the Fidrel you foresaw, but the *end* of the Fidrel, and maybe the end of Travel. I don't know why Isra's here, but it looks like the Kylalnethra are growing, while the Fidrel fail. In this battle of blood, the Fidrel are the losers."

Kyle shrugged, wondering at the clarity of it all. Was it the blow to his head, or the blinding flash of whatever had come from him to save him on the hillside above the Ta'atit Road that brought it together? He had a keen sense of Rupert, close to him. It felt oddly comforting, yet not.

"But what import is such a vision to me?" Talik asked, his hands furiously working the glittering stones with their depictions of the moons on them.

"To lead you here?" Atatha suggested. "Your visions perhaps show that it is wisdom that will prevail, not wyseery."

"You know where we have been," Dakul said. "You are here to keep us from repeating the errors of the past."

"It didn't help with my grandfather," Talik said as he studied his moons. He looked up at Kyle, his eyes seeming so extraordinarily bright in the gloomy cavern. "Perhaps, together, we can unmask the wyseery behind Ruperion's work."

"I will help you," Isra stated. "You will need one who knows wyseery to understand."

"I am thinking of another wyseer." Atatha's words, though soft, brought silence. Kyle glanced from Isra to Atatha. Isra bristled, but then with a curt nod she yielded to Atatha. "This will be a good way to keep Jia here to recover."

"Wil needs a similar diversion," Kyle said as a commotion at the entrance preceded Wilnath and his haggard rearguard. Wilnath's arm had swollen to twice its size and a fever lit his eyes. "I don't know what was in Sethina's parting shot, but it hasn't given up yet."

As the council broke to meet the new arrivals, Kyle sank back, feeling a strange clarity he didn't remember ever having in Metatha before.

Atatha lingered a moment, then stooped low beside him.

"I don't know what happened to you and Jia, Kyle, or, for that matter, to Wil," Atatha said. "It's wyseery, all of it. Somehow, you have either practiced a powerful wyseery, or been a conductor for it. I don't understand. That's why I don't want Isra working with you and Talik. I'm not certain I trust her judgment, or her intent."

Atatha spun away, his green robe sweeping the floor with purpose.

As Kyle's ears strained to hear word of Wilnath's arrival, an image of Rupert planted itself in his thoughts as he considered all that Rupert had ever said about the making of Travel. But it wasn't besotted bagman Rupert that came to mind when Kyle closed his eyes. He saw someone younger and taller, whose black eyes beckoned like an abyss that Kyle couldn't escape.

CHAPTER TWENTY-TWO

The mountain air stung his lungs like the chill fall of snowflakes on his face. It might be summer beside Lake Ta'atit, but high up in the hills beside the spring pond that led … led to a place he didn't want to go, here the seasons were turned on their ear. Jia stood beside him, her knife in her hand, her mouth grimly set. He sensed her fear. He knew it well. It came with his every swim. That fear of being helpless in a place with no friends to call on and nothing familiar. He tapped the pouch that held his Traveling stone, bound to his leg and woven to his belt to prevent its loss in a far world.

"You remember what I told you?" Kyle asked her. "Don't panic or flail or kick. Simply follow me. You need to be very cautious on your return that you don't over swim or you'll come up downstream. Here, that may well be tumbling down a falls or in an underground spring."

Jia nodded and shivered as she dropped her cloak beside the pond, ready to warm her on their return.

"I need to … do something when we return, but not as a manfish, as a man. So follow me closely. When I surface, you surface. Then I will submerge again."

"Be wise in your Travel, Jia," Tiva said. "One eel. It needn't be the largest. Just one. It needn't be alive."

Kyle studied the forest that crowded close to the clearing around the pond. He missed Wilnath's encouraging patter, but Wilnath still battled Sethina's curse, a fever that swept him into delirium and defied Talik and Atatha's ministrations. Eel oil was a fixant, they told him, it made things stronger, more resilient, and somehow it easily replicated itself, like yeast in the sourdough sponge his mother kept on top of the refrigerator. They hoped a drop of that oil would strengthen the small gains they made battling Wilnath's fever. If they must face more Methiliim, they were likely to encounter more such wounds. It seemed so hopeless when one wyseer in defeat could have such a devastating effect on the battle's victorious.

"Kyloreign?" Tiva prodded and he startled, realizing he'd been so lost in his thoughts that Tiva was already fearing for him. "We will await your return."

He took Jia's hand and gave her a small, reassuring smile and gripped a knife in his other hand. He hesitated, remembering his last journey to the eels ... but it wouldn't happen again. His thoughts screamed at him not to go. This wasn't his battle, just wait, wait, wait. But he didn't know for what he should wait. He certainly couldn't tell the anxious wyseers that he had reservations. Was he simply afraid of the eels? Of course he was.

He tugged and he and Jia slipped into the icy spring, and with a flick of his tail he led her deeper, deeper into a murky place devoid of light. He recognized the bitter, metallic taste of this place. He pulled her toward the surface, where a howling wind full of spray slapped him, his lungs seizing in revulsion at the hint of methane and sulfur. The dark night was lit by lightning from low clouds. Something brushed against him. He could barely discern Jia beside him, still clutching his hand.

"We'll never see them coming!" he shouted at her, hoping she could hear him over the wind. He hoped she would tell him to go back. She broke from his grasp.

"It's too dark, I won't find you!" he shouted.

Suddenly the dark fled as a blaze lit in her hands. Before he could exult, the sea erupted in a boil of serpentine backs. Teeth flashed in the light. Suddenly, a giant eel erupted, rearing from the water as if pulled by a line. Instinctively he swung his knife at it, its writhing body pulling the knife free. Jia was beside him again, her hand grasping his shirt.

"Now, now, go, go!" she shouted over and over in his ear as he dived down into the swirl of fangs and slap of eely flesh. He thought he glimpsed small flashes of light beneath the surface, shocks from some electrified eel, or distant lightning strikes, or perhaps even the ghost images of Jia's wyseery.

He swam, urgently, uncertain if Jia had an eel, or what had become of the one he had stabbed or whether either of them had been injured.

He erupted from the pond with a gasp, his heart pounding, as fowl took flight into a blazing bright sky.

Arms were near, but he shook them off. He saw Jia, stunned, a streak of blood on her arm, dragging an eel onto the bank, her knife still wedged in it, but its jaws gaping for the nature of its world.

"Is Kyle—" he heard Jia begin as he sank beneath the surface of the pond, the water angry and cold, his heart still pounding. He felt around the muddy bottom, seeking the upwelling of cold water. He must be careful not to dive or he'd again be among the eels. At last he reached the spring, the sandy spongy soil billowing up at him. Just beyond it, a small shelf of rock jut out protectively over the spring, and there, as he expected, he found the sliver of Baraboo quartzite wedged between stones where Rupert's own logs told Talik he had placed it centuries ago.

He gripped the quartzite and prepared to gasp for air but suddenly the metallic taste was in his mouth. He almost shouted his protest. Had he locked himself out of Metatha? He flailed. The storm had passed, the sky clear to reveal a fractured and cratered moon that lit the sea a sickly yellow. And just there, floating, he found an eel with his knife in it, no sign of any foraging upon it, and no hint of other eels nearby. He grabbed the vile and slimy thing and dived as deep as he could, the yellow light of that sickly moon chasing him.

He reared up from the pool and launched the eel toward the bank, where it fell in reeds, startling ducks from a nest. No clouds of birds rose from the surface, but neither did he find any Kylalnethra.

He clambered from the pool, seeking his green robe beckoning warm and dry with a light layer of snow atop it. He crouched slightly at the sound of a commotion from the forest to the west. He didn't dare dive back in the pool to save himself. He would sooner die. Besides, if everything he understood from Talik and his memories of Rupert was true, he had just closed the portal to that world.

As he stepped onto the bank he felt the sting as air found the long gashes in his calf. An eel's tooth had even broken free and remained lodged in his flesh. He staggered to the green robe and donned it, wondering what had happened to Jia. How much time passed in his few moments in the eel world? Enough passed there from their first journey for the storm to end and the skies to clear. Had they waited for days for him? Had Jia been injured, Tiva hurrying her to safety?

He turned at the sound of a boot against stone, expecting to find Tiva and Jia had merely awaited him in the shelter of the forest.

The breath caught in him, more than travel weariness turning his limbs to lead. Three crimson-robed Methiliim grinned back at him.

CHAPTER TWENTY-THREE

Rupert took deep calming breaths of anticipation as they padded up through the forest, the damp wind in the treetops above warning of how the easterlies from the sea would try to pull them from the bare plateau and rocky trail. Far below, a boil of Kylik-lit surf would froth at the black rocks of shoreline where once a vast marina stood, a water-powered tram swiftly winging people and their goods up the mighty cliff.

They would be most open when the trees gave way to weathered boulder and tufts of grass, the moon marking them to anyone who watched the trail. And those he hoped to meet hated him, reviled him, had named him the destroyer of his Clan. He had always been the master undoer. He must undo again. A tricky feat, for that which he must undo had been set by the master, him.

"They'll kill me." Davath said it softly, his feet stumbling to a halt just as they left the cover of forest.

Rupert lay a reassuring hand on the young man's shoulder. "Now you worry? You said you understood what must be done."

"I also understand I may be in a wyseer's spell," Davath said. "If I lead Metatha's nightmare to Hindlain then have I not committed treason, whether I'm under a spell or not?"

"I used wyseery on you exactly twice. To mend your injuries, and to learn what I needed to know. That is all. You are free to go. Though I had hoped you had come to trust me. And I think you understand why I think you are being foolish. You know what must be done. I must now convince your leaders."

Davath nodded, resigned to a fate that would likely see him floating on the sea in the morning, a feast to a thousand scavenging birds. As the young werran moved on again, his gait revealed his reluctance. He saw Kyle in the man's posture. Reluctant Kyle who always did as the master told him, but hated every moment of it. Rupert chewed on that thought until it was something bitter he had to spit, almost striking a flitterbird hovering beside his shoulder.

Davath had a reason to fear. He had his back to a powerful wyseer, eldest. Yet even Rupert had blundered. It had only been weeks since he had sent Kyle careering into this world to achieve an agenda he'd worked on for decades and centuries with no admission that things might be vastly different, that wyseery might have changed, that there might be cults and legends surrounding Travel. What would be his next blunder? Would he underestimate the wyseery of this world? Rupert was new to second-guessing himself and finding it an unpleasant exercise. He spat again, intentionally striking the flitterbird, which darted away with an angry chirp.

Davath stopped, looking over his shoulder at Rupert a moment before he made a low bird call in the palms of his hands. The response surrounded them and Rupert heard movement coming at them from all sides but the empty space that would plunge him to the rocky shore below. He stared at Davath's back feeling an unfamiliar flicker of fear. He couldn't fail Kyle. He could cast a small spell and Davath would echo whatever Rupert wanted him to say. But even an inexperienced wyseer could see through such a simple spell and immediately doubt him. Instead, Rupert set his shoulders and opened his hands, palm out.

"What traveler walks this path?" the query came.

"It is Davath. We speak the same." Davath said quickly. "I have found a servant of Kyloreign and must bring him to the council."

"Who vouches for this servant? How do we know he is not false?"

"I—I vouch for him," Davath said. "He saved my life. I was almost killed in a skirmish on the Overmount side. He bears news for the council's ears."

"We must give him a name."

"Wisconsin," Rupert replied. He saw a shadowy figure briefly bob its head, turn and dash along the trail with the sureness of a mountain goat.

Only moments passed before the runner returned, with reinforcements. Hands were on Davath, and in an instant, Rupert felt the press of spear points in his side nudging him away from the thunder and mist of the falls and along a path that crept back beneath the eaves of the forest. Vast Lake Ta'atit glimmered, sparkling amid the myriad fowl sleeping on its surface, then disappeared as they descended to deep forest shadows at the feet of the northern cliffs. At last, a moon-washed glade opened around them, edged by the inky blackness of forest. Kylik's light fell on it more brightly than a full Earth moon on fresh snow. He stood, still and certain, waiting. Would they simply execute him? Or would curiosity draw them to address their fears first?

He didn't have long to wonder. He sensed the gathering of wyseers, and slowly, werran filled the clearing. Some of those gathered stood poised to utter a spell, others to loose an arrow. Without even looking he knew where the strongest wyseers were in the gathering, most of them in a small knot that stood apart as they regarded him. Beside him, Davath remained stiff, his chin thrust out as he gazed upon Kylik as if in defiant prayer.

The tease of wyseery brushed against him and Rupert turned to the knot of wyseers that had emerged from the forest shadows. Among them, a slip of a girl in a green mantle that dragged the ground behind her strode up to Davath.

"You are under no spell! What betrayal is this? How could you bring Ruperion to Hindlain!" she demanded of Davath, her fists clenched as if to beat him to the ground.

Rupert heard the gasps of the werran around him, felt the fear, the anger. Some hothead was bound to kill them. Davath hadn't answered yet, the wyseer raised her fist as if to strike.

"You assume I'm Ruperion."

"If you thought `Wisconsin' would send a secret message only to Kyle, you were mistaken," she returned, and he heard in her tone not fear, but anger. "Besides, I recognize you."

Rupert peered at her in the pale light and nodded. "You are Jia, opponent for the soul of my protégé."

Rupert's hands remained out and up. If anything about him startled her, she kept it well hidden. He sensed, too, the wyseery that she likely thought guarded her from anything he might do.

"He found it quite easy to dismiss you."

"Indeed. You seeded the ground well. Since it was never my intent to harm anyone, I did not prepare him for the deceit he would face."

"And you, of all people, the architect of Metatha's woes find deceit surprising? Why did you come? You were warned. Kyle warned you, I know he did. And how?" She cast a glance at Davath, who retained his rigid stance, not acknowledging the physical threat of her so close.

"Do not blame Davath for being open-minded to wise words. There are no spells around him you can see that clearly."

Rupert had to swallow down his urge to let his wrath fall on her impertinence in the face of an elder. The elder.

"I came because I knew Kyle needed me. I came because from his words I saw that things have gone terribly wrong here. I came because I am the maker of Travel wyseery and it is my wyseery that is being corrupted. I came because I am the master undoer and there is undoing to be done. I know Kyle closed the portal to the world of the eels." Rupert smiled a little. "He didn't tell you he was going to do that, did he? It wasn't my guidance alone that led him to that act. He knew it was the wise thing to do, though he nearly died in the trying. And I know you have lost him. I knew you would. I knew, better than you, what would happen if you won him, because the same was done to me. I knew you would use him until there would be nothing left but a body held together by wyseery that you could toss into a portal to serve as your key."

"How dare he address a member of the council this way!" someone muttered from behind him.

Jia waved a hand and absolute silence came instantly but for the wind in the trees. Another small signal sent the encircling guard several paces back, effectively beyond hearing.

"Very nearly that might have happened," she said softly. "Was that your spell, then, that saved him?"

"Saved him? When? He draws on Travel wyseery, but in him it is wild and untrained. I have tried to help him with wyseery, and by revealing what I could in his thoughts, just as you did when you drew him back. But you have cast my guidance in doubt, to his peril. He should never have crossed that portal." Before he could stop himself, his voice rose and took on a note of rebuke. "He had no business entering that sea of eels visible! Do any of you have even the faintest understanding of Travel? That world wasn't even the most perilous he might have been thrust into."

Jia shuddered a moment and glanced back at the council who stood behind her. "We were prepared to protect him," she said. "If the Reign passed these portals in the past—"

"Do you know how long Travelers have been Traveling?" he interrupted, ignoring the angry mutters of those who saw a council member defiled by their enemy's insolence.

"Since the reign of High Chief Despan."

"Incorrect. Despan was only the first Reign to Travel, after the bans. Who do you think advised Despan? That's right, Ruperion. Who do you think created the bans? That's right, Ruperion. Travelers have been Traveling since Ruperion undid the locks. And you would tell me you think you know enough about Travel to know what you are doing? Based on what first-hand knowledge?"

Jia bristled but retained her reserve, even as Rupert felt the heat rising in his face. The arrogance! They stared down history and dismissed it. He noted several of those in the council move closer as if preparing to drive him to his death with their childish wyseery.

"We based it on the lore collected as best we could after your actions brought the destruction of the Valeutans."

"Point scored, but inappropriate," Rupert returned. "When it came to the perilous places, we did not risk the life of a chieftain. We sent his servant. That is how one becomes a Traveling wyseer against the bans, much as you, Jia, have tasted Travel. In your earnest and mistaken fear of the evil Ruperion, you forget that I was a servant to my chieftain, not the leader of my Clan. You also forget that I have been Kyle's uncle, he my etlith. I came here out of fear for Kyle and duty to the woman who raised him as her own, not for me. In ways, not even for Metatha."

"Why come to the Kylalnethra?" Jia asked him, the anger softened in her tone. "You know he isn't here. You put Davath's life at risk. Your own. Did you think we would welcome you with open arms?"

"You welcomed a Traveler. In truth, I am the Traveler." He gave her a small smirk that drew a quizzical look. "You welcomed a Pale priest." He gestured at the man among the council. "In Kyle you found a tool. In the palif, you found history— Yes even from here I can see the aura of a master historian about him. You saw that they might benefit you and brought them among you. Do not give me those wounded looks as if I have somehow insulted you. If you are honest with yourselves you know that it has always been about what you, the Fidrel or Kylalnethra, could gain from them. It is the scavenger's way, and in that it is my fault. If I have done any great harm to Metatha it was not in any action against the Pale. It was the mistake I made thinking I could stop the wyseers' wars with the ultimate undoing. That one moment changed us from an innovative people to a people who are not. Once we built palaces, crafted fine arts and wovens, our sailing ships plied the seas. It took no time to forget, to rely only on the wyseery and forget the rest. Your lore remembers wyseers' tools, not the older knowledge. Do you know why the manfish trees were so important? It had nothing to do with dreams or prophecy. It was because the fruit cured disease and contained critical essences of nutrition.

"Valeutans, Metathans, became scavengers, not users of knowledge, so that they could not remember how to exist without the Traveler. And now you have lost the Traveler, your ultimate tool of hope. I come to you because there is something I can do for you, that will also help me. You do not want Kyle in the hands of the Pale. Too late, that is where he is." A murmur moved among the gathered wyseers.

"I can find him and I can save him," Rupert continued. "But not alone."

"We're to believe the great Ruperion, master wyseer, needs us, the vanquished fools who cannot even manage the Traveler, much less his wyseery? You think we hopeless vagabonds can't fend for ourselves without begging the great Ruperion's aid?" Jia asked.

"Please, Wise Jia," Davath said. "Please don't mock him. He is eldest and greatest among the Valeutan wyseers. Try to imagine what strength it takes to ask those you know wish to kill you for their help."

"I have some familiarity with that," the Pale priest said, coming to Jia's elbow, his gaze locked on Ruperion as if he looked upon history personified, which he did.

"It is different for you, Palif Talik," Jia said softly, not taking her defiant gaze from Rupert. "You had never personally harmed any of us, or given us reason to believe you would. You are a man of the gods and lore, not wyseery, war and politic. Your bond with Martrena vouchsafed you."

"Has Ruperion personally harmed anyone here?" Talik asked. "I don't believe he has lifted a hand against any of you. And as far as I have read he has not personally lifted a hand against any of your ancestors, or, for that matter, mine. We have gone over the histories together, Jia. You have heard from me, the enemy, that the documents make it clear: Ruperion intended no harm to Metathans and may have been banished precisely to stop him from speaking up against the weapon that brought the Withering. It's the same predicament that drove me to abandon all and appeal to my enemy. It was Denalku who gave the orders to collect the weapons, and to use them. Yes, Ruperion was a formidable wyseer five hundred years ago. It was he who had the strength to stop the wyseer wars. It was he who had the power to master Travel. Perhaps his wisdom will help us stop them again."

Rupert found himself staring at his feet. He had never expected to be defended by his enemy. He could still hear the pounding hooves as the horsemen of the Pale thundered over the plains, their battle cries chasing all before them. Woe to the hapless Valeutan they spied on their way. Generations had passed and the horsemen were gone. Yet, only twenty years separated this Pale priest and those who murdered Rupert's people. Yet he spoke so softly, and of mutual goals.

"Wise One, when Kyloreign entered the portal Ruperion fell, I watched over him," Davath said softly. "It was a trance of sorts as he tried to send Kyloreign strength to overcome his weariness and the eel attack and the betray—" Davath paused and glanced at Rupert before turning a kindling anger on Jia. "Why aren't *you* trying to find him and retrieve him?"

"Davath," Rupert said softly.

The man stiffened, his eyes going wide. "Forgive me, Wise One," Davath said to Jia, his head bobbing over his arms.

"I do not believe Jia would willingly do him harm, and I do not believe she chose to lose him," Ruperion said.

Jia inclined her head slightly.

"One could assume it was a simple mistake. Or, it could be, as Davath was about to say, a betrayal."

Rupert heard a pshaw rip through the clearing from someone among the council.

Jia looked over her shoulder as a bent wyseer lay a hand on her arm in the manner of a mentor relieving his etlith.

"Atatha," she said, "Perhaps I am too subjective."

"You've done well," Atatha returned, before appraising Rupert, though his words were for Davath. "What brought you to his defense, Davath? You have been loyal to the werran and the Kylalnethra, and for good reason."

"Yes, Wise One, I have," Davath said. "And I remain so. I was too cowardly to come from hiding to my family's defense."

"No one questions your bravery, Davath, you were only a boy," Atatha said.

Davath inclined his head. "This man could have just forced from me what he wanted to know. I was paralyzed, yet he healed me. After he learned what he wanted, he nursed me through fever, whiling the time with tales about a time he knew, not changed through generations of retelling. And they rang truer than the nursery tales of Ruperion who stole babes from their cradles. He told me it was urgent and I have no reason to doubt him. We both knew I could be judged a traitor for leading him to Hindlain. The demon from our nursery tales gave me leave to go. I chose, instead, to vouch for him before the Kylalnethra council."

Atatha continued staring at Rupert for a long moment. Rupert sensed the man searching him for weakness, plying a deft wyseery that a distracted wyseer might miss. Rupert returned his gaze, and acknowledged the attempt with a slight tilt of his head.

Atatha turned and placed a hand on Davath's shoulder. "Noted and well said, Davath. You are pardoned." Atatha waited for Davath to take his leave, but the werran remained. "You may go, Davath."

"I will stand by him," Davath said simply, again studying Kylik's path across the sky.

"Well, that's just being a fool," Rupert grumbled under his breath. "You're bound to waste a wyseer's efforts and that's just rude."

"You inspire loyalty," Atatha said to Rupert. "Kyloreign didn't want to believe you were the hideous ogre we described."

"I was his mentor, a hard taskmaster to raise a man to be Metathan in a world so unlike Metatha. I'm sure it wouldn't be a great leap for him to conclude I was all that you said. There have been times in my life when I was very much a hideous ogre."

"What shall we do with you?"

"Trust me."

"How can I do that knowing the tales about you?" Atatha said, his words almost a whisper.

"Other worlds revisit their history, knowing that the conqueror writes the history of the conquered, and that the tale told from the oral histories seldom matches the physical evidence. Would it be a leap to believe the Pale wanted you to fear the Traveler? Here, you have a Pale priest, Danat only knows why, and he even admits your tales are not supported."

"You said betrayal," Atatha said softly.

Rupert glanced from Atatha to the gathered council and the ring of guards. "Yes."

"Will you elaborate?"

"Here?" Rupert considered a moment as Atatha inclined his head. "May I ask what became of Kyle's companions? When he at last stepped from the pond, he was alone."

"They were driven away."

"Driven away? Not captured? Not harmed? Methiliim faced them?"

"No, it was Pale soldiers, not the Methiliim," Jia said. "We thought it a patrol. They appeared to take no interest in the pond and simply pursued us. We lost them near the Ridge, then backtracked here for reinforcements. When we returned to the pond, we found a dead eel on the shore, and Kyle's cloak was gone."

"No other sign?"

Jia shook her head.

"Not even his tracks, say in a light dusting of snow that had fallen?" Jia glanced at Atatha.

"And what conclusion did the council reach as to what became of Kyloreign?" Rupert asked softly. He knew the answer. And they knew he knew.

"We assumed that, fed up and finding himself alone and in possession of the Traveling stone, he made his way to Lake Ta'atit and returned to Earth," Atatha said. "Perhaps, his mentor gained his help in coming to Metatha."

"And you know that isn't supported by logic," Rupert said curtly. "And no one wondered that they found no trace of him, or that the Pale would be so inefficient at capturing obviously valuable wyseers, and that they would be patrolling without a wyseer themselves, something that they never do in the old haunts of the Fidrel?" Rupert glanced at the council as a sharp intake of breath showed him that at least Talik knew what he was about to tell them.

"Someone knew you were going to the pond. If you're about to steal something very valuable, and you don't want to be caught, it makes sense to leave the victim believing the object was simply lost, hmm? It leads them to look in all the wrong places, to ignore the obvious signs, to let their conclusions run astray with them. Someone lured his companions away, so that no one would witness what happened next. Someone perhaps bargained in such a way that fellow Valeutans would be unharmed, only the dangerous historical burp that had truly muddled things up would be involved."

Atatha was peering at him, hands clenched, not in anger toward Rupert, he knew that, but that he could see himself that he had been led.

"I saw through Kyle's eyes," Rupert said softly. "When Kyle closed the portal, he was somehow thrown back into the world of the eels. I don't know how. It shouldn't have happened. Perhaps some use of wyseery or maybe it was some coincidental incident. He was in the eel world for moments, bare moments, during which time he found the eel he had killed during his first encounter, floating there with his knife in it. By the time he returned all were gone, and a layer of snow covered his cloak. He tossed the eel ashore, realizing he had been injured by the beasts in that battle, freezing, and Travel weary from that second thrust through the portal. And there, weakened, perhaps in a stupor, he turned to find three Methiliim. How convenient they should be there. Yet, how interesting that they could easily have overpowered the contingent who had been there to protect the Traveler. Yet that contingent had been chased away, unharmed. You can imagine the Methiliim were quite pleased."

Jia had brought her hands up to her face. He could read her dismay so clearly. She existed to serve the Traveler and twice now she'd lost him. He read, too, the honesty of the young wyseer with the Pale colored hair who reached out to comfort her. He quickly scanned most of them for their astonishment, their fear, their dismay and concern. Two were masked from him, though. He peered intently at them, hoping Atatha would mark, too, their strange response.

Just then, something lurched in Rupert and he felt himself staggering, falling. Rupert wallowed, trying to find his feet beneath him. He looked up at Davath, who tried to hold him up. Did the Kylalnethra assault him with some unfamiliar wyseery?

Then suddenly he felt the roar of the water in his ears. "Oh, oh, no." Rupert gasped, trying to claim his feet, seeing it so suddenly. "Kyle, no, no, no."

He could see, feel him. The pungent scents, the fog rising from the lake, a lake that led to—before he could grasp the name from memory, he saw the cauldron, Kyle's arm dripping there into the boiling liquid that steamed up so noxiously it ripped his senses from him. Rupert gasped. He could feel the heat blistering his own flesh, but the image dissolved into a muttered spell uttered over some hapless and green-garbed figure who lay against the cauldron, head askew, blood draining from the neck as the eyes lost their life. And then he felt the tug as he was pulled, pulled toward another world, so stunned he almost allowed himself to follow, to slip away as he had to the world of the eels. The pungent waters, familiar, with a haunting, horrible history. He wanted to scream a warning, but just then, a blinding flash and thunderclap that rang Ruperion's ears threw him to the ground.

He lay there, the silence of the clearing around him. The pale wash of Kylik on his face appeared dull after the blinding flash that ghosted in his eyes as if he had seen it not through his mind's eye but—

"Ruperion," Atatha called as Davath vigorously rubbed his arm. A pungent sulfur on his lip roused him.

"I know how they will go around the bans," Rupert whispered.

"The stone." Atatha said.

Rupert shook his head. "All they need is his blood."

"And Kyle? What of Kyle?" Jia asked.

"Kyle is Traveling."

CHAPTER TWENTY-FOUR

As he broke the surface, Kyle spat out great mouthfuls of sand, gasping for air and choking on grains that swept back into him with each gasp. He crawled upward into a blaze of heat, wading through the sucking sand above an underground stream that once fed an oasis overcome now by shifting dunes.

He felt a prod in his back and saw pale Methil Dwilul, one hand still trying to wipe the sand from his tongue. Dwilul held up the Traveling stone and made a point of showing Kyle that it was in the wyseer's possession, as if there would be any doubt.

"Do I need to bind you?" Dwilul asked, his words thick with sand.

"Where would I go?" Kyle replied with a snarl, gasping harder and harder now as it seemed the air didn't fill his lungs the way he hoped. Nothing but dunes marched away into the horizon. Dunes of white sand, so white it blinded him. Perhaps this had once been the bottom of some sea. "Do you know if this air is breathable? What world is this supposed to be?"

Methil Dwilul gave him a skeptical look. "You are breathing, are you not? This has always been a planet of deserts, and the air has never been easy to breathe."

"Because of the bucket of sand inhaled on the way into it?" Kyle scowled into the blistering whiteness. He forced his eyes shut, seeing the bright red of it through his lids as his eyes watered furiously from the glare and the scratchy grains of sand. "Have you any idea how we're to get back into that underground stream?" He waited for the wyseer's response, but Dwilul had already begun trudging to the top of the first dune. Did the wyseer feel nothing like the weary key?

Dwilul needn't have feared Kyle escaping. The Travel sickness had so worn on him he doubted he could move without help. He'd no more than come up with the eel, having twice traveled to that cursed world, when he was hauled away, forced to march before three gleeful Methiliim. He'd stumbled often, seemingly again much to their delight until they had marched him at least as far as the skirmish where Methil Sethina had died. There they had camped, in the very spot where she'd died, somehow taking strength even from the ground upon which she'd bled.

It didn't take long for Kyle to realize they didn't care if they used him up. They'd be quite happy hauling simply his body, or his head, or even a fingernail if that's all the Reign they needed. He didn't matter at all. At least the Fidrel and Kylalnethra had never wished him ill. Even a hatred of all things Valeutan couldn't explain this callous disregard. Kyle could clearly see that the Methiliim, at least, descended from Valeutan stock. He might have forgiven the Pale soldiers who gave him sour looks now and then. Those soldiers treated him with more deference and consideration than the wyseers who needed him most.

He pulled his green cloak tightly about him to ward off the blazing sun from his raw skin. Whatever atmosphere this world possessed felt inadequate to protect him, its sun seeming far more unforgiving than that of other worlds as if it could bake bare flesh to the bone in minutes.

The novelty and wonderment of seeing new worlds had fled. He couldn't care less what lay over the next rise. It wasn't for him. He was simply a key to the next portal, the next, as many myriad portals as ponds of water in which Rupert had placed a keyhole in generations of Travel. It might be endless.

The sound of slithering sand made a soothing, hissing backdrop that almost lulled him to sleep as he lay against the side of the dip they created as they emerged. A few cool, wet grains had come to the surface with them and he pressed his face to them. Sand shifted, trickled. The ground gurgled beneath him. He tried to rouse himself to one elbow, struggling to open his eyes against a crust of dried sand. He stared in abstract amazement as the sand appeared to boil and bubble but a few yards distant. The boiling sand spread in a broadening ring as if someone had dropped a heavy rock into a lake. Did he rest on quicksand of some sort? Would he be swallowed by some sinkhole? The thought didn't frighten him perhaps as much as it should. Would Methil Dwilul be left here until he became nothing but a desiccated shell clinging to a worthless stone? That didn't trouble him at all.

Suddenly, an adder-like head erupted from the swirling sands. Kyle reared back. Deeply dark eyes in a great white head unpeeled, layer by layer to fix on him a gaze that chilled him to the bone despite the blazing heat. A snake he thought at first, and if so, one to rival the greatest of Earth's snakes. As more and more of the head emerged, it became more lizard-like, the head like a giant white watermelon that arched higher, higher, rising out of the hole as if it planned to stand upon its tail, and still no legs had emerged. At last, its bulk began to crest, becoming a neck of sorts attached to a tremendous mass that made a grinding growling rumbling sound like a colossal machine churning through rock. Then, flippers with giant paddle-like extensions emerged.

It peered down at him. Teeth glinted like icicles as it arched above him, its forward-set eyes not at all sleepy, not at all like some placid herbivore.

Kyle couldn't move. All the adrenalin in him seemed to do no more than pound his heart. He ordered his arms to support him, his knees to bend, but the eyes—so deep and multi-lidded but perhaps the color of dark eggplant—riveted him. He felt powerless to move as the head neared. Its breath came like wet sand and barn lime, the engines of its belly filtering and grinding the sand in search of sustenance. He knew it, as he stared into it. He felt its longing for a watery world in which to swim—

Kyle slammed back against the sand in the same instant as the creature bellowed, its head whipping around toward some nether region that might be a shoulder or flank. A great rent in the white hide spilled fine damp sand and a stronger stench of lime.

Kyle realized he'd regained his will and scrambled aside just as the head whipped toward him and another bolt came from Dwilul's crystal to burn the creature's flesh away. The sand boiled around it as if the body below the surface was a paddle wheel. Its head slammed the ground beside Kyle, a great gasp of sand and dust coating him, before a viscous honey-like liquid began to trickle from its mouth.

"Come, start digging," Dwilul ordered.

Kyle almost jumped out of his skin. He blinked at the wyseer, disentangling himself from the strange paralysis as if he were trying to escape a vat of honey.

"What?"

"Likely its death throes will summon others. Would you like to meet this beast's kin underground? Dig. Now."

Kyle dug at the caked sand near where they had emerged, unable to even sweat in the overwhelming heat. Dwilul delved deeper and deeper with the heel of his staff, Kyle scooping away the loosening sand. They dug several feet before the sand began to feel damp, then moist. Every so often the wyseer would call a halt, listening for the slither of the sand monster or to see if water might pool.

As he dug, Kyle cast a glance at the beast only a few feet away. All the lids were closed and it had almost a milky color to its eyes, like its skin. In death, the air out of it, much of its bulk had sagged, revealing collapsible bones that helped it slither —

"Its spell is powerful even in death," said the wyseer, perhaps allowing just a hint of his own awe to show. "The history says that if you see the uncovered eye, it will enchant you so that you cannot escape."

Kyle nodded, realizing he had stopped digging, mesmerized by the deflated hide and the hint of the deep dark beneath its lids.

"It longs for so much that it lost."

Dwilul didn't respond. He had at last managed to get an inch of water to pool in the bottom of the hole. He grasped Kyle's arm with the hand holding the Traveling stone.

"Now."

Kyle dived as best he could into the tiny trickle of water, expecting to simply come up hard with his head against the sand. Instead, he sort of slapped it like a fish flopping to a deck. He felt the transition struggling to take him, scales and gills aching for moisture, his lungs finding sand. He wormed his way downward, feeling a sense of water further into the sand. Deeper, deeper; at last he found the well of water and almost instantly he arched upward to break the surface of the small lake they had entered.

He gasped. Cool air slapped his face. His eyes strained in the dark of overcast night, a light rain pattering the still lake's surface. They had entered White Dragon Lake in the early hours of a morning with clear skies. How did time travel in the world of sand monsters? White dragons. Had they forgotten what the name meant, or just didn't think him worthy to know what fate he might face?

He flailed a moment before he realized the sandy lake bottom would support him. Though only about hip deep, it was all he could do to wallow to shore, prodded by Dwilul. When he fell to the bank, shivering and numb, he looked briefly around, seeing no sign of the soldiers sent to guard him or the wyseers commanding them. Could he flee before they found them? Nothing mattered. He let himself sag into a stupor where a white beast with violet eyes read the depths of his soul and found nothing there worth noting.

Kyle's head jerked up at the prod of a staff beneath his chin. He blinked. His eyes felt as if they were still coated in sand. Instead a light mist settled in his hair and eyelashes. The mount beneath him stumbled over a rock in the path, shaking Kyle from his doze. He had a brief memory of some horrid liquid being forced down his throat before he had been set upon the mount a scant few hours after the Pale had found them asleep on the far side of the lake. Day had come what seemed like moments later and again it was dark, though a hint of light in the east suggested dawn of another day neared. He felt the strange heaviness, the nausea, the uncertainty, and knew himself to be deep in the throes of Travel sickness.

He found small comfort in seeing that Dwilul wasn't completely impervious. The wyseer dozed on his mount and appeared pale, with little to say of their adventures but that he had returned with the dragon pellets he had sought. They had been there to collect the monster's dung and they hadn't even warned him that he'd very nearly become some magical artifact left to petrify in the sands.

He looked about, finding the sky clear, the moons gone, with just the breadth of Metatha's wondrously dark sky and its stars so bright and sharp. The stars met some great darkness to the north, and as the first hints of the dawn began to brighten the east, he realized that he faced lofty mountain peaks, many white-capped, with a vast mist-shrouded lake at their feet. It stretched west as far as he could see, the smoky surface a pearly blanket brightening by the moment.

He had a dreamy sense of detachment as he studied the vista more like a tourist than a tool used for evil deeds. Some little voice of his own told him he needed to resist the urge to become lost in it. He had a mission, didn't he? Or, he had once. He shuddered, almost losing his balance on his mount, and unpleasant reality hit him hard. He tried to close his eyes again, but the rude prod came again.

They were at the lake's eastern terminus and he realized the deep rumbling he heard was the lake pouring over a scarp, dropping some forty feet to boil over boulders and downed trees, rushing for the Great River and eventually Lake Ta'atit.

"Tell me this lake doesn't have something like eel or dragon in its name," Kyle muttered under his breath, drawing a weak smirk from Dwilul.

"This is Misty Lake," Dwilul said as if he must, not because he wanted to. "We head for the hot springs."

Kyle had an image of himself rising in some boiling geyser, but contained the thought with his own apathy. Nothing mattered at this point. He knew it was Travel sickness that brought on the malaise. If he couldn't find the strength to escape, he would most certainly become nothing but a body.

"We must walk from here, the trail is too rough for our mounts." Dwilul was at his elbow, startling him again as the wyseer tugged him from the beast, which gave an audible and tortured groan that made Kyle shiver within himself. As if sensing his disgust, the macabre mutation of a horse turned its skeletal face toward him. Nothing like a warm expression was in its black eyes.

Kyle lost track of the hard trek through the mist of boulder falls gurgling with steaming spring water, asleep on his feet. At last, about a half mile above the lake, they reached a pool just as the sun broke from the eastern sea. Light gilded the mountain peaks, which glowed in hues of red, black and green, the tendrils of mist slowly rising from the lake's surface to fade into the sky. By degrees the lake revealed its vastness as it stretched west, lapping at the mountains' feet. From here it looked like small ripples mottled its surface, and in places he could see the creamy aqua of glacial melt water mixing into the deep calm of the lake. He knew that as the winds picked up with the day, the fetch on the lake's surface would rival the waves of an ocean.

"There are many hot springs feeding Misty Lake," Dwilul said, his willingness to share information strange and ominous. "This spring leads to a populated world the people called Elnael. Their time moves rapidly, about one thousand years in their time passed since visited by a Traveler. They are a very backward people, living in shelters dug into the mud in the midst of marshes. They may have advanced some in that time. There, we will appear strange of hue and feature and thus we must not be seen. I will make a spell that will make us disappear, to all but each other, but we can still be injured, bumped into, or things we pick up or move will appear to move through space."

Kyle clenched his fists. They had never paid attention to him closely enough to realize he wore the mark of the ilyath. Perhaps that could be an advantage yet. He stared at the pool, wondering what one thousand years became in the hands of a people who didn't wait for a dream to rescue them.

He tested the temperature of the springs. They were hot, but not unbearably so. Like a good bath. He shrugged, and with a slight nudge from Dwilul, dived. The water went from the strong taste of minerals to briny. He popped up into a world so steamy and humid his breath choked up in him.

Sauna-like humidity made him break into an instant sweat, the air almost as saturated as the water as he went buoyant as if the world had a different gravity. He heard a slight humming noise and threw himself beneath the surface as some sort of skimming craft sped overhead. He popped up to find Dwilul wide-eyed and stunned. He kicked so he could rise high enough in the water to see over the light swell and peer through the haze.

"I think I see a bridge," Kyle said, swimming for it as Dwilul followed silently behind. Another skimming craft bore down on them and Kyle turned to face it, peering into the gloomy haze. His jaw dropped and Dwilul turned to stare with such shock he almost bobbed over on his face in the waves.

The creature, or person, for it was clearly some sort of intelligent life, was tall, willowy and hairless with a blue-grey skin that looked shiny in the dim haze. It wore some sort of globe helmet that revealed all of its features, including its long face and almost snoutish nose.

"Are you certain this is breathable air?" Kyle demanded as the skimmer passed by them. "That one's wearing a helmet, like one wears when the air is bad for you."

"That was an Elnaelan!" Dwilul said as if he hadn't heard Kyle. "The lore didn't report such a round clear skin about their heads. Nor could their mounts fly over the water—"

"Shows you what five hundred years could have gotten you if you'd left the wyseery behind and used your brains," Kyle said sourly. "That isn't skin, it's a helmet. It could simply be to protect their heads from an impact, or filter dangerous air. What is it you need to collect here? I don't know if I like floating in a sea I can't see into, in a world where the air may be toxic."

Dwilul was too awed to be much help and Kyle's weariness was seeping up his limbs. He didn't know how much longer he could move. If it hadn't been for a slight current, he never would have made it to the bridge span.

He saw now that it had been crafted of stone, yet rose high above them in a world where either the stone was lighter or the gravity weaker and nature allowed greater elevation. The slender structure almost disappeared above them in the haze. Near shore—actually a shallows of sorts with reeds and stones, and tufts of foliage growing out of it—he saw a giant bubble of glass that glowed with thousands of small lights and more activity than the UW campus on a football weekend. The dome rested on giant pillars that held it at least a hundred feet above the level of the water and shallows, and appeared to connect it with the bridge. A slight sigh above drew Kyle's attention. Another bubble of lighted glass slipped from the dome and shot out across the bridge span until it disappeared in the haze, moving ever upward until, Kyle thought, he might see the barest flash of possible sunlight of a sort on the train before it disappeared.

"Dwilul." Kyle nudged the wyseer. "What are you supposed to be collecting?"

"An Elnaelan."

"What, you aim to kidnap one of them?"

Dwilul turned a suddenly sharp gaze on him. "What of it if we are? They are a lesser people. Not Metathan, clearly. They look more like a sea beast than a man."

"What, you're going to sacrifice a person from another world for your wyseery?" Kyle almost choked the mouthful of water that swept in as he lost his grip on the bridge. "Are you telling me you think the Elnaelans are lesser people because they are more advanced technologically than you?"

Dwilul hesitated. He kept glancing from the high bridge to the glimmering domes, their lights sparkling skyward and shimmering from the water as some sort of nightfall approached.

"The lore described them like animals," Dwilul muttered. "Apparently, in the far past a few were brought back for study and novelty, much as many of the novelties came to Metatha. When the Elnaelans died, which happened quickly as they seemed unable to move on Metatha and soon found it difficult to breathe, we learned that their odd hide and bones held a great power for wyseers."

"In other words, you ground up their dead and used them for some ritual."

"It was no different than grinding up Shestan horn, or eating fish."

Kyle gestured at the glimmering dome city. "Will you contend that they are unintelligent beasts when they have built what you couldn't accomplish?"

Dwilul stared at the city for a long moment and without a word, grabbed Kyle's arm and forced him beneath the waves. As they came up into the heat of the springs, Kyle fumbled around the bottom of the spring for a moment before his need for air, and Dwilul tugging his arm forced him to the surface, without the portal key.

"Where's the Elnaelan?" one of the Methiliim demanded as they pulled themselves from the springs onto a mineral encrusted bank, the sudden weight of the world leaving Kyle too weak to move. The air felt sharp and dry and both of them coughed for several minutes before Dwilul found his breath.

"There's no sign that they still exist," Dwilul stated, gazing intently at Kyle.

"Hmm, disappointing. But we did fear change. Well, you'd better rest up. You'll need to enter Misty Lake tonight."

Kyle sat up and tried to protest but Dwilul silenced him with a backhand to the mouth that threw Kyle to the ground. Kyle started to sputter his protest but suddenly realized from Dwilul's expression that the Traveler must pay for knowing a secret about Dwilul. Kyle's tongue explored a bloody lip. How hard was it for Dwilul to bleed captured Valeutans to death in the cauldrons, if he couldn't even bring home an Elnaelan to die?

"Must it be tonight?" Dwilul asked. "It is wearing on the body to make these Travels."

"Methil Tarcatha sent word demanding to know why we haven't brought him the Traveler yet. He may become suspicious, especially if the courier survives to tell him where he found us. We need to ride for Waymeet tomorrow."

"Could some other go in my place?" Dwilul asked quietly, staring down at the lake that glimmered brightly in the still early morning. "The lore says the Balthysians have a caste society somewhat like the Valeutans and culture on a par with the ancient Pale. Since the Valeutan lore's perspective of the Pale at that time was barbaric and warlike, I … I am uncertain I will be up to my skills as a wyseer. If they have advanced anything like El—like El-earth, it may require more wyseery than I can summon."

"You are experienced. We need speed and experience with opportunities to Travel growing short," the two other wyseers agreed. "You will be better with a few hours rest."

Kyle almost felt sorry for Dwilul, his expression so weary and pathetic.

"Then I shall go," Dwilul whispered and immediately fell to sleep.

Drumbeats echoed a pulse, a throb perhaps, some gut-rumbling, earth-trembling power. Not simply drums. Some carried the hollow voice of bamboo tubes. Some emitted the heartier thumps from timpani to bongo, others the clatter of dried gourds. An undercurrent to the beat emerged. Somewhere deep within himself Kyle realized the pattern intensified, grew urgent, a frenzy raised, a rolling wall of drumming sound like rain or hail on a metal roof, like the monstrous waters of the Great River pounding down to Lake Ta'atit.

The pounding reminded him that he was somewhere. Somewhere he shouldn't be. Somewhere unnatural. He remembered a name, Balthys. It lay beneath Misty Lake, that oddity of warm surface and frigid deeps that smoked into the night. He and Dwilul had looked at each other, neither of them standing certainly. Neither of them strong enough to do this, but each propelled by something they couldn't control and it had been with a strange fatalism that Dwilul had touched his hand to Kyle's arm, almost a gentle prod. And they hadn't so much dived as mostly fallen forward into those troubled waters where glacier met hot spring, the waters tasting clean and metallic. And then, then—

The drumming halted for an instant, an instant that brought Kyle's heart into his throat. He remembered. Clearly. Urgently. He must awake. He must come out of this stupor! Something more than Travel sickness worked here. He had an image of Dwilul and himself, flailing frantically in the calm waters of a lake surrounded by a forest of trees that reached hundreds and hundreds of feet skyward. Dwilul had forgotten to cast his invisibility spell. They had surfaced in the midst of a collection of blood-red fishing canoes, each one of them manned by at least three fair-skinned men who appeared so achingly normal they could have been weekend campers on the Black River. But for the scars carved on their shaved heads, and the black skull tattoos that outlined their faces, and the trophy belts sporting what appeared to be human jawbones, and their brilliant red eyes.

Kyle struggled to surface from this strange dream world. He remembered paddles, trying to duck and dodge as they were wielded like clubs swung at their heads in a demented game of water polo.

The quiet erupted in a wild shout echoed by piercing yells and cat calls and one suffering groan.

At last, Kyle opened one eye to see a night sky with brilliant stars, and streaks of color rippling across it as if it were ablaze, a flickering of greens and blues and violets and reds, whatever this world was, it came equipped with northern lights. The lights played across a tiny stage framed by the giant boles of trees whose canopies formed a semicircle to one side. The open space near his feet might be a lake. The manfish in him sensed the water, longed for it, begged him to find it and go home, any home but this.

He wanted to shake himself free of these strange fancies, but the sickness gripped him hard. He felt a twinge of pain and the heat and crackle of a fire too near and glanced to one side.

His heart leapt to his throat. As someone struck up the drums again, he saw Dwilul on the other side of a growing bonfire, hog tied and stripped, hanging from a pole. A circle of jeering figures in skeleton face masks surrounded him, spitting, punching, pinching, jabbing with small knives so that the blood streaked Dwilul's skin, a threadwork of blood striping him as if all his veins were bared.

Kyle realized he lay in a heap beside the growing bonfire. A rough pole dug under his back and he saw that a hole was being readied for it but a few feet from Dwilul. His feet were being bound and already the rope was tautening as an arm reached for one of Kyle's hands. Instinctively, Kyle had no sense of any self-motive, he flung the other hand at the fire, felt the angry heat against his ilyath scar, heard the man's gasp, and at that moment Kyle grabbed the Balthysian with all his might and flung him at the blaze.

Kyle swung up out of the bonds and sprinted clear as the crowd raced to help the man whose clothing, some sort of woven fiber, had burst into flame.

Kyle sped to Dwilul and fumbled at the knot on his feet.

"Use your wyseery, Dwilul! We've only a moment!" Kyle whispered, staggering as he tried to keep his feet.

"Don't bother, Traveler!" Dwilul's words came in gasps. "You are a far more worthy man than I to even try to save me. I won't survive the journey. And I'm too weak for wyseery. Quick, they're already noticing that I'm talking. Flee! Take the stone! Escape. But don't let the Methiliim find you. Your life will end with Tarcatha. You will be bled into the cauldron to undo the bans."

Kyle was shaking his head, Dwilul's admission a babble in his ears.

"Don't be foolish," Kyle said. "A small wyseer's trick and you're invisible—"

"I cannot walk. Take the stone." Dwilul opened his fist and the stone dropped into Kyle's hand as a cry rose, Balthysians gesturing at the pole Kyle had escaped. Warriors, jawbones rattling at their hips, swept past him along paths into the forest and a lakeside meadow that towered over their heads. As the angry light of the bonfire lit up the night, Kyle could see now the stone knife embedded between Dwilul's shoulder blades, the pulse of blood around it.

"It's a pity," Kyle said, wondering at words that fell from his mouth though he felt speechless. "You showed humanity. There was hope for you. We speak the same."

Kyle aimed for the water, trying to avoid bumping into the furious Balthysians robbed of their spectacle. His mind wandered dangerously close to delirium as an oddly out of tune Anthropology lecture droned through his head like the cavernous lecture hall on Bascom Hill. Was he to be an offering to gods, a sacrifice meant to convey power, or a meal? What would archaeologists make of Dwilul's artifacts and remains?

The sky rippled above. The firelight flared brighter, revealing the hoary boles of ancient trees. Had Rupert seen them as saplings?

Rupert.

He'd fallen to his knees a few feet from the water's edge.

Rupert.

He pictured Ruperion the wyseer, master of magic, ever young and unbent. Urgent words insisted Kyle get up, fool, and just dive in, his tone that of disgust for disrespectful students.

He couldn't dive into the water. He could crawl to it. As it touched the stone in his hand, he felt the water calling him, urging him to breathe a fresh draught of it. He slithered further, reached again, and at last, with the barest flick of tail he swam deep. As deep as he could. And when he tasted the cold depths of Misty Lake, he slowly, only slowly, swam upward.

CHAPTER TWENTY-FIVE

Daylight filtered down through the water to the reaching tendrils of weeds. He surfaced in shallows protected by water-logged grass and brush submerged by glaciers that poured their summer melt water into the lake. The view had changed. The Methiliim were on the other shore in the foothills of the Misty Mountains. From here, the mountains were mirrored, their peaks at his feet, and he could hear the thunder of Misty Lake flowing over the scarp and down river to Lake Ta'atit.

He didn't dare venture out yet. He could see his own flesh was an angry and brilliant red, shot with the tiny magenta lace of broken blood vessels. He doubted he could survive another swim if they found him again. The ilyath burn scabbed and peeled, while the rest of that hand blistered from the fire he'd thrust it into, and the bruises from the paddles the Balthysians had beat him with swelled and throbbed, especially a painful knot on his forehead. He huddled, cold and hungry and exhausted in the cover of the brush, dozing until some flitterbird tugged at his hair. He had never been so miserable, so exhausted, so totally disillusioned.

As the sun slowly worked its way down Misty Lake, Kyle realized, sometimes in his dreams, sometimes in uncomfortable moments of waking, that he had no choice but to set off on his own, without food, water, security or even a map. He'd never survive if he stayed in Metatha. He was too dangerous. Dwilul and his cronies were but one example of opportunists. With the Kylalnethra, it was no different. And if he fell into Methil Tarcatha's hands wyseers would be plundering other worlds left and right, and in the end, likely destroying their own. But they couldn't touch him on Earth

He no longer had Jia's stone to addle his thinking. It was time to go home. Yet, he had no illusion he would be staying there long. Kyle couldn't leave it unresolved, not when he'd been the catalyst. How could they find that balance of power that kept the two from annihilating each other?

When at last he rose from the sodden thicket it was into a shroud of evening mist. The tendrils from the warm surface of the lake gasped at him like the breaths of a sleeping dragon, the slightest hint of fire and brimstone smoldering deep beneath the surface rumbling out at him through the fog.

He let his unsteady feet carry him down the scarp and along the boulder-strewn river. He didn't dare take the road in the event Tarcatha sent yet another messenger for him. His mind told him these things, in an abstract sort of way. He only vaguely registered anything but moving his feet, his arms held awkwardly out to help him balance against the overwhelming swell of the land beneath his feet. Like a ship bucking on the sea, he felt as if the ground beneath him rolled, the rumbling beast beneath Misty Lake sending him off with a growl of good riddance and a gasp of sulfur.

The moons rose and flitted between clouds. Deep shadows hid the landscape long moments before a moon would reappear blazing out at him so suddenly he would almost stumble blindly into a stone or the scragged trees clinging to the margins of the river. The tree margin gave way to deep and trackless prairie that snagged his feet and sent him pitching, often into such a tangle he could barely extricate himself.

He thought of nothing else but following the river to Ta'atit. Follow the river to Ta'atit. It teased his senses, became a singsong chant with a slightly familiar tune but he couldn't even name it. Again he sensed Rupert, seemed to see him gazing intently across a vast space but so close he could almost touch him.

Was Rupert in Metatha? How could he be? He wanted to warn him away from this place of certain death, but he could only mutter under his breath his chant to follow the river to Ta'atit.

He stopped abruptly when another scarp blocked his way. The land before him on this side of the river remained level, but a deep valley opened up on the other bank, the river dropping hundreds of feet down into it and curving away. If he stayed on this side of the river he might be forced to go miles out of his way to descend to the banks again, potentially losing his way in the tall prairie.

As moonset neared, he stared out at the river valley, dozing some but always working the problem. He tried to mark the distance of the trail from the river edge, thinking he had a sense that he could almost see its confluence with the Great River and the road to Ta'atit in a sparkling and misty distance. Following instinct rather than any logic he could summon, he hopped from stone to stone into the middle of the river, then, faced with no more stone, pitched into the hip-deep current, suddenly fearful that he might be transported to yet some other world. He kept his head above the water, sensing that would be key to avoiding Travel. His legs swept from beneath him suddenly and he only barely managed to grasp a branch wedged between boulders and pull himself free moments before the river would have swept him over the falls.

He had to will himself the strength to go on. He dozed again on the far bank, but urgency woke him. He was still too close to Misty Lake. He had to press on.

In the valley he was able to make better progress, and at one point he realized he marched down the middle of a road as if he didn't have a care in the world. He didn't. He simply needed to keep going as his mind wandered through a parade of oddities, of magic and Travel, fish and dragons and eels and always the undercurrent of drums in his ears, pounding out a walking cadence.

Kyle opened his eyes to blazing noon. He lazily noted it, rolled to face away and closed his eyes again. It took a few minutes for whatever had roused him to do so again and at last he sat up. He quickly crawled to the cover of a thicket beside the road he had so brazenly fallen on as the sound of hoof beats echoed back at him from the scarp on the far bank of the river. The brush had just stopped swaying and cracking from his passage when a half dozen mounted Pale soldiers and two wyseers cantered by the very spot where he had lain open to view.

In moments the party and their echoes had passed. Soon they would reach Misty Lake, and likely find those waiting for Kyle and Dwilul. Was Tarcatha one of those who had just passed? Or would these wyseers also hope for a special boon before Tarcatha bled the Traveler?

Kyle kept to the slim shelter of the brush, trees, and tall grass beside the road as he went on, snacking as best he could on unripe berries and oat grass, waterweed and the occasional raw egg from a nest he tripped over. The river remained a companion that sometimes rumbled over short falls, chuckled around boulders, or mildly gurgled as it at last widened near its confluence with the Great River.

As the eastern stars began to edge the horizon and the sun fell behind an angle of the mountains Kyle walked on the open road, both sides gone swampy and treacherous. Near dawn found him crouching for a few hours of rest, hiding in the damp reeds swatting at birds that seemed determined to remove his every hair or loose thread, or to find the salty moisture on his skin.

When he could barely doze for the incessant pecking and plucking, he again took to the road, at last reaching the river as dusk neared. An unmanned ferry bobbed between sturdy poles set deep in the marshy banks. Ropes ran from the poles, around a wheel on the ferry, then to matching poles on the far bank. As dusk lengthened around him, Kyle stepped onto the ferry and turned the heavy wheel to haul the ferry to the far side. He couldn't imagine a more obvious clue for pursuers. How long would they wait for him to surface before they became suspicious? They knew more about Balthys than he did. What if he'd left footprints, broken brush, hadn't buried well enough where he'd relieved himself? What if these wyseers could somehow see him wherever he was?

That gave him a crawling feeling, like when cameras followed him around a convenience store or dressing room, or when it seemed Rupert had climbed inside his head. He shivered with the light sweat he'd earned hauling on the winch. When he stepped onto the south bank of the Great River and the Ta'atit road, the nervous sense of nakedness increased.

This road led to Waymeet, where most of the major roads of Metatha came together, and on its eastern end, the road linked to the great Rim Road to the south. Deep muddy ruts from wagon wheels left a high hump in the middle of the road, where a steady hoof and foot traffic left no foliage. He couldn't remember the last rain that had fallen, but the bottom of each rut remained full of brackish water that left a layer of mud on the cropped grasses beside the road. There was nowhere to hide here, little hope of forage, and every likelihood he would encounter someone more than happy to earn a bounty on the Traveler.

Hesitating only a moment in the deepening shadows of evening, Kyle tethered the ferry fast to the southern shore before continuing on east, thinking only of reaching Ta'atit and home. He had an image of the comfort of his bed, tried to place each item in his room, from the NASCAR posters on the walls to the trophies on his dresser and the photos of friends taped to the mirror. Anything to keep his thoughts from wandering to the images that sought his attention: toothy eels in a stormy sea, the eggplant eyes of a hungry beast, a bloody wyseer tied to a pole.

He stopped suddenly. His senses roused him to waking, to some sound other than his own footsteps. Danat and Kylik had risen, with Siph emerging from Kylik's side, throwing a wash of moonlight onto the road at a point that gnawed at him with its familiarity. The river flowed close to the road on the north, but an older line of eroding riverbank rose over his head to the south, fringed by a few trees and coated with brush. He took a deep breath thick with the strong aroma of herbs and knew White Dragon Lake lay somewhere beyond the ridge line. He swallowed hard, an instant image rearing up in him that made him want to freeze, to gaze upon the wise eyes that made him simply wonder at his own existence.

"There ..." He heard a voice and whipped around so quick he almost fell. He saw three silhouettes against the moonlit river.

His only escape lay in going into the brush, where he wouldn't get far, or leap into the river, which he knew to be deep, swift and treacherous, and might even take him to some far world.

"Kyle," a voice said, a certain gravel and authority in the tone made him hesitate. "It's all right." It took him a moment to realize the words came in English, not Metathan, oddly out of their element in this world.

"Rupert? What are you doing here?"

"I'm here, that's what's important," Rupert said in his closed-subject tone.

Arms took his and he almost staggered back in surprise, trying to shake free, then too stunned to hold himself up when the moonlight shone on their faces.

"Jia, Talik!" he gasped. "How?"

They didn't respond, instead hurrying him into the undergrowth and leading him up the slope. When he caught the glimmer of White Dragon Lake he planted his feet, Jia and Talik tugged at his arms so that he almost fell.

"It's all right, Kyle. The road isn't safe. We need a secluded place to tend to you," Rupert said from behind him.

"White Dragon Lake safe? I don't think so," Kyle muttered, but let them lead him.

At last they settled him on a stump at the top of a slope overlooking the lake. Moss covered the leaf-littered ground, the trees, and gave a cool covering to boulders that still held the barest warmth from the sun. The tall trees made dark silhouettes against the sky, and below the lake glittered like white sands shimmering on a desert. The scent reminded him sharply of northern forests of—

The liquid against his lips burned and stunk of something foul like rotting fish. He tried to spit it out, but Rupert held the wooden cup against his mouth, Jia and Talik firmly gripping his head.

"What are you doing to me!" he choked around the hideous potion.

"Will you take your medicine like a man or a boy," Rupert grumbled at him in English.

Kyle leaned forward to stare at his mentor, ill-defined in the shadows. He almost fell, but not before finding himself awestruck. This was no decrepit wino. He carried himself almost regally, dressed in robes that appeared more natural on him than blue jeans and flannel ever did. His hair had gone almost white and was shaggier than he recalled. He'd be the storybook wizard if he'd grown a beard. Kyle realized he felt warm. It radiated from his belly and worked its way out his limbs. The fog seemed to lift from his thoughts a little.

"Your hair ..."

"Shows you a little magic isn't as benign as you think," Rupert said in English, then switched easily to Metathan Kyle recognized as archaic. He smiled to himself, wondering at this strange expression, one he hadn't used in a long time.

"Yes, Kyle, I'm not so bad after all, eh?"

"What are you doing to me?" The warmth was making him sleepy now, alert but sleepy. His limbs had grown warm, but numb. He wasn't sure he could even move if he tried.

"This is a powerful potion, Kyle. It's restorative and healing. It'll help you safely endure your Travel sickness," Jia was saying somewhere near his leg where she had found the eel wound, something that had made him limp, he recalled, but ... he couldn't remember what ... as Talik tugged at the hair plastered to a lump on his head. They poked and prodded his wounds as if they kneaded a loaf of bread.

"How," Kyle couldn't recall what he was asking, but Rupert seemed to know.

"Before you left Earth, Kyle, I cast a spell at you. I'm sorry. I know you hate that. But it led me to you. I knew you went to Balthys. I saw through your eyes."

"I saw you."

Rupert nodded. "I know you've Traveled a hard road. Travel twice in a week is hard enough, but five times in almost as many days could kill you. To tell the truth, I'm surprised you had the stuff to escape, much less come this far. You never had an athlete's stamina. And it's just plain foolish for them to use you so recklessly. They have the lore to know what worlds the portals lead to, yet they just dumped you in some of the most deadly."

"They don't need me alive," Kyle said slowly, feeling as if he was falling a very long way but that it didn't matter because there was no bottom to strike. "They have a plan to make ...and ... that will be that."

He could barely form words, wasn't even sure if he had spoken clearly enough to be understood. Though he could see them, he wasn't even sure his eyes were open. He had a sense of settling back into a nest of moss and leaves and … a thought struck him hard. He struggled to make his mouth open. "Tarcatha," he managed. "He's come for me … they … I was betrayed. Did you know?"

"Who betrayed you?" He thought it might be Talik's voice. Or was it Rupert's, or Jia's? He couldn't respond and the world swiftly faded into the moonlit sparkles of eggplant eyes.

CHAPTER TWENTY-SIX

Some urgent plea roused Kyle from a deep place where monsters frolicked with the parts of a body torn limb from limb. He sensed Rupert in his head and wyseery in the moment. A blinding flash leaked through his eyelids followed by a thunderclap. He sensed that he had somehow been hidden and should remain still. What was happening?

He heard shouts, tasted leaves in his mouth and felt as if he suffocated, struggling not to move though he desperately wanted to claw free. He recognized Rupert's voice and archaic accent in an incantation that was by the moment lost in blasts and shouts.

Close at hand he made out voices.

"And look what my little bloodbirds brought home tonight."

Someone laughed in a less than humorous tone.

"I wondered where you'd managed to hide yourself. No acolytes to attend you, Palif? No parishioners to anoint your ego? Where are the gods to save you now? What, the Fidrel didn't want you now that your little slave girl lover was dead?"

Kyle forced his eyes open to find himself buried beneath a layer of brush and leaves. To his shock he found only a few feet away two Pale soldiers held Talik between them. Blood streamed down the palif's face from his forehead as he stared defiantly, a half a head taller than his captors, at the wyseer speaking to him.

A ring of wyseers and torch-bearing soldiers gathered and circled them. Kyle was outside the ring looking at the backs of two men but a few feet from him. Someone reported that two wyseers had escaped their trap and soldiers had been sent to pursue them. How could they not see Kyle? Had the ilyath somehow protected him? He went to lift his arm and too late realized his error. The leaves that concealed him rustled. One of the soldiers turned to peer into the night and Kyle froze.

"Tarcatha, have you so abandoned your reason that you would try to destroy your own world?" Talik asked in a voice that though quiet was as strong as if he stood before a thousand supporters. "You are no better than Denalku, trying to use wyseery to destroy—"

"I see your little wyseer friends ran away. They probably tire of your manless words. What a weak little Palif you are, to talk to the High Chieftain of peace and harmony among the peoples and the gods. What have the gods ever done for us? Did they save Metatha from the Withering, from each scourge of the past? What has the hoarding and control of wyseery ever done but hobble those best able to do what they need to? You talk of destroying the world? What foolishness. Is that some argument your gods gave you, worried their followers have given their blood to the competition, that they might finally have what your selfish gods have kept from them?"

Talik stared at him. "Certainly you aren't so simple as to believe you can manipulate a wyseery made by those far greater than yourself," he said softly.

Tarcatha struck so swiftly, Talik fell before Kyle even realized the wyseer had made contact. Tarcatha bent and gripped Talik by the hair, forcing his head back to reveal defiant eyes that blazed darkly in the torchlight.

"Certainly you don't think I care what you think. Where is the Traveler?"

"Why don't you ask your own wyseers? They were the ones who stole him away from the eel pond."

"And I'm sure you just happened to be here tonight on some little errand of chance? We know all about your little network of murdering wyseers. We will deal with them soon enough and have done with this rebellion."

Talik opened his mouth to protest, but Tarcatha splayed his hand out toward him. Talik's mouth shut against his will, only muffled sounds coming from his throat as he struggled against the spell, his lips unable to part.

"I'm tired of your prattle, Talik. I'll leave you your voice, so we can hear your cries for mercy as we bleed you. You should lend great power to the cauldron. Perhaps if we carve the histories from your body, piece by piece, you can cry for the lost wisdom of the ages as it melts away in the potion. Think what great wyseery that might bring to our cauldron!"

Talik's evident shock brought laughter to Tarcatha, and the obedient chuckles of his followers.

"Ah, he wonders at my cruelty, at what twisted thing in my life could make me so forsake all the good things of the world. See, watch his eyes, they are expressive are they not? Perhaps it's the Ruperion in me. Yes, I can trace my line back to his. Perhaps that is the evil in my soul."

Kyle realized Tarcatha was no longer speaking to Talik. His words were for his followers, reassuring those who held the palif with deference and uncertainty. As Tarcatha spoke, they bound Talik. Others gathered firewood, pitched a tent that had no sides and manhandled a heavy cauldron from a cart towed by the mutant horses, then hauled it to the shelter and growing pile of firewood. The flickering torchlight brought back an image of Dwilul, alive yet, as the Balthysians flayed his flesh from his body. He tried to clench his eyes shut to will away the image. But when he opened them again, he still found Tarcatha staring down at the bloodied palif kneeling before him.

"Perhaps I am simply sick of inaction," Tarcatha said as his followers moved through the shadows, their torches glittering from White Dragon Lake like Balthysian fires. "Sick of the simpering of fools who yearly achieve nothing when they could be making this world strong again. Hundreds of worlds, many never even discovered, lead to Metatha. And what do we do? We pray to the moons to bring us health and bountiful crops, and bequeath to them our dead in the unrealized hope we'll get something in return. Instead, we could bring ourselves the goods of other worlds, the powers they would discard, the servants to ease our labor. When the portals are all cast open, there will be no need for Valeutan and Pale to hold each other in hatred. All will have access. But Palifiim hold back progress, whispering in their lords' ears of peace and an end of wyseery. Without wyseery we are no better than the Shestans."

Kyle could see that Talik wanted to protest, but he could only chew his words, unable to utter them. His chest had been bared, Tarcatha jabbing a torch toward one of the histories that spoke so clearly of how the bans on Travel came precisely because the wyseers, left to their own, ran amok in other worlds. That was the very truth Tarcatha hoped to carve away and throw in the pot. With every labored breath of Talik's frustration, that fact of history thrust out at them. But no one but Kyle seemed to see it.

A sharp pain in his side forced a yelp from him, just as a Pale soldier flew to his knees, having tripped over Kyle. They flung the leaves and brush aside, scrambling to distinguish their prize who had clearly been hidden in a spell. A wyseer tapped the empty space that was Kyle and instantly the spell tattered, a sense of Rupert slipping away in a wisp of mist. In moments they had his arms pinned behind him as they thrust him toward Tarcatha.

"Talik, you have brought me a prize!" Tarcatha called when one of his servants searched Kyle and raised the Traveling stone and the pink sliver of Baraboo quartzite that had been the keyhole to the world of the eels. "This will be perfect! What great wyseery could there be but the blood of Danat and the Traveler, blended in my cauldron!"

They bound their two prisoners to a tree as Tarcatha tossed both artifacts into the cauldron without ceremony. A thick, dark liquid splattered the sides, all that remained of lives. How many had been bled away in this pot? Tarcatha muttered to himself as he added herbs and charms and water from the lake. Another wyseer lit the fire beneath the grotesque mixture and soon a coil of noxious steam began to rise.

Kyle sensed Rupert's will bent toward him, weak and faint. Had he been injured? Driven too far away to come to their aid?

Kyle turned to scan the dark woods and found Talik staring at him. The palif looked down at the small vestment of moons hanging from his belt and the tiny little pouch attached to it, then back at Kyle again.

He looked pointedly again. Talik glanced at the cauldron, then back to the vestment. At Kyle, to the vestment, then the cauldron. At last Kyle thought he understood, he stared at the growing flames beneath the pot and the rising steam.

Tarcatha had begun to utter words that made his heart pound with fear though they came too fast and low for him to understand. He could feel the undercurrent of excitement all around, the wyseers peering at the cauldron and Tarcatha as if they expected all their dreams to be realized this day. They had wanted nothing more than to bleed Kyle dry.

Suddenly hands were on them. Ropes cut from them without mind for cutting the flesh beneath, soldiers dragged them toward the cauldron. Kyle's right arm was wrenched out in front of him, two men holding him as a knife slit his arm. They towed him to the steaming cauldron, a rope around his wrist yanked across the cauldron to ensure that his blood dripping from the deep wound in a slow but steady stream went into the pot.

Only slowly did the blood drain, so slow they might now and then need to cut him again. They didn't want it to go too quickly. Tarcatha had many words to say yet. The more suffering, the greater the wyseery, perhaps. Talik, too, was held thus, their blood dripping together into the steaming stench. Tarcatha's words seemed like a nonsensical chant that throbbed against his ears like the drums of the Balthysians. Kyle could only stare at the blood trickling from his arm onto Talik's. The heat of the steam curled the hairs on their arms, raising the sweat on their brows.

The heat. The heat! Through all the addled layers of Travel sickness, the potion Rupert had forced into him and whatever spell Tarcatha wrapped him in, Kyle knew exactly what he had to do. He saw Rupert in his mind nodding, urging him to act, quickly. His right arm felt afire with the flame. He fought down the urge to cry out as blisters rose. And still they gripped him so he couldn't pull away. The rope around his wrist led away through the steam to a man on the other side pulling to keep his arm over the cauldron as the heat grew.

He ripped his ilyath-marked left hand free and grasped Talik's belt, the moons and the tiny pouch hard in his palm, real. Talik let out a groan of desperation. The Methiliim were winning.

Tarcatha continued his spells, tossing in more herbs and leaves and muffled words with each drop of blood, Kyle feeling fainter by the moment, too weak to lift his left arm or pull his right free. He wrapped the chain of moons about his fingers.

Suddenly, he gritted his teeth and thrust his left, moon-wrapped hand into the boiling blood and grasped for the stones he knew to be in there, raising them up, triumphant, as he bellowed out the pain that smashed into his skull.

A flash erupted. The pot roared up in a foam and boil that threw them all back. The soldier holding the ropes to their wrists had fallen and Kyle's arm came to him slowly, as if in a dream. Fire licked up his arms. He felt himself propelled, but unknowing how, his legs rubbery beneath him. A deep voice, as deep as the well to other worlds, intoned words at first unclear to him. They were so old, more archaic even than the Metathan Kyle had learned at Rupert's knee.

"*Ai K'ele e'wak nethral n'atit Danate tarcannen tathral,*" Talik said in resonant words that seemed to make the wicked brew boil more furiously. The liquid spattered, hissing and spitting and burning the flesh of those too near.

"Let my heart be strong to walk and treasure Danat's dark and secret road," Kyle translated to himself, standing numb where he had been pulled back, he realized, by Talik.

"Traveler, we must flee," Talik gasped at him, his words spattering blood from some deep injury within him. "I don't know how long this will hold them."

Kyle blindly looked about him, then realized the furious cauldron continued to boil, frothing and wicked, lapping at and burning those too near, seeming to find an endless wealth of dark liquid to spew, the yelping Pale and Methiliim not even noting what had become of their prey.

"It is the curse of Martrena seeking her enemies. Danat is the abode of the dead, and into their cauldron in the Traveler's hand, went not only a palif's holiest relic, but the ashes of my dear lady, a wyseery herself."

Talik's words conveyed something so strange Kyle trembled, feeling as if he should kneel in the palif's presence.

Talik continued to propel him backward. Kyle stole a look at the palif, strangely lit by fire, his face taken with madness, his hair wild and on end, his beard seeming to curl from his face. The blood streamed down his arm, but he appeared oblivious to it. His bared chest revealed the histories in a relief so brilliant and vivid it captured Kyle's gaze and held it. Talik gripped Kyle by the arm and wrapped a bit of fabric around the knife cut.

"You see me?" Kyle stammered, finding it so difficult to utter a thought, as if the spell that had gripped Talik was instead his.

Talik nodded. "They do not. I don't know how long it will last. They may still have what they need to start over. We must not let them find you. We must return you to your world." Talik cinched tight the bandage. "If he can, Ruperion will try to reach you if he still survives the madness of this night. Trust him. Be strong. We speak the same."

Kyle blinked and realized they stood on the shores of White Dragon Lake, almost stumbling into it with the stone in his hand. The well of water seemed almost a deep purple, calling to him. A sudden image of the white-headed beast rushed up at him from the surface and he turned, gasping as he fell, the cold water threatening to reach above his head.

While most of the Methiliim still stared in amazement at the boiling cauldron, the splash drew Tarcatha's attention his direction. He heard the shout as a staff pointed at him and a blast of white light ripped from it as he scrambled from the lake. The blaze of light skipped up from the water and glanced off Talik, who fell in the shadows.

"Run Kyle. You must!" he gasped.

Kyle ran, amazed his feet could carry him, oblivious to stones and roots that snagged him, branches that whipped his face. He heard explosions behind him. Again he recognized Rupert's voice shouting an incantation. The hissing wail of the cauldron seemed to grow louder, the fire both quenched and fed as a dire and rank smoke filled the little valley.

He looked back, expecting to see Tarcatha still standing beside the cauldron, his arms upraised in fiery anger like some demon rising from the smoke and flames, but the wyseer was gone. He turned and froze. Tarcatha stood before him, his hand splayed out and dripping the smoking blood from the cauldron.

"You have undone much work, Traveler. For what? I'm greater than your Fidrel, than your Palifiim. You may have escaped lesser wyseers sent for you. Why would some trifling exiled Reign think he can possibly escape me?"

Kyle watched as the fist closed, feeling some sorcery close about him until he knew no more.

CHAPTER TWENTY-SEVEN

"Ilyath, how could we not have known." He heard the words, but couldn't place them. Then somewhere deep and panicky within him roused him, like the rumble he felt beneath him.

"Was he trying to make it back to their hidden camps? Perhaps we should simply let him go and follow him there." Another voice.

"We'll deal with them in time." A third voice. "We have allies among them. I think he would have gone for Ta'atit. And I know exactly what he hoped to find there. I have Ruperion's histories. I've studied his many trips into the west of that world. He was going to collect a weapon."

Kyle tried to sputter denial, but he couldn't utter a sound, couldn't open his eyes, or even move. Where was Talik? He felt a cool mist drifting over them. Were they still beside White Dragon Lake?

"If it's to Earth he hopes to Travel, let him go. He will have company."

"Do you think that's wise, Methil Tarcatha? He will be familiar with the place."

"I'm not a fool. He's so Travel sick he won't put up much fight."

"Why not simply bleed him as we planned?" another voice asked. "Then all the portals will be open and the powers will be balanced."

"We must stop this rebellion first and end the Fidrel or Kylalnethra, whatever it is they call themselves this cycle. It will be weeks before I can bring together the spells and artifacts that were wasted so quickly by one counter spell. We must destroy them or we will forever be competing against them, laboring fruitlessly only to have them deny us our due. They would seek a weapon against us. We will have the greater weapon, with our stronger wyseery behind us and they will give up their game and come to us willingly or swiftly die."

"Is it wise to be fetching such weapons? We don't want another Withering."

Kyle couldn't imagine what occurred in the silence. He opened his eyes, suddenly, completely, but the world appeared different, bright and quivery and shrunken as if he wore glasses too strong for his eyes.

"He's coming around," a voice said.

Kyle turned to see two Methiliim regarding him. Three Pale soldiers stood over him, their sabers at the ready. Methil Tarcatha rose from somewhere near his feet to look down at him with what might have been disdain, perhaps even disinterest. How could a Valeutan look upon his own and care not at all? His own. Kyle stumbled over that a moment, wondering when he had decided he was a Valeutan.

"Bind him, guard him, feed him and give him another draught of medicine. I must prepare for the journey," Tarcatha said.

Kyle looked around and realized they were camped at the foot of the western falls, that rumble the pound of water into Lake Ta'atit. And spreading before him, a-flutter with feeding fowl, was the way home. Tarcatha tossed the tiny black stone up in the air and caught it with one hand.

"We will be taking a trip together, you and I," Tarcatha laughed but it was humorless. It chilled Kyle to the soul.

Cool quenching water rushing through him, around him, caressing angry fevered flesh. A deep breath taken that suddenly rushed him, familiar, musty and tannic, the slight sweetness of pesticide, the hint of dark obstacles in his path, of the dark reach of stump and branch, of an old mill looming in the depths, of fear and comfort. At last, he roused himself enough in his stupor to realize he was home.

Kyle blinked in the bright light of noon, gasped the richness of Earth air, and felt the solidity of Earth gravity. He almost grinned at his homecoming, until he heard the splash beside him and felt the tug as

Tarcatha pulled him toward shore. Kyle couldn't even move his limbs in his own defense. He didn't know what kept him from simply sinking into the great dark of Potter's Flowage. How long had it been? Perhaps a few days? Not yet a week? Did his family and friends even realize he'd been gone? It was still autumn here, the longest autumn he could ever recall. It might be October, for the crispness in the air, yet relative warmth of the water and the way golden aspen leaves littered the surface of the flowage. A great blue heron suddenly lifted away from the shore.

Tarcatha gave a heaving tug and pulled Kyle up onto the muddy bank. Down around the bend his house stood out of sight of this place. Was Tarcatha as powerful here? He squinted at him, his eyes barely focusing. The wyseer's crimson robes were tattered with burn holes from the splattering cauldron, the magical mix that had erupted at Kyle's touch. He could see that Tarcatha still hadn't found his wits from the shock of Travel as he peered about him distrustfully, his lip curling at the scent of Kyle's home.

Kyle looked down because the bright sky burned his eyes. A dirty, bloodstained scrap of Talik's robe bound his arm. Red, swollen and blistered, both arms seeped, yet he couldn't feel them, a mercy of his delirium, he imagined. A poultice had slipped from the festering wound on his leg. He stared at it in wonderment. How many years ago in how many worlds had the eel bitten him?

"Predators?" Tarcatha demanded, the Metathan word smashing into Kyle's head.

A foot against Kyle's shoulder jostled him. Kyle realized he was lying on his back as the remnant taste of something unpleasant churned in his stomach.

"I am leaving you here while I attend to my business. It makes no difference whether you are alive or dead, but if predators haul you away, that will matter."

Kyle's mouth and limbs couldn't respond.

"You can shake or nod your head. Your voice I have taken so you won't shout for help, and the strength of your limbs so you cannot flee. You will remain here while I collect what I need."

Then Tarcatha had magic that transcended the portals. Kyle found he could barely swallow as Tarcatha prodded him again, and then with exasperation simply hauled him up against the bole of a tree and used Kyle's own cloak to tie him upright against it.

"The histories say the Dugway is west of here," Tarcatha was muttering as he stared about at the looming forest surrounding the flowage, a place giving way from green to golds, oranges and reds. He checked a purse at his side and to Kyle's amazement weighed American money. "If you are not alive when I return, well, good death to you." Tarcatha swept a hand upward and was gone.

Kyle thought he sensed the man continuing to hover over him a moment, then move away. How did he intend to reach Dugway? What did he hope to find there? How many days could Kyle survive tied to a tree?

The sun glimmered in that buttery autumn haze, the leaves blazing and burning, rattling a little in a pleasant breeze as the frogs resumed their chorus and the birds chattered and geese honked. The racket smashed into his skull. He had to shut his eyes, silent and unmoving but a few paces and a shout from home.

CHAPTER TWENTY-EIGHT

"**I** am sorry. Tarcatha seemed untouched by the wyseery. There was nothing I could do," Talik said. Jia held the palif's hand, nodding assurance.

Rupert didn't raise his head from his hands. He felt weary. He had failed. His wyseery had failed to fight off the Methiliim and they simply wiped away the strongest of wyseery he'd woven about Kyle to protect him from detection and harm as if they swept cobwebs from their path. How could he stop this madness if his strongest spells couldn't hold?

It didn't help that he was already drained by the wyseery that kept Metatha from imploding around them, kept the portals from screaming open. Didn't those fools realize the portals went both ways? Remove the ban and sand dragons, eels and Balthysians could come through as easily as wyseers. What pestilence, what banes of all living things might move with seeming ease between worlds? There were worlds Rupert had never even found. Something so innocent-seeming as a fish swimming from one world to another had brought the pestilence of the Withering in its pocket. What worse horrors might there be unrecorded?

Rupert scanned the small glade they rested in, yearning for more warmth than the meager sun could lend him. He spied Davath on one edge of the clearing standing watch as they tended Talik. Barul dozed against a tree out of earshot. The two werran had found the palif dazed and feverish and huddled in a thicket near White Dragon Lake, a place littered with the bodies of the dead and the smoking ruins of wyseery like none seen since the great wars of Metatha's past. Talik only knew he'd told Kyle to flee as he fell, and had last seen him floundering in White Dragon Lake.

What possible hope did he have of saving this world when the powers of the four of them had barely stopped Tarcatha from destroying the portals? Kyle's will to thrust his hand into the boiling cauldron with the symbol of Danat in hand, while Rupert and Jia and even Talik with his own odd brand of wyseery combined their efforts on the cauldron, had been for nothing if Tarcatha remained free. He was the one who had the greatest lore behind him.

Rupert hadn't counted on Martrena. That was a curiosity he might ponder for eternity and not solve. And all that they had expended, they had gained nothing, well, a little more than nothing: they had stalled Tarcatha's inevitable success.

Rupert struggled to untangle the murk of his contact with Kyle. There was no sense of the sand world in this contact and it was a place Rupert would never forget. He hadn't plunged into White Dragon Lake then. Did Tarcatha suspect that Rupert had tied himself to Kyle to track him? Had they somehow muddied that contact?

"Why do they gather there?" Jia asked quietly, swinging her arm toward the vast expanse of Lake Ta'atit in the valley below them where Methiliim had begun arriving, pitching their tents and setting up their fires. "I would have expected them to again put the fire to the cauldron. Do they need some difficult-to-acquire elixir?"

Rupert straightened and stared out at the lake, wishing for a pair of binoculars so he could count the enemy on the far shore. He swallowed hard. He knew that smell, that taste.

"The question should be, what is it that Tarcatha would want from Earth," Rupert said softly.

"Earth!" Talik straightened. "You think they plan to Travel to—"

"Not plan, they have gone. And now, I must follow them."

"How?" Jia demanded, her gaze narrowing on him.

He almost laughed. "You are absurd in your suspicions! Do you still think me your nursery villain, your cosmic evil? Of course I can Travel. How do you think I came here? How do you think I came to be there before? I am the first Traveler, and the maker of the bans. Do you think I would be so foolish as to trap myself in a spell I couldn't undo?"

"If you could Travel so easily, how come you never did so before?" Jia asked, her cheeks going red.

He held up the small pendant Kyle had found in the ruins of his master's house. Jia's mouth fell open as recognition dawned.

Talik was nodding. "The great wyseery was never performed without a back door. After Denalku's fall, the Pale searched for years, and suspected the Fidrel harbored the key, always fearing they would use it to reopen the portals. In Ruperion's journals we found references to a mysterious 'kokapelli' but it was a code word with no meaning."

"It meant this pendant that I found in my Travels on Earth. It is crafted with turquoise, a power stone and silver, a strengthening metal. The figure is part of the mythology of one of Earth's clans. It was an excellent anchor for the ban. Kyle thought it was Jia's white stone that brought him home. It was not. This is what will take me to him. Tarcatha must be stopped. He is a student of my history and I think he plans to find his own weapon of Withering to use for purposes he likely thinks quite noble. The spells he called upon, the herbs he chose, the wyseery he made were all like pages torn from my own book. And I meticulously recorded my long history of researching Earth's military complex and her great destructive weapons." He acknowledged the question mark on Jia's brow. "How do you think I made my first great mistake? It was in an arrogance, not unlike Tarcatha's, with nobler goals."

Rupert stood heavily. "I must go before it is too late."

He'd no more than gathered up his wyseer's oddments into his bag when Davath snapped two sticks together.

Barul's head jerked up, and the wyseers and Talik whipped around to find Davath pointing down slope. Pale soldiers raced uphill on their twisted mounts. Arrows flew around them, skittering among branches, thudding into the ground.

The force threw Rupert to the ground just as the rip of pain raced from his shoulder to his brain. He tried to scramble up, but that moment a mount leapt over him, he saw the shadow of the hoof descending, and knew no more.

"Here!" Jia called, a little too loud, a tremor of panic slipping into her voice. "Oh no, no," she muttered as she knelt beside the grizzled wyseer so pale among the leaf litter. Davath was at her side in an instant, almost pushing a wyseer aside to place a hand against Ruperion's throat.

"He's alive," Davath said, tugging at the wyseer's cape.

"But not for long," Jia said softly, pulling Davath's hands away. He had almost ripped the arrow from the wound. Already blood pooled in Ruperion's clothing. "Ruperion!" she said loudly beside his ear. "You must wake!"

The eyes remained closed, but the lips moved.

"He calls for Danat to give him a star," Talik said from beside her, the palif reaching for Ruperion's forehead, where he left a circular smudge of dirt.

"Kyle needs you, Ruperion. Tarcatha will bring another Withering!" Jia heard her words as if standing beside herself, watching a petulant child make demands from a wyseer. "You promised to protect Kyloreign, to undo all these wrongs! We need you!"

Ruperion's mouth stopped its whispered prayer, and his dark eyes opened, seeming so distant, not like the sharp and predatory gaze that could raise the gooseflesh. He looked from Davath, to her, to Talik, and touched on Barul who stood back, uncertain, his gaze sweeping over the churned ground of their battle. Jia caught the distant movement of a riderless mount trailing its reins as it grazed in a glade. Nearer, another beast stood gamely above its rider, who lay with twisted neck upon the ground. Further into the wood more forms remained.

"Ruperion, you are dying," Jia said. "What do we do?"

"You do not let me die," he said in what might have been a whisper but struck her thunderclap loud.

"You bleed from a serious wound. I don't dare remove the arrow. We have no skills to mend such an injury."

"In my purse there is an elixir, a very potent elixir. Davath knows it. One not to be wasted. One drop, only one, mixed with five parts eel oil, four parts Shestan horn. Remove the arrow, apply it to a poultice, and perform a binding spell—you do at least know how to do that?"

His words came out as a teacher guiding the hands of a small child to carry a wounded songbird. She searched his wyseery bag, sifting through small leaf bundles, pouches, vials, and bark-bound packets waiting for Davath's nod at the unfamiliar substance in a very ancient vial. "I find no eel oil," she said.

"Eel oil is necessary."

"It will take me a day to reach Hindlain and return."

"Then you had better go now."

Jia hesitated only a moment before she leapt away. She raced for Hindlain as if the Pale rode on her heels. She thought of nothing but wings beating at her back, her feet racing over air, the branches peeling back from her, the stones rolling away from her path. Now and then she'd splash through a creek and pause long enough to splash water in her face and drink deeply, refilling the gourds that banged at her hips, holding her sides and gasping as she imagined what her failure might mean. Only Ruperion could stop Tarcatha from returning to Metatha with yet another threat of annihilation. What else could he be seeking there? They could make it, she knew, if they could save Ruperion. She had a hazy sense of the time in Kyle's world, how it seemed to drag in that place so hours became days.

As she ran ever on she almost imagined herself beating the ripples of water to shore, the Traveler only just breaking the surface as she raced ahead to undo what might be done. Undoing, as Ruperion called his spells. Undo nature to free her sinews, give her speed greater than any she could imagine.

Cramping muscles in the end slowed her to a limping walk-trot long before she crept toward the mouth of Hindlain, a dark cloudy night making the sea and falls a formless rush of noise, a black emptiness on the edge of her path. Practiced years of stealth left no trace of even these hurried steps as she passed.

"Hold!"

"It is Jia," she gasped, imagining the torchlight must not be strong enough to reveal her features as she rested, hands on knees and sucked for air for a moment before proceeding.

"You will hold." She heard hurried footsteps on the stone, startled by the coldness in the tone. She'd been gone a week, no more. She couldn't imagine what could possibly have happened. A spear crossed her chest, stopping her. Then she saw Wilnath's familiar features revealed in the torchlight as he approached.

"You fools, it's Jia," he grumbled as he took her in a rough embrace, peering at her as if her face could reveal her story.

"Our orders don't come from you, Wise One," the werran guard returned.

Jia stared over her shoulder at the guard as Wilnath led her on, finding the response strangely insulting, and not a little unnerving.

"Jia, your timing couldn't be better," Wilnath whispered as he led her behind the veil of falls into the warm cavern. Heads popped up to mark her arrival, glances quickly averted. The only face that stared without hesitation at her was Danathea's and—Jia startled at the realization—she could clearly see that some wyseery was about Talik's niece. Danathea raised her hand to cover her mouth, with a slight nod.

"What is going on here, Wil?" Jia asked, wishing she had the time to wonder how Danathea came to be unseen, and yet how it could be that Jia saw her but not those Danathea feared enough to hide from in wyseery among wyseers.

"The voices of reason are losing. Atatha and Isra are at odds. The Kylalnethra lose Hindlain."

"I don't have time to deal with this, Wil. We—"

"Oh, I'm sure you can make time for the council." Isra's words were like ice. Jia turned to find Isra flanked by several wyseers of the old Fidrel Council, all with smug expressions as they peered at her as if looking upon an insolent child. "There has been a notable loss of discipline when the ranks of young and novice wyseers suspect they are above the laws of their elders. Well it is stopped now. The rebellious Kylalnethra are through. It is time you remember you are a Fidrel wyseer. I recall your role in the betrayal of the Fidrel. I'm willing to consider reduced punishment if you recant your foolishness and prove your innocence."

Jia couldn't stop her mouth from falling open. "Where is Atatha, I must speak to him."

"You'll see him in good time. Where is the Traveler?"

Jia didn't need to even sift Isra's words. The woman made no pretense of hiding the spellcraft she used. Jia had no choice but to answer.

"Kyle is captured. I don't have time for politics and protocol. I need eel oil, and now."

The murmurs rose, Wilnath staring at her with his Pale eyes stark. She had dared to counter Isra with the same spell, with the arrogance of an equal. Jia had to trust her own instincts. She didn't have time. Too much was at stake.

Isra stared a moment. "Thus, the danger we feared comes true. He's been no help to us, only to them. Now he's gone from us. Betrayed likely by the very enemy among us, this Talik and Ruperion." Isra almost spat the names.

"No," Jia stated firmly, catching Danathea out of the corner of her eye, the girl signaling caution. Jia didn't have time for caution. "Talik and Ruperion sacrificed more than I. Ruperion is injured and dying. He needs attention or we will lose him. Kyle's been taken by Tarcatha to Earth and we fear he's there to again find some weapon of Withering. Without Ruperion we can't stop him."

"But if Ruperion dies, perhaps so will end the bans and we will not have this foolish hierarchy of haves and have nots. All wyseers will be free to gather the tools they need to."

"You can't end the bans! Not without closing the portals first. You don't know what you'll unleash. You might be opening the gates for those creatures to enter this world as well!"

"Jia, you have overstated your power. You are but a novice and out of fondness for you I have been tolerant, but my tolerance is at an end."

She ignored Wilnath's warning shake of the head, but Jia couldn't stop the anger. The weariness of her race to Hindlain fled as she stood up straighter.

"Where is Atatha?" she demanded.

"Taken ill," Isra said. A motion of her hand drew two werran to Jia's side. They gripped her arms hard.

"Who authorized you to wear a headdress in the council of Kylalnethra?" Jia demanded.

"You do not listen closely, child. Kylalnethra? We are united again, the Fidrel."

"Wil, I need eel oil. This is foolish. I must return." She felt the tug as the werran pulled her backward. "Where is Atatha? There is a traitor among us. Kyle was betrayed. By Isra!" Jia's voice was rising to a shriek and she didn't mind thinking hard on her power stone and lending so much volume to her words that they echoed throughout the caverns, reaching every ear.

"Is that a betrayal or a saving?" Isra asked calmly. "You are dallying with things well beyond you, child."

"Just how did you communicate with the Pale, Isra? Did you tell them exactly where they could capture Kyle? How did they know just where in all Metatha to be, to find us, when no one could have known what Ruperion saw? How was it Tiva and I escaped swarms of Pale when three Methiliim captured the Traveler?"

"Enough." Isra raised her hand and Jia struggled, choking to regain her voice and failing. Didn't anyone see that she used an unnatural wyseery to command her silence thus? A Pale wyseery. She glared at Isra, wishing for the rocks to break from the ceiling and smash into the vile woman's head. But that was a spell more like a Pale wyseer to cast. She wanted to ask Isra where she found the blood for her abominable rituals, where she stored her cauldrons, how she could claim to be Fidrel and betray the Traveler to whom they had sworn. But her throat closed with each thought of speech, making her gasp for breath, choking so that she sagged in the werrans' grip.

"Jia is a traitor who first made us vulnerable to the Traveler's evil and brought Ruperion back to this world through her conniving. All who have heard her heard the ravings of a fool caught in a trap and begging and lying to gain her release. You will disregard any words she said."

Jia stared in amazement. Certainly all the other wyseers present sensed the spells wrapped around Isra's words, spells of compulsion, spells that gave the werran holding her arms the justification to drag her rudely, for they heard truth only from Isra.

The back of the cavern did not have so lofty a roof, its floor the sandy soils of an old spring dried up over the years. And back here she found only the cave birds staring with their pink-shot eyes at the torches of the werran, and the faint light that reached back from the living quarters near the cavern mouth. There she found Atatha, tossing on a mat of sweat-damp rushes, his skin an angry red, and knew he was in a prison of wyseery she didn't have the skill to overcome.

How did Isra dare trust werran guards to watch over wyseers? Jia studied their stony faces and could just detect the hint, the barest whiff of treachery. Isra held them under her spell, completely. And of course wyseers couldn't be trusted to watch over wyseers. They would see what she had done to Atatha. Where were the voices of reason? What of Tiva and Dakul, Wilnath? She couldn't believe that Wil would turn to Isra, not when he had been one of the first to turn away, hot with the passion of Kylalnethra, a passion that had fired so many of their followers. They had fought and bled for this cause! Did it fade and fail so quickly? Was it some poison of Methil Sethina's still festering in him?

Perhaps these last remnants of the Valeutan wise deserved to huddle in caves. They waited five hundred years to rise up, and then gave up all they believed when in two years' time they hadn't yet won. And in the meantime, Ruperion was dying, and likely Kyle as well. In the end, Tarcatha would bring on another Withering. She had no doubt he had no intention of making the world an overflowing garden of wyseer's tools for all who simply wished them.

Jia paced, her teeth grinding her impatience, her muscles screaming as they stiffened from her run. Her stomach growled with hunger, her throat burned for the water pounding so near. She couldn't simply sit here and let everything happen, let Isra defeat the passion. They had waited five hundred years for the Traveler! She brushed against the wall, startling a cave bird. She hesitated, staring at where it huddled as it ruffled its feathers and gave her a cross look. She rummaged among Atatha's robes, knowing where he had always hidden his cache of the most secret elixirs against a casual Pale search.

The false hem of his cloak easily opened and within she felt about for the odd vial or packet, at last finding what she needed. She tore a strip off her own frayed coat and scratched words of warning on it with the droppings of cave birds. She stared at one of the birds, a particularly black one that appeared sleek and strong. It ruffled, it looked away, it stared back, and at last, it fluttered down onto her outstretched arm. She bound the vial to its leg and blew a breath into its ear. She closed her eyes, gripping the stone in her pocket, imagining her voice uttering words that needed to be said. Swiftly, the bird rose and shot from the cavern.

CHAPTER TWENTY-NINE

Wilnath paced near the entrance of the cavern. He had to do something, but didn't know what he dared. Isra had used strong words, so strong he feared it was already too late to alter this horrible path. And what had Jia said of the Traveler, of Talik and Ruperion? They couldn't let it all end like this!

A bird shot by his ear and he caught a glimpse of the small slip of green fabric bound to its leg. He stepped out into the night and watched as it navigated, following a path as it sped from the cavern toward the west.

He turned, ducking back against a tree a moment before subtle footsteps carried two figures out of the reach of the spray of the falls and the thunder that might have forced them to shout. Instead their voices were low, the kind of low that made Wilnath go as still as he possibly could.

"They are dangerous."

Wilnath felt the heat rush his face as he recognized Isra's voice.

"Our hold is tenuous as long as there are heroes to worship. They must be revealed in their bald treason."

"We have no evidence," Tiva responded.

"No evidence? Consorting with Ruperion? Do not the Pale hold the Travel stone now, after a Pale spy came among us?"

"But that isn't how it happened."

"Are you in league, Tiva? Do you know what consequences they face for having done this wrong to the Fidrel?"

Wilnath peered at the two figures and knew that Tiva had chosen her silence, just as Wil had many times since Isra had come and begun to assert herself among the Kylalnethra.

"Do not make me regret trusting you, Tiva. When they are gone …"

"Exile?" There was something guarded in Tiva's stance.

"I thought we might exchange them for good will."

"That is a death sentence, Isra! They will be bled for the cauldrons. Haven't we lost enough good Valeutans and wyseers to this?"

"You're trying my patience, Tiva. A lasting peace, an easing of the burdens of all our people, no more random assaults, aren't these freedoms worth but two lives when so many have gone before?"

"And we're to believe the Methiliim will stop with their sacrifices simply because we give them but two people whose blood will be gone in a short time?"

"This is where you are out of your depth, Tiva. Once the bans are gone, and that will be soon, there will be no need for the Methiliim to cast their lot with evil. They will have access to the powerful tools of other worlds, not tempt fates by mangling the natural order here. Oh think how much such changes will mean to Fidrel lives!"

"But what is the purpose of the Fidrel now, if not preparing for a Traveler to arrive?"

"Well we will again regain our natural place in the order of Metatha, Tiva. We will be the guiding leaders of people, mending their ills, arbitrating their disputes."

"Isra, that was how the bans came in the first place. They didn't work."

"Ah, but that was before we saw and learned from the alternative. What an incentive it is to control yourselves when you know how bad it can become if you don't."

Tiva didn't speak, but Wil had no doubt she was thinking just as he was. Isra had been in league all along. She was delivering them to the Pale, five hundred years after their defeat, but most surely. Were they to believe the Pale would simply turn the rule over to wyseers, that the Methiliim would openly embrace the Fidrel, that the Pale would invite Valeutans into their lives?

Wilnath lifted his head. He thought he'd heard a whisper, the slightest wordless message reaching his ears. There, again, a spell tickled against his ear. It was Jia, grown more powerful than even Wil had realized if she could guide a cave bird and simultaneously use wyseery to defy Isra's silencing spell.

The message was clear, so incredibly clear, it was the one thing that could move him to action.

"Atatha is dying."

Even as his heart pounded in denial, the blood rushed him. An icy calmness stole over him, as if he had stepped outside his body and now manipulated himself as if he were moving power stones about in a spell.

Wilnath backed into the dark, then crept behind sentries who watched for their enemies approaching from the forest, not from their own camp. His ears roared long after he had left behind the thundering falls and wind-tossed headland. Atatha was the father he had never known, the wyseer who had marked him adept and chosen him from among all those dark-haired Valeutans with their loving families. Atatha chose him. Wilnath the outcast, his Pale blood so visible in his features. And everyone knew that the Pale couldn't learn wyseery. Yet Atatha chose him, saw in him, knew that Wilnath could rise above the cursed blood in his stock. He might not be the most skilled of wyseers, but he passed his levels and that was more than any other half-Pale had ever accomplished.

Wilnath bumped against the bole of a tree, startling himself. He'd been almost running. He realized, by the way the breath ripped at him, but he hadn't even been watching his path, yet followed it as if Jia guided him as she had the bird. How had Jia placed her whisper in his head? Where did he think he was going? He simply let his feet carry him, his body tuned to the sounds of Metatha.

With every pause to catch his breath, leaning against trees and clutching his side, he wondered what wyseery Jia had used to make the journey to Hindlain so swiftly. Or had she been that swift. How much time had passed since Ruperion had been injured? Was he already dead? And Atatha? And what of Kyle—

He stumbled into the clearing blazing with afternoon sun, coming up short to find Davath's arrow poised to pierce him in the chest. His mind reeled at the sudden brightness when it seemed he'd been running through the night forever. When had day come? His chest heaved, the sweat slick on him as he sank to his knees, clutching his side. Talik stared at him in silence as he tended a fallen Ruperion, who huddled beneath a bloodstained cloak, still alive, but feverish and pale. The cave bird let out a disturbed squawk from the dark shade of a boulder, its head tucked beneath its wing, and a small reward of grubs neatly piled before it. The cave bird, he was the messenger.

"Jia's held prisoner, and Atatha, she says Atatha's dying of wyseery," Wilnath gasped out, accepting water from Barul's gourd, his hand trembling so that most of it spilled down his chin.

"Prisoner, why?" Talik asked, settling a reassuring hand on Ruperion, who tried to rouse himself.

"Isra. She's named you all traitors. She's taken over the council and says the Kylalnethra are over. Jia accused her openly of betraying Kyle, twice, which Isra fails to deny. Isra intends to arrange a trade with Tarcatha to open the portals." Wilnath's words tumbled from him, desperate.

"I left Danathea. What will they do to her?" Talik muttered. He shook his head. "What of the other council members? Certainly the werran aren't allowing such foolishness."

"Talik," Ruperion said, his voice a whisper. "You underestimate Isra's craft and ambition. I wondered when we'd learn her motive for rejoining the Kylalnethra. They are powerless to resist her. Dissenters, like Wilnath, were forced to follow or risk her setting the werran upon them. Likely this is why Atatha is a prisoner."

"We must do something! She's killing him. Maybe if you come back with me, it'll stall her, we can get help to Atatha."

"Wilnath you aren't thinking," Talik said gently. "She isn't going to trust you. She'll simply hold us prisoner until Tarcatha returns and it will be too late."

"But what now? We can't just …" The last reserves of Wilnath's strength wavered then, hearing his own pleas sounding to him like those of a child.

"I know it's hard to accept, but our priority must first be to stop Tarcatha. Ruperion can do it. But as you see, Ruperion is fighting another battle now. This time it will be Danat … and perhaps a little Kylik, we must count on, not wyseery."

Wilnath hated the words he heard coming from the palif but felt the energy that had propelled him here draining, wondering if that overwhelming sense of hopelessness was his alone. The tiny whisper of Jia's spell had fallen oddly silent.

"We must count on Palif Talik to stop Tarcatha," Ruperion admitted in a whisper. "But time in that world creeps by, an hour for a Metathan day. Tarcatha does not yet have so great a lead that I can't find him. There is a powerful wyseery that if any young wyseer can use, it will be Jia. She's skilled indeed. I must leave it to her to accomplish. I am stretched too thin to do much more than ask the moons to bring me healing."

Ruperion gestured and Davath was beside him in an instant, the wyseer's bag open to Ruperion's groping hand. It emerged with a sliver of almost clear glass, pinkish in this light, opaque.

"This is a very special power stone from a place called Baraboo. Talik has made a healing potion at my direction. Take one part of it and bind it in manfish leaf about this stone and send the cave bird back to Jia. It is all that I can do, and probably more than I can handle. Do you know any diversion spells?"

Wilnath nodded, staring at the wyseer who so calmly assessed this world falling apart.

"It would be wise for you to ward Talik and the two werran, lest they fall prey as those with Isra have."

"Will she know what to do with it?" Wilnath asked as he scrounged in his bag for a limp manfish leaf and gently spread the potion on the leaf, then using a thread of his green robe, bound the leaf about the stone. When he looked up, still awaiting a response, he found the old wyseer's eyes closed. How many generations they had vested such hatred in this single man, and he lay here, vulnerable, his sleep halfway his death, and their futures were still wholly in his hands.

CHAPTER THIRTY

A flutter of wings stirred the dark. It had been dark forever, it seemed. The torches had sputtered out and since Isra had not commanded that they be lit again, they were not. Jia mentally tried to calculate how much time had passed since Wilnath had begun his journey. It had been night when she returned. It seemed it would never cease to be night.

She shifted a little, so that she could again check Atatha's pulse, a fluttery thing like a wounded bird struggling to escape a net. Heat rose from him as if from a banked fire, too much heat for one so old. A dry heat and silence. Her hand brushed against something feathery soft and she startled. She felt the spidery claws of a bird foot against her skin as it hopped upon her wrist. She gently felt for the string that bound a leaf pack to its leathery leg. How would she find light to read by? If she attempted wyseery, certainly the guards would be upon her. She let her fingers probe the object as the bird rejoined its fellows in the eaves of the cave, a rustling and disturbance of the dark that seemed as if it came from a vast void that belied what the light had shown her of a low grotto.

The packet was clearly some wyseery. She recognized the soft underside of manfish leaf. Power emanated from the tiny packet, something that tingled her fingertips, sent heat pulsating up her arm. A sniff revealed pungent eel oil in its essence. Then she had the strangest sense of Ruperion's wisdom in its crafting, Wilnath's hesitant hand in the desperate making and the faith of Talik in its essence, a power that seemed at once deeper and older than even the wyseery of Ruperion.

In the darkness, nothing to break the shadows apart, no edges to separate her fancy from reality, she turned inward. She'd been here before, long ago, when she had sought understanding for things so strange. Suddenly, she snapped the package open. The potent paste clung to the leaf and the power stone gave off the faintest light. And she knew, just knew instantly what she must do, that this inward way was always the way, had always been the key to knowing what she must know and seeing what she must see. It was how she had followed Kyle's journey to Earth, and how she had drawn him back. It was how she'd guided the cave bird and Wilnath. It seemed like forever since she had listened to the wiser self within, even though to a lesser degree she'd done it even this day. And even as she realized it, she sensed the faintest hint of Ruperion, could almost see him with a raised eyebrow as if it had been so plainly obvious that he asked what had taken her so long to figure it out.

Clutching the sharp glow of stone in her hand, she gently spread the paste upon Atatha's chest. How did she know? She knew that she just knew. The light grew around her, around them, emanating from the stone in her hand and the paste she spread. The eyes of cave birds emerged as small green and pink pinpricks against the grotto walls. If the glow brightened, certainly guards would see it leaking around the dark covering over the grotto entrance. Would it brighten beyond, illuminating the narrow chasm and at last into the vast cavern, dwarfing the light of all those torches? She thought of Ruperion as she gently spread the paste, seeing the hawkish gaze that sometimes reminded her of Atatha, how the villain the Fidrel had long dared not even name had so gently ministered Kyloreign. She pictured him lifting a newborn from the frigid black waters of a far world, felt his love for his homeland, his devotion to his people and family, and desperation to make right what he could. She thought she saw a nod, somewhere, some hint that perhaps she truly did touch him in this inward journey, as he had pursued Kyle from world to world, as she had clung to Kyle's link to her white stone. What wyseery Ruperion wielded! The Fidrel had forgotten so much. Blood didn't need to be part of the power.

Atatha took a deep breath. Another. A hand shot up and clutched hers holding the power stone above his forehead.

Suddenly something snapped in her head, a blinding pain that made her gasp and she could see the spells being broken, the frayed ends coiling back like a rope stretched beyond endurance. Her throat relaxed, her mouth opening with ease as speech returned to her. Atatha blinked and looked up at her. What did he see in the faint light, huddled in a damp corner of this blackened cave? Did her eyes glow like the cave birds, bathed in the oddity of the pinkish light thrown by the stone? She still felt Ruperion, so present within her, her own self still moving slowly through a place she seldom traveled.

"This is a worthy effort," Atatha whispered to her.

She held up her hand, gesturing with her head toward where guards stood beyond the curtain.

She bent to his ear and whispered in ragged breaths the awful tale of what Isra and Tarcatha had done. They must escape. Both knew it. But Atatha could barely sit up without her help and they had many guards to overcome.

Jia wasn't sure how much was her initiative, how much Atatha's, how much Ruperion's, her very movements slow and methodical, instinctive. She clenched the stone in her hand, gripped it so that its sharp edges dug into her palm, keeping her present in the moment and hiding the glow. She gathered up the oddments she'd found within his cloak and they crept toward the doorway, her one arm steadying Atatha. They paused each time a scuff of the stony floor came loud enough to make the green eyes light along the walls, or dark feathers shuffle with disgust.

She paused for long moments at the opening, considering the scents that came around the curtain, the feel of the air, the least little hint of the muffled sounds of life in the caverns. She had never concentrated with such purpose. Not when she had been forced to sneak into a Pale encampment to become an adept, not in her years of stealth and rebellion, never. A depth deeper than she knew she could go loomed before her, tempting her, opening up the possibilities of what more she might discover about herself if she simply leaped. Yet, in the same instant, that weak and distant sense of Ruperion seemed to be holding out a cautioning hand as if to advise such exploration be saved for later. Atatha was watching her. She could feel that uniquely Atatha gaze. Did he know? Had he found this depth, and this was simply a step she should be learning as a wyseer? Or was he wondering at what kept her standing so frozen in the blackness of the caverns, the strange rumble always under foot of great falls pounding the sea somewhere far below?

At last she straightened, certain in the picture she saw from the sounds she heard, the currents she felt. Two werran stood between them and the water-carved chasm that served as a corridor to the inhabited portion of the caverns. One dozed as he stood. The other was preoccupied in his thoughts. How did she know this? She simply knew. Beyond, the hubbub of life remained subdued compared to the liveliness she had known before Isra's return. She wondered again how Danathea hid among so many wyseers unseen. Should she somehow try to slip Talik's niece out with them? She knew she couldn't. If truly unseen, she probably could leave far easier than Jia and Atatha. Jia held out her hand, the stone shining through the flesh to reveal bloody red and pink.

"Break. Sleep." She whispered, simply. And knew, without checking, that Isra's spell had shattered and the werran would wake in a few hours, stunned to know what task had been set to them.

She hesitated only a moment, wondering if it was her wyseery or Ruperion's that came through. It didn't really matter at this moment. What mattered was she and Atatha must escape before they were bled into a cauldron.

Atatha moved slowly at first, as they pushed through the curtain and into the passageway. In the dim light of a spare candle almost expired she saw the two werran slumped to the floor in their path. They stepped over them, hugging the shadows as they passed the candle and rounded the corridor to the cavern.

They stopped in the long shadow thrown by a pillar of melted stone. How she wished now for a bit of the ilyath wyseery. They had a ten-span to cross to the next crevice in which they could hide, then another five- or ten-span to reach the mouth of the cavern. Would they be more noticed by dashing, or by creeping?

Jia glanced at Atatha, whose eyebrows arched at her. He jerked his head toward the small cluster of wyseers hovering near Isra. They couldn't possibly miss seeing the fugitives once they left the shadows. And two werran stood near the cave mouth. Had it all been a hopeless exercise?

Jia shrugged, then felt Atatha's pressure against her side, urging her forward. They truly had nothing to lose. Bled into a cauldron or cut down by the wyseery of their own? Jia thought she'd find the latter a more satisfying death.

Jia took a deep breath and stepped boldly from the shadows, striding toward the next cover with purpose. From the corner of her eye, she could see the animation as Isra polled a circle of wyseers, her attention moving ever nearer to their path. Tiva's gaze fell on them, her mouth fell open then clamped shut. Jia cringed, waiting for the shout of alarm. But instead Tiva turned to Dakul who stood behind several others, his position opposite the cavern's mouth.

"State your allegiance, Dakul!" Tiva shouted suddenly, her voice drawing all eyes in the cavern toward the diminutive elder whose expression went pale at the accusation. Jia thought certainly that Dakul, too, had to see them. His eyes widened at her a moment, then he turned on Tiva, returning the accusation, their words startling cave birds and drawing the bored, curious and simply nosy to close the circle around them.

Atatha nudged Jia and they headed for cover at an almost run, then dashed again for the cavern door, stumbling to a halt when the two werran crossed their spears to block the exit.

"Hold!" one shouted.

"Break, sleep!" Jia hissed, thrusting her bloody red hand toward his face. She and Atatha pressed on as the two werran sank toward the floor. But suddenly there was a thunderclap that rose above the falls. It raised the hairs on Jia's neck. Isra strode toward them, her hand held outward in a motion that made Jia's blood run cold.

Jia and Atatha backed away, the falls roaring at their backs, the path narrow and slick.

She had to concentrate, to give it every element of her attention, even as her certain death marched toward her with a storm crow's gaze.

"Break!" Jia shouted, a word with so much more strength behind it than she could even imagine, the word ripping from her throat so that she tasted blood. The effort made her sway a bit, almost lose her balance, and for a moment, she leaned on Atatha.

Isra laughed and held up her hands to show she stood unscathed. But the word hadn't been meant for Isra, but for the hundreds of werran and wyseers behind her. Jia sensed Atatha gathering himself, heard some muttered curse beneath his breath and she almost felt as if he leant her his strength. That moment, Isra thrust her hand from her, and though at least eight paces remained between them, Jia felt the force of hands throwing her backward toward the lip of the ledge. The falls roared at her back, the spray drenching her; the scent of wet and the fertile waters of Ta'atit Lake infused her thoughts, the pounding water sending its own wind back at her as it tumbled at least eighty-span to the boiling surface of the sea.

Without Atatha's counter spell, thrown hastily, they both would have been blown into the torrent. The gap narrowed and as Jia regained her balance, Isra lay hands on her. From Isra's other hand came a sudden blast that struck Atatha full in the face, glancing off and striking Jia like daggers of fractured stone. In that moment, she had the briefest image of blood blooming across Atatha's face. In what must be the longest instant she had ever lived, she felt herself falling backward into the thunder of water. She grabbed for that steady force that had gripped her, grasped arm and fabric. She knew she fell, and Atatha. The pressure of water slammed her, swept her with it. She sensed the writhing fear in the arm of Isra she gripped, pulled, and dragged down with her.

Jia didn't panic. She let go of Isra in that heartbeat of eternity as they fell toward certain death. She gripped the token Rupert had sent her and climbed deep into her soul, at first to hide from the inevitable that she knew would come. Then, in that last spark of certain thought, she sought her body's memory of its evolution and that sensation she had felt as she swam to the world of the eels and back. To think scales, silvery fins, a twist of tail, gills flaring wide, the arch of desperation as it struggled against the current pulling it into the depths of a Metathan sea.

CHAPTER THIRTY-ONE

The familiar and musty scent filled Rupert's lungs, the world growing dim and dark as he rose slowly to find the sun low over Potter's Flowage, throwing up a golden glow with juts of black stump breaking the buttery ripples. Six days he'd fought to regain his strength, giving Tarcatha six hours' lead on him. They could be anywhere by now. But certainly Tarcatha could never have imagined the world he arrived in. How far could he have gone in six hours, disoriented in a modern world that moved so swiftly in its relative slowness, and speaking alien languages? And just what would Rupert do when he finally faced him?

Rupert scanned the shore, stunned to discover Kyle leaning against a tree, his head lolling forward to his chest. He hesitated a moment, everything frozen in one caught breath, before his wyseer's sense told him it wasn't a lifeless body he had discovered.

Travel weariness settled deep into a body already worn by his battle with death as he waded through the mucky shallows, water snakes slithering and frogs leaping at his every step, ages of mud tugging at his feet. It seemed strange all the life that leapt from around him, the insects, the reptiles and amphibians. Despite its many fowl, Metatha seemed a sterile, silent place now.

He sloshed to Kyle's side, his noisy passage silencing the wild racket of the Black River bottomlands, but not at all rousing Kyle.

Tarcatha had left him to die. He could see the spells wound tightly about the young man whose own mentor had tricked him into peril. Tarcatha didn't need a living Reign. Only his body, and his blood.

When Rupert untied the robe that held the young man against the tree trunk, Kyle sagged, the tree sap grasping at his tunic where Kyle's struggle had scuffed and wounded the bark. Rupert didn't have time to be gentle, yet Kyle had become like a fragile bubble that might burst at the least touch.

Rupert tried to find the young man's unfocused gaze. "It's my fault, Kyle. I— I seem destined to bring Metatha to the brink of disaster with my own selfish fear."

"Oh yes, fear," he said as if Kyle had the words to protest. He dug in his wyseer's purse and made a small paste of herbs and added the barest pinch of precious powder. "I was too afraid to say no to Denalku's madness, and too afraid to see what legacy I'd left to my home, a place you couldn't imagine to remember. I should have gone with you. And look where we are. Sure, the Methiliim were a fanatical lot before they got their hands on you, but ..."

Kyle's gaze had hardened on him and Rupert didn't finish the thought. He pressed the paste into Kyle's mouth, muttering the spells he had never truly forgotten. Tarcatha's wyseery was strong, each tendril seeming to double back and rethread itself as soon as Rupert undid it. He'd never encountered such spells, stronger than anything he'd ever tried to undo. In the bad days of Metatha before he'd banned Travel he'd come to prominence through his skills in undoing the worst acts of the wyseer wars. But Tarcatha's wyseery wasn't natural. It followed its own laws in the twisted way that benign things brought out of their own environments can be turned into something deadly. At the same time, there was something different about Kyle, too, as if the impurities had burned away leaving behind a man who only vaguely resembled what he had been. Was it the ilyath mark that hinted of some lurking wyseery beneath it all? Something Tarcatha hadn't touched, something Ruperion couldn't touch? Was that the mark of Atatha, or the mark of a Traveler?

Ruperion took a deep breath. He felt torn between worlds with too many spells scattered across the void. At last he added a power stone, knowing that it would only draw that much more from what little strength he had left. He gently stroked the cold stone against the angry red skin of Kyle's throat, both men sweating in the silent battle against unseen bonds. He could feel the way Kyle tried to break the bonds with the sheer force of his will. The last of autumn's cold weather mosquitoes flocked to their heat, clouds of them in each breath Rupert took. At last, Kyle lurched forward into Rupert's arms from the force of his own struggle, a guttural shout of breath giving him back his voice.

"Dugway," Kyle gasped. "I don't know why or where that is … He has money. He … he seems to know what to do."

Rupert went chill, the sweat on his skin raising gooseflesh. In the destruction of Denalku's Reign the Pale hadn't destroyed everything. Talik proved that. But someone had known to seek and whisked into hiding Ruperion's logs of two hundred years of Travel. To how many wyseers had it been handed down? Tarcatha had claimed some descendancy from the famed Ruperion. Had it been his own family who kept the damning tales that could undo Metatha?

Rupert tried to pull Kyle to his feet, but the eel-bitten leg gave way beneath him. Rupert struggled to get an arm around the rail-thin young man and staggered under the weight as he followed an uneven path along Potter's Flowage.

"He thinks I sought a weapon of Withering," Kyle whispered in Metathan, correcting himself to English as he continued. "He wanted to beat me to it."

Ruperion found himself hushing Kyle's apology for allowing himself to be so easily manipulated, thinking of so many youthful apologies he'd heard seemingly eons ago when he tended the childish scrapes and bruises. It was stronger, nearer, than his memory of his own son, now long gone.

When Rupert banged through the door of the Nelson home, Betty Nelson dropped the basket of laundry in her arms and rushed to open the door to Kyle's room.

Before Betty could speak, Rupert cut her off.

"He's weak and needs some tending, mostly rest. There's a very, very bad man looking for him. Whatever you do, don't try to stop Tarcatha yourself." Rupert added that last as much for Kyle as Betty. It was all coming from so far away, a roar in his ears of water, of the blood of exertion, of the wearying of Travel and wyseery.

He realized he stood before Betty, whose mouth hung open with dozens of unexpressed questions fighting to escape. How would he face Tarcatha when he could barely command his thoughts to remain in the present? He clasped his hands and forced himself to find his center as the first of Betty's questions came pouring out.

"No, I don't need a hospital," he heard Kyle say firmly at some question Rupert hadn't heard. Kyle seemed like too much of a man to be in this boy's room and bed. But a few weeks, years ago, it had been. The posters and trophies, the cartoons and bumper stickers pinned to a bulletin board, seemed childish and trite when worlds hovered on the brink of annihilation.

"I'll be back as soon as I can," Rupert said. "I don't know what I can do. He's stronger than I am. If he's gone for Dugway, he's looking for a military base in Utah. He's pretty resourceful. I don't doubt he'll find his way there. The important thing is he not find you. He needs you to get home. Hide, run, escape. Life matters not to him."

Rupert hesitated a moment as Betty's questions grew louder. He heard a door shut and Paul Nelson's voice asking what was going on.

Betty had a hold of Rupert's sleeve, a Metathan wyseer's robe that seemed to suddenly draw her notice as she then looked to her son dressed in a Metathan garb. She stammered to silence. Rupert gently removed her hand as Paul came to the door and simply stared, his mouth forming a hard line, his glance at Rupert hard and stabbing.

"You'll need to do some explaining to your parents. I told your mother what I could, but, well, you know."

He pushed past Paul who was still struggling to find words as Betty began to peel the soiled clothes from Kyle's back. Rupert strode from the house to his little shack on the edge of the property. Already trembling with Travel sickness and far too much wyseery expended already, he donned dry jeans and a t-shirt, grabbed cash and the keys to his truck. He slammed open the old tackle box that served as his wyseer's purse on Earth, picking through the dried herbs and stones and other oddments he'd collected over his long exile. He swept what he needed into his wyseer's purse and tucked a change of clothes, a toothbrush and other necessities of this world into a small canvas bag. He was old and he knew it. He'd spent too many years nursing his wine, and a grudge, letting Betty's cooking gather above his belt. Tarcatha was young, strong, filled with his illicit wyseery and the power of a leader on a mission. Rupert had nothing to beat him with but home-field advantage, and if Tarcatha had spent years memorizing his logs, even that was a slim advantage.

CHAPTER THIRTY-TWO

The Great Salt Lake spread forbidding and vast beneath him, glittering with moon and starlight as they prepared to land. City lights ended abruptly in a deep dark that hinted of certain death for a manfish. It all seemed a blur. Just hours ago he'd been in a Metathan forest watching the red cliffs overlooking Ta'atit emerge and the fowl on the lake's surface rouse themselves with the dawn. He couldn't even remember the wild drive to Minneapolis and his frenzied attempts to make an already boarding 10 p.m. flight to Salt Lake City that would have him on the ground at 1 a.m. local. He kept checking his watch. Again, again. Fourteen hours. What had Tarcatha accomplished in fourteen hours on Earth? And what of Metatha? Another week had passed.

Rupert roused himself from his meditative stare out the window and gripped the collection of stones and the Kokopelli in his pocket. He sensed it there, somewhere beneath him, the Traveling stone. West of the lofty Wasatch Range, over the brown and barren Quirrh Mountains, past Tooele and its depot of rusting chemical weapons that even Denalku hadn't dared to pilfer, through mountain pass and over paths the Donner Party once trod, there nudging into the Great Salt Lake Desert waited Dugway Proving Ground. It would take more wyseery to cross that expanse, to pass through guarded gates and concertina-wire enclosures. Rupert had already readied his own little spell, cousin to the ilyath, that he'd need to pass unseen. Had Tarcatha only just arrived? Did he seek a means of travel to Dugway, in no rush because he knew he alone possessed the means for Travel? Or had he been there and back?

As Rupert was preparing to land in Salt Lake City, had his plane already begun its descent to Minneapolis? How could Tarcatha move so quickly, so secretively through this strange world with its strange language? It had taken years for Rupert to perfect behavior to not attract attention to himself. It had taken years to learn the language, to read it, to unravel the mysteries of another world. Had Tarcatha gleaned this much from Rupert's logs, or was it some greater wyseery that allowed him to so quickly master what had taken Rupert Metathan generations to accomplish?

As he gripped the stones, he sensed the Travel stone closing, nearer and nearer. Did Tarcatha sense him? What would he face?

When he stepped off the plane, he quickly found a restroom and slipped into a stall. The door latch was loose, but he perched on the back of the toilet stool, laying out his magic oddments, oblivious to the sounds of voices, travelers coming and going, urinals flushing, the sounds of the custodian unlocking the towel dispensers. At last he flicked his lighter beneath the tiny sliver of ilyath that would render him invisible. A tiny curl of smoke rose and he heard, seemingly distant, someone telling someone that smoking wasn't permitted here. He let the wyseery wash through him as the smoke of the ilyath curled upward and he breathed it in deeply.

He felt tentative again. Too much wyseery pulled him apart. Wyseery across a void. Wyseery that tied him to Kyle, to the ilyath, to the Traveling stone. The door to the bathroom stall opened suddenly and a custodian blinked at him. Rupert tucked the sliver of ilyath into his pocket as the custodian eyed the disembodied breath of smoke dissolving above Rupert's head. The man shook his head and went back to his work, eyeing the empty stall in the mirror as Rupert slipped out the open doorway into the terminal.

He froze. There at the empty gate at which Rupert had just arrived stood a tall man in a crimson cloak, staring about him suspiciously as he peered at the schedule showing the return flight departure time for Minneapolis. Tarcatha looked down at the scrap of paper in his hands, then peered at the words, as if uncertain what they said but knowing what they should look like. A few travelers and staff moved through the terminal. No one looked at this man in his strange outfit. A custodian brushed against him, apparently startled to have bumped into anything. Rupert realized that Tarcatha, too, had the wyseery to make himself unseen. If not for the seeing stone in Rupert's pocket, he, too, would not see Tarcatha.

One hour had passed. Another whole day on Metatha. In three hours the flight would board again. Three more Metathan days. The dual clock never seemed silent in Rupert's head. Someone opened the jetway door and Tarcatha slipped through before it shut with a slam. Rupert found a seat near the window where he could see if Tarcatha at any point left the plane other than through the jetway door, and waited. Could Tarcatha read time in this world? Did he know how long it would be before the craft took off again?

The wee hours of night crept across the airport, the occasional flight taking off or landing, but at a pace slowing to the point it almost, but didn't quite, stop. There was a weighty silence in the cavernous place. The weariness was so entrenched! He felt his breathing slow, sensed the way his mind wandered into places better left untouched. He sensed the way little pieces of him trickled away with each touch of his wyseery, the little bit of him in each portal, in the people he'd met on Metatha, in Kyle.

Tarcatha was him, he decided, as he contemplated the reflection in the night-blackened window of the empty seat he occupied. In Tarcatha, he faced himself as a younger man, for certainly the Methiliim had learned all of Rupert's own craft from the elder's logs. Centuries of wisdom he'd recorded in the scribbly hand of a wyseer too caught up in the sheer wyseery of it to contemplate the rights and wrongs of what he did. He had kept up his logs as if he left something for posterity, like some presidential library that others would peruse to marvel at his skill and how the future had come from him. He'd recorded how he cased Dugway, how they planned to steal a weapon and return it to Metatha to at last stop the Pale.

What an arrogant wyseer he had been, drunk on his power! He had been the guiding hand of Valeutan chieftains for hundreds of years. He was Metatha. Many paths. It was almost as if he had been chosen to make Metatha what it was. He had thought that once. Perhaps, deep down, he still did. Or fancied he did. Indeed, Metatha's future had much owed to him. Danat give him a gallon glass of wine to let him forget it all.

Had Tarcatha understood all of it? Tarcatha had an added edge, that forbidden power that came from bending the natural out of sorts, using his blood sacrifices to lend power to each spell, to use the sheer wickedness of profane action to add that special magical property that had so abhorred the Metathans of ancient times. The Metathans were slow to rise up to what disgusted them, but it could be done. Once, Pale and Valeutan had gathered to the banners of the Palifiim to purge all the wyseers in their own bloody retribution. It was the very thing that made Talik so dangerous to the Methiliim. It was the thing that could tempt Isra. For peoples so caught up in the wrongs of their past, the Metathans seemed too willing to repeat them.

Rupert shook himself, trying to peer past the reflection of empty seats in the terminal window. Would Tarcatha recognize him? If he could find an open seat he might appear just like any other traveler to a wyseer with a seeing stone. Unless Tarcatha had a way of sensing the wyseery about him. Rupert wasn't even sure how much of his wyseery would stand the magicless landscapes of Earth. It would be nearing dawn when the flight departed and late morning when they landed. If he dared wait until Tarcatha reached the Black River Forest to try to stop him, it might be too risky. He might ferret out Kyle and this chase would be for nothing.

How had Tarcatha reached the airport from Potter's Flowage?

He realized he'd dozed when the intercom announced that the flight was about to begin boarding. He sat up suddenly, seeing a sparsely peopled waiting area, a few weary travelers gripping their coffees as they milled about the gate, as others disappeared around the bend of the jetway to board. Dawn was trying to creep over the mountains somewhere. He shook himself, but the Travel weariness still clung. It would take more than a two-hour catnap.

The flight wasn't full. At first he couldn't see Tarcatha and a moment of panic almost sent him racing out of the plane. But the Travel stone was so close he could almost touch it. Then he saw the red cloak peeking from behind a bulkhead where Tarcatha stood out of the way until all the passengers were seated. Rupert kept his gaze on the seats ahead as he passed, Tarcatha studied him with a stony gaze, but he was doing that to all the passengers. Rupert took a seat a few rows behind Tarcatha, watching as the wyseer eyed those around him with his mouth curled in distaste.

What had he found? Had Dugway changed in all these years? Perhaps they no longer had that secretive little closet of horrors. Did he come back to find Kyle and make him help? Or had he instead found some other tool of Withering?

Rupert shook himself. He had to grip his fancy. The airplane was already in the air and he didn't remember the final preparations or even the takeoff. Flight attendants were moving though the cabin collecting empty trays. Was he dozing? He glanced at his watch again, stunned to find they were two hours into the flight. Sun glinted off the wings as the plane flew above the tops of morning storms thundering over the plains like the saber-wielding horsemen of the Pale kicking up tornadoes of dust in their wake...

He needed to get a grip! He shoved his hand in his pocket, seeking the warmth of the power stone. There.

He saw Tarcatha tense. Rupert let the stones drop from his fingers and watched as Tarcatha carefully studied passengers around him, as if looking for something familiar. Rupert slid down in his seat as Tarcatha's scrutiny drew near. Not here, not on the airplane. Rupert needed a few more hours yet to catch his wind, to somehow stop this strange sense of wyseery dividing him into tiny ilyath slivers like wood chips struck from his soul.

He jerked alert to find Tarcatha peering down at him, his face a mixture of glee and rage.

"Ruperion!" Tarcatha spat the name as if he hurled a dart and Rupert felt it strike his temple as if it had been a blow. Several passengers turned at the sound of a voice where no one stood.

Rupert lurched forward, throwing Tarcatha back, then ran through the airplane toward the galley where he might have room to maneuver. Tarcatha fell against passengers, who startled from their reading, then quickly regained his feet and raced after Rupert. As Tarcatha rounded the bulkhead wall, he ripped aside the curtain and Rupert tossed a pot of hot coffee into the wyseer's face. Tarcatha bellowed.

A buzz of voices rose in the cabin at the torn galley curtain and the coffee erupting from nowhere. Rupert backed away as Tarcatha extended his hand. Rupert dodged aside. Something smashed into him as a force meant to kill blasted into a wing exit door. A hissing roar followed, then a blast as the door peeled away from the plane. Rupert felt himself falling toward the space, the force of his powerstone and a shouted spell anchoring him to the deck as blankets, pillows, papers and luggage were sucked out of the plane, oxygen masks falling, screams ripping through the airplane. The plane veered sharply, descending rapidly.

The cold penetrated, the pressure sucking the wind from Rupert with such force he expected to see his own lungs blowing out through the bright hole. It was only moments and he could feel himself slowing as the plane turned inside out. He felt invulnerable as his blood raced through him in search of oxygen. He found Tarcatha anchored to a bulkhead nearby, his tattered crimson robes billowing about him.

The plane fell. The screams became a white noise like the roar of air over the wings, the shudder of the plane. Rupert laughed suddenly, giddy, crazed, as he raised a stone and threw a curse at Tarcatha. Tarcatha ducked, throwing back a blast that struck the bulkhead, leaving an indentation the size of a watermelon.

Rupert launched at the wyseer, picturing himself like a wild cat leaping at its prey, a raptor closing its talons. He fell hard on Tarcatha, the air whistling from the surprised wyseer through a flutter of lips. Rupert laughed in that wild giddiness of oxygen starvation. Tarcatha guffawed as he choked on Rupert's weight. Rupert tried to smash Tarcatha's head against the cast frame of a seat, but he couldn't seem to pick the man's head up from the floor. He teetered, laughing, unable to pull in the breath he needed. Tarcatha swiped at him, his spells flying haphazardly, ineffective as he bungled his thoughts.

Fitfully they batted at one another like kittens at play, rolling about in the tossing airplane. Rupert grasped Tarcatha's crimson robe, pulling it free. He reached for the medicine pouch, hoping to fling it toward the hole in the world, the hole that continued to draw papers into the air, that made the crimson robe dance about the cabin by itself.

At last Rupert started to regain his sense of place, of motive. Through fuzzy double vision he suddenly saw the wide-eyed passengers, oxygen masks to their faces, staring at Tarcatha's Methiliim robe settling to the floor. Rupert's head pounded as the plane finally descended toward a runway, the oxygen rushing his blood.

In that moment of revelation, Tarcatha threw him toward the open door. Rupert grabbed the wyseer by the hair, a roaring bellow in his ear and the Methiliim's own spell kept them both from tumbling out onto the wing and the tarmac speeding by.

The plane lurched as its wheels touched, emergency vehicles chasing after the plane as the engines roared and it slowed its race down the runway. Rupert gripped his power stone muttering the ancient Metathan words to untie the strands holding Tarcatha's medicine pouch to his belt. The purse began to fall away.

Tarcatha shouted a reply lost in the tumult of frightened passengers and roaring sirens. A flash of light shot at him and Rupert dodged aside at the last moment. Tarcatha was already gone when he opened his eyes. He saw the movement out onto the wing and raced after him. Blood ran down his cheek. How badly was he hurt? His head throbbed, his movements weak and jerky. The plane came to a stop as he stepped onto the wing, and he almost fell to the tarmac below. Tarcatha leaped onto the roof of an emergency vehicle, then swung to the ground. Rupert followed suit, forgetting he was a far older man. He landed wrong, almost falling from the roof to the ground, and hobbled away, dodging the flocking emergency vehicles to reach the safety of a median between runways. He couldn't see Tarcatha anywhere, but he recognized the Minneapolis airport. Potter's Flowage, and Kyle, were a bit over two hours away in Rupert's rusty old pickup. How long would it take Tarcatha?

CHAPTER THIRTY-THREE

Kyle had that surreal sense of waking from a dream not sure whether it had been real or not. He lounged in his father's recliner with his bandaged leg propped up on pillows, pillows to cushion his injured arms, and the channel changer in his hand. He'd slept through the night in a real bed, so soundly he didn't even rumple the covers. Now he was just digesting his second breakfast and the comfort of a cup of coffee. Surreal.

His mother watched him. He could tell by her expression that his answers to her questions didn't satisfy her, even though he answered her probably more truthfully than he had about anything since he was a small boy. He still hadn't touched the questions he had for her. What was it about Rupert that had made her lie to him? They seemed irrelevant now. He was home. This was home. If he just didn't have that nagging sense of time passing somewhere, racing by, people he cared about at risk, a world that might, or might not, bind the universe together in the hands of madmen.

The channel changer took him nowhere he felt like stopping. Everything was too loud and disturbing, as if he couldn't concentrate, on what he wasn't sure. He clicked again.

"The passengers on United Flight 1190 from Salt Lake City can't quite agree on the cause of their emergency landing at Minneapolis at nine forty this morning. Was it an encounter with a UFO? A mid-air collision? A poltergeist? Some breach into a parallel universe? Or a secret military experiment gone awry? Whatever it was, most consider it a miracle that they landed at all," a reporter on CNN said with a wry twist to her mouth as if she had decided this was the quaint and quirky feature story, not a lead story about a near tragedy averted.

Kyle sat up, sucking in a breath he couldn't seem to exhale. He turned up the volume.

"No major injuries were reported among the one hundred passengers and crew on the 757, despite the doors literally blowing off the plane as it began its approach to Minneapolis. One passenger suffered a mild heart attack when a red cape apparently danced through the cabin. Passengers report hearing an unknown language coming out of nowhere. Some claim they were struck by unseen objects and that a coffee pot flew through the air moments before the doors blew at thirty-one thousand feet."

The camera zoomed in from a great distance turning the plane into a mirage of emergency vehicles, a mangled airplane door and there in the shadowy interior, much magnified, someone stuffing a crimson robe into an evidence bag.

"FAA investigators have been called in, but no officials are willing yet to explain just what happened, or speculate for the record."

"Mom, I gotta go," Kyle said. "Remember what Rupert said about a very bad man? That was him. The guy in the red cape. I imagine Rupert found him. I don't know who won, but if it wasn't Rupert, serious trouble's coming for me."

"Kyle, you're ill. You—" She stopped, staring at him with her mouth working a moment, then she looked away. "Where are you going?"

"Madison. If Tarcatha finds me he'll use me, dead or alive, to return to Metatha with the means to destroy civilizations. Whatever you do, don't tell anyone where I am. I'm not going to have a lot of time. Minneapolis at nine forty … it won't take him long to find out I'm not where I'm supposed to be."

"You can't do this alone. Let me call your father. You—"

"Mom, there's no one to help me if Uncle Rupert can't! I know this is asking a lot, but you just have to trust me, and Rupert."

Kyle almost fell over when his mother pulled him into a rough hug, then pushed away, just shaking her head and biting her lip to keep her from spilling whatever it was she desperately needed to say. He couldn't find his keys … had he left them in Madison with the car? His mother pulled them from her purse. He dashed out, at a loss for a moment where to find his car before he saw that someone had parked it in the garage. Before he could back out his mother was there again, thrusting spare bandages, food and a change of clothes through the window.

He wondered how long she stood in the driveway watching after he'd driven out of sight.

The drive to Madison never passed so fast. He should be thinking about what he needed to do there. Hide from Tarcatha. Lay low somehow. But the clock on the dash seemed to spin out of control. Every time he looked minutes had sped by. He heard the news at ten-thirty. Suddenly it was eleven, then twelve. He was probably only an hour ahead of … What happened on that airplane? Were they tripping over the invisible body of a man who really didn't belong in this world, dressed in blue jeans, looking a little careworn?

Kyle had to force down a knot in his throat. He wasn't sure what it was he swallowed, a well-earned fear of Tarcatha maybe, or worry for Uncle Rupert. Uncle.

"Man, Nelson, what is it with you?" Ripp thrust his face in the car window as Kyle pulled up to the curb. His grin turned to stunned surprise as he took in the ugly burns on Kyle's arms.

"Wood stove accident," Kyle said as he tried to push the door open against his roommate.

"Dude, you're a regular pratfall. I figured you'd show up. That weird uncle of yours called. I don't remember giving him my mobile—"

"When?" Kyle demanded.

"Hour ago. Said we hadn't seen you in a couple of days. He said he'd try again later."

An hour. He had survived then—

"Then your mom texts, says, to tell you, watch out. He figured it out, somehow knew where you'd be. He's coming, she says. Wish I'd known that before, I'd have just hung up on your uncle. Like, maybe you should give all these people *your* number."

"Oh man, how did he figure it out?" Kyle leaned against the car door. "What's he flying, a freakin' broom? Rupert doesn't have a cell phone. Did he say how I could get a hold of him?"

Ripp squinted at him. "You're confusing me. Aren't you trying to lose your uncle?"

"I need to reach Rupert. There's a guy looking for me. Bad dude. I have something he wants—"

"The knifing ... is this like a drug thing? I mean, we can put up with a lot of your crap but I'm not going to get kicked out of school over—"

"Don't be stupid, Ripp. What's someplace Rupert would recognize in an instant if he saw a picture of it?"

"The Capitol? Bascom Hill?"

Kyle shook his head. "Too recognizable. Something only someone who has been here would know."

"The Terrace? State Street's obvious."

Kyle nodded. "I gotta take a walk. If anyone comes, even Rupert, you haven't seen me."

"Your car's here."

Kyle looked at it. "Yeah."

"You're going to have to spill it one of these days," Ripp called at his back as he strode away, limping slightly from the rub of his jeans against the bandaged eel bite. He fumbled to fit his car keys in the pocket of the unfamiliar and restrictive jeans he wore, already crowded with the small Metathan purse he'd stuffed in his pocket. His fingers recognized the sharp point of the sliver of quartzite, the portal key to the eel world that he'd plucked from Tarcatha's cauldron. It felt hot to the touch, like an ember, as if it recalled the boiling cauldron. He pulled it out and studied it, the heat so great it almost seemed to radiate, warming his face despite the crisp autumn breeze. Suddenly, he had an image of Tarcatha uttering his ancient spells, binding spells, over the boiling cauldron. Kyle dropped the stone in the gutter and kicked it so that it skittered through the grate into the storm sewer.

State Street hadn't changed. Why would it? This entire world-hopping odyssey was closing in on only a month, years in Metathan time. He tried to mentally calculate how time had passed but he'd been to so many worlds where the time had been lost ... so much had slipped away from him.

He sat on a street-side bench, staring pointedly at the gyro sandwich shop, the tinny Greek music piped into the street beginning to fray his nerves. He ignored a strolling guitar player who sang off key, almost in his face, in search of a little cash, and the buses that belched by every few minutes to block his view of the gyro shop's marquis. He might have dozed, or perhaps he simply had become entranced by the twang and rumble of State. He started as if from a doze, hearing Rupert's voice in his head and sensing someone looking for him.

He turned to find Rupert carefully strolling down the street toward him, too deliberate to appear normal, but certainly not out of place among the street life despite his disheveled appearance.

Rupert stopped in his tracks a few feet away when he realized Kyle watched him.

"You see me?"

"Yeah, shouldn't I?"

"I'm visible?"

"Well, I see you."

The guitarist gave Kyle an odd look and moved to a different bench. Rupert waved his hands in front of the man's face, then regarded Kyle with that chilling gaze that seemed to peer so deep within him.

"So, what are we gonna do?" Kyle asked.

"We're going to draw him somewhere on our terms."

"How?"

"I think he has linked a spell to some object about you, much as I tracked you," Rupert said as he guided Kyle off State Street along Broom, away from campus. They passed Dayton, where he could see Rupert's truck parked askew in the driveway in front of his house, blocking the sidewalk. They paused for only a moment in a dark doorway, as Rupert touched a lighter to Kyle's palm.

"You're limping," Kyle said.

"So are you."

"You know, you look like Hell."

"I'm too old for this. And I really could use a drink. In five hundred years you'd have thought some Metathan would have discovered fermentation."

"So, what happened? I saw the news."

"Let's just say he's saving me for later, a cat letting the mouse think it escaped before it pounces again. He really is stronger than I am. Even in my youth he would have been a worthy challenge."

"Where are we headed?"

"To the Point off Olin. It's the most private place I could think of around here."

"Maybe we should take a cab?"

Rupert gave him that odd gaze again. He picked up his pace a bit so it was all Kyle could do to keep up. His leg began to throb.

"Kyle, I didn't have the magic to face him. Certainly not the stamina. This ... it could be the death of me. Whatever happens, you can't let Tarcatha go home. I don't know if he was successful on his trip or not. Metatha couldn't withstand another assault like ... like what made the Withering. Like what I did to it. It was Anthrax, Kyle, from Dugway Proving Ground, the military grade stuff, powerful, resilient. That's what Denalku had me fetch to him. And I planned it all out in advance and wrote it all down in my logs, step by step so that some twentieth grandson could study it, and do all of it again. Dugway held more things, evil things, he might have laid his hands upon. And even you, you are a weapon of mass destruction in his hands, too. What he wants to do, throw the portals wide open, it'll be a two-way street. Anything could bumble in, or out, good and bad. It comes down to not just stopping Tarcatha, but then closing the portals, ending Travel."

"But what can I do if you can't stop him? Why doesn't he understand the risk of the open portals? Or of another Withering?"

Rupert gave him a long look, then looked away.

"He didn't make the magic. He isn't intimate with it. You simply mustn't let him have you. The problem is that Valeutan Travel magic was more about easing life's daily burdens. Wrongheaded, but still basic. The goal was to improve lives. This, this bloodletting is about conquest and power and malice. Taking out Tarcatha alone won't end it. He's the leader, and most powerful, but I'm betting his prodigy know what to do and are waiting with their cauldrons for Tarcatha's return. If you returned alone, they'd still know what to do."

They paused, waiting for the light to change so they could cross John Nolen Drive to the lakeshore bike path. Late sunlight glittered from a light chop on Lake Monona as a few anglers in fishing boats trolled along the riprapped shoreline but a few feet from the traffic thundering over the causeway bridges. They had at least another half mile to hike before they'd reach the wild peninsula across the lake from the city's isthmus.

Kyle shook himself as another surreal moment struck him, flanked by traffic and bass boats to contemplate a magic battle on another world. But it was never away from his thoughts, even without Jia's white stone, even without her in his head all of Metatha was there. He marked his internal clock now to the Metathan clock.

"I ditched the portal stone. I think he was using it to track me. It's in the storm sewer under Dayton. What's going to draw him out here?" Kyle asked as they dodged bicycles and joggers on the trail.

"I'll need you. We'll be drawing the stone to us, not Tarcatha. You have to be the conduit, Kyle, because I'm growing too weak. I know you hate it when I push you into something and you don't know all the details. I think that last push was probably the least forgivable, but I can't tell you what's going to happen or how I'm going to do it. It's magic. And how it works here, well, you've seen. It might, it might not. Wyseery failed me in that airplane. There was nothing I could do. Nothing. I threw a coffeepot at him. That was about it. I don't know what will happen."

Kyle was still tripping over what might have been a Metathan apology.

"You've gotten yourself all bound up in Travel magic. It's plain to me as that Valeutan nose on your face, and likely to Tarcatha as well."

Rupert was slipping from English to Metathan and back, and finally settled into Metathan as if already steeling himself for the spells he must recite.

"But then, I opened the portals," Rupert was saying. "They're as much me as my son was, my wyseery laced through them all. And I see it in you, feel it in you, my wyseery, spread across ... worlds. No wonder I can't conjure up the least of beasts to face this demon. I need to tap a bit of my wyseery in you, that wild unpredictable thing you've let out of control now and then. I don't know what will happen. It may be all we can do. I keep trying to undo my errors of arrogance and they just keep accelerating."

Kyle gave him a look out of the corner of his eye. There was something different about Rupert. That irascible side of him subdued. Ruperion had indeed brought the Withering to Metatha, and never forgiven himself for it. And now, through Tarcatha, he feared he was about to do it again.

They walked in silence up an old cement drive that ran beneath the arching eaves of untended and wild wood in the midst of a city. Once this park had been a portage point for local tribes who left their mounds and artifacts scattered across its bluffs and shores. Much of the wood then became farmland or pasture. Now, the farms and families long gone, it had become the unruly tangle of re-growth in the midst of a city, a wild place but for the few signs of illicit trysts and the old foundations that had been family homes.

They walked until the noise of the causeway faded into the trills of wildlife. Rupert stopped in the midst of a clearing at the top of a hill, a place that may once have been field or pasture, perhaps restored prairie, now simply frost-killed weeds and brush that grabbed at their feet if they strayed off the paths of those before them. Rupert settled with a bamboo thicket and the remnants of long crumbled foundations at his back. The canes clattered in a light breeze as a steady waterfall of leaves sifted down from the edges of the clearing and flocks of blackbirds rose and fell, swirling in eddies as they gathered to move south.

Rupert sat cross-legged on a hump of moss-covered foundation and began arranging a collection of stones. Some Kyle already recognized for their role in Metathan wyseery. Rupert poured into the ring of stones a handful of brightly colored marbles that looked vaguely familiar, then sprinkled over it all a small dusting of powder. Kyle felt it, the strength of a wyseer's power like the blast of the lightning he'd felt in Metatha when his anger had ... had—

"Careful, Kyle. Don't try to do anything. Just be my conduit."

Kyle startled, realizing he had frozen in place, his fists and teeth clenched, staring into the thicket of bamboo as if he peered into an eggplant gaze that drew him places he couldn't go. He shook out his hands and settled down beside Rupert. If the wyseer continued to murmur words, Kyle lost track of them. Time spun away from him, his thoughts lost in trying to calculate how long since he had left Metatha. They were invisible here in the clearing, the ilyath itching in his palm, stones held in his open hands where Rupert placed them, the power tingling through his limbs. He imagined Jia, saw her slowly turning away from him, tossing her feather-laced braids, seeing her swaying, dancing beside a fire, becoming the manfish, the Kokopelli, then in a flash of silvery blue of moons' light, she was gone. He slowly roused himself, sensing something, hearing the silence of the canes clacking together and only an occasional bird call.

Kyle opened his eyes. The sun had set, but the brightness of the gloaming remained, lending deep shadows to the woods around them. Rupert had fallen silent and stared toward where the path emerged from the woods.

Kyle froze. "Tell me, does he teleport or what?"

Tarcatha gazed across the small clearing at them.

Rupert didn't have a chance to reply. Without warning a blast like a small bolt of lightning ripped at them. Whatever protective barrier Rupert had built around them lay in tatters. Kyle could see it as if he were looking at the shredded curtain sheers in an abandoned house, or tufts of dandelion seed wafting away in the breeze.

Tarcatha strode toward them, legs and arms bared to the cold without his crimson tunic. Certainly Tarcatha remained invisible, but Kyle could see him, could feel the malice in the man. Rupert gripped Kyle's wrist like a vise. He shouted what almost sounded like the Metathan greeting, *na he pata*. Something yanked in Kyle's gut, wrenching at Rupert's words. The goldenrod and browning grasses of the clearing lay flat before them, a wind pouring from them like some giant downdraft from a wall cloud.

Tarcatha braced. Wind shredded his clothing, ripped weeds up in clods and pelted him with dirt, pebbles and fragments of foundation stone. A bamboo cane drove into him, lodged in his shoulder a moment before the wind ripped away the rest of the stalk, leaving a bloody stub behind. It was only an instant, the wind scouring the ground to the dirt as if a tornado had torn through, before Tarcatha raised his hand and without even a word, the wind curled back at them.

Rupert's grip had become hot and slick. In the fading light, Kyle saw littering the bared topsoil dozens of arrowheads brought to the surface by decades of frost heaves. It was a passing thought, his mouth falling open at the sight, but he barely registered it before he felt that strange tug in his gut as if he were being sucked up like the dregs through a straw. Rupert worked some other trickery, something he couldn't see.

The bamboo burst into flame behind them, a furious inferno that licked at their backs and threatened to overcome the circle of stones Rupert had placed. Rupert remained unmoved. Tarcatha had closed the gap now, crossing the bared turf unhindered by undergrowth. Kyle sensed the battle, noted how Rupert's features struggled as he took on an almost bird-like aspect, his hawkish features for a moment accompanied by feathers before he settled back into the weary old man, a little paler, with a sheen of sweat on his forehead.

"Face me, old man. You called me out. Or can you not face me without your little tool?" Tarcatha taunted as he drew the flames toward them, as if the fire fed on the air alone.

"You impress me, Tarcatha. You are such an adept student of my work. Yet you fail to see the obvious flaws in your method."

Rupert's words were calm, unruffled. But again Kyle felt the tug of something in his gut. What was Rupert up to?

"See I know cauldrons. You know that. You are a student of me. It's a false god that in the end corrodes your soul. You know what I did to open the portals. But you misunderstand. It wasn't the blood of innocents I used. I used blood more powerful. My own. Isn't that the greater sacrifice? When we give of ourselves to better others—"

Tarcatha had his hands on Rupert so suddenly Kyle wasn't sure what had hit him. Rupert's fall beneath the bulk of Tarcatha yanked

Kyle to the ground. The Methiliim wyseer's hands tightened around Rupert's throat, Rupert's blood going hot in Tarcatha's grip. Kyle could feel it, Rupert's grip on his wrist like an iron searing into his flesh. Blue and white light flicked about them, beating back the reaching flames of the burning bamboo. Kyle's guts heaved, his head pounding with such intensity as Rupert drew his strength from him. Distantly he knew Tarcatha tried to pry Rupert's grip from Kyle's arm. How long before both of them succumbed, their blood boiled away? He had the instant's image of the cauldron, of the way Martrena's ashes and Talik's moons had made it boil, froth, erupt.

He concentrated on that moment, that instant when he had delved his hand into the boiling blood of Methiliim victims, his own blood, Talik's, that of so many others before them. He imagined her, Martrena, her dark hair swirling up about her as if she were a furious black wind. The moons lit her face, but left her eyes in shadow, mysterious, as if they were no longer there and she saw with something else.

A bellow almost roused him from his thoughts. He could feel only Rupert's grip, as strong as ever, on his wrist. He felt the great weight of something against him, his arm wrenching, twisting, but it was almost as if he felt it at a distance. He was watching Martrena. She held something in her hands: Talik's little trio of moons. Light flared from Kylik, so brilliant it dwarfed the other moons, growing too great to look upon. He tried to turn away, but she held him with her black stare. Suddenly Martrena's veil of hair had become Jia's feathery braids tossing as she turned, her hair going briefly and brilliantly white and gold as if fired by Kylik's light, before they resettled inky dark on her shoulders.

A black stony beach stretched before him, so far, so long. Black stones washed smooth by a black sea fed by a black river, black waves breaking over black sands beneath a sky devoid of moon or star, it seemed he looked upon the beginning, so far back there was nothing but the power of the stones. A great flash of light blinded him, and stones rose from the beach to the sky, flaring white, brilliant, to settle in the black heavens. Or were the heavens the sea, and the stones sparkled in its depths? In the dark he could see nothing of up or down, only the darkness and in it still Martrena stood there, dangling the moons from their chain, her silent dark gaze penetrating into him, deeper, deeper.

A knife of pain ripped through him, so sharp and sudden he knew he screamed. He was losing it, losing the image. Something about the image. Martrena pointed to his feet, where a white stone blazed like a star. He reached down and grasped it in his fist, its edges not smoothed by the sea's fury, but sharp and biting.

His eyes flew open to find Tarcatha standing over him, wild eyed and bloody, revealed in the fading orange light of the burning bamboo. His clothes were gone. The wyseer's skin had sprouted a filigree of blood as if a thousand tiny daggers had ripped him. A flash of sight showed him Dwilul in the Balthysian fire ring, and then it was gone. Tarcatha was nothing but blood, in places his skin had almost charred from whatever conflagration had struck him.

Rupert? Rupert! The wyseer no longer gripped Kyle's wrist which was swollen and bruised. The wyseer had fallen still and pale, the palm of the hand that had held Kyle blistered and open.

Kyle couldn't speak, couldn't move, could only stare. Tarcatha furiously searched for something, his breaths coming out as puffs of steam as he moved away from the firelight in search of, in search of … Kyle knew. Rupert had blown the Travel stone away from Tarcatha, into the pile of debris that had swept into the very forest.

Kyle tried to sit up. He needed to check Rupert. No, he needed to flee. Why had no one come to investigate the fire, the lights? Shouldn't the police or fire department be here? He must escape before Tarcatha could use him. He could barely move his right arm, the arm Rupert had gripped, putting out his left hand to support himself, only to find that fist clenched and bloody, in it a whitish quartz arrowhead streaked red with his own blood.

Suddenly a force yanked him around. Tarcatha held out his muddy wyseer's purse, gripped it in his fist like a trophy that would never be taken from him. In it would be the Travel stone, and what else? Had Tarcatha pilfered some atrocity he would unleash on the Valeuta? With the barest of effort he threw Kyle to his feet like some fairy tale giant.

"Remember, only your body is of use to me." The words ripped from Tarcatha's throat, hoarse and raw. Kyle swayed a moment, looking from Rupert to the scattered circle of stones and at last to Tarcatha's angry eyes. His head felt so empty and he realized Rupert's spell in him had been broken. Was it because the old man had … had …

"No," Kyle said and tried to sag to the ground, with purpose. The soil felt hot, as if Rupert's wind had been a firestorm. Suddenly, his tongue locked up in his mouth. Tarcatha's wyseery left a metallic taste.

Tarcatha simply yanked him up again with an impatient waggle of his finger, as if this had simply been a contest, not a battle critical to the survival of a people, or their world, or universe, or Kyle. But this time as Kyle came to his feet he slashed his bloody fist at Tarcatha's head, shouting a denial silently in his head, a denial of every indignity suffered by him, or in his name for generations of Fidrel. And for Rupert.

Tarcatha tipped his head to the side to avert a blow to the eyes. Kyle's fist met the man's neck and slashed with a force of desperation. The arrowhead ripped across the wyseer's neck just as Kyle felt that something, the world growing crimson before his eyes, that roar in his head of wild wyseery.

Kyle fell hard, awash in the odor of blood, slick with it. Tarcatha stood above him for the briefest instant as if his body couldn't conceive defeat. Then he sank to the ground in the puddle of blood pouring from a rent no arrowhead had ripped in his throat, a force that almost severed his head from his body.

At first, Kyle couldn't move, unsure if Tarcatha might yet rise again like some monster from a horror film. At last he let the arrowhead fall and tugged the purse from Tarcatha's hand. After a moment's hesitation he tucked the bloody arrowhead in the purse and looked within for some possibly broken vial of anthrax. He found nothing but herbs and pebbles.

He had to crawl over the hot ground to reach Rupert, unsure if he had the strength to stand. He couldn't feel his arms, couldn't feel anything. Rupert had to be dead. He was so pale, his features smooth and careless, nothing like the intimidating character of Kyle's youth.

For a panicked moment, Kyle searched for a pulse, Rupert certainly long departed on his final swim. Danat guide him. What would he do then? He didn't know how to stop the madness on Metatha.

"Not so easy, old man," Kyle muttered as he found a pulse. "Remember, this is your party."

Rupert didn't respond. Kyle sat for a long minute weighing his options in the dying light of the burning bamboo. He struggled to order his thoughts, finding them sluggish. There was Kim, but if she didn't like taking care of an unexplained knife wound, she wasn't going to be much help with an invisible wyseer covered in burns. And was Rupert still invisible? Was Kyle? He wasn't sure, but couldn't imagine getting far if they weren't.

Only a hundred yards distant, Lake Monona could easily take him back to Metatha to find some wyseer to help him. Would wyseery heal Rupert? Or did he really need a hospital? Could Rupert even survive the swim in his condition? Kyle sensed he couldn't because didn't the Travel require a bit of Rupert's own wyseery? It might very well be the last straw, and they might rise in the midst of Tarcatha's men. Then what? If he simply went alone from here, he and some wyseer would have to find a way back to Madison, only to find Rupert dead already. He couldn't imagine asking Ripp and O'Malley to harbor his bloody uncle after the things he'd said. What he needed was home. Never before had that musty flowage beckoned with such promise.

At last, Kyle struggled to hoist Rupert to his shoulder. He barely took a step and stumbled, his knees giving way and piling him into the hot earth. He wanted to cry with the helpless frustration of it. He couldn't feel his grip, it gave way several times as he tugged Rupert's t-shirt up beneath his arms, slung the back of the shirt over Rupert's head to form a loop across his chest and pulled. He dragged the wyseer, stopping often to rest, ears ringing, head throbbing and his breaths ripping the night like little shrieks. Could he even survive the swim for help himself? Kyle couldn't imagine having the strength to even surface. He had a sense that something in him was broken, but he wasn't sure what, something that made him alien to himself, out of sorts. What had Rupert done to him?

He knew, without looking any deeper that the carnage that had swirled about him while he wandered with Martrena was his doing, through Rupert, through himself, it was all part of it. All the magic had come together, Rupert had said that, the Travel magic ... and more. Did Rupert realize something had happened to Kyle when he thrust his hand into that stew of Martrena's ashes, magical stones and the Metathan moons? Kyle wasn't sure what it was, but something ... something permitted a decidedly unmagical Reign to see invisible wyseers, and to call on some rending force that could sever a man's head with just a shout.

Kyle stopped then and retched, empty, dry heaving into the dark shadows of the windy wood.

Time slipped beyond reckoning as Kyle first hauled Rupert to the edge of the parking lot, then hiked over the causeway to the isthmus and retrieved his car. Then, with the last of his strength he managed to stuff Rupert into the back seat, gently pillowing the old man's head with an old towel. Days, weeks, had passed in Metatha.

As he sat at the light, ready to pick up the Beltline and then the Interstate north to Potter's Flowage, he noted the strange look from the driver in a pickup beside him. He peered down into the car, face all scrunched up. Kyle glanced in the rear-view mirror and saw nothing but the lights of cars pulling up behind him. He felt around in the bag of food his mother had sent him, finding a bottle of water. He splashed the ilyath scar in the palm of his hand, then drained the rest of the bottle. As the light turned, he glanced into the back seat at the deathly still wyseer he shouldn't be able to see. What had they done? What had he become? As the minutes ticked by, what was happening in Metatha?

CHAPTER THIRTY-FOUR

The glassy surface of Potter's Flowage reflected starlight and almost had that slightly transparent quality of a two-way mirror. Kyle peered into the water. What would keep him from bumbling right back into another cauldron? He felt too weary for this. Midnight, a little past. A month since Rupert left Metatha, five weeks since Kyle and Tarcatha had departed. Did Methiliim still wait beside Ta'atit? Kyle felt as if he'd gone all those five weeks of Metathan time without rest or food, though it was only this morning he'd eaten two breakfasts and snacked as he drove. He'd munched only minutes ago again, but it never seemed enough to quench his hunger, no sleep enough to ease his weakness. He didn't even remember much of the drive home but the sense that he was swimming through a dark tunnel, the cold wind whipping through the car keeping him barely awake.

Tarcatha was gone now. He'd killed him, not with rogue magic alone, but with purpose. He hadn't slashed the man's throat hoping to slow him. Kyle swallowed hard, feeling that nausea rising up in him again.

A flash of light made him cringe. The yellow light from the doorway reached far across the yard to where he regarded the stumps.

"Kyle, I don't know what to do," his mother said softly. She touched his hand, the hand that had killed a man. He shook himself. He looked up at her. "Maybe I should try to find someone who knows more about …"

"Who do you know who knows about wounded wizards? Bit of a stretch, Mom," he said softly, no sarcasm, none of the sneer that had often come to his expression when he spoke to his mother about Rupert.

He'd dug through the wyseer's pockets after settling him on his own bed in his mother's house and found that little sliver of wood that reminded him so much of the manfish pipe Atatha had crafted so long ago. When he removed it, he'd heard his mother gasp. Rupert had come among the visible.

"I need a wizard to tend a wizard. I don't even know what happened to him, or what can be done. It could be he just needs rest, but too much is riding on this to not be certain."

"So you're going to go to this Metatha."

He turned and looked at her. How did she absorb all this? What had she thought for all those years of Rupert's strange stories and language and—

"What did he tell you when you adopted me?" Kyle asked, suddenly realizing he'd asked the question aloud. "How could you do it without a birth certificate?"

Betty Nelson hugged him, blood and all, and held him so fiercely he winced.

"He told us you were something precious and endangered. That someone had killed your parents and might come after you, too. That we must keep you hidden and secret. I don't know why we believed him. Now that I know ... well, maybe he just made us. We always suspected something military, the way he talked and how, before you came along, he'd disappear for weeks at a time. Maybe we felt like we were doing our duty. He gave us money, bought this house for us. It was hard to dismiss. After a few months, Rupert brought papers identifying him as your natural surviving parent, probate documents and, well, I guess we sort of wondered how he got them but convinced ourselves they were legitimate because we already loved you. He wanted to be in your life, but thought we were better suited to raising you because a child should have parents, he said, who would always be there. He offered to pay your way, but we said no. We wanted to be your true parents and he agreed."

Kyle stared out at the water. Rupert had done for him what he couldn't even do for his own son. How many times had Rupert tried to tell him about sacrifices he'd made for his people, and Kyle had just rolled his eyes and dismissed it as more stories meant to manipulate him? Had Rupert's son wondered what became of his father? Did he know he was the Traveler, locked away in another world? Or did he watch Lake Ta'atit fill and wonder if his father might one day rise to the surface, bloated and... Kyle shook himself and fought back a shiver, not so much from the chill night as Travel sickness settling into his soul.

"If you watch closely, you'll see something strange. If all goes well, I'll be back within a few hours, perhaps sooner."

Kyle didn't move immediately. His mother let go of him, but he still didn't move, feeling as if his feet were setting roots. When he'd first Traveled, Rupert had pushed him. He'd plunged in, confused, losing his bearing in his attempt to swim to the surface, but each time he'd done so he'd moved deeper, deeper. He needed to do that now. He couldn't come up in Ta'atit. He must again rise in that vast sea of Metatha, close enough to not wear himself out on the swim, but not so close that he'd be immediately seen or dashed on the rocks.

Kyle stepped carefully to the edge of the bank, knowing the water here dropped off only gradually. Yet he dived into the bare foot of water at the bank, knowing it would be enough. He felt the water rush his lungs and kicked, kicked, kicked, hard as he had when he had struggled to surface that day. He went deeper, angling ever deeper. He kicked again, again. How many times had he kicked that first time? Then he hesitated just a moment before slithering, letting something like his shoulders wriggle him upward into the briny welcome of the Metathan sea.

This time he didn't emerge into a flock of waterbirds. He was too close to the current of the falls where a few giant fowl, sleek and arrow-like, dived for stunned fish. Afternoon shadows already shaded the face of the land and water.

Kyle pulled hard, letting the waves help him fight the current, and at last he waded ashore and stumbled to the cover of scrubby trees clinging to the base of the scarp.

It took him several hours to find his way up the steep face, passing the hints of past forays by the denizens of Hindlain to this place to fish or gather seaweed, the two staples of their meals. But no one appeared to have passed this way recently. He caught no hint of smoke falling down the cliff face to him from Kylalnethra cookfires. He tripped over something and pulled from the black sand a crimson cloak. He froze a moment, his heart pounding in his ears. It could have come over the falls. It could have washed here from any point. But it hadn't. He knew. How did he know?

A broken arrow balanced on a small ledge of fractured rock. A shredded bit of fabric balanced atop a tuft of grass and a slashed purse hung by one string from the twig of a weathered bush. The pale glint of late sky shone back at him from a sword or long dagger, with a double-edged blade, its looped hilt wrapped with tanned, tattooed avian skin still dimpled with the holes of feathers. He eyed the weapon only a moment before hooking the hilt loop on the belt of his jeans.

The thunder of the falls covered several missteps that sent stone clattering to the beach far below. At last, he crawled the last few feet up onto the narrow path that led into Hindlain. Small plants sprouted in the path. Kyle steeled himself for what he must do. He'd walked these lands both unafraid and terrified, but always feeling like some alien detritus. Somehow Metatha had grown into him, become a part of him. He sensed the world about him, felt a keen belonging, and more. He had friends here. He couldn't even feign disinterest. And his physical state now as he leaned hard on his knees to regain his breath, made all those past maladies inconsequential. He couldn't curl up and bemoan his weariness. Rupert needed him. Metatha needed him.

Kyle carefully edged along the path, hugging the wall and placing each step so he didn't crush new growth or leave a footprint in mist-dampened soil. The scent of the falls greeted him like homecoming, the mist settling in his hair and clothing and dripping from the end of his nose. Moss clung to the sheer rock walls, small red flowers blooming on the ends of delicate stalks.

He froze when something glimmered at him from near the entrance to the cavern. He edged nearer, his heart in his throat as he unhooked the sword and slipped his hand within the hilt loop. No one challenged his approach. The glimmer came again and Kyle stopped, his mouth falling open to see that the walls of the cavern had become the black glass of obsidian, all of it glimmering in the faint light entering the cavern. There, on the floor, rippled sand and debris told the tale of some great deluge that flooded the cavern. A few broken casks had come to rest in a corner around a stony pillar. The wall hangings had ripped free to collect where an eddy half buried them in sand. And there, he could see clearly, water urns had fused to the walls of the cavern.

The place stunk of wyseery. He didn't know how he pulled that scent out from all others, but he could. What had happened to the Kylalnethra? Had Wilnath and Jia perished in this deluge? What of Talik and Danathea and loyal Barul? Old Atatha, and Davath, the werran so devoted to Rupert? A small chest lay broken near his feet, half buried in sand. He nudged it to find a store of stones, vials and small covered pots still intact. Had the Pale at last destroyed the Valeutan wyseers as they had hoped to so long ago? The Valeutans were so poor, certainly they wouldn't have left a single magical item behind if they had survived.

Again he froze as he became certain he heard the scuff of a foot against the sandy floor of the cavern. He swung the sword up in front of him, certain he wouldn't know what to do with it but to use it like a bat, and whirled to find a cloaked figure standing boldly in the cavern opening, the waterfall glimmering behind.

"Well met, Kyloreign," a vaguely familiar voice said in Metathan as two more figures moved out of the shadows beside the entrance, their hands on the hilts of swords.

Kyle closed his eyes a moment certain he had been lured into a trap as surely as Tarcatha had tracked him across worlds. He felt it building in him, marveled at how he knew it was there.

"No!"

The shout didn't come from him. It came from somewhere far away. He slipped into himself, found a place so deep and dark he must be amongst the moldering ruins at the bottom of Potter's Flowage.

Then, he found that strange place within himself where Martrena still danced on the starry black night.

CHAPTER THIRTY-FIVE

She sat still, her mind in her hands, holding it out before her. She had seen the tiny seeds of night. And more. She must understand. Talik sat beside her, his niece Danathea giving only the slightest of rustles as she looked through the scrolls. Her blond locks had grown out to cover the toplock she'd worn as Talik's student, and fell across her face now. She'd bound a few feathers into it, like the Valeutans. Somehow Danathea had managed to remain unseen by even the greatest wyseers, yet Jia had seen … had seen …

Jia shook her head.

"I am distracted," she said, letting her hands fall and perhaps let her mind roll away into the brush to rouse a quiver of birds into the bright afternoon sky.

"What was it you saw that distracted you," Talik asked softly.

"Danathea's hair," Jia said, giving the startled girl a sad smile. "Sorry. I just can't concentrate anymore."

"No, no. That isn't such a strange thing, really. What about her hair?"

"When I returned to Hindlain I saw her, and saw the sense of wyseery about her. She seemed to have blended in, despite her obvious difference. Why didn't Isra ever take note of her, imprison her, use her against you? Why wasn't she seen as dangerous? Why didn't anyone notice her missing or, many being wyseers, simply notice her?"

Talik smiled a little and nodded at Danathea.

"Wise one, the word 'seen' is the key. They didn't see me," Danathea said softly. "I was raised by a Valeutan Fidrel and a Danatan Palif. One can't escape learning survival skills in such a setting."

"But I saw you. How?" Jia blinked at her. She knew ancient wyseers could, using the ilyath, make themselves unseen. But a Pale student of Danat?

"Perhaps you were looking? Perhaps no one expected her to be unseen, so no one looked for her with a seeing stone?" Talik posed his theories as questions. "Perhaps others did see her, but chose to keep quiet? And then," he gave Danathea a quick smile, "Perhaps Danathea is exceptionally adept at her craft. Jia, you would never claim you could become a fish without the Travel stone. Yet that is most certainly the transformation that saved you. There are many mysteries of the mind and the gods and the wyseery that we never discover because we assume they are impossible."

"Yet I still don't understand why Atatha or Isra didn't use such a spell to save themselves."

"Perhaps they thought it impossible? You say it is impossible that the things you have been seeing could be. Yet, we know you have already done the impossible. You need to open your mind as you did in the past. Then, you knew that you were divided of mind and Traveling with the Traveler. Then you knew that Ruperion guided you. You knew."

"But that was the Travel wyseery, the power of my stone, that's what did it then," Jia said, not sure herself if she believed it.

"Perhaps it is the Travel wyseery again that draws you. Remember the cauldron. In it went Martrena, the Travel stone, the moons of a palif. All bound together in one grand wyseery."

"Into which Kyle thrust his hand," Jia muttered. "But that explains any strangeness about Kyloreign. Not why I should see the strange images I see, or how Ruperion could … could, make me a fish. And that is another point, knowing that it was Ruperion in my thoughts."

"Ruperion is the Travel wyseery, Jia," Talik said softly. "And you have touched that wyseery yourself when you drew Kyle back here. You are connected. May forever be so." He had opened his robe slightly, to gesture to the small tattoo there on his side that showed a great circle of men and fish spinning about the image Ruperion had named Kokopelli.

Jia frowned, missing Atatha's brusque teachings. The burly palif was too patient and easy with her. She swallowed hard. She still couldn't think of Atatha without seeing the way the blood obliterated his face that last moment, and then he was gone. And she had been thrust into the pounding force of falling water, but able to breathe, able to swim, to slowly find her way to shore and emerge unscathed near the broken body of Isra. But Atatha had not. Shouldn't he have known, too, how to do this thing, this strange transcendence of her person? Or had that blow, that awful blow, been the end for him? Would he still be alive if she hadn't tried to spirit him away?

She sat up a little so she could peer over the brush to the distant sea beyond. She could still taste how the fresh water had grown briny, made her choke on its suddenness. And then the way the air had roared into her lungs and she had cried out with the pain of it. And Ruperion had been there, in her head. He'd been there often in the last month since he had gone in search of Kyle.

All was silent now. And that, too, was something she needed to explain to herself. She hadn't felt herself since then. She had awakened with the horrible sickening sense that ... that ... that something had crawled inside her mind to slowly feed upon her. Not Ruperion, though. He was simply gone. She tried to hold her hands out again, to again place her head in her palms to consider the turnings of her mind, but at that moment she felt it.

"He's back," she whispered.

"Tarcatha?" Talik looked around as if the wyseer was about to crash from the cover of the brush.

"Kyle. I sense him. This is ... I— I— He's here."

"We must send scouts to Ta'atit to protect him. The Methiliim are —"

"No... I see the midnight beach, night's buttons." She looked up, seeing the way Talik peered at her as if uncertain of her faculties. "He's out there." She pointed at the sea. "He would know Ta'atit is guarded."

At a motion from Talik, Danathea rose and dashed away. Jia gathered up her robe and the rush mat she'd sat upon for her meditation. As she rose, three werran stepped from cover, two to flank her, one to precede her, the latter waiting for her instructions as if she were some great personage, a chieftain, a priestess.

"Wise One, you are too open to view," Davath said softly from his position behind her.

Jia inclined her head.

"May I suggest the Grove?" Talik said with that odd deference so many used with her. What was so different now? Because she had survived when others had died?

She let herself be led to the thick grove in which the survivors of Hindlain had found respite. She felt so strange, so other ...

"Is he alone?" Talik asked as they followed secretive paths guarded by stone-faced werran, many of them with still-fresh scars of a battle so astounding that simply recalling it made the breath catch in her throat.

She could still smell that scent of forged metal in the air, the strange smoke rising from the Methiliim wyseery that blew apart flesh, shattered stone, could raise flames in the falls of Ta'atit. And in the midst of it, she alone had stood, stunned, her hair filigreed with golden feathers and sea beads that marked the miracles of her wyseery, facing those Isra had called to betray them. The walls had melted around them, flaming rock pelting them. The falls had suddenly come thundering through the cavern roof. Those who escaped, those with the means to work enough wyseery to spare themselves, emerged to face Pale soldiers blocking the narrow paths to Hindlain. The very thing that had made it a hidden fortress, now made it a trap.

"Is he alone?" Talik asked again, gently prodding.

She shook herself. "I have only the faintest sense of him. And none of Ruperion."

Talik took her hand gently in his. "You worry on Ruperion's absence often. Perhaps you no longer need his help, and he has ended his bond."

"Perhaps," Jia said softly.

The Grove loomed before them, its shadows deep and welcoming, a dark place, like so many of the dark places the wise of the Valeutans had been forced to gather over the centuries. This one seemed the darkest, the most bleak. Remnants of the Kylalnethra and Fidrel had pitched tents and lean-tos from their cloaks, starting over as ever they did, as they always had. Did the Methiliim simply bide their time before pursuing them again? They had to know where they had fled. Their wyseery was too strong to not sense where others feebly dabbled in the arts.

So feeble it had seemed. Hindlain melting and rushing about them, people thrown about like leaves on a storm-tossed sea. Alone, Jia had stood in the midst of the chaos, ignoring the waters that rushed about her ankles, rose to her knees. She had sensed Ruperion in her then, Ruperion giving her strength, telling her to be strong, to do what she must for she could do it, she had already done it. She had the strength, the power, and she could touch the true wyseery of Metatha if she only left all her rote learning aside and simply applied what she knew, what she had always known.

And with that, she had simply closed her eyes, turned her head to the ceiling and recalled the Hindlain of old, the cavern lit with a soft glow of lanterns and torches, the murmurs of her people, the thunder of water beyond a veil. Whatever trance she had entered barely allowed her to even register that the water no longer threatened to pull her from her feet. She thrust her arms from herself, imagining herself pushing the Methiliim intruders into the falls that had swallowed Atatha and Isra. She had cried out then, in words that echoed far back. She called on the path for which Atatha had been named, the path that linked worlds and bound them, that had been so powerful it must be controlled by Travel, the path the gods had set upon the land when they made the world firm and made it abide by laws that the Methiliim corrupted, that Travel corrupted.

"Wise One?" She looked up sharply, swallowing hard to find she stood in her shelter in the Grove. Manfish trees were the pillars, and from their lowest branches had been slung a roof and a rear wall of sorts that sheltered her from the wind. At the base of the tree, she had invited Talik to place his altar stone. It was white, like Jia's stone. A power stone.

Danathea stood before her, the girl oddly visible in a way Jia had never seen her before. Dappled sunshine fell on her Pale gold hair. It was she who had spoken with such deference, to one who had simply been a soldier of the Kylalnethra.

Talik squeezed her hand and Jia nodded.

"There is no sign of him. Wilnath asks if you saw a premonition, a concurrence, or perhaps a memory?"

"He's here," Jia said again as she sank onto a rush mat and leaned back against the bole of a manfish tree.

Birds scattered from her every move as they picked at the dug-up pebble-sized eggs of a delver bird. She closed her eyes and saw again Hindlain, as she had seen it last, destroyed, empty of all the life and hope it had once been. She looked up at it from below, seeing no signs of warmth or light, and the remnants of battles, feeling a cold fear in her gut—

"Hindlain." She looked up at Talik, then to Danathea. "He went to Hindlain."

She closed her eyes and heard the rustle of Danathea's departure, the slap of her feet on the ground.

Did Kyle see the handiwork that had been hers, the strange wyseery that couldn't be? When she had opened her eyes, the roof of the cavern had closed, the Methiliim were standing their ground, one of them eyeing her with an arched brow and a smirk on his face.

She didn't know. That was what she kept coming back to. She didn't know how she did it. She didn't know how she survived when Atatha didn't. She didn't know how she could stop the carnage, when no one else could. She didn't know how she withstood the combined assault of three Methiliim wyseers, who had bent their will for death on her and yet she stood unscathed. She sensed a bit of Ruperion, yet, at the same time, something else, something familiar, but different. Something that made her head hurt to contemplate.

And simply for surviving she held this post of deference, no better than Isra perhaps with her strange wyseery, her unnatural ways. Talik claimed she had saved her people. She didn't know how. She had simply stayed alive. She had driven them back along the path. One had fallen to his death. The other two had backed from her. Why had they backed away from her? What had they seen? And behind her were the survivors, so few.

And since then, since then she had been ... when Ruperion fell silent, in that moment, she had thought of Kyle, of Ruperion, had thought—

Something strange had crawled within her then. She felt as if it consumed her will to move, it consumed her sense of time, of place, as if she were caught in that manfish world of water and couldn't emerge into the air of any world, but only see the sky from beneath.

"Jia, you must put your head back on your shoulders."

Talik's voice. How could a Danat priest be so wise in the ways of the wyseery, a wyseery Jia keenly sensed that most Fidrel had never come to know? Had Martrena so marked him? Martrena. How was it she could see her standing there, a shadow on the great black strand, a stranger she knew so intimately—

She nodded and with effort took a deep breath and looked into Talik's gaze. "Our savior returns. What shall we make of that?" she asked softly.

She didn't hear the answer. Instead she saw Martrena again, Atatha's true daughter. Had they found one another in Danat's world of the dead? Or did Atatha wander unhomed for having forsaken the gods?

"Wise One ..." It was Talik's voice again. He was always here for her. So close, so gentle. "You must wake, we need you."

Jia shook herself, shedding the disorientation as she tried to calculate the time by the angle of the sun, mark the collection of curious who stood around outside her tiny sanctuary, and note the grave look on Talik's face.

She sat up, startled that she had drifted into sleep. It seemed she did that often since, since ... since she had expended so much of herself, Talik had said.

She let Talik help her to her feet and there she saw what had brought the survivors to gather around her. It was Wilnath who stood before her, his face covered in bloody welts as he kept his gaze averted from her. He her elder, her brother in Atatha's house, yet he deferred to her.

"What happened?" she asked, reaching out to touch his face. "There's wyseery in this."

He jerked his head toward the burden held between two werran. "I think we startled him."

He nodded and the two werran came forward, bearing Kyle on a litter of bent saplings.

"Kyloreign did that?" she asked softly.

A murmur of fear rose among those gathered. Wondering voices asked if Kyle had turned against them if he attacked Wilnath. Others suggested he was a Methiliim imposter.

"Enough!" Jia said, not realizing how her voice would carry, and with what power it would strike their ears. Heads bowed in deference.

She hated this!

"Bring him here and have him made comfortable. Talik and Wil, I need your help, the rest of you certainly have something to do."

Talik's hand was on her arm, guiding her to the rush mats Wilnath had placed beside Kyle. She looked upon the familiar face of the young man she had befriended so long ago. Some of her people now feared they had been led astray to believe in Kyloreign. She wondered herself if they should have placed so much hope in one man. Hadn't Kyle himself said so much? Victory had seemed so easy when the Pale were an untried foe.

She bit her lip. He was steeped in wyseery. She lifted one arm, burned, blistered, his wrist and hand so swollen she wondered if it might not be crushed inside. His clothes bore faded bloodstains.

"Wil?" Jia looked up at him, expectant.

"He was in Hindlain, as you said. He had just found a chest full of stones and potions and it had his attention. I think we startled him. He simply closed his eyes and the next thing I knew there's a rain of stones flying into us, not little pebbles, but hefty chunks of rock pulled from the floor of the cavern. Then he just sank to the ground and we couldn't rouse him."

Wilnath fingered a particularly large welt on his forehead. "It's our own fault. He probably couldn't tell who we were. And we certainly didn't expect, well ..."

"He's overwhelmed," Jia announced then. "Travel sickness, wyseery, and … more. He needs rest, but that is not what we can give him now. He had a reason for risking all to return. And we must find out why he came alone."

Jia unstopped a small pottery flask she wore at her side and sniffed it, her lips curling involuntarily at the foul stench. She said a few small words to herself, gripping a power stone in one hand as with the other she poured a little of the flask's contents into Kyle's mouth, held open by Wilnath.

Kyle's eyes flickered and he coughed a moment, before falling still again. Jia listened intently to his breaths, pulled a lid up and peered at his eye, then motioned for Wilnath to open Kyle's lips again. She dribbled a few more drops into Kyle's mouth. He groaned, coughed, swung one hand at them then fell still again.

Jia glanced at Talik. He whispered something under his breath that sent Danathea again rifling through scrolls as if she sought some answer in the fragments of paper they had rescued from Waymeet.

Again Jia muttered under her breath. She thought of Rupert, but no image of him came. There, a sense of someone … Martrena. She swept her hands out from her, sending stones spiraling into the sky like swirls of smoke from a campfire.

"Wil, where is his Travel stone?" Jia asked without opening her eyes.

She felt something pressed into her hand and at the small sound from Danathea, she looked down to find a purse in her hand, clearly Pale-made. Racing horses trimmed its edges, the bold strokes of mountain flanking plain. The purse was stiff, coated in mud and dirt, perhaps blood. She opened it and found within a wyseer's collection of stones and herbs, and the black stone that had brought him here. She took up his left arm, finding his ilyath-scarred palm with a fresh and ragged slice in it and pressed the stone into his hand, clasping it with hers to hold the stone between their palms. Again she appealed to her spells and the burning liquid Talik poured for her.

He fought like some cornered blood bird trying to bite its way free of a net. He didn't know who was in his head and thought only to not fall prey to… She sensed that wild wyseery in him again. Instead she gripped his hand harder, imagining a pot removed from the fire, the bubbles abating, the surface calming, the steam rising, then dissipating.

She opened her eyes to find him looking at her.

"Where's Tarcatha?" she asked.

"Dead." He mouthed the word. She nodded, curtly, silencing the murmurs growing around her with a quick glare and signaled Wilnath to dribble water in his mouth.

"Ruperion?"

"Dying. Need help. I can't." Kyle closed his eyes again.

Talik waved an herb under Kyle's nose, the man rousing to escape the scent that so resembled a bloated corpse.

"Need a wyseer to him."

"You can't Travel again," Jia said firmly as he struggled to rise.

"He'll die. If not for him, Tarcatha would … It's not over yet. He knows how to stop it."

Jia bit her lip again. That was why Ruperion remained so silent in her head. Was it too late already?

"What's not over? What must he stop?" Wilnath asked.

"Tarcatha was just one. They'll just find another leader, and another. The portals must be closed." Kyle's words were gaining strength, desperation. He tried to sit up, and failed.

"We don't want to end Travel, do we?" Wilnath asked. "That's what we were awaiting, that's why we wanted Kyloreign, the opportunity to be on an even footing with the Pale."

Jia silenced him with a look. "We owe Ruperion a great debt. If not for him, we would have all been destroyed," Jia said.

"Who among the wyseers even has the skills to help him?" Wilnath asked.

"I do," Jia said.

"Jia, the journey could kill you, and … him. You have yet to recover," Talik said in that gentle tone of his. She peered more closely at the palif, feeling strangely light-headed from just the little wyseery she'd employed to rouse Kyle, but at the same time so incredibly perceptive. Talik's hand had taken hers again. It felt warm, comforting.

"I doubt we could get near Ta'atit without being seen," Wilnath said.

"It doesn't have to be you," Talik said. "Tiva and Dakul are mending, they might be strong enough."

"Yes, it must be me," Jia returned, leaning into him to struggle to her feet. "And there are ways to reach Lake Ta'atit unseen. Even Danathea knows them."

"How long?" Kyle asked.

"Since your return? But a few hours."

"We must go now."

"Traveler, you need rest," Talik said. "How many days passed in that other world since you left? You haven't even begun to heal and here you have many new injuries." He gently lifted Kyle's right arm, leaving it when the Traveler winced and paled. "I think you've broken something in your arm. I don't know how you can contemplate—"

"What incredible wyseery it must have taken to defeat Tarcatha," Jia said. "Ruperion is in grave need. But how will I go unseen?" She watched Kyle a long moment. His eyes were closed. Did he search his memory, or had he succumbed to his sickness?

"Do you remember how to create the ilyath?" Kyle asked without opening his eyes. "That is where we start."

As Danathea hurried to find each item Jia asked for and Talik gently tended the Traveler, Jia wondered briefly if they were fools. They would attempt a spell she had never performed to sneak by heavily armed camps of those likely using a seeing stone to see right through any wyseery they might concoct. And then to Travel again so soon, would he even be able to lead her?

As if he heard her thoughts he suddenly reached out and snagged her arm.

"We will come up in a musty lake full of old stumps. You will need to reach the shore to the sun. There you'll find a house. That is where you must go to find Ruperion. My parents will be caring for him. Don't forget how to become visible."

"Where will you be?" Wilnath asked, giving Kyle that skeptical look that would have made her angry if it had been directed her way.

"In a stupor on the bank. Sinking to the bottom, too spent to even float." Kyle said with enough sarcasm to draw a smile, but Jia feared it might be too close to the truth.

Somehow Kyle kept up, relying on Davath and Wilnath as she walked beside Danathea and Talik. When had she come to trust them so?

She looked up, stunned, to find they had reached the ridge above Lake Ta'atit. Talik and Danathea smoothed a place for her to hide in the cover of brush that fringed an outcrop of rock. She wanted to wave them away. She'd lived her life in the dirt of this valley with no one to sweep clean the ground for her before. What had changed?

A soft touch brought her upward, from somewhere. She realized her hands were fists in her lap, her jaw clenched as she stared into nothing. She couldn't seem to stay in the moment, she felt pulled, pulled somewhere and … again that soft touch on her arm. Talik? She opened her eyes into the bright glitter of light. It wasn't Talik. He and Wilnath had crept down the ridge line in their search to mark Pale sentries.

She turned, blinking slowly, moving with a dragging precision that marked each heartbeat. Kyle was peering intently at her, his hand on her arm.

"Focus on me," he said softly. She heard it, but no one else could possibly have heard those words. Had he uttered them? Had his lips moved or did he speak in her head? She tried to shake her head, to clear the murk of … this strange sense of … time staggered in her.

"Jia, please, try harder." Again she blinked. She tried to open her mouth but words were hung up in her throat, no, someplace deeper, locked as if by a spell.

"She's been like this for a few days. Slipping away." It was Danathea's voice. Staggered moments gave it a staccato feeling like beater birds drumming their wings beside their nests to ward off predators.

"I think she's caught in a wyseery … of Tarcatha's," Kyle said and it rang so clear in her ears that she had a sharp moment of understanding, her head bobbing. Did they see that? Did they see that she understood?

"There's something about Travel wyseery, Jia. It comes through Rupert and so much of what is wyseery links back to him. Including the ilyath. I don't know what Tarcatha did to him, but wyseery is a part of it and you're part of the wyseery. You and Martrena, Rupert, it all goes together."

Jia heard clearly now, even Danathea's mumbled reply, maybe words from Talik or Wilnath.

"If you can't do it, I can help," Kyle was saying. "I need the ilyath, Wil."

Heated words followed. She could tell though she could hear no one but Kyle as he would patiently, or was it wearily, reply that they were running out of time. Was that fear she sensed in Wilnath? Why? Martrena stood upon the waters, her palms up as the stars rained down into them like tiny sparks from the sky. Then, she realized, it wasn't star sparks, but shattered moons. Kylik had smashed into Danat, the old blue face splintering and crumbling, sending bits of itself to rain upon Martrena and the strange dark sparkling waters while Kylik moved on as if leaving the old beside the road. What did it mean? If only she could be free of this strange prison in her head. She'd been somewhere like this before, long ago, when Kyle fell home with her white stone in his pocket. But it hadn't been her stone, had it, as much as the little figure he'd found in the ruins of a great wyseer's house.

The water lay so dark now about her, the stones black. Were those the ancient battlements protruding from the darkened waters, or were those stumps of trees long gone to decay? She took a deep breath, so deep she thought it would never fill her, that all the air of the world would rip into her. It had a strange musty odor, a bitterness that made no sense, but so cool, so evenly it flowed into her, soothed the fever of her uncertainty.

She sputtered, coughed, felt the rip of air in her lungs and opened her eyes to see a liquid light above her dissolve into a distant moon. It struck her then that she was in water, deep enough that she must flail to stay above it. Her hand struck hard against the hard-soft of a stump just beneath the water. She clung with one hand a moment before she realized it was Kyle that lay in the water beside her, still.

She pulled at his shirt and he floated to her easily. She could make out the shapes of trees and struggled a few feet toward shore until she found soft bottom and the uneven footing of moldering branches. She dragged him behind her. She realized suddenly that she was back in her head again, for the moment.

As she stumbled ashore her exertions were not enough to stop the shiver of cold air striking her, nor her panic to see how pale he looked in the weak moonlight. She was on Earth. She had swum to Earth. What strange place was this that she had dreamt of since first she'd met the Traveler!

Kyle was so still. She listened for his breaths, finding none. She pumped at his chest, slapped his face, forced a breath into him before he coughed and a gasp of water emerged from his mouth. Then coughs came more furiously and he rolled, alive.

Toward the rising sun or moon she was supposed to go to find Ruperion. She studied the moon for a long time, but it didn't seem to move. The stars weren't the same. She sniffed at the air and caught the faintest scent of smoke for a brief instant before the calm swept it away from her. If she peered hard she could make out the water stretching far away on one side. No glimmer of fire light. So she must go the other direction, around the small bend in the bank.

She couldn't rouse Kyle and did her best to cover him with pine needles, leaves and dried grass to keep him from the cold as at last she gingerly stepped up onto the crest of the bank and found a worn little footpath. In moments she could see it, a light glimmering through the trees. But this was no firelight.

She clenched her fists and let the sliver of ilyath drop into her purse. She couldn't let the wonders of the world stop her. She must keep to her mission. A wooden building rose, two levels at least, taller than the caverns of Hindlain with its peaked roof. Certainly it was even bigger than the small inn at Overmount. The clearing around it had been grazed as if by Pale mounts and there now she saw the fire trapped in glass above a door, a few tiny birds smashed against the glass, trying to reach the flames.

Before she could touch it the door yanked open, a spill of light almost blinding her, warmth racing out at her. She froze, unable to even think to save herself.

"Kyle?" the woman called, looking past her.

Jia tried to tell the woman where she'd left him, but the woman looked at her without comprehension. At last the woman spoke again, but her words made no sense. Kyle hadn't prepared her for this.

"Ruperion?" Jia asked.

"Ah! Rupert …" The woman was nodding, taking her by the arm, leading her into the warmth.

Jia's head swam in the bright light, her limbs barely moving of their own will as she looked upon a box of moving pictures and other oddities all about her. At last a door opened and she stepped in. She could smell it, the sickness, all about her, the stench of wyseery gone foul. She knelt beside the old wyseer. She could see the power in him, feel it emanating from him. He was the source of it. Would it all end with Rupert? What would then become of the wyseers of Metatha? Was that the secret of it all? As long as he remained in this world on this time, wyseery would never end? She tried to shake away the strange ramblings that threatened to overtake her again.

The woman held something out to her and at first Jia didn't understand. It was a green box, made out of some strange material and with a handle on top. The woman set it down and opened the latch. When the odd little box opened, with cascading trays that popped out as if she'd flushed a bird from a bush, she had to smile her gratefulness. Of course a wyseer like Ruperion would need such a mysterious box for his treasures. She had never seen such a store of wyseery arrayed with such neatness and plenty. It lacked only two things, the treasure Kyle had paid so dearly to bring back—eel oil, and the mysterious elixir that had saved the life of Davath, Ruperion himself and even Atatha. She still possessed the tiniest essence of it.

She studied the wyseer for a long time. If she closed her eyes, she could see Martrena dancing among the stones, fragments of Danat snowing to the black stone beneath her feet. Martrena reached down,

down into the darkest sands at her feet and nudged. There, the glimmer of pink. Jia opened her eyes and took the pink stone from the box and set it on Ruperion's brow, remembering now in what order the essences must touch his tongue, how to set power stones on his closed eyelids, and one above his heart. Over all, the woman hovered. Now and then mumbling something in that strange, grunted language. She had disappeared, returning with candles and a wyseery fire for lighting them, as if she knew what a wyseer needed.

At last, Jia held the wyseer's hand. She had found no injury so deep that it would kill him, and she could tell that the woman had already tended what wounds he had far better than Jia ever could. It was inside him that Tarcatha had done his wounding. It was the draining of his wyseery and some knotting, tangling spell that hadn't died with him, it was the spell that had begun to twist at Jia's own sense of being. She expected the small pink stone to glow, as it had in Hindlain. But hadn't Kyle told her that there was no wyseery in this world? Would her craft be for nothing?

When she mumbled the words she knew she must, her call to the paths of Metatha to open, to take her on the journey to Ruperion, for the first time she realized what Kyle had been telling her … Ruperion was the wyseery! He had made it him. All that they invoked had been him. He was the key, and her appeal went directly to him, to unlock, to let her in, to let her draw upon him. He seemed to sink deeper, as if she was forcing more of him out of him to heal himself.

What had he done when he hadn't the strength to face Tarcatha? She had an image of Talik examining Kyle's crushed arm.

"Kyle!" she said more to herself, her eyes flying open.

She took the woman by the hand, leading her into the night. Kyle must have roused himself from the covering of leaves. He'd thrown them off and now lay sweating in the cold night. Even as the woman clucked and cried over him, they tried to lift him, but he was more than they could handle. They roused him to a point where he could lean on them and stumble back to the house. Would she have to steal the last spark of Kyle's life to save Ruperion? That hardly seemed fair. From what she'd learned of Kyle, that was what Ruperion had been doing all along, honing a tool. Just as the Fidrel had spent their existence preparing to use that tool.

When they returned to Ruperion she settled Kyle beside Ruperion. Jia placed Kyle's battered wrist in Ruperion's hand, forcing the wyseer's bandaged hand to bend about Kyle's wrist. She placed her hand atop them both, and again closed her eyes, letting the candles send their warmth and scent into the room. The stillness of the moment slowed her heart, let her look far inside, past dancing Martrena who seemed so constant in her thoughts to the distant Kylik about to set.

Again she muttered her words, called on Metatha's paths to guide her on a healing journey. She felt it coming, sensed it rushing at her like a diving bird plummeting from the sky to strike an unsuspecting fish. And then it smashed into her and radiated up her arm, pounded into her skull with such ferocity she thought she might scream. Her mouth was open, was she screaming, talking, was she even breathing?

On the dark beach, Martrena spun in a mad dance among the sparks and stars and embers of Danat.

"What have you done to me!" Jia shouted into the dark wyseery that spun about her.

"*You have done a wyseer's work.*" The voice came into her head, unrecognizable. Deep it seemed, familiar, but not.

"This is some bloodcraft."

"*No. You call upon the pure power that existed from the beginning. It is not your wyseery. It is that which makes Metatha what it is. It needs no blood or cauldrons.*"

"But what am I to do? I don't know what to do. I lost my mentor. I am changed and remade into something unknown and odd. Who will teach me what I need to know to help my people, to help these fallen, to fight the Pale without becoming them?"

The silence in Jia's head was deafening, as if even the beating of her heart could no longer be uttered against it. Martrena's dance spun her wild mane up like a veil to conceal the sky, leaving Jia alone in absolute darkness.

CHAPTER THIRTY-SIX

The twitter of birds roused him from where he'd dropped when moonset brought deep night about them. Dawn played in the canopy as birds swirled through the branches and fluttered like falling leaves to the ground, only to swirl upward again as if in a draft. He could just lay here and watch, let it fill his time for hours, forever. Puffs of cloud ran pink before the dawn, high above a flock of giant westerlies moved ahead of the dawn, racing to seek the cover of cave and deep wood to hide them from the brightness of day.

"If we gather our powers, and with you and Ruperion, we'll be able to destroy them. Tarcatha was their strongest, the rest will be easy." Wilnath's voice carried to him.

"No, Wil. First we make Travel unavailable," Jia said. "The portals must be closed."

Kyle roused himself to one elbow to see Rupert give a small nod of approval to Jia, the tiniest hint of a smile around his lips. Had Rupert ever given him such a benevolent smile?

Rupert looked up at him that moment and gave him a smirk. Kyle knew what that expression meant. It meant that unlike Kyle, Jia didn't have solid rock for a brain. With a snort Kyle rose, ignoring the protest of aches and pains. He pulled the blanket around him and moved closer, Talik making room for him.

Wilnath sat across from Jia, a circle drawn in the dirt between them, the remaining Kylalnethra gathered about beneath the canopy of the Grove waiting to hear what would become of them.

"Then they'll have the wyseery and we'll have nothing," Wilnath protested.

"It'll be a forever battle if we don't. We must."

"This isn't a one-person decision, Jia. You may lead the council, but it isn't a council of one."

Kyle saw several of the wyseers gathered cover their mouth at Wilnath's insolence. Jia could have reprimanded him, ordered him out of the discussion, even banished him. Instead, she plucked a gold feather from her hair and began twirling it between her fingers as she looked just above it at Wil. Rupert was almost grinning.

Wilnath bit his lip, looked away, then down at his hands.

"Forgive me Wise One. It is the passion for this battle that makes me speak so," Wilnath said.

"I know that, Wil," Jia said. "The wyseery isn't just about Travel. It's about Metatha. The portals need not be open for us to call on the wyseery in them."

"But that's what the Methiliim do!" someone protested from the anonymity of the crowd.

Jia immediately picked out the wyseer, who appeared startled to be skewered by her gaze, as softly as she wielded it.

"It is not what the Methiliim do," she said again, wyseery coating her words, and silence returning to the crowd. She turned back to Wilnath. "I saw a vision, of a vast black beach lapped by dark waters. That's the void, the place beyond, the true beginning and end, the womb of the universe. And I went there. There, Danat and Kylik did battle and the way of the old ended. Kylik was victorious."

"That would seem to say that the way of the Traveler was correct," Wilnath said.

"It would seem that way," Jia returned easily. "If that was all there was. But even as Danat, the keeper of the traditions and the home of the dead, rained from the sky, crumbled and wounded and lost to us, so Kylik set. And darkness filled the sky. But it wasn't a true dark. There were the tiny lights of Danat falling yet, and the glimmer of stars in the roof of the world and those were the memories of those who have gone before. They rained down, ever down onto the dark beach and were swept away by the waves, washed clean of the world."

"You say then that the world comes to an end?" Tiva asked.

"No, only that we must start over. That the ways we have known cannot continue. That we have held our grudges for our dead too long. We must look deeper into our roots to understand our place in this world, in the web of worlds. As Ruperion once said, we have forgotten our lore. And as the Traveler told us so many times, we must for once rely on ourselves."

Kyle wasn't ready for all eyes to turn on him. There he sat, mouth agape as Jia's words fell into him, putting things together for him. He glanced at Talik, the palif nodding ever so slightly, his face turned skyward and eyes closed as if he clung to each word.

"Talik, how does this fit with your prophecies?" Kyle whispered, his words carrying so that Jia and Rupert turned to study the white-robed Pale among them.

"Neatly," his blue eyes flicked open to regard them. "Neatly."

Just then, a werran raced into the Grove, waving his spear wildly.

"Quick, Pale!" Davath pulled Jia and Rupert to their feet as one, both of them struggling to keep up as Davath led them away. Others scattered in different directions, the crowded Grove giving way to silence in seeming moments.

"Come, Traveler!" Barul tugged at him and Kyle stumbled to follow.

He let the werran lead him deeper into the forested mountains overlooking Ta'atit. Soon the air gasped out of him as the exertion caught up with long weeks of deprivation. Only hours ago he had been lying in a stupor on the banks of Potter's Flowage. Only hours ago, Jia's wyseery had plucked him from the silence of nothing and plunged him into knowledge, of things too deep to perceive, of wyseery and world-making and the roots of existence. That was where they had to go to find Rupert. He didn't understand it. None of it made sense, but neither did wyseery.

They had fought to unbind Rupert from some spell-wrought prison Tarcatha had built and knew the three of them were linked by some wyseery that extended all the way back to the roots of the world. He had surfaced then, for that was how it felt, come awake in his room with his gills wide to find air, and his mother asleep in her chair, the candle burned low. And Jia, ghostly and almost transparent had opened her eyes but a moment before they rolled back in her head.

When at last he woke again, it was to find himself in his own bed, Jia asleep on a sleeping bag beside him, Rupert speaking with Kyle's mother in the hallway, their voices low and easy, as if nothing had happened. If it hadn't been for the stench of wyseery in his room, the sense that he had again somehow changed, he would have wondered if any of it had happened at all.

But time passed in Metatha. And the more of it that passed, the more likely someone would begin to wonder what had become of Tarcatha, and the Traveler, and Ruperion. And soon Rupert was rousing them and again they must Travel, again they must move on to another time, another place. Jia had paused long enough to stare silently at the TV, her eyes wide. As they ate a quick breakfast, she marveled at each item in the kitchen, at the radio, at sausages and toast and butter, and almost fainted when a phone rang.

Child-like and awed she'd gazed about her as if newborn to the world and he'd wanted to laugh, but couldn't quite, recalling their long day talking about the wonders of worlds that don't know their own magic.

In Metatha, here she had changed too. They revered her, adored her, paid her homage like the Reign once reserved for Denalku and Ruperion.

Kyle stumbled and skittered several feet down the rocky slope, startled to find himself alone. Barul lay still a few paces above him. Kyle hesitated only a moment before he realized that only a Pale could have felled him so. He thought he caught a glint, a glimpse of crimson among the trees. He ran down the slope, chiding himself for not paying attention, for relying too much on others.

His infected leg gave way beneath him again and he stumbled again, falling down slope in a slither of stone, leaf and soil. He came up on his feet again, almost falling when he planted all his weight on his bad leg.

He could hear nothing but his own heartbeat. He didn't even know where to go for safety. He followed the lay of the ridge, the terrain pulling him down and west to an area that looked vaguely familiar. He didn't want to be on the shores of Ta'atit where he might fall easily in the hands of the Methiliim. He ducked into heavy undergrowth, certain he sounded like a crashing bull as he thundered up the slope to a narrow plain where the wooded slopes gave way to meadow fringed by trees.

In the midst of it lay a pond, a familiar pond but he couldn't think of the name. He turned, seeing a crimson robe, a staff pointed toward him, a blaze of light. He leapt for the water, and swam for his life, but not before he felt the blow strike him in the back. He imagined bloody bubbles pulsing up from him, of being gobbled up by some predatory fish, ripped apart by some giant muskie.

Instead, he surfaced in the tiny spring at the base of a quiet valley of Shesta. He stumbled to the grassy bank and collapsed before he could hit the ground.

CHAPTER THIRTY-SEVEN

In his head Kyle smiled. Martrena was pulling bouquets from the palms of her hands like some carnival magician or a clown in a parade. Each bouquet was larger, more ornate. At last she revealed a rainbow of birds that fled for the sky, streaming away from her, hundreds and hundreds of them. The sun sparkled on a sea turned almost bright white, while at her feet were the washed black stones, the giant driftwood trees littering the shore behind her, but not ominous now. Now they were so starkly beautiful it stole his breath away. She smiled, laughed, danced as the birds flowed from her.

Finally she turned and looked directly at him and waggled a finger, as if he had been spying on her unawares. The color fled into memory, the sky rolling in black and dark, the surf calming until there was nothing but the dark world of beginnings around her. She gave him a sad smile, then bent and plucked a pink feather up from the darkness and held it out. It glimmered, not a feather at all, but a sliver of pink stone.

Baraboo quartzite.

The name shot into his head, from where he didn't know. Was it Rupert again? He opened his eyes to discover that a herd of Shestan cattle had surrounded him. The creatures that might be a cross between buffalo and wildebeest paid him little attention. How long had he slept? Not nearly long enough, he knew. He felt that squishy sense of not being quite right as he sat up. The animals snorted and blew and slowly moved away.

At least he hadn't fled into the world of the eels, or even that of the Balthysians. Red cliffs loomed above him, a verdant prairie rolled away from him. It felt so idyllic he could just settle back into the prairie and sleep. He had no mission this time to saw off the horns of beasts or gather herbs from high cliff faces. He could just look at this place like a haven. The moment he returned to Metatha, he knew he'd be surrounded by crimson-robed Methiliim.

Rest. He'd wake in time.

Was that Rupert calling across worlds to him or his own common sense? How much time passed in Shesta to Metatha time?

It didn't matter. He needed the rest to do what he must do.

Kyle moved a little away from the herd and settled back in to sleep the deepest sleep he'd ever slept.

Again, Martrena came to him. She was in him. He knew that. She was under his skin, in his blood. His blood, Talik's, the blood of countless dead, had been in that cauldron, with the Travel stone and an anchoring power stone, the powerful Baraboo quartzite, and the vestment of moons and Martrena's ashes. That brew had burned him, boiled up his skin, sloughed it away as he raised his hand triumphantly. Tarcatha's words had been some spell. But Talik's had been older, from the roots of the world, from the days when the worship of Danat and the homes of the dead were the strongest wyseery.

How did he know?

He knew.

Somehow everything goddish and wyseerish had centered on the last Reign, a reluctant Metathan. He must seek his answers in the roots of the world. That was what Martrena's dances had been telling them. A power so old, so primal, that it could defeat the wicked work of cauldrons. It was already in him. It had been since that day his rage had killed a man when he hadn't even raised a hand. He'd been Travel weary and weak then, too. Now he was even more weary, more at one with Danat's time, when he would be called home to the moon.

But if he lived on Earth how would he come home to Danat? What a strange thought.

Danat would know. First he had to close the portals.

But then how would he come home?

Danat would know. Kylik would lead him, Siph witness it. The time was come to close the portals, undo it all. He had to bring together the oldest, the strongest, the powers of wyseery. He had to do it, because he was the power. He could do it, if he called deep, deep into the roots of Metatha. He was the last Reign. He was of Metatha. He was a thing of older times. He could do it, if he just tried.

Whose words were in his head?

Deafening silence.

Kyle opened his eyes. A starry sky spread above him, so bright and clear, with stars so brilliant they stole his breath away. He sensed the beasts resting in the deep grass, their soft sleeping grunts like some heartbeat of the land. He stepped carefully as he moved among them, seeking the small spring that once had been revered here, before. Before. How did he know about before?

He stopped. He would have only a moment. He had to think it through clearly. What words would he use?

The oldest.

What actions would he take?

He must be swift.

What would happen then?

It was best if he didn't know.

He hesitated. That wasn't the answer he expected. Was he losing his mind to have a conversation in his head like this?

Did it matter?

How long had he slept?

If long enough it didn't matter. His rest would come. He must do what he must.

He looked across the prairie of Shesta, oddly lit in starlight so bright he expected a bright moon hid somewhere. If the Methiliim threw the portals wide, what would come of such places?

What had become of the people of Shesta? Did they still graze their cattle or had all succumbed to Denalku's whim?

Kyle turned and dived into the spring. He swam deep knowing the little shallow pond would barely conceal him. The pink feather would be at the deepest point, deep in the muck of centuries. And there his hand grasped the Baraboo quartzite. He lurched from the water in a sudden move, erupting half man, half fish, changing so rapidly that those who would see him most certainly couldn't move for the shock.

In that instant, Kyle shouted the words he knew he must. How he knew he didn't ask. He simply spoke: "*Danatatha na kylalnethra achlimen pata tathral. Tarcannen d'atit'et palifir!*"

He heard words, thought he sensed some call of wyseery nearby but he plunged on. He had only a moment.

He brought his two hands together, the black Travel stone slamming into the anchor stone, power stone. The snap of stone rapping stone cracked like thunder and the quartzite glowed, flaring brighter and brighter so that Kyle could no longer bear to hold his eyes open. He thought the light would engulf his arm, him, he stood there, his arms in the air, the glow of light blooming out from him. At last, he flung the stone high into the air and shouted again, for emphasis, "*'et palifir!*"

The water of the tiny pond behind him bubbled. The stone spun upward, flaring like a sun lassoed from the sky.

"*Na he pata,*" Kyle whispered to the dark image before his vision, to the strange sense he had of flying high above the land. Through the eyes of a westerly, perhaps, he saw the portals of Metatha bubbling, closing, the womb of the universe closed to all but the gods and those moving to life and death.

The stone reached its apex and fell. Kyle held out his hand, the hand that held the Travel stone. When the two came together, he had the instant's sense of white-hot light, then knew no more.

CHAPTER THIRTY-EIGHT

The darkness was complete, though perhaps some sense of darker moved before him. It wasn't frightening, simply nothing. Just dark. He drew it to him, embraced its offer of eternal forgetfulness.

"That is a road to come. It is not for you now."

The darkness had spoken to him. Or … had Ruperion again climbed into his thoughts?

"The portals are closed. I can't go home." He wasn't sure if he'd spoken it, or merely thought it.

"You are home."

He reached for the forgetful darkness, stretching his battered hands toward it. He didn't want to think or play games of semantics. He simply wanted to sleep, forever.

"Forever is a long time."

Who waded through his thoughts?

"You forget so quickly the lessons learned."

He was becoming irritated by this nagging voice. Why wouldn't it just let him sleep?

"You are asleep."

Then this dream was becoming tedious.

"That is what forever is about, tedium."

"Why are you bothering me!" Did he shout it?

"You have things yet to do."

"I think I've done plenty."

"And you did all of it alone, did you?"

The tone. It had to be Rupert. Would Rupert torment him for the rest of his death, harassing him with inane questions and snap quizzes on arcane languages of worlds that no longer mattered? Yes he'd done it alone, except for the nagging voices that came into his head and invaded his dreams. Couldn't a man simply die in peace?

"Who said anything about dying? You think you've had suffering? How many hundreds of years of living have you done? You have a long life yet to endure."

"Well that's certainly the kind of thing that makes me just want to leap into life with both feet."

"Let go. The time will come. It is not yet."

He didn't know why, but he let go. He realized he'd been clinging to the darkness, some edge of the beyond, a lip he couldn't see beyond. The water was about to close over his head. He could feel it, cold and unpleasant, seeping upward, about to send him Traveling again. Hadn't he Traveled enough? Hadn't he closed the portals? Enough already!

He opened his eyes with a gasp, then shut them tightly against a light that seemed to blaze out like a new sun. Light leaking in around the corners.

"It's okay, Kyle, you can open your eyes." The words were English. He opened his eyes, expecting to find his mother had flipped the light on in his room and—

The sky above him was that dusky pink of predawn. A dark figure loomed over him now, a silhouette against the sky. He was surrounded, he saw, by shadowy figures. Kyle lay in a circle of stones and he could still feel the heat of them abating. They had been blazing with light, hadn't they, flaring like the anchor stone had moments before—

He couldn't move. He tried to raise his head, tried to lift his arms.

"You've had a long journey Traveler, it is time to rest." Talik's voice?

"Sleep now, Kyloreign and we'll stew a blue for your waking," the light words belied the gravity of the tone. Jia, it had to be. He was about to speak when he sensed it. They weren't speaking to him. They were performing some wyseery. Hadn't wyseery ended with Travel?

He thought he heard a chuckle in his head. *"You chose your words of unmaking wisely, Kyle. It is a great wyseery indeed. And now it resides in you."*

He tried to sort out those last words. Were they in his head or from the circle of figures around him? The more he pondered it, the more certain he was that he couldn't. At last, he gave in to the wyseery he felt swirling around him. Let them sleep him. Let them spell him. It didn't matter anymore.

This time when he closed his eyes the darkness was less complete. Nothing moved there. Nothing spoke. There was simply nothing. And at long last, the Traveler slept.

"What I wouldn't give for a glass of wine about now, but that isn't all that likely to ever happen now, is it?" The words, in English, nudged him closer to the green-gold light on his lids. Was this the hereafter on Danat and he was destined to share eternity with Rupert?

"No. There'd be wine in the hereafter."

Kyle forced his eyes open to find the wyseer, still in t-shirt and blue jeans, leaning against the trunk of a manfish tree only a few feet away. Kyle glanced around, recognizing trees, a glade, perhaps it wasn't all that far from the pond portal to Shesta. Some sort of white cloth hung overhead, filtering the sun that dribbled through the canopy. Then back to Rupert who wore a white beard now, his hair longer than he remembered and pulled into two braids bound with gold feathers. He stared at the old wyseer, the man's hair so completely white, no hint of pepper remained even from the jet black it once had been.

"How long?" Kyle managed, finding his throat dry and scratchy. Something pressed against his lips and he startled to find Danathea beside him, ready to tip a gourd. A rich nectar, cool and sweet, refreshed him.

Rupert gave him a strange look, not his measuring gaze, not the scheming one, but perhaps wistful? One eyebrow had hooked up a little, the salt and pepper black slash an accent mark to those dark eyes. The wyseer snorted a bit.

"Knock it off, Rupert, get out of my head," Kyle grumbled in English. He tried to rise to one elbow but couldn't seem to lift himself. It was almost as if his limbs wouldn't respond.

"Don't be concerned. You're still mending," Rupert said. As he spoke, Rupert moved his hand and Kyle realized the wyseer had been holding his wrist, where scars marked the burns that should be—

"How long?"

"The mark of a Traveler. Remember how obsessed I was with the passage of time? How you scoffed at the old, besotted fool. It's been a while, Kyle."

Again Kyle tried to rouse himself, but Rupert lay his hand on his brow.

"You have endured more than I ever would have asked you and we've only called you back from Danat. Just take it easy. There's no rush."

"Because the portals are closed and I can never go home." Kyle scrunched his eyes shut. "What an idiot. Was that you in my head, making me do this? Why did you do this to me?"

"I called you back to the living. I thought you'd like that," Rupert said softly. Too careful yet. Was he yet so sick that Rupert would be gentle with him?

Rupert chuckled, eerily reminding him of those long-ago days before he began some tale of Metatha to the anxious ears of the Nelson clan.

"No, before that, telling me what to do with the portal stone." Again, Danathea pressed that sweet nectar to his lips and he drank it hungrily, feeling stronger already.

"I'd take the credit, but it wasn't me. I think I know what you ... experienced. I was trying to find you and I met ..." Rupert faltered, sat silent for so long Kyle nudged him to see if he was still awake. "I met a greater power than me, and, well, that is rare, isn't it?"

A commotion drew their attention, Danathea tensing and looking over her shoulder, Rupert craning his neck a moment before settling back against the tree trunk.

"Much has happened while you slept, Kyle." Rupert continued, his English sounding strange in a place where birds swarmed like insects to taste of the sweat or salt on his body or to tug at the seeds still on the rush bed beneath him. "The Methiliim were none too pleased to see the portals boiling shut across Metatha. Without the Travel magic they're no better than any other wizard or priest who calls hopefully upon some greater power, uncertain what will come of it."

"Except you," Kyle said. "What wizardry did you use to bring me back from the dead?"

"Well, your words of unmaking were well chosen. There will always be magic in Metatha. It just isn't the Travel magic of Ruperion. It's the magic I tapped when I tamed Travel. You have hidden it again. Look." Rupert held up the black stone he had clung to since birth. "This is your Travel stone. It's useless now. It would take you nowhere." He held out the small Kokopelli anchor stone. "And this is merely an historical artifact now. To be revered simply for what it meant to an occupied people."

"So without the magic?"

"Metathans again fight Metathans. But this time, there is a Talik in our corner. He has gone to his grandfather and appealed to his wisdom. Talik isn't the mere palif he would seem anymore either. He has his own magic, doesn't he?"

"Does he?"

"Oh yes," Rupert said with that strange smile again. "When you reached into the cauldron to retrieve the Traveling stone, you tapped into something very old, Metatha's original magic. That's the power I used so long ago. Metatha was always a place of portals, but they were difficult to mine, they took great magic each time they were breached. The Travel magic consolidated them, brought powers from elsewhere in the universe to bear on Metatha's own special place. But I brought no such powerful pantheon together in my appeals as you did in yours. You called on the gods of old, new-made powers, the magic of Travel, all of it. All of it! And they replied. It is … unprecedented. You did far better than I gave you credit for, Kyle. When I sent you here, it was with no such expectation."

"Wise One," Danathea said softly, making a small sign to Rupert.

"Jia comes. She has been coming to visit you each day, even though she's been leading the battle against the last of the Methiliim. Most of them slipped away when the realization came that it was over. They still practice an unnatural art, but we have taken their prize from them. There are a few hold outs and we hope that soon Talik will prove successful with a message from the Atannate."

Kyle shook his head. There was a buzzing in his ears, the edges of the world growing dark again. He wanted to know more. What time was it at Potter's Flowage? Why couldn't he move?

"Easy, Kyle, you are only just returned. Let the healing come to you." Jia's words in Metathan startled him, brought the light back for just a moment. He forced his eyes open. She, too, stood before him with white hair like an elder, not the young woman she was, her hair still bound in gold feathers. A healing scar crept from her cheek to somewhere behind her ear and her eyes appeared so tired in her face. But the presence had returned. She was there. She didn't wander in the strange world of trance and wyseery.

"I am so pleased to find you wakened. But they have tired you already. You are indeed a treasure now, Kyloreign. We honor you. We speak the same."

Jia bobbed her head, an expression he hadn't seen in so long. He grabbed Rupert's hand as the old wyseer moved to leave.

"Why am I a treasure?" he demanded in English.

Rupert gave him that Rupert smile, the one with so much more behind it than humor.

"I was the Travel magic, Kyle. It was me. Anyone who tapped it, tapped me. Remember how stretched I became, how I needed help focusing because so much of that wyseer's war was pulling me apart? It pulled Jia apart, because she tapped it. It sent you into your strange visions. Do you recall your words of unmaking? `Danat's followers, follow now instead the light road, unmake the Traveler's road. Hide this treasure among the wise.' What possessed you?"

Kyle shook his head.

"It's you, now. You fool. It's you."

CHAPTER THIRTY-NINE

Kyle stared out over Lake Ta'atit, watching the birds gather, lift into the sky, find some field or meadow in which to feed, then return, their din a constant racket in his thoughts. How long had he sat here staring, waiting, waiting for something, he wasn't sure what. Nothing was going to change. He was Metathan now. He'd seen to that. There was no home to return to. There was work to be done, a world to rebuild, peace to be formed. But from those things, Kyle remained removed. He'd found his place, yet he hadn't. He felt like he had a foot planted in each world and someone was pushing the door shut against one ankle.

He glanced over his shoulder. Rupert hummed merrily to himself as he worked to ferment yet another batch of manfish juice. Did Rupert, too, find the slow pace of Metatha unnerving? Why else would he want to deaden it with a manfish wine? Somewhere behind him the trail led up to Hindlain, where Jia and Wilnath and the rest of the council, excepting its most famous and most wise, worked out the future of the world. Talik was there, as envoy of the Atannate, and with him had come the greatest of the wyseers who had been lured to the false wyseery of the Methiliim. They worked out the tedious rules of wyseery in a new world where the Valeutans were again no better or worse than the Pale if they kept to their valleys and the Pale kept to their plains. They talked, too, about knowledge, and how they would relearn the lore of Metatha.

"If only I could just go home. It's so close."

"Heh, I wouldn't want to be swimming into that flowage in November. What's the point?"

"November!" Kyle stared at Rupert. How long had he been here now? Where had time passed? What did his parents think? What had happened that last night when he and Jia and Rupert—

He didn't think, he simply dived. The water closed over his head like so many other swims he had taken as he tried to regain his strength. But this time was different. He thought of home. He thought how he wanted to be there and ... with a strange suddenness he realized he was breathing, and tasting and the tannic flavor of Potter's Flowage rushed his lungs. He surfaced to find the sky gray and blustery, a cold wind ripping the last leaves from the trees. The cold water crept into his limbs, chilling him so deeply he thought he couldn't move. He ducked beneath the water and in a moment he swam among the ruins of Ta'atit. He rose along the bank, only a few paces from where Rupert peered into the water, his mouth half open, his eyes bright with excitement.

"How did that happen, Rupert?" Kyle asked.

"It happened?"

Kyle nodded as he waded ashore.

"You have become the traveling stone. The wyseery is in you."

"Now they'll really want my blood."

"Not if they don't know about it. Go home to Wisconsin. I can tell them anything you want. Besides, if it's you, now, putting you somewhere safe and slow wouldn't be such a bad thing. Let's just hope you aren't hit by a bus."

"And what about you?"

Kyle realized he'd laid a hand on Rupert's shoulder. He started to pull his hand away, but Rupert grasped his wrist before he could move, a gentle grasp, one that forced him to recall how they had fought as one in their battle against Tarcatha.

"I hope you can forgive me, Kyle. I used you hard. It was never personal. That's the hard part. It was always the mission. I always worked for Denalku, for my people. I tried to tell you so many times and I never could find the words. By the time I knew what to say, I knew I'd lost you." Rupert didn't say anything for a long, time, then gave him a light push toward the water. "Come back to visit, bring a good merlot or cabernet. Come and get me when I'm decrepit and ready to collect Social Security and bide my old age beside the fire with a good glass. By then, perhaps I can help my people learn to learn for themselves, learn to build and think."

"But haven't they become my people, too?" Kyle asked softly.

He saw a flash of gold and knew Jia would be standing up on the ridge overlooking the lake. Did she hold Talik's hand as she was prone to do when thinking most deeply?

"I've never been a Nelson, or ever fit in. And when I was there I always wanted to be somewhere else. But when here, I've most missed there. I don't know what it is I want, Rupert. I miss my family, but I think, too, I'd miss, well, you … and Jia and Wil and these insufferable birds." He flicked away a bird that was trying to sample the water on his skin.

"You must figure out what you want, Kyle. You've sat here and pined for home. And you sat there and pined for here. I can't give you the answer."

"I would like to work for greater good, here, to help mend the things I helped make wrong. But I also have some fences to mend and some explanations to give. I'd like to hang out at the Terrace and thank my roomies. But, maybe I …"

"Maybe visit carefully," Rupert said quietly. "Don't wait too long. You'll find all those you know and care for will be gone in only a few months' time. But then, you too are trapped in the Traveler's time, aren't you? You'll never forget what time it is here."

Kyle looked over his shoulder toward the hillside that led up to Hindlain. He thought he discerned Jia in the crowd of thoughts that always seemed ready to crash into his head. He had the strangest sense that he saw Talik's tattoos before his eyes, in motion, as if he followed a history timeline and as he took each step he could look back and see how each move he made would appear in the history. He saw the image of the manfish, encircled, still the key to Metatha.

"Goodbye," he whispered. "Forgive me, this Traveler must go home."

He dove. The water closed over his head and in an instant he bumped against an old stump, felt the deep chill of late autumn creeping into his bones. None of the old weariness struck him, as it should. He swam easily to shore, the leaves crunching beneath his feet having their earthly sound, his breath puffing out in a steam as a slate-gray sky rolled overhead.

He could smell the wood smoke wafting toward him, lingering among the boles of trees he'd scampered among as a youth. There, he passed the spot where so long ago Rupert had sent him on this journey. A raucous passage of geese overhead were mirrored on the flowage's face, where the tentative first ice crept from shore.

At last, he tugged the back door open and entered the kitchen, unable to keep himself from grinning from ear to ear as he caught a whiff of the beer batter and the oil heating up to cook the fish in.

"Mom, I'm home," he said softly as she turned to find him dripping and shivering in the entry.

A snap of cards shuffling called attention to his father at the table, his mouth set in a line as he looked from his wife to his son. One of his brothers-in-law was fetching a beer, ready to settle at the table.

"Rupert?" his father grunted.

"He'll be away for a while, couple of months," Kyle said. "I'll probably go visit him in a week or two. Deal me in?"

His father looked at his mother. She grinned and let the fish drop into the oil so that it roiled up, boiling and spitting and furious, like a cauldron filled with wild magic.

"Get into something dry and pull up a chair, then." His father's voice was gruff, but it cracked. He sensed it, knew. Perhaps a little Metathan magic worked here as well.

As he settled at the table in the cozy kitchen, warm in a flannel shirt and jeans that fit too loosely, the cards slid across the table, the oil clattering like rain on the black stones of a Metathan beach. The chatter of his brother-in-law going on about the buck he'd missed on the archery opener, the feel of the cards in his hand and the beer his mother set down beside him. He couldn't stop grinning. It felt … right. Metatha was there, coursing in his veins, in scars that had healed despite his short time away. It was there in that strange backbeat in his soul, that told him how time raced in other places. He must always be torn between worlds. That's where he belonged, in the middle, swimming, the manfish.

"Hearts," he said to his father with a grin as he threw out the jack.

About the Author

A former journalist, editor, and farmer, M. Turville Heitz's short fiction appeared in anthologies and magazines before she took a break to collect a PhD and teach science and technical communications to undergrads. *Black River* is her first published novel. She lives on a defunct farm near Madison, Wisconsin where she coddles chickens and is kept by cats. She can be found on social media at MegT@bsky.social

Curious about other Crossroad Press books? Stop by our website:
http://crossroadpress.com
We offer quality writing
in digital, audio, and print formats.

Subscribe to our newsletter on the website homepage and receive a
free eBook.

www.ingramcontent.com/pod-product-compliance
Lightning Source LLC
Chambersburg PA
CBHW021437240626
47153CB00001B/191